The

CHARIK

Something Dark and Evil

by Robert C. Wahl

Copyright © 2014 Robert C. Wahl

All rights reserved.

ISBN: 1494721449

IBSN-13: 978-1494721442

To good friends
Jerry and Carolyn
brother and sister at heart

evil — adj. 2. Causing injury, ruin, or pain: HARMFUL. 3. Marked by or indicating future misfortune: OMINOUS. 5. Marked by anger or spite: MALICIOUS — n. 1. A cause of harm, misfortune or destruction

*"I have often heard the sound of a vanished voice
and felt the touch of a vanished hand."*

— Sir Arthur Conan Doyle (1927)

Prologue

The deputy called for the stakeout not knowing what to expect. There had been only one homicide in the county all year, eleven robberies, a rash of lesser crimes. Nothing overt or extreme. The city and county and outlying towns were about as crime free as any community could be. Until recently.

As of yesterday, six random attacks on livestock had been reported, scattered outside a valley. The manner in which they were mauled and killed caused widespread fear and many a sleepless night for farmers.

The evidence pointed to a farm as the *nesting ground*. None of the attacks, oddly enough, occurred there.

This morning the deputy followed a lone set of tracks embedded in the dry, rich soil. He placed a hand inside the imprint. There was room to spare, maybe four to five inches. At the top were claw marks, five digits. It appeared to be the track of a bear. Not just any bear, a specimen unlike any other. There was contradictory evidence, however. Other factors revealed an abnormality. The curvature of the claw. The size and proportion. And the width of the heel. All of which were freakishly large.

The same exact imprint was found at all four locations. Same abnormality, size, width, everything. Same killing scene existed as well. The gore, however, had grown steadily worse. It was almost like the predator was trying to outdo itself, when actually it was probably just becoming bolder. The signs of aggressiveness were growing as well. Six kills didn't seem to whet an insatiable appetite. It was the deputy's duty to prevent kill number seven.

No. What he was dealing with here was no ordinary bear.

He studied the surrounding darkness with a cautious eye, relieved that a fellow deputy, the 'shooter,' was sitting in another patrol car parked nearby. The shooter had a Heckler and Koch assault rifle with laser lens, range finder, and night vision capability.

A technician occupied the rear seat of the deputy's patrol car, with a modified version of a laptop resting on his knees. The lead deputy stood by the driver's door, holding what looked like a radar gun, a cone-shaped devise with handle, battery, cable, and antennae.

From the back seat the technician said, "I'll do one more sweep."

The deputy raised the cone. Held it over his head. The cone did a three-sixty. Circled once like the second hand of a clock. Only faster.

"You sure this thing works?" he asked.

"Sure as hell hope so," the technician replied. "It took six years of research."

The deputy stood at the entrance to the state park, half a mile from the nesting ground. He glanced at his watch. The park had been closed since dusk, more than four hours. The attacks all took place after dark. He could feel the tension mounting in the cool night air. Conditions were changing. Not *weather* conditions. A mood, an indefinable presence seemed to cling to the darkness. He listened to the night as the technician pulled information from the computer, waited, and watched the screen.

"Well?"

"All pretty much clear, except..." The technician hesitated, his eyes cast deep in the computer's refracted glow. "Lots of deer. Raccoons. Rabbits. Christ. Everywhere you look..."

"Not worried about deer or rabbits," the deputy interrupted. "Concentrate on something larger."

"There's nothing else to report...so far. No wait. There's a pack of coyotes..."

"Not worried about coyotes. Coyotes can't bring down a horse. There's something else out there."

To the north, about a mile away, was a freeway. They could hear the distant drone of diesel engines and tread from heavy rigs rolling over asphalt.

A wisp of wind blew through the trees.

The technician made a popping sound with his lips, like he'd discovered something. "Incoming car," he declared. "Approaching from the west. Moving fast." He waited, watching the screen. "Ah-ha. What's this? Something's happening east of us..." He paused, eyes brimming with intensity. "...Near the nesting ground."

"What is it?"

The technician's voice was veiled in mystery, his eyes lost in the reflective pool of the screen. "Just a second. The computer's running through the data now."

"For Christ sake, Pete. Lock on. Lock on and identify!"

"Computer's locked on. It's just...just...what in the hell is going on? Can't identify the source. It's...emerging..."

"What's emerging? Where did it come from?"

"I don't know. Let me try something."

Fingers flew across the keyboard.

The deputy glanced to his right at the sound of a door opening. The shooter got out of his car. Raised the assault rifle, took a wide stance, placed the butt of the weapon tight against his shoulder, propped his elbows on the hood of the car.

The lead deputy whispered loudly, "It's got to come from somewhere, Pete. It didn't just drop out of the sky."

Frustration began to creep into Pete's voice. "I know. The computer's doing a quick analysis. Hold on. Still analyzing. Coming from...huh? What the heck. Can't be. Computer says it's coming from *below*."

"Below what?"

"Just below. Beneath the ground. It's moving, expanding, getting larger. The car—it's about two miles away. Entering the Watch Zone."

"Forget about the car! Focus on the thing that's emerging."

"Still checking." The technician tapped a few more keys. "Huh? What now? The middle of the screen has gone blank, completely black. Hold on." His hands typed faster. He sat back, looked at the screen, confused.

"So basically the machine is useless. Is that what you're saying?"

"No, no. It's telling us a lot. Something's disrupting the heat patterns, masking them. It's moving...still moving. Heading east. Following the road. Oh, no. What's it doing? Loosing contact. It's fading...fading..."

"Is it living or an object, Pete? What is it?"

"I don't know."

"Have the computer clarify, make a guess!"

"I can't. There's not enough information."

"Is it dangerous?"

"Can't answer that," said Pete. "The computer's thinking, trying to formulate a response. Uh-oh. No way! That can't happen!" He threw up his hands.

"What can't happen?"

"The computer morphed. Died. Shut itself off."

"Shut itself off?"

"Not completely. There's a black hole, a blank circle...center of the screen...it's...it's expanding...covering the entire screen. Wait! The computer's printing something out."

The deputy waited.

The technician paused, wondering if there was an electronic malfunction, a virus he didn't detect. Having developed the system, he knew the computer inside and out. He knew it was programmed to collect data, identify, track, and make a scientific, factual, and statistical analysis one hundred percent of the time. It was incapable of doing anything less. It recognized only one classification when all else failed.

Appearing at the bottom of the screen was a nine-letter word—

"P-h-e-n-o-m-e-n-a."

Chapter 1

Into the solitude of night...

Through the rolling hills the yellow cab raced. For miles around it was all farmland. No street lights. No house lights. Just a deserted stretch of earth and sky where the spring air ushered in a wave of country freshness, dark and star-lit, with high beams stabbing out at the highway.

The driver peered at a passing road sign—*Dangerous Curves Ahead*—and shifted uncomfortably in his seat. Something didn't seem quite right. Ever since the ride began he had been troubled by a number of nagging questions. Why would anyone take a taxi, pay an outrageous fare, and travel more than eighty miles at this late hour? He figured either the person was scared, desperate for a ride, or running from the law. There had to be a catch to it and the more he thought about it the less he liked it.

The clock read: twelve minutes past midnight. There was movement in the back seat. A lighted dial from a cell phone cast an iridescent glow across the passenger's face. The young man appeared to be the very picture of health, a strapping sort with chiseled face brimming with vitality and boyish good looks. This was his fifth or sixth attempt at making a call, all unsuccessful. Frustrated, he shut the phone off and tossed it aside on the seat.

"None of my business, sport," remarked the driver, "but you haven't said two words since we left the airport."

David Macklin sat in civilian clothes, looking out the window, distracted. He was returning home to a lonely heartbroken father and a farm heavily in debt.

"Everything all right back there?"

No, David thought to himself. Not since he received a text from his sister a few days ago. No details. No emails. No phone calls. Just three letters—*SOS*—waiting once he got back on board ship. And no communication since. That was the most disturbing part. No communication.

He stared out the window, worried, restless.

"Hey, soldier. You okay?"

David woke from a daze. "A little eager to get home is all. How did you know I was in the military?"

The driver laughed. "You kiddin' me? Look at you. Only thing missin' is the uniform." All at once he changed expression. "Oh, oh. What happened here?" He tapped the screen to the navigational system mounted to the dash. The screen had gone blank. "Huh, this is weird. It was working a few seconds ago." Frowning in disappointment, he unplugged the cord and sat back.

Up a long steep hill, the road flattened out. They drove past a lighted gate, the entrance to Fallen Oaks State Park. Two county sheriff patrol cars blocked the entranceway. One officer stood outside by the driver's door, holding what looked like a radar gun. A second man sat in the back seat, his face aglow, a ghostly blend of green and blue reflected in the darkness. Another officer had an assault rifle propped over the hood of the second car. All three turned their heads to look, appearing to have more than just a casual interest in the passing vehicle.

Relieved by the presence of the cops, the cab driver relaxed, removed a cigarette from his shirt pocket, stuck it in his mouth, and lit it. The flame shed light across the visor, revealing a license and identification card with the name Charles 'Red' Phillips stenciled in black. Exhaling a thick plume of smoke, Red grumbled with a slight wheeze, "Now why in the world would they be looking for speeders this time of night? And why the rifle?"

There was no reaction from the back seat. David was still watching the patrolmen. But the driver was right. Why was the guy holding a rifle—an assault rifle at that? What was he aiming at?

Just as the taxi made the next curve, a flasher from a patrol car flickered on and off. Just once.

Was it a signal? An attempt to get their attention?

"Not much of a talker, are ya'?" said Red.

"What?"

"Nothing." Red yawned and turned on the radio. A gospel station was playing *Rock of Ages*. The broadcast was intermittent, fading in and out. He pushed the seek button, cigarette dangling from the edge of his mouth. He found mostly static amid snatches of songs. Going back and forth across the dial, he ran the full range of frequencies, always with the same result. The signals were either too weak or nonexistent, so he snapped the volume off. Sat back. Took a long drag of the cigarette and watched the road through a thick haze of smoke.

Headlights flashed across a weathered sign badly in need of repair—*Welcome to Wine Country.* A tenth of a mile farther, leaning on rusted posts, the wood rotted, letters faded, was a second sign—*GlenRiver Vineyards & Winery.*

David wasn't paying attention to the road. Through a break in the trees, he noticed a light shining in the window of a log cabin. He caught only a glimpse of it, but was surprised to see anything at all since the building had been abandoned for years as well as the winery next to it. GlenRiver hadn't made wine of any variety in more than sixty years.

So who was in the cabin?—he wondered. More importantly, *why?*

"The house—how far?" asked Red.

"A mile ahead," said David. "On your right."

The taxi followed the contour of the highway, winding left, winding right, drifting back and forth continuously, never moving in a straight line.

The meter read: $298. And ticking.

"Have you noticed?" Red asked. "No traffic. Haven't seen a car since we left the freeway. Huh, this is strange. Really strange."

David looked over his shoulder, then straight ahead without saying a word. He knew he was on a road not heavily traveled. It entered a valley, an isolated stretch of cropland, remote to travelers. But not to see any cars or trucks whatsoever was strange indeed.

Red crushed the cigarette out in the ashtray. When he looked up, his eyes widened and head jerked forward. All at once he slammed on the brakes, turned the wheel right, then left. The taxi lurched, the front end dipping, tires skidding. David was thrown against the shoulder restraint as the taxi swerved into the lane, slowing down.

"What in blazes...?!" Red exclaimed.

Only a few feet from the bumper, dark shapes scurried across the highway, eyes aglow, caught in the projection of the headlamps, disappearing into the darkness.

"Why happened?" David cried.

"Wolves! Lucky I didn't run 'em over."

"We don't have wolves in Ohio."

"Sure looked like wolves to me."

Red wiped a bead of sweat from his forehead while his eyes wandered back and forth. Whatever he saw was gone now, but it only seemed to make him more nervous.

"Feel that?" he said. There was an audible catch in his throat. "Can you feel *that?*"

David watched and listened. Felt with his senses.

The night was astir with warm, moist currents of air gushing past the window.

"No," said David. "I don't feel anything."

"Well, I do." A thought seemed to trigger a reaction. Red's voice took on a tone of gravity, of trepidation. "I don't like this. We're gittin' outta here."

Off the taxi flew, foot clamped hard on the accelerator. Wheels spun, leaving a trail of hot rubber on the road. By the time they were cruising in fifth gear, Red was feeling much better. He pulled out another cigarette. Raised it to his mouth. Flicked a lighter. Held the trembling flame to the tip.

A bump suddenly rocked the car.

The cigarette fell onto his lap, spilling hot ashes everywhere. He panicked, slapping at his pants as the cab came crashing down against the pavement.

David braced for an impact by grabbing the safety handle above the rear passenger window.

Somehow Red maintained control of the taxi. Tires hugged the blacktop close to the centerline, headlights veering up and down as the rocking motion stabilized.

"I swear, there was nothin' on the road!" he declared, both hands now gripping the steering wheel. "Not a damn thing! I was looking right at it. Right at it!"

The cab shuddered again, the undercarriage lifting, then dropping with a jarring abruptness.

"What the hell!"

Metal scraped asphalt. The car bounced, the suspension flexing, straining as the stability control kicked in. Amazingly, Red managed to avoid an accident. The vehicle sped around a bend on two wheels, over a hill, righted itself, and descended into another stretch of pavement leading into a valley.

"You all right?" asked Red.

David kept quiet…his eyes riveted to the road.

The quick descent plunged them into a pocket of dampness, light fog that floated past unexpectedly.

The cabbie slowed down. "Whoa, where did this come from?"

One moment the night was clear. Now it wasn't. The fog thickened as they progressed. Deep veils of gray mist hung in the air with a distinctive odor, a staleness, like egg water. The headlights, even on high, couldn't penetrate it. Visibility was limited, the road in essence a blind path. The car slowed from fifty to thirty, though it was difficult to judge. The effect was eerie, almost supernatural, as all motion appeared to cease. Both the cabbie and David leaned forward, trying to see.

The dashboard flickered. The radio came on by itself, jumping from station to station. Excerpts boomed through the speakers, one right after another, from guitar rhythms to symphonies, resonating in erratic spurts. Vocals were drowned out by orchestras, George Gershwin's *Rhapsody in Blue*' by a preacher shouting a sermon, all of it coming while neither Red nor David could see a thing.

Something flashed. A burst of light struck their eyes.

"Look out!" David yelled. "Stop!"

Too late.

Oncoming headlamps sliced through the mist at high speed. A ton and a half of steel came hurtling forward like a projectile, horn blasting. Tires skidded. Metal struck metal, a glancing collision, side to side as the two cars slammed together. Glass shattered upon impact. David's head snapped to his right, hitting the window. He felt a violent shake, felt the cab go plunging downward. The windshield popped, then burst as pieces scattered everywhere. A body went flying through it. The driver wasn't wearing his seat belt. David was. He braced one hand against the front seat. The other gripped the safety handle. The taxi went sliding on its side, bouncing along at a decelerating pace, the ground looming no more than a foot from his face when grille and fender met a solid object. The air bags deployed, the vehicle heaving like a dying animal, metal twisting, screeching, static buzzing from the radio as the engine stopped.

For one brief moment, squinting through the broken windshield, David thought he saw something, a shape of some kind, barely distinguishable—rising.

Maybe he was imagining it. But it hung there, floating, hovering, vague yet slightly incandescent, languishing in a shroud.

Then light, motion, everything faded away. He felt his breath give out.

His eyes closed.

A distant rumble accentuated the night. It sounded like an explosion.

The meter read: $301. And holding.

Chapter 2

The air remained clouded, filled with nebulous haze.
Despite being in a state of shock and woozy from the blow to his head, David found himself standing at the edge of the highway. For some reason he felt a sense of urgency, a need to run. He didn't remember leaving the taxi or at what precise moment he saw her. It was difficult to tell what she was wearing. Her dress seemed to blend in with the surroundings. Her long hair trailed as though it were windswept, as did the scarf hanging from her neck.
He found himself in pursuit of her while staggering up through a ditch in fog so thick he couldn't tell where he was. Ground, trees, sky, everything was blotted out by the elements. Behind him, from the road, he heard a strange hissing noise—either a radiator overheating or tires deflating—followed by a loud continuous crunching of metal, like a large aluminum container slowly being crushed. This gave him reason to pause. As he did, the woman he was pursuing disappeared. Everything went quiet, so quiet he could hear his heart thumping in his chest.
All at once he felt a coldness at his back. His pulse quickened and skin tingled as perspiration ran down his face. He was afraid to move. Every instinct, all his training, told him not to turn around, that he was in danger.
Ahead, no more than ten steps away, the woman reappeared—like she had materialized out of thin air. She seemed to be motioning to him, either beckoning to come closer or warning him to stay away. At the same time he heard another sound that made him freeze. Imperceptibly at first, mounting steadily, it was heavy, rhythmic. After a few heart-stopping seconds, he realized it was long, deep breaths. And they weren't coming from him or the woman, but somewhere else. In the dimness, a huge shadow fell. The breathing grew louder, closer. He turned, and gaping up into the night, he shrieked, certain he was going to die when—
A hand touched his shoulder.
He jerked forward as he woke up, his body trembling, his chest heaving.
"Easy there, sleepyhead." The voice withdrew to the side of the room. "Some nightmare that must have been. For a moment I thought you were gonna jump out of your skin. What you need is a

little sunshine."

Gasping, David felt a mattress beneath him and clutched it firmly in both hands. He was lying in a hospital bed.

A middle-aged nurse cast a glance in his direction as he opened the window blinds. "Gotta nasty bruise there, young man."

He sat up, wearing hospital whites. "How did I get here?"

"By ambulance. Don't you remember? You had an accident."

He touched the sheet, the mattress, the bar at the edge of the bed to make sure he wasn't dreaming.

"They found you wandering through a field," the nurse said.

His brow furrowed in confusion. "The cab driver—how is he?"

"Not as fortunate as you. He died en route to the hospital. The other driver, poor thing...she didn't make it that far."

David reached for a bandage wrapped around his head, suddenly conscious of the pain. "Other driver?"

"Yes. You're lucky to be alive. The second car exploded, went up in flames. The driver...she a...unfortunately was burned beyond recognition." The nurse hurried across the room and paused by the door. "Need any medication, aspirin? Feeling any discomfort?"

"No, I'm fine," he said without conviction.

"Lie back. Get some rest. I'll be at the nurses' station down the hall. Someone's outside to see you." She opened the door and leaned into the hallway. "Officer, he's awake. You may come in now."

The nurse left the room and a man in uniform appeared, a sheriff's deputy—starched blue shirt, badge, gun, holster. A stocky man about thirty years of age, well-groomed, hair cut short, military style. David recognized him instantly. The nametag read: *Thomas Duckett*.

"Hi, Tom."

"David." The deputy sat down, placed his hat on his knee. "Good to see you. Feeling better?"

David nodded.

The deputy glanced around the room before settling back in the chair. "Last time I saw you, you were playing center field for Ohio Southern. How long has it been? Six, seven years?"

"Something like that."

"Coach says you were the best recruit he ever had. Speaking of which, I heard you joined the Navy. Navy Seals, I believe."

The patient acknowledged it with a half-hearted shrug of his shoulders. He didn't feel like making small talk. "You're here because of the accident, I take it."

Tom rubbed his jaw as if contemplating tact. "I am. Other than a mild concussion, the doctor said you're doing okay. Too bad we can't say the same for the driver. Apparently he wasn't wearing a seat belt. Were you?"

"Yes."

"I won't take up much of your time. Mind if I ask a couple of questions?"

"No, go ahead."

"I'm trying to determine what happened. Did the other driver hit you or was it the other way around?"

David slipped the covers aside and sat on the edge of the bed. "I'm not really sure."

"Anything stand out in your mind?"

David arched his back, groaned, and said, "A few things. Mostly the strangeness of it…"

"Of what?"

"Everything. The whole experience."

"Could you be more specific?"

"Well, for one thing I saw two county patrol cars sitting by the entrance to the park, monitoring traffic, but there was no traffic to speak of. One of the patrolmen had an assault rifle. Why an assault rifle? What was he expecting? And then later we ran into some fog. Couldn't see a thing until the last second when the headlights hit us. I heard the horn, and bam! The two cars slammed together."

"Did you see anything you'd consider… unusual?"

Soreness swept across David's shoulder. He massaged it. "Only the fog. It was weird. One second the sky was clear. The next, there it was. Excuse me. I have to call my sister." He reached for a telephone sitting on a bedside table.

"I already did," said Tom. "She should be here in a few minutes. Do you remember what happened to the driver?"

David replaced the phone. "Vaguely. Things got a little fuzzy for a while."

"Details, descriptions—anything would help."

"Now that I think about it, I do remember one thing. The headlights of the oncoming car…at the last second they veered hard to the left. Like she was trying to avoid hitting something."

"Into your lane?"

"I think so."

"That would explain the skid marks, the violent turn. And the cab driver?"

"Once I saw the headlights, I braced against the front seat. The windshield snapped. Maybe not snapped. *Sucked out* is more like it."

Tom leaned forward in his chair. "What do you mean, 'sucked out'?"

"This'll sound crazy. The glass—it shattered upon impact. But the pieces flew *out*, not down and in like you'd expect. Our momentum was carrying us forward, not backward. The fragments broke like they were being pulled from the opposite direction. It was almost like the driver was lifted from the car. Where was the body found?"

Tom took out a pen and notepad and started writing hard and fast. "Eighty feet in front of the taxi. Hmmm. That adds a little twist to things."

"Twist?"

"The body, where it was in relation to the car. Since the vehicle was moving forward, his body should have been found behind the vehicle, not ahead of it, not when we found fragments, glass chips from the windshield well back where the taxi first slid. There was a difference of more than a hundred and sixty feet. The body, it appears, was carried. Not dragged. Carried. His arms and legs were broken, so I doubt he could walk or crawl. It doesn't add up. Lots of things don't add up."

"Such as?"

"The condition of the taxi."

"What about it?"

"It was crushed. Like it had been in one of those compactors you find in a junkyard. Good thing you got out when you did. You do remember getting out, what you were doing when I approached, don't you?"

David tried to piece together bits of memory He had lapses that went completely blank. "No," he replied. "I don't remember getting out or seeing you. But I had this...this weird feeling I was going to die."

"Why do you say that?"

"I don't know. I just...*know*."

"Was it something you saw?"

"No."

"Something you felt?"

"I can't explain it. The moment we entered the fog...everything after that was like a dream. I couldn't get my bearings."

"Do you know you were in a state of shock when I found you... out walking around?"

"I was?"

"You wouldn't talk. Your eyes were open, but I'm not sure you could see anything."

"I don't remember."

"Soon as I got to you, you collapsed. My partner and I had had to carry you to the patrol car. At what point were you conscious?"

"After I got out of the taxi."

"After? How long after?"

"I don't know. I don't know how far I walked I never looked back."

Tom noticed the young man's confidence was shaken. "Why not? Why were you in shock?"

"Why else? I hit my head."

"Let me rephrase it. You weren't in shock. You were panic-stricken."

"Same difference."

"No. Shock would be a result of the crash. Panic-stricken refers to something else. People don't go walking around with that kind of expression, so scared they can't talk. There has to be a reason."

David was about to comment when a knock came at the door. The nurse poked her head in. "A Miss Eileen Macklin is here to see the patient."

Both men stood up.

"Tell her to wait," said Tom. "Give us a second." He cupped the brim of his hat. "One thing bothers me, David. We had checkpoints, random patrols out looking for drunk drivers, speeders, and according to my sources, there were no sightings of fog anywhere else. Only in that one area. I find that rather peculiar, don't you?"

David was intrigued by the choice of the word, *sightings*. It carried with it certain implications, none of which he was willing to accept. "I know what I saw," he said, a bit puzzled.

"No, no," said Tom. "I'm not questioning that. I saw the same thing you did. I'm only making an observation. Guess that's it. I won't bother you any longer." He walked to the door. "Oh. We found your suitcase in the trunk of the cab—a bit flattened, I'm afraid. You'll find your belongings in the closet. By the way, where are you staying? At your dad's place or your sister's?"

"My dad's."

"Well, nice to see you, David. Good luck." Tom thought for a moment, then turned at the last second. "One last thing. Wilfredo Pinoza. I assume you know him?"

"Freddie? Of course. He's worked for my father off and on for years. Why do you ask?"

"He's come up missing. Last person to see him was his ex-wife."

David froze while reaching inside the closet. "Missing?"

"Poof. Gone. Without a trace."

"Freddie wouldn't just leave and not say anything."

"That's what your father said. We've looked everywhere. Put the word out at the usual places. Bars, restaurants, gas stations. So far, nothing."

"That's strange. Do you think something's happened to him?"

"Put it this way. No good can come from any disappearance, especially when we have no clues." Tom watched the patient dump the contents of a paper bag onto the bed and go rummaging through them for a shirt and pair of pants. "If I have any more questions, I'd like to stop by if you don't mind."

David nodded and slipped into a pair of blue jeans. "Sure. Any time."

Tom took a step and hesitated. "Oh. One word of caution, David. There've been a number of incidents around your place that…well, I'll let your sister explain it. I'm not at liberty to comment further. Let's just say, the Sheriff is thinking of imposing a curfew in that part of the county. You might want to reconsider where you stay. Same goes for your father. I can't convince him that it's unsafe to stay at his place. But it is."

"Unsafe?"

"Talk to your sister." Tom put his hat on, opened the door, gestured to someone, tipped his hat in one direction, then the other before exiting.

With a rush of anticipation, Elly Macklin walked in. "Nice headband." She grinned and gave David a hug.

He stepped back and took a good, long look at her. She was tall, athletic, auburn-haired, dressed in khaki shorts and lavender angora sweater, sleeves rolled up to the elbows. When she smiled, dimples accented the edges of her mouth.

David studied her eyes. They betrayed her. She may have been smiling on the outside, but not on the inside.

"Why didn't you tell me you were coming?" she asked.

"I did. I sent texts, emails. Called at least half a dozen times."

"I didn't get any messages."

"I know. The phones—they're all messed up." He remembered leaving his cell phone in the taxi. He cussed under his breath and waved her to the door. "We need to talk. Let's get out of here."

He hurried to the bed, threw on a red flannel work shirt, tennis shoes, stuffing the remainder of the clothes in the paper bag, grabbed it, and slipped his wallet in his back pocket.

"You didn't tell me Freddie was missing."

Her smile faded. "I'm afraid there are a lot of things I haven't told you."

Chapter 3

The back road was rough, pitted with ruts as the Jeep went rolling…shaking over it.

"Where are you taking me?" asked David.

"Be patient. We're almost there."

The ride home was about to be interrupted. Mistwood, Ohio—the county seat and largest city in Bertram County, also residence to the university and hospital—was seventeen miles from Macklin Farms, seventeen miles of rich, gentle-sloping croplands neatly manicured by tractors and combines to the middle of GlenRiver Valley, regarded as one of the most scenic and fertile pieces of property in the state. Elly chose a deliberate route for a reason. Her yellow Jeep Wrangler, top down in sixty-degree weather, was heading southwest. Blue skies, early morning sun at their backs, they drove to a hill bordering their father's farm and stopped along the graveled side road overlooking the valley.

Elly cut the engine and said, "Okay. There's no easy way to put this. We might as well start with *that*." She nodded at the valley below.

Green undulating hills stretching for miles were divided by a steep-banked river running east to west. In the distance, impossible to overlook, was a railroad bridge lying in ruins, half submerged in the river. The middle section looked as if a bomb had struck it, leaving a huge gap where the girders, track, and main leg of the foundation had caved in.

David snapped his head back. "Holy…"

Elly waited so he could he absorb the impact. "Investigators have been crawling all over the place since Monday. Guess what they found? Nothing. Not a trace of explosives. No heat marks, burns. No basic weaknesses in the structure. Cracks, breaks, faults—none of that. A report issued last year said the bridge and foundation were still fundamentally sound."

"So what happened?"

"Good question. No one knows. Dad was asleep. Said he didn't hear a thing."

"That's crazy. It had to be explosives. You can tell just looking at it."

"Evidence doesn't lie, David. Anyway, the cause is immaterial.

You know what it means, don't you?"

He knew all too well. The bridge allowed the transport of grain to and from a complex of storage elevators located on the other side of the valley. A nonfunctioning bridge meant product couldn't be shipped by boxcar to the railroad yards in Cincinnati. No transport, no product. No profit.

David felt a sickening twinge in the pit of his stomach.

Elly's anxiety level went up. "The real killer came yesterday when the entire staff, outside of management, quit. Just walked off the job without a word. Most of them wouldn't return my calls. If they did, all I got was the run around, a bunch of lame excuses. One guy acted like he was kinda...spooked or something."

"That's weird."

"Trust me. It gets weirder. The weather hasn't been cooperating either. If it doesn't rain soon, we'll be in deep, deep trouble. Dad's hurting for cash so much he rented Aunt Blanche's old place to a sharecropper, a hog farmer."

"What?" David could feel the blood rushing to his face. "Since when?"

"Since Monday. His name is Paul Heidtman. A real creep, hard-core ex-marine. You know how you can look into someone's eyes and tell they can't be trusted? He's that type of guy. Frankly, until this week I didn't think things could get any worse. That's why dad had to take out a second loan...liquidate assets for home repairs, payroll, insurance, and back taxes."

David shook his head. "This is not good. Not good at all. Caddo's still working, I hope."

He was referring to a family friend, a full-blooded Indian who lived in the basement of the farmhouse.

"Oh, he's still working all right, but boy, oh, boy..." Elly let out a sarcastic laugh. "He's getting stranger and stranger every day."

"How so?"

"He keeps to himself all the time. Comes and goes whenever he pleases. Sometimes he'll work sunup to sundown. Two, three days in a row. Other times—after dark, weekends—he just...vanishes."

"What do you mean, 'vanishes'?"

"He leaves. Disappears. Outside of work I can never find him. And when I do, he's always reading, studying, or doing research on the internet. When I ask him about it, he becomes evasive. It's like he's trying to hide something."

"He's not married to the job, El. How's dad holding up?"

She grabbed the steering wheel and took a deep breath. "Not well, I'm afraid. I said I wasn't going to do this."

"Do what?"

"Be emotional."

But emotional she was. She paused as her eyes swelled with tears and throat constricted in a gag-flex. "He...started drinking again. The hard stuff. The other night when I stopped by...he was passed out on the kitchen floor, holding an empty whiskey bottle. Swore he'd never do it again. Two days later I found another bottle. Not a drop left. He doesn't date. Hardly knows what a woman looks like. Won't take money or discuss how he's doing. Work, sleep, and drink—that's all he does."

She sucked in the emotion and continued, "I thought I could help. Now I'm not so sure. Uncle Mark..."—she pretended to laugh—"good ol' Uncle Mark. He and the bank got together and hired a bunch of lawyers. They've been sending letters, asking for records, documents, bills, receipts, tax statements. They've even threatened to sue. Legally, anything short of blackmail, they're looking for ways to harass him."

"Why?"

"Delinquent loans. But it's just a trick, a ploy. What they really want is land, anything they can get their grubby mitts on. Dad has never defaulted on anything in his life. And these are the same people who've cheated him blind. Petty stuff. Nuisance claims. Based on implication, innuendo, supposition, lies. You name it and they're throwing it up against the wall to see if it sticks. If it wasn't for the bank, clever manipulation by lawyers, they'd call it extortion."

"Extortion?"

"Uncle Mark is trying to steal the farm—by whatever means he can."

David was in shock. He could see why she was so upset. Who wouldn't be? For a moment he thought she lost her objectivity. But not now.

Blackmail. Extortion. Theft of property?

He expected bad news, but nothing like this. Not of this magnitude anyway. He felt a sudden pang of guilt. After all, he was partly to blame for the financial mess. If he had stayed at home instead of joining the Navy, perhaps some or all of it could have been avoided.

Elly was nearing the breaking point. "Now dad's discovered poker on the internet. Texas Hold 'em. Plays almost every night. Doctor says he's a manic depressive...compulsive gambler. Put 'em together and you've got a big, big problem. Throw in drugs and you've got a lethal combination. Just look inside his medicine cabinet and you'll find antidepressants, Vicodin, pills for stress, cholesterol, high blood pressure, headaches. God knows what else. Says he can't sleep at night unless he takes something. And during the day, like I said, all he does is work. Add a few shots of bourbon and he's a train wreck waiting to happen. I'm afraid he may be suicidal, David. He might die of loneliness or depression. I do what I can, but I go to school and work almost seventy hours a week."

David put a reassuring hand on her shoulder.

Calmly as she could, Elly reached into the glove compartment, removed a tissue, wiped her eyes, and took a few seconds to collect herself. "Sorry. I'm not very good at this." She drew a deep breath and proceeded, "One of my professors...she's beautiful, a widow. I had it all set up, a casual date at a restaurant in town. What does dad do? Drinks. Passes out on the couch at home! Blew her off completely. God, what a fiasco that was." She stared off into space, fighting back the tears." It's so sad. Remember the old home movies...the scene where mom was dancing in the backyard?"

He nodded.

"Well, dad put it to music. Procol Harem. *Whiter Shade of Pale...*"

David could hear the haunting melody: *'We skipped the light fandango. Turned cartwheels across the floor. I was feelin' kinda seasick. But the crowd called out for more...'*

He remembered when he and his sister were little, the nights Dora would crawl into Elly's bed or his and they'd curl up together and she'd lull them to sleep, humming or quietly singing a song by Joni Mitchell, Joan Baez, Procol Harem, or reading a children's book—*Cobweb Castle, The Grinch Who Stole Christmas.* Or she'd tell a bedtime story, making it up as she went.

God, how he missed her.

"Dad plays it almost every night," said Elly. "He sits there in front of the bedroom TV, staring as she dances barefoot, wearing that yellow sundress. Sometimes I can't get the lyrics out of my head." Almost unconsciously, Elly whispered, "*...That her face at first was just ghostly...*"—and ended it by singing—"*...turned a w-h-i-t-e-r s-h-a-d-e of p-a-l-e.*"

It was just like their mother used to sing it—soft and sweet.

David felt a lump in his throat.

Elly steeled herself from heartache and said, "Nice way to welcome you home, huh David?" She dabbed her eyes with Kleenex.

David reached across the seat and touched her arm. "You okay?"

She forced a smile. "Yeah. The crazy thing is, there might be a silver lining in all this."

At that point David was ready to latch onto something, anything. "What's that?"

"A company out of Toledo wants to build a golf course. Guess where?"

He shrugged.

"*Birch Run.*"

David reacted without so much as a flinch, but inside he was cringing. "Why would anybody want to put a golf course up there?"

"My sentiment exactly. Caddo goes up there all the time. Why, I have no idea. A couple of days ago it was practically a done deal. As of now, there's no guarantee. Everybody seems a little uptight lately. Come here. I want to show you something." She looked to her left, at a fenced-in power station. She opened the door and walked across the road with David fast on her heels. She pointed at the transformer. "See that? Notice anything?"

David examined the power grid. Wires, cables, utility lines intersected. It looked like a gigantic metal spider web, woven at angles, divided into squares, encircling a gray box about fifteen feet long and seven feet high. Warning signs, attached to the fence, ringed around the structure. Everything else appeared normal, except the housing.

"What the…" David uttered, amazed.

"That, dear brother, is forged sheet metal, a quarter inch thick."

They locked their eyes onto the housing, a cast iron power unit that was dented and partially misshapen. It looked as if someone had taken a giant mallet or wrecking ball and whacked the sides of it—front, back, north, and south—only as Elly explained it, there was no evidence of impact.

"Not a scratch anywhere. No one knows how it happened. See the fence? It's new. So are the cables and wires. Half the county was blacked out. Tuesday night a neighbor said he saw electricity… smoke shooting out, a great big shower of sparks and in the middle some kind of weird light. Like heat lightning. A guy with the power company said there's nothing in the system that could melt wire. The company claims nothing is wrong. Everything's working perfectly. It's not the system, not the transformer, but something else. Something *outside* that caused the damage."

David didn't say a word. He listened as she kept bantering on about neglect—neglect by county officials, the Sheriff's Department, anyone involved with the investigations.

"Neglect," she said, "to issue a public statement." Her anxiety was evidenced by the fact there was little conjecture as well, none from a media standpoint.

His mind kept wandering at this imposing thought.

"David!" She waved a hand in front of his face. "Are you listening? I said, there hasn't been one eyewitness. Just rumors about things seen at night, never during the day."

"What kind of things?"

Her shoulders slumped in frustration. "I don't know. Vague references. Sightings. I live in town, remember? They only seem to occur on this side of the county."

A hundred questions raced through his head at once. Before he could get a word in edgewise, she dropped another bomb—

"One more thing. Something's attacking the livestock."

"Attacking the..."

"There's been at least six killings we know of...at four separate locations. Different nights. Mauled the exact same way. Gutted. Half eaten. Body parts scattered everywhere. Two other animals are reportedly missing. Presumed dead—eaten—bones and all."

"What kind of animal would do a thing like that?"

"That's what everybody is asking. I've heard everything from a grizzly to a mountain lion."

"A grizzly? Hasn't been a bear around here since grandpa died."

"It's all conjecture. I visited a scene where a cow was killed. Never seen anything like it. The fangs had to be three inches long. Huge chunks were taken in a single bite. We've got a real nasty creature wandering around out there. Whatever it is, it's nocturnal. It feeds at night, has a bite radius twice the size of anything I know of. Another thing. I analyzed a hair and piece of skin, as did a colleague and professor at the university. We all concurred. The hair, we believe, is from a mammal. The skin, from a human."

"Anything else?"

Elly took a sip of water from a plastic container and that seemed to settle her down. "Coyotes. We have a problem with coyotes. Sometimes you can hear them at night. The scary thing is, they may have rabies. They act more aggressive than they should."

"They need to be hunted down and killed."

"Captured and treated, David. Not killed."

Elly—animal right's activist. Lover of animals.

David expected no less from her. He remembered the cab driver mistaking a pack of coyotes for wolves. "So what does dad make of all this?"

Elly shook her head. "Nothing. He denies everything. He's been denying things for years."

"What do you mean?"

"Mom. He acts like she's still alive. After seven years? Sooner or later he has to face up to the fact she's dead." Elly wiped her nose with tissue. "Wish I knew what to do. A friend of mine, a reporter—she keeps asking questions, but the Sheriff's Department is keeping everyone in the dark. To avoid panic, I guess. But don't they understand? Not knowing is just as bad. Maybe worse. Talk to Caddo, David. He's hiding something. Why else does he behave the way he does?"

He led her to the car and gestured to the door. "Tell me about it on the way home."

As he climbed into the seat, he couldn't help but reflect upon the longtime Macklin employee—

Caddo—if ever there was a more enigmatic man on the planet...

The thought almost made David laugh.

If it hadn't been for the accident last night, he wouldn't have believed half of what he had heard. Then again, twice this morning in separate conversations, the word "sighting" had been used. Coincidence? Perhaps it was too early to tell. Given the circumstances, David was beginning to wonder if he had experienced a sighting himself. Somehow he wasn't sure if his naval training, or any training for that matter, could have prepared him for this.

He glanced at Elly as she started the engine. "Who else goes up to Birch Run besides Caddo?"

"No one."

"How do you know?"

"No reason to. It's not like we're using the land for anything." She shifted the transmission into *drive*. "Maybe he's got a secret stash of pot up there." The Jeep lurched forward, scattering dust and gravel as her voice rose above the engine. "I swear sometimes he acts like he's stoned."

Chapter 4

In the late 1700's, Stewart Macklin and his wife, Elizabeth, immigrated to the United States from Great Britain where agriculture had been a family tradition for generations. Like his father before him, Stewart toiled in the fields doing backbreaking work day after day. Unable to support a family in the manner in which he had hoped, he realized better opportunities awaited elsewhere, so he and his wife sailed across the Atlantic. Then west, aboard wagon trains and riverboats, they explored a wilderness and upon their arrival in Ohio before it was a state, the young man, eager and full of ambition, sought a location relatively unpopulated in a region that bore a climate similar to England where he could apply his various agricultural skills and dreams. A month later, Macklin Farms was founded in a valley so beautiful, so unspoiled by civilization, his bride upon seeing it for the first time said, "Seems a shame to be putting a spade to it."

But put a spade to it they did—first as a logging business and then as a crop farm. It grew and grew. Its boundaries spread south beyond Little Bass River, northward across what is now Bertram County, while east and west the property extended for miles. During its heyday, the amount of land swelled to ten thousand acres, stretching across hills, forests, rivers, and lakes. Bit by bit the acreage dwindled. Land was sold, lost during the Depression, or given to charity—Fallen Oaks State Park being a prime example. In all, it was a storied history, propagated by 'Poppa' Wil Macklin during World War II and inherited to this day by Richard, the latest in a long line of descendants who alone kept ownership intact and the Macklin dream alive on twenty-five hundred acres, the remaining legacy of an ever-shrinking empire.

That sense of history was never lost to David whenever he returned home. It was a place where people worked hard, had a genuine respect for nature, a place rich with history dating back to the Indians, infused with an atmosphere unique to itself—isolated, peaceful, and quiet. Those were the impressions he had whenever he saw the rustic, three-story house by the highway, the barn beside it, the twin silos, and massive old barn sitting at the top of the hill. He felt guilty about joining the Navy a year out of high school and he wasn't sure which was more compelling—his desire to be independent and travel the world, or how the spirit of the land affected him, drew him in. Macklin Farms was ingrained in his soul and that, he knew, would never change. Homecoming, especially on this day, tore him in opposite directions.

Elly hit the brakes, bringing the Jeep to a stop. David swept his gaze across the gentle terrain running along Route 2, the freshly plowed fields, furrows in perfect alignment, the cattle yard to their left, heifers and cows standing idly, grazing on spring grass. A Midwestern farm at planting time. Trees budding. Splotches of green sprouting from bushes. Sunshine. You could almost hear the corn seeds popping open.

Nature engaged in the miracle of spring…

It was David's favorite time of year, when baseball reigns, when expectations take over and everyone believes they're a kid again. He could remember warm mornings in April when he woke up so excited he went running through the fields at dawn, tossing a ball up in the air, waiting for it, glove in hand, judging the wind, arc, speed, the motion of it as it was coming down, never once afraid of it hitting his head. At that age you embraced baseball, reveled in it, revered everything about the game, never conscious of how deeply rooted it became, not while you were a kid. You may have said you loved it, may have even believed it, and indeed it was true, but the real love affair came later when you were older, when you could recall the youthful passion, the excitement exhibited by someone inspired by the wonders of sport. As a boy, naïve to the complexities of the world, you were only aware of the purity of baseball. As a man, baseball exemplified a longing for innocence, a longing to be a kid again.

And nothing rekindled his love of baseball more than the farm. The two were inseparable. David was always moved by the serenity of GlenRiver Valley and surrounding hills. Together they summoned up a wealth of emotions.

Elly reached across the seat and touched his shoulder. "You okay?"

He looked at the old Victorian house with its red brick siding, gabled porch, and ornate styling. Images flooded through his head all at once, one of them in particular. "Just thinking of dad. Living here by himself. All this land. Sometimes I wonder if it was a curse to inherit so much. Every time I come home I think about the day I left."

"Stop it," said Elly. "We've had this discussion before, remember? You're entitled to live your life—however you want." She studied him a moment, then put the Jeep in reverse. "I'll come back later. You two could use some time alone."

David opened the passenger door. With his bag of clothes in hand, he stood at the foot of the driveway while the Wrangler drove away. The sound of a distant engine drew his attention. Recognizable by a shock of shoulder-length white hair and customary army-issue khaki shirt, Caddo was sitting on a tractor, plowing the east field.

To the left of the driveway, the doors to the lower barn were open, revealing a tarp that covered a '57 Chevy truck he and his father had restored. At the far end of the driveway, an old gray Jeep Cherokee was parked beside a chicken coup, a drab cinder-blocked building where a flock was clucking contentedly.

From behind the house two black cocker spaniels suddenly appeared, scampering forward, barking. When they realized who the visitor was, they ran up to him, tails wagging, eyes full of joy, and started jumping up and down.

"Hey, Roscoe! Cinders! Miss your old pal? Huh? Where's the love? Show me the love. *Y-e-a-h-h-h.*"

He bent down and petted them as they nuzzled his legs. They danced, drooled, and skipped around, lavishing him with puppy dog affection. Roscoe rolled onto his back, kicked his legs in the air, and began pumping his paws, while Cinders, distinguished from her brother by the patch of white on her neck, was not to be outdone. Whimpering playfully, she got down low, eyes shining, tongue sticking out, and did some goofy dance, hopping side to side, her cropped tail jiggling faster than a rattlesnake's.

David didn't dare put his face close to hers. No way. If he did, she'd lick him like crazy. And if he smiled or laughed, she'd lick harder and faster until his cheeks were raw. A licker. Smoocher. That was Cinders.

If only dogs could smile.

"Where's dad? Come on. Show me where dad is."

Reacting as if they understood, the cockers went running lickity-split toward the back of the house.

Attired in overalls and rubber wading boots, Richard was digging inside a fenced-in garden soaked in mud and water.

"Hi ya', Pops."

Richard turned. His face went from frustration to surprise. "Oh, my God!" He sloshed through the mud, a grin growing wider with each approaching step. After opening the gate, they embraced. "Well, well. Good to see you, David. Good to see you. What brings you home?" There was a certain amount of awkwardness at first—due to a year and half of separation—but that was dispelled by the usual chitchat. Finally, Richard said, "What did you do to your head?"

David reached up and absentmindedly touched his bandage.

"Long story." He offered a shortened version, adding, "I was the lucky one. I walked away. The cab driver didn't."

Richard frowned as if something was bothering him. David noticed it, but kept the conversation light and casual until he asked, "Where do you suppose Freddie is? I heard he's been missing for almost a week now."

"Wish I knew," said Richard. "Who told you he was missing?"

"Tom Duckett. He came to the hospital. Gave me the third degree about the accident. I can't believe Freddie would just...up and disappear."

"Unfortunately, that seems to be the case. Everybody was brought in. Police, Highway Patrol, county Deputies, even the Ohio Bureau of Investigation. Freddie left two grocery bags sitting on the kitchen counter. Not something you'd do if you're planning to disappear, is it?"

"Why would agents from the Ohio Bureau of Investigation get involved?"

"That's a good question."

"Freddie, a concern of the state? It doesn't make sense."

There was a commotion inside the fence, a gurgle of water as it leaked from a pump.

"Looks like you got a water problem there," said David.

"Yeah," said Richard. He glanced at the garden. Roscoe was standing in a puddle of water, sniffing around. "You know, it's kinda strange. I had a dream about that pump last night. Couldn't shut it off. Now look. Hey, Roscoe. Get outta there!"

The cocker spaniel came splashing out the gate, tail wagging, mud oozing underfoot. Richard stroked his back with a gloved hand.

"Pipe must've have sprung a leak," remarked David.

"Maybe," said Richard. He removed a rag from his back pocket and wiped the dog's paws with it. "Well couldn't have much water in it. Haven't had rain for seven weeks. Musta leaked all night."

David noticed a difference in his father. Richard had aged considerably in the last two years. He had a scratchy two day-old beard. His thinning hair was unkempt. Dark, puffy circles under his eyes indicated a lack of sleep. He looked as if he had lost twenty pounds or so.

Richard released the spaniel and stuffed the grimy cloth in his back pocket. "So a...you and Elly...been keeping in touch, I hope. Forgive the old man. Too much to do around here."

"Yes, sir."

Richard leaned against a fence post and crossed his arms. "And?"

The younger Macklin shrugged. "What?"

"Come on, David. You're here for a reason. Not that I'm complaining. You're always welcome. Any time."

"I'm not sure what you mean."

Richard smiled. "I know your sister—how she thinks, how she feels. She's a worrier, like her mother. And when she worries, she talks. About this place. Me. She's concerned."

"Maybe she has a right to be."

"Maybe so. I won't deny it. But every year we seem to survive. Has she told you about the golf course?"

David nodded.

"Four hundred acres this side of the winery. Land's no good for farming. Too hilly. Better suited for golf. Or so they say. I haven't written or called because…well, it was supposed to be a surprise."

"I understand."

"If you don't like the idea, we'll forget about it and move on."

David saw an opening and jumped in. "It's your call. What if they cancel, what then? It's not like we're getting rich these days. If the grain elevators go out of business, that's really gonna hurt."

"If that happens, I'll just have to cut costs…suck it up."

"So where do we stand…financially?"

"Let's put it this way. If I go under, so does the bank. Too much invested for that to happen."

Not satisfied by the answer, David pressed the issue further, "Are we in hock? Or in the black?"

"Well, last year we lost a little over ten grand. Most of that has been paid off. This year, God willing, if we get any rain…let's just say I'm optimistic. Hell, I have to be. I'm a farmer. One profitable season can erase a ton of debt. Aw, heck. What am I doing—boring you with this stuff? You're supposed to enjoy yourself while you're here. Go have fun. Eat breakfast. See some friends."

After a few parting remarks, Richard assumed the conversation was over. He sloshed through the mud into the garden and picked up a shovel.

David wasn't ready to leave just yet. "Want some help?"

"Nah. First day home…you kiddin'? Go eat breakfast."

"What if Freddie's not found? That just leaves Caddo and you."

"Unfortunately, there's not much I can do about that."

"Aren't you going to hire any part-time help?"

"Not anytime soon. Now harvest time, that's another story."

"Dad, two guys can't run a farm this big. What about the other businesses?"

Richard forced a smile. "I'm not worried about the other businesses. The nursery will be making a profit soon and in a couple of months I'll be leasing the quarries and selling stone to Canada. Now get out of here. Enjoy yourself. I've got work to do."

David watched his father go digging around the pump. The garden existed as long as he could remember, a family tradition filled with tomatoes, green beans, onions, celery, three kinds of peppers, okra, lettuce, cabbage, and tended over with care, love, and heartbreak. Each time Richard removed a shovel full of mud, he grunted. He dug faster and faster. It was almost like he had a strange affinity toward it, a strained and compulsive attraction.

David couldn't help but ask, "Dad, why do you keep a garden? There's a lot of other stuff you could be doing."

With eyebrows raised, Richard cried, "Why a...your mother, she always worked this garden. She loved it. That's why I do it, son. That's why. For your mother."

As David turned to leave, he heard Richard say, "If I forgot to mention it, glad to have you home, David. There's homemade jelly in the refrigerator. And bacon, smoke-cured. Your favorite."

That's when it hit him—the guilt, the sadness, the overpowering concern David had for his father. And that's when it also dawned on him: Nothing was mentioned about the bridge, the blackout, or the killing of livestock.

Chapter 5

Showered, shaved, sans the head bandage, David finished off the bacon and eggs, threw the pans and plate in the dishwasher, and stood by the kitchen steps leading to the basement where Caddo maintained modest living quarters. David peered out the window and saw the Indian seated on the tractor. He respected privacy, but curiosity drove him downstairs.

It was a cramped compartment, hidden behind a storage and utility room filled with boxes, water heater, and furnace. A far door led to the outside. Caddo's bed was tucked against a back wall next to a shower, toilet, and sink stall. The furnishings consisted of unstained furniture and an old picture tube TV gathering dust. A handmade sash rug of native American design covered the floor. If David didn't know the occupant, the place would have depressed anyone else. Not Caddo. He never complained about anything.

After turning on an overhead light, David walked over to a desk and opened a drawer. Inside was a purple heart Caddo received in Vietnam while enlisted in the Army Special Forces. Nothing else was unusual except for a small clay pipe, which had a sticky brown residue coating the bowl. One sniff and it gave off a distinctive odor, a sweet smokiness—undoubtedly marijuana or hashish.

"Caddo. You old devil, you."

David browsed a bookcase next, which contained an eclectic mixture of reading materials, essays on world events, a Sherlock Holmes' novel, and biographies of Adolf Hitler and Osama bin Laden. Apparently, Caddo had a myriad of interests, leaning toward mystery and conflict. But perhaps the most telling aspect of his life—other than the sash rug lying on the floor—was missing. Specifically, books or items relating to his heritage. No artifacts, belongings, decorations suggesting he was Indian.

David searched the bookcase to see if he had overlooked anything. On the bottom shelf he found an old book, bound in a tan-brown cover, which he lifted and pulled loose. After wiping the dust from the edges, he cradled it. In gold, embossed letters, a bit faded, he read the title: *Ghost Dance—The Cults, Rituals, and Practices of the American Indian.* He leafed through the pages, noting there were passages highlighted in yellow magic marker.

A door slammed upstairs.

Startled, David jumped, then cursed—barely louder than a whisper—and heard his father shout, "David!" He quickly replaced the book and tiptoed into the storage room.

A shadow darted past the stairwell.

"Down here!"

The shadow reappeared, Richard in dungarees, holding a crescent wrench. "Going to the hardware store, son. Pump needs a new O-ring and pump arm. Also need to buy some fence wire. What're you doing down there?"

Boxes shook. David was shaking them on purpose. "Um... looking for my baseball cards."

"They're upstairs in your closet where they've always been."

David switched off the light. Trudged up the steps. "I forgot. Why do you need fence wire?"

Richard looked at him as if his brains were leaking out. "Coyotes. Snuck in and killed a calf the other night. Have you eaten yet?"

"Half a slab of bacon and six scrambled eggs. I'll help when you get back."

"You know the rule. First day home, relax. I don't want you lifting a finger. You can come along if you like?"

"No, thanks. Thought I'd look around. Go for a drive. See how the truck's holding up."

"Oh, by the way—guess who bought a car?"

One person came to mind, someone who had never owned a car. "Caddo?"

Richard smiled. "Yes, sir. Bought it when he started datin' a waitress in town. Beat-up, old rusted American Motors' Pacer. God-awful color. Isn't worth the nickel he paid for it."

David's jaw fell open. "Caddo *is* dating?"

"Hot'n heavy. And, boy, is she a pistol."

"Wow, I can't believe it. I haven't seen a Pacer since I was a kid."

Richard laughed, "Now that may be a problem. It's stranded on 223 just past the grain elevators. Won't start. Do me a favor. Tell Caddo to some spread hay for the cattle. Keys to the pickup are hanging in the kitchen closet. I'm going to get cleaned up."

Once the water was running in his father's bathroom, David dialed information on the kitchen cordless. "Hello...Mistwood, Ohio...I need the number to Don's Towing Service."

* * *

You can't live in the country and not wear boots. The good earth was made to be trampled on wearing thick, solid leather. With every step, accompanied by two black cocker spaniels, David felt as if he was reverting to his youth. After all, it's where he learned everything firsthand—from riding a bike, swimming in Little Bass River, giving birth to a baby calf. Every day brought new and unexpected discoveries. And the one person who helped guide him through much of it sat on an old worn out machine belching exhaust fumes.

Seated on the tractor with his back turned, Caddo didn't see the young man approaching. A sharp left of the steering wheel and there David stood—hands on waist, wearing blue jeans, red flannel shirt, and a smile from ear to ear.

"*Kiriki.*"

The word was drowned out by the hum of the tractor. Caddo popped the clutch, pumped the brake pedal while the engine sputtered. When he glanced at David, there was a hint of a smile in that broad, tanned face.

"Well, aren't you going to say anything?" said David.

"I did. You just didn't hear me." Caddo leaned a big paw across the steering wheel.

"Looks like you lost some weight," said David.

A slow nod.

"Heard you have a girlfriend."

Another nod.

"What's her name?"

"Irene."

"Where does she work?"

"Jake's Country Café."

"Is it serious?"

A shrug of the shoulders.

Damn, this is hard—David thought to himself. Not that he expected it to be easy. He decided to take the initiative by talking about the Navy. Taking college courses on the internet. Small talk. He wasn't very good at it. If nothing else, Caddo was a good listener. A shrug here and nod there. Once in a while David would inject a question just for the heck of it. Each time he would position himself just so, to where he could see the road facing west. He counted the minutes and chatted, relaying his father's message. After that, he got down to business—

"I hear there's been a few incidents lately. A fallen bridge. The blackout. What do you suppose caused those things?"

Caddo raised both his hands, palms up, in an I-don't-know gesture.

"Strange how there can be sightings, but no witnesses," said David.

The farmhand ignored the comment, leaned back, and pointed at David. "How'd you hit your head?"

Sensing it was a ploy intended to change the subject, David gave a brief description of the accident, ending with a question. "You didn't happen to hear anything around midnight, did you?"

Caddo acted as if he didn't understand the question.

A horn sounded. Richard's Jeep pulled onto the highway, heading east toward town.

David checked his watch, wondering why he was being given such a cold reception. It had been a year and a half since he'd seen Caddo...decades since Caddo and his father had returned from Vietnam. Based on that alone, he thought there might be a spark of emotion somewhere.

Why the sudden indifference? Was Caddo hiding something, like Elly said? If so, what...and for what reason?

After a few minutes of verbal shoe tapping, David saw the tow truck coming down the highway. "Dad told me you bought a car? Is that it?"

The truck was hauling a brown AMC Pacer. The truck slowed down as it approached the house, then turned into the driveway.

"Not many of those around," said Caddo. "Yep, that's it."

"Get down. Let me take the wheel. Tell the driver to pull it into the barn. What's the problem? Why won't the car start?"

Uncertain of what to do, the burly Indian remained seated.

"Don't worry," said David. "I paid the tow. Get down."

"You sure?"

"Heck yes, I'm sure. It's about time I did some work."

As soon as Caddo's feet hit the ground, he started walking. Roscoe and Cinders followed, noses pressed to the turf, tails jiggling.

David tossed a set of keys. "Here, take the Chevy. In case you need to go into town for parts."

Caddo tossed the keys back—"No time for repairs."— and kept walking.

"Hey, you haven't told me why the car won't start."

"Wiring's shot. Lightning must have hit it."

Chapter 6

The tractor shook and rattled. The engine whined in rhythm to the thumps of the exhaust pipe cap. After an hour of riding the old John Deere, David felt a numbness come to his backside.

Doing idle labor, he found, created a dichotomy of extremes. While seated, remaining inactive in a physical sense, times like these made his mind more active. He thought about his childhood mostly, playing baseball, which led to a scholarship at Ohio Southern.

Whatever the interest, when at home, his thoughts always gravitated to his mother.

How tragic her death was. Bedridden with cancer. Strong despite the pain. The sustaining memory was when she was healthy. The way she laughed, how she played the piano, fingers gently caressing the keys. Her love of Broadway music, rock 'n roll, the Moody Blues. Melodies by George Gershwin. *Stairway to Paradise* echoing through the house. The incredible talent she displayed while painting portraits, still-lifes, and abstracts. Her devotion to art. How gracefully she expressed herself. Dora truly was an inspiration. That's why the loss hurt so much. She was someone you could never forget. Memories of her existed everywhere he looked. And no-where was it more in evidence than in the old barn sitting on top of the hill.

He remembered the day Dora took out her easel, brushes, and tubes of oil. He was a scrawny five-year-old full of curiosity and admiration for his mother. It was a gorgeous spring day. He sat with his elbows on his knees, chin on fists under the shade of an oak tree, eyes riveted to the canvas as the subject took on form and texture one stroke at a time.

Whenever he watched Dora paint, a feeling of contentment came over him. The brushstrokes were like fingers massaging the skin—so soothing to the touch. It was fascinating to see how the shapes evolved, the colors blended. The paintbrush was hypnotic in her hand. A swirl here, dab there, and the dreary old structure was transformed. *Old Serenity*—she called it.

She was aware of the enjoyment he took from watching her. She played upon it, nurtured it, took comfort in it herself. Such an innocent thing—this shared bliss between mother and son. The same quiet peacefulness he felt then he could feel now.

He was reliving the moment when he noticed a small black speck darting across the sky. It was joined by another, then another. At first he thought they were vultures. He cut the engine. No, they were crows. The biggest crows he'd ever seen. They began to squawk as they circled above, wings outstretched in effortless flight. He shaded his eyes and glared into the sun. About a half dozen birds flew over the field, drifting, gliding, their movement like vultures hovering over a dead animal. They spiraled down in ever-decreasing circles, wings spread, claws extended. One of them landed. The rest followed. A slew of black falling bodies hit the ground softly, their heads bobbing like little jackhammers, pecking the dirt.

   David found himself running. He started yelling, waving his arms. With a loud *whoomph*, wings took flight. The flock leapt into the air. A straggler stayed behind. David took a clod of dirt and hurled a near strike. The crow squawked in protest and, with one big thrust, threw itself skyward.

   He stood staring at the ground. Bodies were scattered everywhere, lying in clumps of brown plumage, feathers torn from wings, from backs, exposing skin of a pinkish pallor. They were sparrows. Dead sparrows. He bent down and inspected one. Its neck was broken or, in its lifeless state, appeared to be broken. He looked for teeth or claw marks or small punctures made from shotgun pellets, but saw none. He felt for indentations in the body. It was soft. He went to the next bird, another, then another and each had died the exact same way—without wounds, scratches, or apparent reason.

   There was no logical explanation for it. What could kill a flock of birds? He doubted chemicals or any form of gas. Nothing of that sort, or that lethal, existed on the farm. No animal could surprise birds grounded at the same time, or while they were in flight. It just wasn't possible. And what other kind of bird was capable of killing so many without the urge to eat them? No bird or animal killed for the sake of killing. They did it out of hunger or fear, and whatever did this couldn't possibly feel threatened by a flock of harmless sparrows.

   If the evidence didn't lie in twisted lumps all around him, he wouldn't have believed it. What did this? More importantly, why?

   A gust of wind stirred the grass. He came out of his momentary trance. The crows were still airborne. Maintaining a vigil sixty feet high, they swooped in graceful arcs back and forth, cawing, the flutter of wings barely audible. Then, by some quirk of nature, as if orchestrated, they began to alight one by one on the roof of the structure towering over the hill. The pattern was repeated over and over. A single landing was trailed by another until the sky was clear and the crows had found a perch.

   David was awestruck. He had never seen anything like it. A half dozen birds sat motionless in perfect silence on the rooftop. But it wasn't just the crows that interested him, but what they rested upon. Captivated, he walked up the hill. Somehow the massive, mottled gray barn didn't have the allure of his mother's painting. Close up, Old Serenity portrayed something more sinister, a place where rats crawled and bats slept.

The barn was a family fixture, an heirloom, a monument of rubble owing its existence to sentimentality. Other than the old farm equipment crammed inside it, it served no purpose. It hadn't been used in decades, but it still stood in spite of wind, rain, snow, and blistering heat. To withstand the elements for as long as it did was a testament to his grandfather's skill as a builder and carpenter. And while the tarnish of age had taken its toll, David could easily picture how it looked when it was built—from cedar-shingled roof, red oak siding, to the exterior support beams cut from walnut.

David found himself drawn to it, a morbid fascination perhaps. He wasn't watching where he was going when he stumbled over a metal stake stuck in the ground. Weeds and grass encircled the area, but the place where he stumbled was trampled like a well-worn path. At the top of the stake a feather was tied with twine, its plumage speckled umber with light tans running from edge to edge. A pile of ashes surrounded the stake. He dug his fingers into the soot and extracted a tooth, charred and curved, slightly larger than a thumbnail. Digging deeper, he found a strap or belt about the size of a snake, which crumbled in his hands. It had the texture of incinerated leather. There were markings on what remained, a design of some kind, geometric in shape. When he stepped back, he noticed it was a pit, which had all the trappings of an Indian ceremony. The question was—what purpose did it serve?

Before he could give it further thought, a sound distracted him. It came from the barn, somewhere up high, near the rafters. It wasn't a panel grating against the wind. There was no wind to speak of. Then he heard it again, a light scraping sound, as though claws or wings were scratching against a hard surface. The origin appeared to come from the hayloft where an access door was pinned shut, a door designed as a passageway for the stockpiling of hay. Above it was a rusted iron pulley hinged on the outside wall, harnessed with rope and claw flange to assist in the lifting of the bales. The rope dangled a few feet from the ground. David remembered swinging from it when he was kid. He was also a hundred pounds lighter back then.

He walked closer. The sound in the hayloft continued, only it was broken by a tiny squeal no louder than a whisper.

David tested the rope to see if it could support his weight, then proceeded to climb. The pulley arm flexed. Rusted nails strained against rotted wood. There was another squeal. He lifted himself hand over hand. The pulley arm was bending like a fishing rod, dipping up and down. The loft noises became more pronounced, scraping across the floorboards. He lifted himself higher. His grip was tenuous. The pulley arm swerved on its axis. His body swung closer to the wall. The hinged bar was within reach. So was the loft door. He freed his right hand, then hooked his left forearm over the bar and could see his hand shaking. The door handle was only an arm's length away. He reached, wondering what in the hell he was doing, afraid to open the door, terrified the bar supporting him would break any second.

His fingers nervously coiled around the latch-handle.

The loft went deathly quiet.

Chapter 7

"David, what're you doing up there?"

The door shot open.

A screech!

Something pounced.

Wings slapped his face. A giant blur leapt into the air, flapping, grazing his left cheek. Something sharp pecked his cheekbone.

Dogs were barking.

The pulley arm snapped.

Dead weight. Two hundred pounds of bone and muscle hit the ground, feet first. He fell one story, but it felt as if he'd been dropped from a skyscraper. The impact jolted his body as he rolled onto his back.

Elly was laughing, Roscoe and Cinders woofing in confusion.

If it wasn't for the shock and pain, David would have been laughing, too.

"You okay?" giggled Elly.

David hopped to his feet and limped around, checking out body parts, seeing if he left anything on the ground. "Damn, El. Don't sneak up on me like that."

"Scared of a little old barn owl, David?" She held a hand over her mouth, burping out laughs between her fingers.

David hobbled stiff legged, hunched over like a crippled old man. He was playacting, but the performance was brilliant.

Elly caught her breath. "Please. Would you…a-hoo-hoo…stop!? What in the world were you doing up there?"

He stretched backward, forward, side-to-side. Did a deep knee bend. "Exercising. What do you think I was doing?"

She stood with arms folded, smirking. "You could have killed yourself."

"Yeah well, that was the plan." He walked over to the pit. "Come here. Check this out." The dogs had their noses pressed close to the turf, sniffing. "I found this buried in the ashes." He tossed her the charred tooth, underhanded. "What do you make of it?"

She examined it. "It's a tooth. From a dog or coyote I think." She bent down and looked at the feather tied to the stake.

Roscoe and Cinders, meanwhile, picked up a scent and disappeared down the hill while Elly stirred the ashes with a stick.

Underneath, she found a ring of pellets blackened by fire. From the way the pellets were positioned, at one time they had to be connected. "Beads? A ritual?" She stood up, wondering aloud, "Caddo?"

"That would be my guess."

The spaniels started barking.

There was a flutter of wings. Cawing. Crows went scattering, leaping into the air.

Elly ran. David walked. The dogs were sniffing around the base of the hill. Elly stopped when she saw the dead sparrows lying on the ground and peered up at him with a look of sadness.

David shrugged. "Don't ask me. I can't explain it."

Overhead, the crows were circling. Silently.

Elly cupped a dead bird in her hand with Cinders' nose practically touching it. "I don't understand."

David shook his head, then watched her gently lay the sparrow in the grass. Words weren't necessary. Death, whatever the form, upset his sister—whether it was a squirrel or a rat. Her love of animals, after all, was the focus of her studies. With one more semester to go, working as a graduate assistant at Ohio Southern, Elly was about to receive her veterinary degree. David was proud of her, proud of the fact she was first in her class, on scholarship throughout her collegiate career. He also knew what she was thinking, so he went jogging toward the lower barn.

"Where you going?"

"You want to bury them, don't you?"

She watched him leave, shadowed by Roscoe. David ran with a swagger, a baseball trot after hitting a home run. She'd seen him hit countless home runs. Had witnessed that familiar gait of his rounding the bases. She pictured him running across the field of a big stadium, thousands of people cheering. They were cheering for a tall, broad-shouldered young man, legs a bit bowlegged like a cowboy's, boyish face smiling beneath the bill of the cap. He was tipping the cap to the crowd.

Her heart ached.

It ached whenever she thought of the missed opportunity, the dream her brother never realized, though the talent existed in raw abundance. If given a chance, there was no telling how far he could have gone. Fame and fortune were distinct possibilities.

If only their mother hadn't died. If he'd only stayed in school. If life were only fair. If, if, if...

Elly realized it was more painful for those around him to see such potential go to waste than it was for David. There was no self-pity. He embraced everything with a sense of innocence, always with a positive attitude. There wasn't a negative bone in his body. That's what she loved about him. He was a child in a man's body.

Which reminded her of a call she was supposed to make. She removed a cell phone from her hip pocket and tapped in a number. It rang twice.

"Hello."

"He's here, Coach." She listened, said uh-huh a few times, giggled, then listened some more. "Will do," she tittered. "Ten minutes? Okay. See ya' bye."

After disconnecting, she gathered up the sparrows, cupping them to her breast, and placed them in a pile. After David returned with the shovel, he dug a hole and buried the birds as Roscoe and Cinders sniffed the mound of dirt.

The sun broke through the clouds, unveiling a beautiful afternoon.

Elly slipped an arm through David's, led him to the house, and asked, "When was the last time you had a date?"

"A *date* date? As in *pick-her-up, go-to-a-movie, dinner-candlelight* kind of a date?"

"Yeah."

"Well, let's see...a tour of duty in the Pacific, another in the Middle East. Mmmm...oh, about two years I'd say."

With a heavy dose of sarcasm, Elly said, "You've been celibate for two years?"

He fluttered his eyes and cooed, "I'm saving myself. Waiting for a nice girl to sweep me off my feet."

"Yeah, right." Elly fought the urge to laugh. "Well, I have a friend, the reporter I told you about. I want you to meet her."

He grinned. "Always the matchmaker."

"Always the bachelor."

"What's her name?"

"Alexa Wilde. I think you'll like her."

"Oh, yeah?"

Using reverse psychology, Elly teased, "Come to think of it, things probably wouldn't work out."

"Why not?"

"She has one big flaw."

David craned his neck. "No teeth? Lips? What?"

"She's cursed."

"As in *voodoo*?"

"As in *gorgeous...drop dead*. But I'm warning you. No leering. Three things to remember, David. Charm, wit, intelligence. Undress her with your eyes and you're history. Understand?"

"So when's the big occasion?"

"Occasion?"

"When do I meet her?"

"Soon."

They walked arm in arm.

David craned his neck again, a devilish grin forming on his lips. "Charm, huh? Least I have one of the three. So...other than being stunningly hot, what's she like?"

"Um..." Elly thought for a moment. "Tough. Sassy. Not afraid of anyone. A bit cynical at times. Maybe it's because she's a reporter. She writes a column for the college newspaper. *On the Wilde Side.*"

He had the look of a fish about to swallow the bait. "Beautiful cynic with a touch of wild. I like it."

"Smart as a whip, too. Problem is, she carries a full load of classes and works for two newspapers. But I guess you're not interested."

"Maybe I am. Maybe I'm not."

Elly stopped when she saw a red high-top conversion van approaching. "Shoot! Almost forgot. You already have a date."

"Jeez. Woulda been nice if you asked me."

"No, no. Not with Alexa. It's not really a date date."

The driver of the van slowed down and honked. A bald, chubby-faced man put his arm out the window and waved, holding a baseball cap.

David narrowed his eyes. "Hmmm. Wonder how he knew I was here."

Elly gave his rear-end a good hard slap. When he tried to return the favor, she started dodging one way, then the other, snickering and giggling with Roscoe and Cinders barking, leaping up and down at their feet.

It may have been fleeting, but it was one of those moments when David realized there was no place he'd rather be.

Chapter 8

Elly ran up to the old guy wearing the baseball cap. He was standing next to another man. Both were waiting on the driveway. She stopped short, staring at him appraisingly, hands on hips, tapping her foot. She smiled and launched into his arms. "Stumpy!" She made it sound like *yippie!*

Ed Kragan was a potbellied, hairless stump of a man. Hence his nickname. As a coach, he was a fierce old buzzard who, away from the field, was gregarious and fun loving. On the field, he was an intense, fist-pumping competitor. His players loved him. His rivals practically soiled their britches. Forty years working one job. His won/loss record for the Ohio Southern Tigers was unmatched anywhere in the country. If there were an inch of talent in a ball-player, he'd stretch it to a foot. He won on sheer grit, out-maneuvering opponents at every opportunity. He was also known as a prankster, someone who could embarrass and make you laugh at the same time. And today Ed Kragan had something up his sleeve, not as a coach, but as a schemer, plotter, a maker of mischief. Although he was retired, he'd been retained by the university as an unpaid consultant, cheerleader, and motivator, all packaged under one cap, with an OSU logo—Ohio Southern University—stitched above the bill.

Stumpy laughed, held Elly in his arms, and quipped, "If this won't make my wife jealous, I don't know what will." He glanced over her shoulder. "Who's that behind you?"

David walked up, grinning. "Hi ya', Stumps."

"Hayseed, good to see you." Stumpy stood back and stared at him from head to toe. "By golly! Look at you. Nice bump you got there. Heard you had a little accident." To the other guy he said, "Let's call Cincinnati, Joe. Bengals need a linebacker." After that, Stumpy made the introductions.

The other guy, a Mr. Joe Reid, was a frumpy, bespectacled fellow who shook hands like he was working a water pump. His hair looked frazzled, like it had been rescued from a vacuum cleaner.

Half-mocking, Stumpy said, "Joe here…he's a scout for the Detroit ball club. Them little kittens up yonder in that sissy league. Anyway, he's taking a look at a pitcher in town, a Buckeye, kid by the name of…what was it, Joe?"

"Mike Venebar."

"Yeah. One…big…mean…string bean. Six-foot-eight. No bigger than a toothpick. Couldn't weigh more than half a sack of potatoes. Second Team All-American. Anyway, he's pitchin' today against you know who. Big bad boys from Ohio State and us scrawny little chickens from Ohio Southern. I'd like you to be there if you're not doing anything. And bring your baseball shoes."

Elly was burping out laughs between her fingers.

David leaned over, chuckling, shaking his head. "My baseball shoes?"

Stumpy threw up his arms. "What? You know how to tie shoelaces, don't you?"

David waved a finger. "Something's up with you, Coach. What is it?"

Stumpy held his hands to his chest—"Moi?"—and slapped a cigar in his mouth. "Tell him, Joe."

"Ed's arranged it so you could take a few swings. See how you do against Venebar."

"Me?" cried David. "Against an All-American? I haven't touched a baseball in over a year."

"Scared, are ya'?" said Stumpy. "That's not the David Macklin I know."

"It's not that I don't want to, Coach. This is my first day home. I'm here to help my dad. Maybe next week."

"Huh-uh. There is no next week." Stumpy was distracted. He saw a car pulling into the driveway. "What's this? A convention?"

Everyone turned to look. It was an old candy-apple red Saab convertible. Sitting in the driver's seat was a young woman. When she got out, all three men stood with their jaws hanging.

David was star struck. Hit by a bolt of lightning.

Elly cleared her throat and looked disapprovingly at her brother. "Hi, Alexa." Elly slipped an arm under Alexa's and led her to the little group and made the introductions.

Alexa was a stunner. Short raven hair. Complexion as smooth as cream. She wore a clingy, black cotton sweater and tight blue jeans. Her green eyes could melt butter, and when she spoke, her accent dripped with honey-cured barbeque, southern style. "Pleased to meet y'all."

Ed reached out, cupped her hand, and wouldn't let go. "I can guarantee you, young lady, the pleasure is all mine. Are you the one who writes for the newspaper?"

"Yes, sir."

"Good stuff. Don't pull any punches, do you?"

"I try not to." Alexa held David's gaze for a second.

Stumpy and Joe Reid realized they were playing second fiddle. Make that third fiddle. Hell, they weren't even in the band.

Ed tipped his cap. "Yes, indeed. The pleasure is all mine." He did a half bow with his neck. Alexa did a half curtsy. "David, if you change your mind…two o'clock…at the ball field. And bring your baseball shoes. Joe and I got a game to catch."

Everyone said goodbye, except David. He walked beside the girls, never taking his eyes off Alexa.

Left in the lurch, the old coach stood wistfully dreaming of younger days.

Joe Reid wiped his glasses. "Piece of work, Ed. You could be arrested for what you're thinking."

"Ain't dead yet, Joe." Stumpy winked, slapped the cigar back in his mouth, and started chomping. "Look at that, will ya'." He watched as David glided alongside both women. "Wow! Without so much as a goodbye. Hayseed's been stung. Snake bit by the venom of love."

"So much for that bird-brained idea," said Joe.

"Get in the van and shut up," said Stumpy. A minute later they were driving away.

Meanwhile, the two young ladies and David were embroiled in a conversation. Elly explained, "Coach tried to get David a major league tryout when he was in college. Things didn't pan out. Today was his big chance. It's in his DNA."

"What is?" asked Alexa.

"Taking risks. Some people jump out of airplanes, wrestle alligators, others…come on, David. Help me out here."

Self-promotion not being one of his assets, David kept quiet.

His sister, on the other hand, was just warming up—

"As you can see, my brother doesn't like talking about himself."

"I noticed," said Alexa as she put on a pair of sunglasses. Whenever she assumed the role of reporter, she had a tendency to squint. "Chance at doing what?"

"David was asked to play against a big time pitcher, but passed."

"I don't blame you, David," said Alexa. "I'd be afraid of striking out, too."

"Him? Afraid?" giggled Elly. "Try scuba diving in shark infested waters. Now that's scary."

"Did you?" inquired Alexa.

"Did I what?" said David.

"Scuba dive in sharp infested waters?"

Once again Elly came to his rescue. "You kidding. Navy Seals do all kinds of crazy stuff."

"Like what?"

"Demolitions. Calisthenics day and night. Jumping outta airplanes at ten thousand feet. Sniper fire. Crawling through jungles. And just for kicks, they do this Iron-Man triathlete thing. David's won it two years in a row." Elly slapped him on the back. "Jump in any time, David."

Blushing, he scratched his head, absentmindedly running his fingers over the bump on his head.

"Wow. That's really swollen," said Alexa. "How did you do that?"

The cornpone in David came out. "Uh, an accident?"

Alexa's face lit up. "You mean the one last night? On Route 2?"

David stood, open mouthed. "How'd you know…?"

"I'm a reporter! I heard the call on the scanner, asking for an ambulance."

"At midnight?" Elly shot back.

"I work late," said Alexa. Her cell phone rang. She reached into her pocket and glanced at the number to see who the caller was. "Excuse me. This'll only take a second." She turned and started whispering.

David darted a look at his sister. "Would you stop? You're embarrassing me."

"I was just teasing, having some fun."

"Yeah, well, what am I supposed to do if she asks more questions?"

"Lie. Act stupid. Shouldn't be hard for you to do."

"Ow."

Alexa paced back and forth, talking quietly, then disconnected. "Sorry. My boss. He wants to know if you could tell us about the accident."

Brother and sister exchanged glances.

"Not much to tell," said David. "Long trip. I slept through most of it."

Alexa wasn't buying it. "Did you know both drivers were killed?"

"Yes."

"But you have no recollection of anything else…how it happened?"

"Can't comment about something I don't know."

"I suppose not." Alexa was in a bit of a snit, frustrated by the turn of events the past week. She was about to express those frustrations, but instead switched gears. "I have a favor to ask you, David. I write a column for the school newspaper. I'd like you to be the subject of my next article."

"Me?"

"Yes, you. I write about students, faculty, anyone associated with the university, past or present. People have no idea what it's like to be a Navy Seal. The places you've traveled, the experiences…that would make for a great story."

He was mortified. David Macklin, a celebrity? His words captured in print for thousands of people to read?

What if I make an idiot of myself?

"You don't have to decide right now," said Alexa. "Think about it and let me know. Still having supper this evening, Eileen?"

"Sure am," beamed Elly. "Seven o'clock. Sharp."

"What can I bring?"

"Just yourself."

Alexa jerked a thumb in the other direction. "Sorry to cut this short, but work is calling. Gotta run." She started walking away, stopped, and smiled. "Oh. And, Eileen, you were right. See ya' bye." She went marching toward the Saab convertible, her hips firm and athletic, slightly swaying.

Elly nudged her brother. "Easy, boy. Easy."

He was caught staring. "I like it when southern women say 'supper.' Sounds sexy."

Elly rolled her eyes—"Oh, brother."—then mimicked Alexa. "Work is calling. Gotta run. See ya' bye." Her voice trailed away as she headed toward her car. "Oh. And try not to drool during supper, okay David. She hates it when men make a fuss over her."

"Hey," he called out. "What did she mean when she said 'you were right?' Right about what?"

"She was talking about you. She thinks you're cute. But don't let it go to your head, David. Remember. Wit, charm, intelligence."

Chapter 9

David had a bounce in his step as he approached the lower barn. Ten years ago he found an old run-down truck. Paid two hundred bucks for it. The day he bought it, it wouldn't start, squirrels were nesting in the radiator. The tires were shot. There was more rust on the body than metal and virtually no paint. For two and a half winters he and his father spent a small fortune restoring it. Over the course of a decade it had fallen into neglect again. But the urge to see it, no matter its condition, still thrilled him.

Once he slipped the tarp away, his eyes almost shot out of his skull. The pickup had a fresh coat of deep blue metallic paint, waxed to a sheen so lustrous you could see your reflection in it. The door handles and trim glistened like star mist. The seats and dash had been reconditioned. Chrome wheels, chrome grill, chrome body side steps, chrome exhaust, chrome everything. Wow! Contrasted against the richest blue he'd ever seen, it looked better today than it did when it rolled out of the factory.

David jumped in and turned the key. The engine roared to life like a NASCAR on nitroglycerin. When he looked under the hood he found a modified 6.1 litre Hemi V-8, which produced 425 horses. Just revving it up got his adrenalin going. He estimated the cost at around $20,000. While pleased with the result, he couldn't believe his father would spend that kind of money—on a truck no less.

He hopped into the driver's seat. Opened the glove compartment. Pulled out a disc. Slid it into the disc player. Popped the five-speed transmission into first. Drove down the driveway, music blaring from the ten-inch speakers. With the windows down, he sang at the top of his lungs—

"Get your motor running…running down the highway…"

* * *

Mistwood was a typical, small Ohio town. The architecture, mostly mid-twentieth century. The buildings and houses, heavily tree lined. Everything had an aura of innocence, the simplicity of hardworking people.

Jake's Country Café wasn't hard to find. All he had to do was stop and ask. The restaurant was located at the corner of South and Erie in a strip mall called Trotter's Market Place between a coffee shop, bakery, delicatessen, and vegetable stand.

It was late afternoon when David entered the café. Only a few people were eating. Two waitresses scurried about, keeping busy. One in her early thirties, sad-faced, homely, and overweight. The other in her mid-forties, slightly plump yet pleasing, a fireball of energy. The latter moved with cat-quick feet.

David sat in a booth. Soon the fireball came whizzing past.

"Excuse me. Is Irene working today?"

She stopped, swiveled, leaned against the table, all in one motion. "No one calls me Irene." She pointed at her nametag. It said 'Bubbles.' "What can I get for you, sweetie? A menu? Coffee?"

"Just coffee, please. Sugar and cream."

"Oooo, baby. I like it when you talk like that. Bubbles' Special comin' up." She hurried away and returned, holding a steamy cup of mocha.

David peeked into it. What's a Bubbles' Special?"

"It's sweet, the color of light chocolate. Like me!"

He smiled. He couldn't help himself. He liked her already. Offering his hand, he introduced himself. "David Macklin."

She shook it. "Caddo's friend? Macklin Farms?"

He nodded.

She hugged him to her ample breasts. "Oh, my god. It's little Davey, all growed up. Lord, where you been, sugar?" Her voice rose to a high squeal as she squeezed harder. "It's about time." She released him and smacked her lips upside his head. "Pleased to meet ya'." She stepped back, one hand on her hip. "Um-hmm. Lookin' good. Back from the Navy, I take it. Nice to have you home. Boy like you deserves somethin' *extra* special. Don't go nowhere." She hustled away and returned with a plateful of lemon meringue pie, the meringue piled three inches high. "Here, smother your face in this!"

"Thanks. If you have a second..."—David gestured to a seat opposite him—"I'd like to talk to you."

She slid into the booth, like a swan gliding through water. Eyes wide, perky. A cheerful, good woman. Her nickname suited her perfectly.

"Mind if I call you Irene?"

"Sweetheart, you can call me whatever you want. We're practically family. Caddo sure talks a lot about you."

"He does?"

"Like you were his son. Bet you're drivin' a blue '57 Chevy pickup just about showroom new. He and your daddy spent the winter reconditionin' it. Went to every junkyard from here to Cincinnati. Even ordered parts from some fancy catalogue."

David gulped and blinked both eyes. "Really? How's Caddo doing by the way?"

"Fine, I guess. Haven't seen much of him lately. Man's busier than a jackrabbit in springtime." She winked and fanned herself with the order pad.

He grinned.

Her half-moon eyes glowed flirtatiously. "Not complainin' mind you. Been busy myself. How's your daddy doin'?"

"Good." David fiddled with the coffee cup, wondering how to begin the conversation. "Hope…a…you don't mind me asking…you and Caddo, how long you two been together?"

"Goin' on a year. That man sure took a shine to me right away. But…oh, heck. I might as well confess. I asked him straight out one night. Hey, big fella, wanna go out on a date? He just smiled and laughed. And boom! Like I was hit on the head with a sledgehammer. Been datin' ever since."

"How'd you two meet?"

"Three booths down. He and your daddy—they come in, eat every Sunday ever since the place opened."

"Dad's loss. Caddo's gain."

She blushed. "Me and your daddy? Honey, you kiddin'? He's still married to your momma. God rest her soul. Your daddy, he's a hard nut to crack."

"What do you mean?"

"He don't say much. Tips well. Don't bother nobody. Those two—they're as thick as brothers."

"I've often wondered why that is."

"Why what is?"

"They're so close."

"Shoot. Ain't no mystery to it. When bullets come flyin' at you, it kinda makes people tight. Know what I mean?"

From the kitchen someone hollered, "Hey, Bubs! Can't make money sitting there jabbering all day." A skinny-necked man wearing a grease-soaked apron stood behind the serving station, watching.

"Aw, hush up, Jake!" Irene snapped. "Haven't taken a break all day. If I quit, you'd be out of business." She turned and lowered her voice. "Jake's a funny old bird. Thinks he's boss."

"Maybe I should leave," said David.

"And be lettin' that pie go to waste? You crazy? Dig in! I made it myself."

David took a bite. Soft, fluffy. Magnificent. With his mouth half full, he garbled, "Tastes so good…makes your tongue wanna slap your brains out."

That made her happy. She patted her hair, giggled, and batted her eyelashes, blushing like a schoolgirl just kissed.

Two bites later, David said, "Listen. I came here to..." He had a hard time expressing it. He took a swig of coffee. "I...a...just want to..."

"Spit it out, honey! And I don't mean pie."

He swallowed, then leveled his gaze at her. "Don't mean to get too personal, but...have you noticed any change in Caddo lately, in his behavior, attitude, or in any of the conservations you've had with him?"

"No."

Her left eye twitched. A dead giveaway.

"Irene, look at me."

She raised her big brown eyes. "Well, maybe a little," she confessed.

The front door opened. Two couples walked in. Seated themselves three booths down. Irene glanced at her watch. It was half past four, start of the dinner hour. Jake arched his skinny neck, staring... waiting.

David leaned closer. "Look, something's happening at the farm."

"What?" Both of Irene's eyes twitched.

"It's different," said David. "I can't quite put my finger on it. It's...it's like being in a room you've been in your whole life, seeing the furniture and knowing something's out of place. You can't figure out what it is. You've got a feeling something's changed. A bad analogy maybe. But that's the impression I have about the farm. And Caddo. He's not the same. Not like he was anyway. I'm not saying bad. Just different. Quieter. More...secretive."

"Not around me, he ain't."

"That speaks well of you. Let me ask you something. Does he seem worried? Has he mentioned anything odd or peculiar that might have caught you by surprise?"

"I don't know, Kiriki. Maybe I shouldn't..."

"What did you say?" he interrupted, snapping his head back. "Kiriki? Where did you hear that?"

"From Caddo. That's what he calls you."

"Do you know what it means?"

"Of course. It means Bright Eyes. Dreamer."

David's mind was racing. "You were about to say...?"

Her eyes roamed around the room.

"Please, it's important," said David.

She started to speak, hesitated, then mumbled, "He's worried."

"About...?"

"Your father."

"What about him?"

"The drought. He's worried about the drought."

David knew it wasn't that. The real issue wasn't the drought, although a long dry spell could ruin a harvest. Something else was on her mind.

"Hey, Bubs!" Jake cried. "Customers. Table six!"

Irene slid to the edge of the seat. "We'll talk later, hun."

She was about to stand up when David grabbed her arm. "You said we're practically family. I know Caddo. Not as well as you maybe. We've been friends for a long time. Help me understand something. Is there anything he's told you, anything about himself? The farm? My father?"

Bubbles was torn Indecisive. She didn't know what to say.

David leaned closer. "Listen, I would never do anything to hurt your relationship. Never. I know it's not easy to trust someone you just met. But you have no idea how important this is. So I ask you again, have you noticed any change in Caddo lately, either in his behavior or any of the conversations you've had with him?"

"No."

"You're not convincing me, Irene. Look at me." He reached across the table and put a hand over hers. "I need your help."

"Why?"

"I don't know if I can explain it. It's here..." He tapped his chest, just below the sternum, where the heart was. "I can feel it. Something bad is going to happen. I just know it. Unless we can prevent it. You, me, Caddo. Whoever."

Their eyes met. "Okay. You gotta promise...you didn't hear it from me."

David raised his right hand. "Promise."

"If you breathe a word of this, I'll hunt you down and put a hurtin' on you, ya' hear?"

"Yes, ma'm."

She took a deep breath and said, "Okay. It's true. Somethin' is botherin' him. He hardly ever eats." She toyed with a ring on her wedding finger, an opal surrounded by a cluster of diamonds. She took another breath and said, "Says he found an Indian burial ground. A tribe I never heard of. Won't say where. Talks a lot about what it's like to be an Indian. But that's just Caddo. He's proud of who he is. That's all I can say. Gotta go, darlin', or Jake'll have a fit."

"Wait. Let me borrow your pen." David wrote Elly's cell phone number on a napkin and handed it back to her. "In case you want to talk."

Bubbles slid from the booth. Walked over to the table where the two couples were sitting. Within seconds, she was taking orders and making them laugh.

Chapter 10

Music rang out across the countryside so loud birds leapt from the trees like quail from buckshot. The truck sped along an unpaved back road, the undercarriage shaking, vibrating from the washboard bumps beneath.

It wasn't always called Birch Run. Didn't have much in the way of trees either, not since the logging business stripped away the elms, maples, and oaks. Some people still referred to it as *Indian Hills* because of a little known tribe that once lived and hunted there.

The name *Birch Run* was derived from a dispute during the Civil War when a small cavalry regiment from the north, led by Colonel Jacob Birch, met up with a group of riders dressed in civilian clothes. There were rumors of secret rebel detachments being sent to blow up a munitions factory up state. After a few questions, Colonel Birch grew suspicious of their accents. A fight broke out. The chase led to a tiny stretch of marsh below a hill where the civilians were hunted down and killed.

Situated between Little Bass River, at the western edge of Macklin Farms, half a mile from Route 2, lay a series of larger hills extending to the Ohio River, the most prominent being Birch Run. Whatever term you used, Indian Hills or Birch Run, at its base a tall ring of wilderness grass grew.

David drove to the bottom of a dirt road beside the marsh and stopped, letting the engine run. To his left a trailer sat in the middle of a field. He shut off the engine and walked the rest of the way.

The door to the trailer was unlocked so he knocked and walked in. A drafting table, charts, graphs, and surveying equipment were scattered about the front room. Near a hallway, leading to a back bedroom, was a desk with a small stack of papers on top. He shuffled through them, reading at random when he noticed a piece of stationery—'From the office of Mark Treshler.' He read the first paragraph and threw the letter down in disgust.

He felt like kicking chairs, the table, turning the place upside down. Instead, he slammed the door and ran to his truck. As he drove off, dirt went flying from the spinning tires. When he reached the base of the hill, he killed the engine, got out, found a crude walkway made of planks laid end to end, extending across the wetlands, and stepped across it.

* * *

The pitcher had just pitched a two-hitter. The Buckeyes won ten to zip. Mike Venebar sent the Ohio Southern Tigers home with their tails between their legs.

Joe Reid and Ed Kragan were hungry. Food always had a way of fighting off depression for Stumpy. Retired or not, he never enjoyed it when his team got spanked. A good ham steak cured most anything and Ed drove his guest in his high-top conversion van straight to Jake's Country Cafe where his favorite waitress worked. They sat in a booth and were waiting for their order.

Joe Reid lit a cigarette and inhaled. "I understand your compassion, Ed. One thing bothers me about the Macklin kid. You may have all the talent in the world, but if you have one major flaw—lack of heart, drink too much, have no self-control or discipline—you'll never make it."

"And what, pray tell, do you think he's missing?"

"How blunt do you want me to be?" Joe asked.

"Blunt like an axe."

"Okay." After a second puff, Joe said, "Trust me. I know from experience how hard it is when a parent dies. The problem is, he played only one year. Maybe he has a heart as big as Texas, but it was deflated big time when his mother died. I can understand a week, a month, a year. But never to play again?" He took another drag, exhaling with a slight wheeze. "The kid has no motivation. Sorry. I deal in judgments and that's mine."

Bubbles sidled up to the table and plunked down two glasses, milk for Ed, water for Joe. "No smokin' in the diner, sir. Would you like a salad or apple sauce?"

"No thanks," replied Joe. "Sorry." He put the cigarette out in a saucer.

As soon as she left, Stumpy responded to Joe's earlier comment. "So you deal in judgments, do you? What in the hell do you think I do? I know the boy. He didn't quit. He stopped playing because of his father. The old man started drinking. The farm fell into neglect. David took over until his dad got sober. Richard's a good man. He knows what he did was wrong. His wife's death devastated him. Devastated everyone. That's why he encouraged David to join the Navy."

"So who's idea was it? The boy's or the father's?"

"A little of both. I told them a scholarship was available any time they asked. Richard told me David needed to get away, leave home before it dragged him down. They'd sacrifice anything for each other. No, sir. If I was measuring heart, I'd begin with those two. Hell, the entire family for that matter. The daughter's as bright as sunshine. Just like her mother."

Joe Reid puffed on an unlit cigarette and said, "I know you're dead set on giving this kid a tryout. Let's assume he has the talent. First of all, he's no spring chicken any more. How old is he? Twenty-six, twenty-seven?"

"Close enough."

"That alone puts him *w-a-y* behind. Strike one. Strike two. He hasn't played organized ball in how many years? Six or seven?"

"Joe, the boy thrives on adversity. He loves challenges. I've seen him do things at age twelve most men can't do."

"Let me finish," said Joe. "Odds being what they are, maybe the numbers will convince you. Each year every major league team scouts hundreds of players, drafts...oh, let's say between fifty and sixty. Dozens more are given minor league tryouts. After this year's draft, we'll have two hundred players on our farm rosters. Take any position, except pitcher, and you're competing against fifteen others, all expecting to play in the Big Leagues. The youngest ones are so immature they eat potato chips for breakfast. They're away from home for months at a time. They travel in buses night in and night out, stay in the worst hotels, get injured, get lonely, get sick and tired of the travel, the frustration, not to mention most of them can't afford a girlfriend. Christ, they can't live on what we pay 'em. No, Ed. I'm afraid David Macklin can't cut it. Now that Ohio State pitcher, he can. Know why? 'Cause he's mean. Thoroughly committed."

Slumping in his seat, Ed remarked, "So you've already called strike three before the first pitch is thrown. Is that it?"

"I call 'em as I see 'em. It's better to be discouraged now than broken-hearted later. Believe me, I've seen good men go bad because their dreams were shattered."

Ed removed a cigar from his shirt pocket, slid a band from it, drummed the cigar on the tabletop. "Did I tell you what the kid does?"

Joe stubbed the unlit cigarette in the saucer. "Yeah. You said he was in the Navy."

"Not just the Navy, Joe. Navy Seals. Wanna know how big his heart is? I'll tell you how big it is. I've been keeping tabs on him ever since he left home. Talked to officers in charge of training, big brass wherever he's gone. And everybody said the same thing. If the Navy had a thousand more like him, you could get rid of the Army, Air Force, Marines, and you'd still have one hell of a fighting machine."

"Ed..."

"No, I listened to you. Now you listen to me." Ed had the cigar in his fist and was pounding his fist on the table. "I talked to a training instructor by phone. He said before the program began he bet another officer that sooner or later he'd break David. He made him do twice as many pushups as everybody else. Got in his face, screamed at him, put him through combat swims for three hours at a time in water so cold his skin turned blue. Made him row twice as hard, twice as long as everybody else. Put him through endless hours of mental strain with practically no sleep, made his group carry a big rubber pontoon raft up and down the beach morning, noon, and night. He explored every weakness. Exposed him to the point of exhaustion. And you know what? The instructor told me he'd seen hundreds of recruits in his time, thousands, but no one, not one single person endured what David did. The kid never whined, never complained. The more the instructor threw at him, the stronger David became. And wherever he's gone, from the commander on down to the enlisted men, David's gotten nothing but respect. Damn good leader I'm told. Most modest, unassuming, good-natured kid you'll ever meet. Tough, too. I'd love to have him as my son."

"I'm sure you would, Ed. I'm sure you would. But if you want my advice, leave him alone. Baseball has passed him by."

"Passed him by, huh," said Ed, with a deadpanned look on his face. "You don't become a Seal because you're a lame-dick wuss-ass, afraid of a piece of cowhide. Let me tell you something. He doesn't go parading around what he does in the military. Don't know how many tours of duty he's done, what missions or where he's been. He's extremely private about those things. But I'll tell you this. There was this jihadist, militant extremist in the Middle East holed up in some radical stronghold somewhere. The military wanted him captured. They choose David to lead a hand-picked crew of special forces. This was a few years after Osama Bin-Laden. Anyway, they sent in all these drones on bombing missions, exploding all around this stronghold as a diversion while David and his guys parachuted in, in the middle of the night. Shrapnel flyin' everywhere! Bombs explodin'! Boom, boom boom! Ten guys runnin' through the streets quiet as church mice. I won't belabor the details, but they got their guy. Captured him alive. Drugged him and killed twenty of his armed guards. Now that jihadist leader is holed up somewhere in the states, squawking like a baby, thanks to David. Took guts to do that. Yeah, baseball has passed him by all right. Yep. Just like one of those fastballs you think he can't hit. And let me tell you something else. Strange stuff is going on where his father lives. Cattle being killed, horses, pigs. More than I know of. But if I had to pick one guy...one guy in the state of Ohio who could root out the problem,

I'd pick David. I'd let him fight a battle for me any day."

Joe sat there quietly and said, "Let it go, Ed. Let it go."

Stumpy thought about it as he swallowed more milk. He needed something stronger. He realized pro ball was a fairy tale to most young men. None of his players had reached the majors. David, the best of the lot, was his last chance. Stumpy waved to Bubbles.

"What is it, sweetie? Ham steaks comin' right up."

"No hurry, Bubs. I'd like a beer. And give my friend here the same. Bud Lites if you got 'em."

"Wow," Bubbles cried. "I never knowed you to drink."

"I'm retired. I can do whatever I want. Tell Joe here...never mind. I forgot. You never met him."

"Met who?"

"David Macklin."

"Sure have. Just left here an hour ago."

"What's your impression?"

"Oooo, baby! Whatever he's sellin', I'm buyin'."

Stumpy leaned forward, hovering over the table, eyes fixed on Joe Reid. "See? You know what strings to pull. I don't care how you do it. All I'm asking for is a tryout. Hell, it doesn't have to be anybody else but you and me. We'll put him through the paces, time his speed, test his reflexes, put him in a batting cage, and crank up the machine. By God, we wrote the book on this stuff! What do you say, Joe?"

Joe removed his glasses, rubbed his eyes, his chin, scratched the back of his neck like he was trying to scratch away the idea. He did more scratching than a dog has fleas. After a while, he took out another cigarette, lit it, remembered he wasn't supposed to smoke, snuck a puff anyway, put it out in the saucer, and wheezed, "When?"

"Damn, Joe! You get better looking every second. Hurry up with those beers, Bubbles! I'm gonna drink the son of a bitch pretty!"

With that, Stumpy slapped the cigar between his chubby lips.

Joe Reid roared with laughter, pointing, unable to speak.

Stumpy looked down his nose and saw the smashed remains of his cigar, dangling from his mouth.

Chapter 11

It wasn't quite like the Hatfields and McCoys. They hadn't taken up arms and shot at anybody. But it was reminiscent of an old family feud. Only in this case the feud was born and bred in southern Ohio.

It started out to be just a harmless research paper for graduate studies, an overview of the politics and financial makeup of Bertram County. Three families basically had been the dominant forces since the county's inception. It began with the Bertrams who established a mortician business, furniture and casket making company known throughout the Midwest. As the power and influence of the Bertrams faded, the Macklins and Treshlers became the prominent leaders of the community. But because of jealousy, greed, and political infighting their once close-knit relationship deteriorated to the point where neither side would have anything to do with the other.

Alexa Wilde was well equipped for such research. An army brat for most of her life, moving predominantly in the South, she took an interest in local history, acquainting herself with the places and cities in which she lived. It became a hobby of sorts and she used that knowledge to make friends and adapt to an existence of hopping from city to city.

Her research took her to the county library where she combed through the archives, digging up tidbits from local newspapers and magazines under the guise of compiling a historical perspective when actually she was doing the legwork for an investigative piece exposing county corruption, corporate manipulation, fraud, and unethical business practices both past and present. As her research progressed, it was becoming clearer and clearer who were the good guys and who were the bad.

As she sat in a cubicle behind the bookshelves, she flipped through a microfilm screen which stored past editions of the county newspaper, the *Bertram County Sentinel*. When she found what she was looking for, she smiled and turned to her laptop and wrote—

> *This is a story of two men. Wil Macklin, co-founder of First Farmers State Bank, and his good friend, William Treshler. When Wall Street collapsed, Wil Macklin personally made good what customers lost. He*

> *literally gave away the bank by donating shares of stock to those in need and those heading down the path to bankruptcy. He paid out a fortune. Cash as well as land. Cash from his own personal account and land that had been in the family for generations.*
>
> *That's when good friend, William Treshler stepped in. Unbeknownst to Wil Macklin, Treshler met with shareholders behind closed doors and convinced them to sell their stock—to him. Not exactly a crime. But to do that to a friend?*

Yummy—Alexa said to herself. She knew full well it wasn't a news story per se, more of an indictment against William Treshler's underhandedness. Despite the lack of objectivity, she hit the *send* button in her e-mail.

Her stomach growled. She was getting hungry. She closed her laptop, opened a yellow legal notepad, and referred to a page listing the stories she was working on. "One…two…three. Four…five… oh, my god!…six!"

Things were getting hectic.

One question remained. Should she run the bank takeover story as is, an uninspired piece that didn't point fingers? Or go with the newer version and run the risk of angering one of the most powerful families in the state? On the surface the decision looked easy enough. Only an idiot would throw herself in the path of an oncoming truck, steered by none other than Mark Treshler, owner of a trucking company by the name of *Fleet Merchant*. But Alexa was hardnosed. She chose to leave the decision to her editor, Sam.

She heard footsteps, the patter of tiny feet. At the same time her cell phone rang.

A petite, rosy-cheeked, gray-haired lady, with bifocals balanced on the tip of her nose, stuck her head around the corner of the cubicle, grinning like a pixie. "Ah-ha. There you are."

Alexa held up a finger and spoke into the phone, "Hello, Sam. Just a second." To the older lady she said, "Hi, Mae."

Mae pushed the glasses up the bridge of her nose. "Sorry to interrupt you. But I have the information you wanted."

"Great. Could you make me a copy?"

"Certainly. Come to my desk and I'll have it ready."

"Thanks. I'll be there as soon as I get off the phone." Once Mae was gone, Alexa said, "All right, Sam. What do you have?"

"The interview tomorrow is all set up. The only thing you have to do is call Treshler's secretary and confirm. She wanted to know who's responsible for the *History Today* pieces. I told her it was written by the editorial staff. I thought it best not to single anyone out. And frankly I don't think it's very smart to do the interview until we have more information. You're walking into a lion's den, unarmed."

"He's a bully, Sam. Don't worry. I'll handle it with kid gloves."

"Yeah. With rocks in the gloves, you mean. How about David Macklin? Did you get a chance to meet him?"

"I did."

"What did he have to say?"

"Not much. He said he was asleep through most of it."

"Didn't have much luck at this end either," said Sam. "The sheriff is stalling. I put a few feelers out." Papers rustled. Sam was shuffling through his notes. "I found out where they keep the wrecks and impounded cars. One of us should check it out."

"Us? You mean *me*."

"Are you wearing a skirt?"

"A what?"

"Can't climb a fence wearing a skirt."

"Very funny. What about Max? What did he say about the front-page piece?"

The phone went silent. When Sam spoke, it was with a tone of regret. "Ah...he...a...moved it."

"To where?"

"The back page."

"He what!?" Alexa shrieked.

"What can I say? He owns the newspaper."

"Yeah? Tell him to look up *gonads* in the dictionary 'cause he doesn't have any."

"My, my. Aren't we getting huffy. He said it was too sensational for our modest publication. So he tweaked it a little. Tamed it down."

"Took the guts out of it is what he did."

"Alex, raising awareness is one thing. Scaring the hell out of our readers is another."

"He didn't...tell me he didn't take my name off it."

Sam's voice dripped with apology. "Had to. He did it to protect you."

"I've worked hard, Sam."

"So keep working and stop complaining. You love this...love stirring things up. Think about it. If there's a backlash, the paper's responsible, not you. It's bad enough that we're publishing it.

Sensationalism doesn't sit well with me."

"It's not sensational, Sam. It's factual. We have a handful of dead animals, a missing person, and head of the veterinary school of medicine saying the bite is twice the size of anything he's ever seen. How is that not factual? Hell, yes, it's sensational! But in terms of content, not because we twisted the facts around."

"All right, all right," said Sam. "You're preaching to the choir, kiddo. I like what Max did, though. By moving it to the back page, we softened the impact. If that's it, I suggest we run with what we have. You agree?"

"Could it wait a few hours? I'm having dinner tonight with the Macklins. Might have something to add if I can get David or his father to talk."

Sam chuckled, "I'll wait 'til Hell freezes over if I have to."

"Nine o'clock will do just fine, Sam."

"Okay. Anything else?"

"Which of the *History Today* pieces are we running?"

"Black Monday. The day the stock market crashed."

"Good," said Alexa. "I was hoping you'd go with that."

"Why?"

"I have this thing for the Macklins. Oh and Sam. Check your email."

Chapter 12

David found a multitude of things. Rabbit holes. A litter of spotted skunks. Snakes hiding under rocks, in the bushes, in the grass. An arrowhead. Not much else. More importantly, he found another ceremonial pit, complete with ashes and feathered stake. Caddo's presence was everywhere, as evidenced by the small excavations, patches of soil where the grass and weeds had been dug up. Perhaps Caddo was taking soil samples to see how fertile the soil was. Throughout the time David was aware of another presence, too, as if someone were watching him.

As he returned to the truck, he heard the rumble of a diesel engine. A white Ford pickup cut across the field and parked by the trailer. Two men got out, looked at David, then entered the trailer. Two minutes later, David was knocking on the door.

A middle-aged man wearing a green windbreaker and Masters golf hat opened the door. He had a thin mustache and flattened nose like a boxer's.

"Can I help you?"

The trailer was raised on cement blocks. David stood on the lower step, squinting into the sun. "Hi. I'm David Macklin. I understand you've been talking to my father about a golf course."

"Why, yes. We certainly have. Nice piece of property you have. I'm Jack Lorrigan, the architect." They shook hands. Lorrigan's partner, dressed in denim, came to the door. "This is my partner, Matt. Nice set of wheels. What year?"

"Fifty-seven."

"Excellent restoration."

"Thanks." After a few formalities, David got down to business by addressing the land to their right. "So what hole would you put there?"

"Too early to tell," answered Jack. "But if I had to guess, our version of Amen Corner. Most interesting part of the golf course."

"What makes it interesting?"

Both men laughed.

"Craziest winds I've ever encountered," said Jack. "Never know what direction it's gonna blow. Sorta like Amen Corner. You familiar with Amen Corner? It's in Augusta where they play the Masters. Three of the toughest, most seductive holes in golf. They may look easy, but they're not. I imagine that same seductiveness can be applied here."

David shaded his eyes and gestured to the outlying field. "What about the spot behind us?"

"What about it?"

"I was wondering what you thought of it."

Matt spoke up for the first time. "Look around. There's something different about this place. It has a different feel to it, a different mood. Almost like it has eyes or something. Hate to use the word *mystical*, but that's the first thing that comes to mind."

"Forgive him," said Jack. "A couple of beers and he gets light-headed. There's eighteen holes here somewhere. We just have to find them."

Subtly, David was trying to steer the conversation in another direction. "Any problems? Anything we can help you with?"

"No," said Lorrigan. "We just have to deal with the usual red tape. We need permits to get permits these days."

"I assume you're going ahead with it then?"

"Can't say just yet."

"Why not?"

"Several reasons. Don't want to overextend ourselves. We're very picky about what we do. We're also into restoration, consulting, installing irrigation systems. At the moment we're working on four projects, all in a slow economy. The time element and business climate are one thing."

"The other...?"

"With respect to this course, we're still in the planning stages. Aside from the red tape, there's cost projections, contractors to hire, a price to be agreed upon. The design may take weeks, depending on what direction we take. Should we bankroll the project ourselves? Find investors? Plant more trees? Dig a few ponds? So you see, there's quite a bit of work to do."

"I can imagine."

"Even the most promising courses are high-risk these days. But we have two things in our favor. A limited number of courses in the area. And your property makes it very appealing. We're also doing a feasibility study through the university's marketing department to find out how much interest there is."

"Outside of what you do, this 'red tape,' what factors into it?"

"Well, first there are state and local ordinances to consider, not to mention environmental issues."

"Like what?" said David.

"We have to provide proof that we're not upsetting the ecology or tampering with the habitat of some animal or protected species."

"Like a wetlands or a marsh?"

"If a local, state, or national agency or government can justify its protection by law."

"As it does with the land over there, to our right?"

"Like I said, at this point nothing's been decided."

"Really? Aren't you forgetting something?"

"Not that I'm aware of."

"Isn't there a lawsuit pending, undermining the project?"

Jack seemed tongue-tied all of a sudden.

"It's my understanding," said David, "the state is putting up a fight. I'm pretty sure my uncle is behind it. Didn't he make a counter offer, proposing a piece of his property to compete with ours?"

"Who's your uncle?"

"Mark Treshler." Jack looked at Matt and Matt looked at Jack while David continued, "Before you say anything, I'm on your side, okay. I happen to know you're being forced into considering another site. How it's being transacted...well, that's where I have a problem."

In some peculiar way, Lorrigan found the whole thing amusing. He tugged at the bill of his hat and said, "Intriguing scenario, young man. Don't stop on our behalf."

"The injunction is based on environmental concerns, right? My uncle found an obscure law, brought it to the state's attention. At the same time, thanks to your study, he realized a need for a golf course. Being the opportunist he is, with the connections he has, and having a company with an established reputation already in the area, meaning you...well, that made it very easy for him, didn't it? The lawsuit is nothing more than a delay tactic. I'm not here to judge. Just to offer my assistance if you care to do business with us."

"What did you say your name was?" said Jack.

"David."

"Well, David, I must say, you've helped make for an interesting last couple of days."

"Oh? How so?"

"The property surrounding us, the valley—it's created quite a commotion. Someone's playing games with us. Our power keeps cutting out. Blueprints have come up missing. Paperwork. All kinds of stuff. Our trailer's been ransacked twice. Somebody with bare feet has been trampling through mud, walking through every room. There's no lock on the door, but after today there will be. This lawsuit you mentioned—where did you hear about it?"

Ducking the issue, David replied, "Sorry. I can't reveal the source."

"Tell him about the Indian," said Matt.

Jack gave him a look that could kill.

David's curiosity was instantly aroused. "Caddo?"

Lorrigan shook his head and muttered, "Nice, Grady. Real nice."

"What about him?"

Jack explained, "He came to us the other day to ask if we'd keep a certain piece of property off limits."

"What property? Where?"

"He didn't say. Not specifically."

"Yes, he did," Matt blurted out. "He said it was near the old abandoned buildings. And he didn't ask. He more or less told us."

Jack gave Matt another one of *those* looks.

"Did he say *why* the property was off limits?" asked David.

"Not really."

"Tell him," said Matt. "It's no skin off our teeth. He said it was '*hallowed ground*,' or something like that."

Lorrigan grimaced, obviously displeased by the remark. "My friend is guilty of letting the cat out of the bag, I'm afraid. To be honest, I found the whole thing kinda strange."

"In what way?"

"The Indian. When he came to us, he said it was in the strictest of confidence. Of course, that being the case, we've broken our promise, haven't we? Thanks to Matt. And I disagree. What he said was a request. He wasn't pushy or anything."

"I understand. The lawsuit—do you think there's any merit to it?"

"Difficult to say. When it comes to the law, anything's possible. If we have to, we'll design around it. It's not the first time we've dealt with environmental issues. It sure does put a crimp on how we proceed, though."

"So how do you proceed?"

Lorrigan hitched up his pants like a famous golfer about to take charge in a tournament. Come inside, David. Not that anybody's listening. But I'd like to continue this in private. I've got a strange, strange feeling. Always do about this time of day."

Chapter 13

As a reporter, tenacity was Alexa Wilde's most valued asset. When she wanted something, she went after it like a crazed bloodhound on the trail of a wounded animal.

She found the compound where the wrecks and impounded cars and trucks were towed. It was hidden behind a seven-foot-tall wooden fence, adjacent to public playground and Dairy Queen.

She was eating a chocolate fudge sundae as she cased the perimeter. She walked around it for half a block and found a maintenance shed butted up against the fence. There was a small crack between the fence and shed. As she peered through it, she saw a gate swing open at the far end. Three cars drove in, a county sheriff's patrol car and two sedans. Six men got out and walked toward her. She recognized Tom Duckett. He was the only one wearing a uniform. The others wore dark suits and communication devices. Their manner of dress and the way they carried themselves screamed *cop*.

Static buzzed from a car radio, interrupted by an occasional message from a dispatcher. The men were talking as they walked closer. At the last second they turned to her left, out of sight. There was a sound as if someone were stripping a sheet from a bed. A camera clicked. The men were mumbling. Alexa fished out a notepad, laid the sundae aside, and eavesdropped.

A few seconds later a man said, "You identified the registration, I take it."

"Yes, sir," said Tom Duckett.

She recognized the inflection of Tom's voice.

The man who spoke did so with a tone of authority. Alexa assumed he was the agent in charge.

"What I can't figure out," he remarked, "is how it got like this. No accident I've ever seen could cause this type of damage. How in the hell did the passenger walk away?"

No one was willing to comment.

The lead agent asked, "Brian, do you agree with the initial report?"

"Kind of hard to say," said Brian.

No one else said a word.

"Come on!" declared the agent. "Don't we have anything to go on? Any evidence? Any clues? Steel doesn't bend like that. Imagine the amount of pressure it took to do that."

More mumblings. Alexa heard crunches, shoes stepping on gravel...more clicks from a camera.

"When did you file this, Tom?" the agent inquired.

"Early this morning."

"And the other deputy—he can back it up?"

"Yes, sir. The Sheriff asked us to file separate reports, so he could compare stories...get an accurate account."

Papers rustled as pages were being turned. "Says here you set up watch at the park's entrance, looking for speeders, drunk drivers. Why two cars? Why there?"

"Security in numbers," Duckett explained. "Earlier reports indicate the majority of the incidents occurred within a two and a half mile radius, between the park and a utility station. The animal attacks were confined to a much wider distance, ten to twelve miles. Almost to the city."

"I take it then, you weren't really looking for speeders or drunk drivers."

"No, sir. Our main objective was to inform headquarters if we saw anything unusual or suspicious. Other units remained on standby all night. If I may, sir. There's one thing I didn't put in the report. Each night the range keeps moving farther and farther out. So far it's confined to the rural areas. I'd hate to think what would happen if it reaches the city."

The agent flipped through more pages and said, "The surviving passenger, you interviewed him this morning?"

"Soon as he woke up."

"Huh. Not much to go on."

"No, sir. He didn't have much to say."

"Last night, what was he doing when you found him?"

"Nothing. Just standing there with this blank look on his face. His head was bleeding. I asked him if he was all right. He couldn't talk. When I walked him to the patrol car, he passed out."

Alexa was writing furiously. She was so excited she got a case of the hiccups and had to hold her breath.

"I don't know," said the agent. "I'm completely...I mean *completely* in the dark—about everything! The only thing unusual I can see in your reports, Tom, is how vague they are. There's not a shred of evidence...about anything. You and your people obviously don't have a clue. Is that right? Or did I miss something?"

If Tom answered, it wasn't very loud.

"What's that?" said the agent. "I didn't hear you."

"That's correct," said Tom.

"So, essentially, we have nothing. Just rumors. Eleven incidents we know of. No eyewitnesses. Or none we can rely on. A fallen bridge. What else?" More pages were being turned as the agent continued, "A utility station that, for some unknown reason, caught fire and shut down. A two-car accident at midnight. One car exploded, killing a woman while the cab driver was thrown from the taxi. In the process every bone in his body was broken. We have one missing person, presumably dead, another six or seven instances of livestock being attacked. In two cases, practically eaten whole. The tracks appear to be those of a bear, only twice as large, and—and," the agent's voice was rising, "the tracks suddenly disappeared right in the middle of a cornfield! That about sums it up, right?"

Someone said, "If they *are* bear tracks."

"Oh, Jesus. What else could they be?" the agent snapped. "And the lab techs—when are they expected?"

"Any time," said Tom. "The sheriff called Columbus this morning."

"Can't wait to read their reports. And the surveillance team?"

"E.T.A.—about two o'clock. One of them is already here. He was with us at the stakeout last night. The rest should arrive sometime today or tomorrow afternoon."

"Can't wait to hear what they come up with. Half a million bucks for a surveillance van. Jesus. Somebody's pissing the state's money away. Okay, Brian…Roy. Cover this back up and let's get rolling."

Alexa waited until the men left. She grabbed a fence rail with one hand, a downspout to the shed with the other and climbed up and over the fence with surprising agility. Two minutes later, she removed a car cover and was taking pictures with her cell phone of a compacted piece of metal about the size of a king-sized bed and a charred wreck beside it.

* * *

After seeing the light in the window of the log cabin last night, David thought he'd do a quick drive-by and see how the place was holding up.

Accessible by two roads, the cabin and winery were located just east of Fallen Oaks State Park. He took a dirt road and stopped between the two buildings. The view was in stark contrast to what he remembered years ago. The lane was no longer overgrown with weeds and the condition of both buildings was amazingly good despite years of neglect. His grandfather designed structures to last. The proof lay in the construction.

The winery was built of brick, painted an off-white. The roof was made of slate, not just any slate, but the variety found in older homes, each slab weighing as much as twelve pounds. The frames, therefore, had to be incredibly strong. Only treated, tempered steel of the highest quality was used. The only evidence of neglect was the boarded-up windows.

Sprawled against the backdrop of the park, the winery was a replica of a French chateau. Deep slanted roof. Dual chimneys. Rounded towers at each corner. Standing two and a half stories tall, it stretched nearly the length of a football field. And that was above ground. Below ground, a cavernous cellar extended in all directions. A wraparound driveway led to a rear loading dock. Out front, greeting visitors, was a fountain shaped like an oversized birdbath. The trouble was, there were no visitors any more. At the base of the fountain a rusted sign read: '*GlenRiver Winery, Macklin Bros. Est. 1936.*

To the left of the winery was a vineyard, consisting of vines hanging from trellises and vine posts, measuring about eighty rows long, forty rows deep, not growing in the wild, but cultivated, hearty, and green, bursting with leaves and buds that would eventually become grapes. David couldn't believe it. Throughout the patch not a weed could be seen. The grounds appeared to be manicured. The grass was mowed, the wilderness tamed.

Was this the work of Caddo, too?—he thought.

Even though the last batches of wine were made more than sixty years ago, he could almost smell them fermenting in the oak barrels buried deep in the wine cellar. He often wondered if any wine remained. If so, was it still drinkable? Rich? Smooth? Full-bodied? Aromatic?

What a waste!

As he drove toward the highway, the log cabin rose out of a stand of trees, marking an era when Macklin wealth was at its peak. The cabin, or "winemaker's shack" as the family referred to it, was originally constructed as a temporary residence for a wine producer, a Frenchman who found Ohio too unsophisticated for his taste. While the job was never filled, Wil Macklin often slept there and found it a pleasant retreat, so the cabin remained as a home to visitors and family. As a kid, David loved it and often played there, so for him the drive-by was a nostalgic look at the past.

He was tempted to stop and evaluate the property more closely, but it was getting late. He had to shower and shave yet.

Satisfied he'd seen enough, he gunned the engine and drove away, anxious and giddy. Just like a kid on his first date.

Chapter 14

Elly loved to cook. She just didn't have the opportunity. The more she thought about it, dinner at the farm didn't seem like such a good idea. Too many things could go wrong. The impending nightfall, less than two hours away, weighed heavily on her mind. Caddo's quiet, unsociable manner didn't help. And she could smell alcohol on her father's breath. He wasn't drunk, but it was only six-thirty. Still plenty of time to toss down a few more shots. She found a fresh bottle of Jack Daniels hidden in the kitchen cupboard.

She laid five placemats on the dining room table. Shrimp Creole, with each ingredient cut, peeled, and put aside in bowls, was ready for the saucepan. An oil and vinaigrette salad and carafe of Chardonnay were stored in the refrigerator while saffroned rice awaited the steamer.

Static buzzed from a cordless speakerphone resting by the sink.

Richard's voice came on: "Elly, have you seen David?"

She picked up the phone. "No. Not yet. Where are you?"

"Out in the cattle yard. Putting up fence wire."

"Get cleaned up. You don't have much time. And wear something besides blue jeans and overalls, please. Don't forget to tell Caddo. He's invited, too. Where is he?"

"Here with me." Richard paused while there were murmurings in the background. "Sorry. Said he can't make it. He has other plans."

"Oh, no. No excuses. I expect him to be here and ready in half an hour."

Richard passed the word along, then said. "All right. Says he'll be there. Do me a favor. There's a telephone number written on a notepad on my night table. Would you get it? I need to order more fence wire."

"Sure. Just a second."

Carrying the cordless, she hurried into the bedroom. A photograph of her mother sat on a night table where she found the notepad. Elly repeated the number and hung up. As she was about to leave she noticed a drawer ajar. She closed it, became curious, reopened it, and found a stack of letters written by Dora to Richard while he was in Vietnam. Beneath the letters was a book titled *The Phenomena of Revenants* with a letter tucked inside the dust jacket. She had no idea what a revenant was, but opened the letter and saw it was a recent correspondence from a law firm in Columbus. She removed the letter and unfolded it. Immediately, her heart sank. She became angrier and angrier the more she read. All at once her attention was broken. Through the window she saw a blue truck drive up and stop on the driveway. It was the '57 Chevy. She replaced the book and letter in the nightstand, ran into the kitchen, and greeted David as he entered the house through the side kitchen door.

"Hi, El." He kissed her cheek. "Gonna take a quick shower. Mmmm. Smells good." He rushed down the hall, leapt up the steps, taking three at a time.

While the rice was simmering, the guest arrived right on schedule. Twenty minutes later, five people were seated, wolfing down hotly spiced, tomato pureed Creole in wine sauce and garlic. Make that four people. Not five. Caddo pretended to eat by stirring his plate with a fork.

"Something wrong, Caddo? I made it especially for you."

He slumped down in his chair like a little kid. "No, ma'm. It's all good. Stomach's a bit upset. Can't keep anything down."

"Ma'm? That makes me sound old."

"Okay...*Elly*."

"No wonder your stomach's upset. You look like you haven't eaten for days. Try one bite. Please. For me."

Caddo knew he shouldn't have accepted the invitation. Not to eat was rude. But denying her invitation was an insult. He considered the former the lesser of two evils. But there was another reason he couldn't eat. He just couldn't explain why. "Can't," he said. "I apologize. Maybe you could freeze it and I'll eat it in a couple of days. Wouldn't mind another glass of ice tea though."

Once the pitcher was passed, the wolfing continued. Dinner was delicious, the affair lightened by Chardonnay. Everyone had a good time, including the spaniels who sat at opposite ends of the table, ears perked, eyes alert, waiting for food scraps.

At the conclusion of dinner, Alexa sat back and said, "Oh, I'm stuffed. Great supper, Eileen. Thank you." She dabbed her lips with a napkin, then turned to Richard. "Mr. Macklin, I love your paintings. The two in the hallway remind me of something I might see in a museum."

Richard smiled. "Glad you like them."

"The use of color and shade...the attention to detail—wow! I'm impressed. The painting behind you..."—she pointed at a picture of a boy and girl sitting on a horse—"who was the artist?"

"My wife. Unfortunately, she's no longer with us. Painting was one of her great passions. I have a collection in the front room if you'd care to look."

"I'd love to. Where did she study?"

"She didn't. She was self-taught."

Alexa got up, walked past the table to the wall and viewed the painting more closely, pausing at the bottom at the right hand corner where the signature was. "Dora. Huh. She was good. Really, really good."

"We called her Dode. Named after her grandmother, Doreen Treshler."

"As in *Treshler Construction*?"

Caddo slid his chair back, excusing himself. One question altered the mood.

"Yes," said Richard, "The kids were six and nine when she painted it. They rode that horse morning, noon, and night. He was our only venture into thoroughbred racing. Fleet Merchant was his name."

"Fleet Merchant? As in *the trucking company*?"

Richard nodded. "My brother-in-law, Mark, borrowed him for breeding purposes. Dumbest thing I ever did. Never got the horse back. That's how Mark and his father got started in the horse business."

"How awful," remarked Alexa. "I've heard they've done quite well in the horse business."

That elicited a few suppressed coughs around the room. Chairs squeaked. David grunted. And Richard Macklin responded with a half-hearted laugh, "Ha. You have no idea."

"Oh?" said Alexa. "If you don't mind me asking, what kind of money are we talking about?"

"Don't know exactly," answered Richard. "But Fleet Merchant made a fortune as a stud. Sired two champions, a stable full of incredible horses. In a span of…what?…twelve years they've won something like twenty races. So yes, I'd say my brother-in-law has done pretty well."

Alexa pressed the issue further. "Didn't you have a contract? Did you know he was going into the breeding business?"

"It was mentioned," said Richard. "We shook hands. That was our contract. I'd rather not get into it."

David and Elly exchanged glances.

David cleared his throat. "Okay, what's for dessert?"

Elly had a chagrined look on her face. "Nuts! I knew I forgot something."

He pushed himself away from the table. "Couldn't eat more if I had to." Tugging at his belt, he added, "Well, looks like I'm in charge of the dishes."

Alexa volunteered to help, but Richard wouldn't have it. "Oh no, young lady. Guests are few and far between in this house. You're coming with me."

"I'll clear the table," said Elly.

The guest smiled, slipped an arm through Richard's, and together they waltzed out the door. At the end of the hallway he flipped on the light switch. "This is our pride and joy."

Alexa was stunned by what she saw and smelled. It was more of a shrine than a gallery, nicely decorated with stained oak panels. Spot lighting from the ceiling projected onto an assortment of paintings. A love seat with end tables and reading lamps were the only furnishings. An easel sat in a corner with dozens of ribbons taped to the frame. Inside the frame was a blown-up photograph of a woman in her early 30's. She was wearing a yellow sundress and matching bonnet, doing a mock pirouette, with one hand on the hat, the other hand on her hip—body turned, back erect—posing in a manner that would be the envy of most models. Not only was she beautiful, her face had a refreshingly innocent quality as well, as evidenced by her smile.

"Oh my," cried Alexa. "This is unbelievable!" She looked at Richard. He could barely hold back the tears. "This is amazing! And the scent. Mmmm. Smells like wild flowers. Wow! Look at those!"

She was staring at a series of portraits—one of Richard as a handsome young man, another of Eileen, David, and Caddo—striking resemblances all. There were three other portraits—of two older gentlemen and a lady. Most of the paintings, however, captured landscapes or subjects of a less personal nature. A flowered meadow in springtime. Sailboats anchored in a harbor. Two black cocker spaniel puppies asleep in a cardboard box. An old rustic barn sitting atop a hill.

"Is this...?" Alexa motioned to the barn out back.

"It is."

"It's so...big."

"My grandfather and father had big ambitions. They built a barn and stables under one roof. Sixteen stalls, eight to a side, for sixteen thoroughbreds. A shop and fireplace for a blacksmith. Hayloft. Everything was made to order, under strict specifications, using the best materials. Cedar mostly That's why it's still standing. They even had plans for a racetrack, a hundred acres where the horses could run."

"What happened?"

"The Depression. Banks defaulted. Only two horses ever slept in the barn. Work horses. Not thoroughbreds."

Alexa moved to the next portrait. "Who's this?"

"My father, Wil. Everyone called him *Poppa*. Never said a bad word about anyone. They say if he met you once he remembered your name. He died a year and half after I was born."

"And this?"

"My mother, Carolyn. Nicest woman on the planet. She was always doing something for others. Baking cookies. Raising money for charities. She loved to sing in the church choir."

"And the guy with the curly hair?"

"That...well..." Richard laughed, "that was Edgar Allen Poe's grandson."

"Really?"

"No. Just kidding. He was a kind of a vagabond, a gypsy. Traveled everywhere...throughout the world in search of the strange and bizarre. What a character he was."

"What was his name?"

"Henry Purdy. *Hank the Willie*, they called him. Historian, poet, writer. Poppa's closest friend."

Alexa's eyes blazed with interest. "He looks so...fascinating. Funny."

"Funny as in odd. He was that. Oddball Hank. Lived in the basement where Caddo lives now. Never had a steady job. Musta had money the way he traveled. Wrote for a local newspaper, travel magazines. Even got published a few times. Some of his books are still in the basement."

"What did he write about?"

Richard laughed. "Weird stuff. Mostly things with a darker side. He loved mysteries. Fancied himself a novelist. Like Poe."

Alexa examined the painting. Crooked nose. Sunken eyes. Wild curly hair. Thick mustache. A hint of a smile. He resembled a young, affable Albert Einstein.

"Now there's someone you don't see nowadays. Was he alive when your wife painted this?"

"No. She did it from a photograph. Of all the people she painted, she considered Willie the most challenging. Mostly because of his eyes."

Alexa stepped closer to the photograph of Dora. "She's beautiful! I can see why you loved her so much. How long were you married?"

"Not long enough."

They stood before the easel, gazing in silence. Alexa could see tears in his eyes. Richard looked away and wiped a cheek.

She took him by the arm and led him slowly past the paintings. Each elicited a response, either in admiration of the content, style, or versatility of the artist. Eventually, they came to the foot of the love seat where they sat down. Alexa took the opportunity to delve deeper into the lives of the Macklins and Willie. Richard happily obliged.

After all, he hadn't received this much attention from a beautiful woman in years.

Elly, meanwhile, crept down the hall to listen. She eavesdropped for a minute or so, then withdrew to the kitchen. David was drying a frying pan when she whispered—

"Boy, you can tell she's a reporter."

"Why do you say that?"

"She asks an awful lot of questions."

David hung the frying pan on a hook above the stove. "There's something you should know. I drove around the farm today and talked to the architect. There's a letter in his trailer from Uncle Mark." He explained the content of the letter and said, "No court's going to validate his claim. The lawsuit is a joke, a trick to delay the project. Legally, he doesn't have a leg to stand on."

"Unfortunately, we have another problem," said Elly. "I found a letter in dad's nightstand from a law firm in Columbus, demanding payment of the loan."

"How much?"

"Sixteen-five."

The news hit David like a punch in the gut. He had to suppress his anger. "I'll call the bank tomorrow…see if I can get an extension."

"What are we going to do, David?"

"First thing, we get Uncle Mark off our back."

"And how do we do that?"

"In the Navy we have a saying. '*Define the objective. Collect data. Analyze. Strategize. Then Execute.*' That's what we'll do."

"What do you have in mind?"

"I don't know yet."

Elly said something, but he wasn't listening.

"David."

"What?"

"I said, go drag her butt away from dad. I didn't invite Alexa here so you could wash dishes with your sister."

A thought occurred to David. His mood changed. He came out of it upbeat, inspired. "I don't know, El. Maybe I shouldn't."

"Why not?"

He pointed at the edge of his mouth. "Look."

"Look at what?"

"This. Right here."

She leaned closer. "What are you talking about?"

"This! See this?"

"I don't see anything."

He stuck out his chin and pointed at his lower lip. "Look closer. Help me, El! Help me! I'm drooling!"

She giggled. "You idiot. I have a question. Do you know what a revenant is?"

"Nope. I have a question. Where are the marshmallows and Graham crackers?"

"Why?"

"Dessert. If you want me to drag her butt away from dad, I need a reason."

Cinders and Roscoe stood by the kitchen door, staring out the screen, growling.

Dusk was underway. Blue skies were being supplanted by gray.

Nighttime loomed like a shadow, waiting.

Chapter 15

It was Alexa's suggestion to eat outside by the old barn. She said it would top off a perfect evening. Elly and David weren't about to object. Neither were Cinders or Roscoe. S'mores were their favorite food. Richard politely declined. Nobody knew where Caddo went.

The tiny stick fire along the hillside flickered just enough to light up their faces. It was a star-filled, moonlit evening. Quiet. Nothing but the soft reverberation of cricket song to serenade the night.

Seated in lawn chairs around the ceremonial pit, they huddled close to the fire. Scrawny branches dipped in marshmallow extended like fishing rods, the tips barely touching the flames. No one bothered with the crackers or chocolate. A few treats were saved for the dogs. Instead, they played a game when they were kids. *'Feed your neighbor'* it was called. Once the marshmallow caught fire, a gooey chunk was dangled in front of someone's mouth. The person had to blow out the flames and eat it without using their hands. Sometimes it got a little wicked. The recipient often received a dose of melted marshmallow on the tip of their nose or side of their cheek.

Alexa tortured David right off the bat. Not by accident she slapped a gob of crispy whiteness onto his cheek, then did it again.

"Time out!" he cried. "Foul! That was a double whacker! What's the penalty for a double whacker, El?"

Elly was doubled over, burping out laughs like a hyena with hiccups.

Now David had two globs of whiteness on his face. Cheek and chin.

"Come on. What's the penalty? Tell her about the tongue teaser, El."

Elly was almost in tears. Between sobs she said, "Sorry, Alex. You...*hoo-hoo*...have to...lick them off!"

Calm as can be, Alexa got up, took two steps, bent down, plucked both smears clean, using her lips and tongue. To David's astonishment and great delight, she whispered, "Close your eyes," and gave him a peck on the lips.

Oh, boy. He felt dizzy. The game had turned sensual. Poor, shy, cornpone David. His face was burning hot, melting like the marshmallow sliding down Alexa's gullet.

"David, you're blushing," giggled Elly.

Intoxicated is what he was. Bitten by the most potent of aphrodisiacs. A beautiful young woman. *Aw-shucks* was written all over his face.

Alexa returned to her lawn chair and sat down as if nothing had happened. Roscoe snuggled up, begging for attention.

"Couldn't ask for a more beautiful night," she sighed as she stroked his back.

It was hard to tell who was smitten more—Roscoe or David. Needless to say they were smitten in different ways.

The campfire crackled, sending hot ashes streaking into the air. The moon was nearly full, waxing like a big, bright, beautiful cabbage. It shone with an amber essence, almost surreal. A single, sparse cloud floated above. No one said a word until Alexa spoke again—

"You know, I was really impressed by your mother's paintings. Especially the portraits. How do you paint what someone looks like, make the eyes so perfect, a chin so right? The one she did of Henry Purdy was amazing. What a strange nickname, *Hank the Willie*. How do you suppose he got that?"

Elly looked at David and David looked at her. "Go ahead," said Elly.

David dangled another marshmallow close to the flames. "Probably because of his attraction to the '*Dark Arts*.'"

"Come again."

"Dark Arts. That's what he wrote about, how he got his nickname. You've heard the expression, '*giving the willies*?' Well, that's what he did. Scared the willies out of people."

"You're joking."

"Nope. One of my favorite stories about Willie had to do with his first experience, what he called his 'baptism into the occult.' He was nineteen when he fought in World War I. After the war, he remained in Europe, traveling abroad. For three days he stayed alone in an old Scottish castle. One night while getting ready for bed, he heard voices in the hallway. When he went to look, no one was there. As he was about to fall asleep, the bedroom door creaked open. He heard footsteps in the room...shuffling...coming towards the bed...heavy breathing. He freaked. The lights were out, but he could tell the room was empty. The footsteps came closer. The shuffling moved past the bed. The closet door opened slowly...then slammed shut!" David slapped his hands together. "That's the day Henry's life changed and he became Willie. Until he died, that's what he did. Chased ghosts."

Elly and Alexa sat there enthralled and slightly creeped out.

"He even wrote a book about ghosts," said David. "Several in fact.

About divine intervention, life after death, spiritualism. He mentioned famous people with similar beliefs, similar experiences."

Alexa scooted forward in her chair. "Famous? Who?"

"The most famous was probably Sir Arthur Conan Doyle, the English novelist who wrote the Sherlock Holmes' mysteries. He and Willie met in London at a writer's conference. Conan Doyle frequented a house owned by a gypsy. He took Willie and a friend there for a séance. Pretty wild stuff."

"Wild in what way?" Alexa asked.

"Two things happened. Willie claimed they talked to someone who died, not like we're talking here, but through a spiritualist, a medium, in this case the gypsy. The dead person was Conan Doyle's mother and he asked a question only she could answer."

"Fascinating. You said there were two things."

"The gypsy was a palm reader. She read the palm of Sir Arthur's friend, a guy named Sir Charles Blake. She became so upset she refused to divulge a single word. As they were leaving, Sir Arthur followed her into a back room and asked her to write down what she saw, so she did. She stuck a note in an envelope, sealed it with wax, and told him not to open it until the following Sunday. A week later, Sir Charles Blake died of a massive heart attack inside an old manor house. The house was supposedly haunted. Sir Arthur read the gypsy's note the next morning. She predicted to the exact hour and day what would happen. The cause of death: heart attack induced by severely impacted trauma. Blake died of complete and utter terror."

"Yikes," groaned Alexa. "I'll never have my palm read."

"Remind me to stay away from castles and old manor houses," said Elly.

David removed a stick from the fire. Another marshmallow had melted. He tossed it into his mouth, chewed, and swallowed. "Maybe the most interesting thing about Hank was his adventurous spirit. He was drawn to dangerous and exotic places. The pyramids, Bagdad, Marrakech, the Middle East. He visited ancient Mayan tombs to study the crypts of the dead. Toured the world with archeologists and discovered ancient artifacts, centuries-old cities buried in the Himalayas. Things like that. He told my grandfather he was drawn to the region because of its sordid history. Like he'd lived here before. He was an explorer in the truest sense of the word, a world traveler, or as a friend and fellow writer once said—'Seeker of the Wild and Wicked.'"

Elly leaned forward in her chair, her eyes rolling to the side. "Shhhh! Listen!" She indicated to her right, then to her left. "It stopped."

Alexa mimicked every move. "What stopped?"

"The crickets. I just realized...crickets don't come out in April. They come out in May or June."

Both dogs were asleep. Cinders woofed. She was dreaming. Roscoe woke up as if touched by an invisible hand. His head jutted upward, ears raised like antennae.

"Easy, boy," cautioned Alexa. "What is it?"

The evening had grown quiet, stilled by the absence of wind. A distant truck rolled down the highway. Roscoe yawned, rested his head on his paws, then jumped to his feet when David picked up a kerosene lamp. David struck a match, lit the wick, and turned the valve to high, casting a warm glow beyond the pit.

Elly looked at her brother. "Where are you going?"

"We need more wood. Fire's getting low." He pulled a long-nosed pistol from a blanket resting by his feet and laid it on the lawn chair. "Compliments of Mr. Smith and Mr. Wesson."

"David!" Elly protested. "You know I hate guns. Why did you bring that *thing* up here?"

"Never know when you might need it." He walked away, carrying the lamp, with Roscoe frolicking at his feet.

As he left, he heard Alexa say. "Okay, I confess. I knew about Hank all along. There's an article in the library he wrote. You should read it."

"Why?" asked Elly.

"What you heard is tame in comparison."

Chapter 16

Red oaks and sugar maples formed a barrier beyond the old barn. Branches and twigs littered the ground, a result of the strong spring winds that blew in late April. The light reached out at an angle, so wherever a twig or branch was embedded, it looked like a snake gnarled and curled in a petrified state. There were a lot of petrified snakes.

While he was gathering wood for the fire, David noticed the lamp flame trembling inside the globe even though he had filled the container half an hour ago. The wind wasn't blowing, yet the light kept brightening and dimming like a strobe lamp. About that time he heard a dull scraping noise coming from the structure to his left. The light became secondary. The noise, more compelling.

At the base of the wall, he bent to listen. The scraping continued, reminiscent of the barn owl in the hayloft, only this time it was more suggestive of a rat digging against a floorboard. The trouble was, there were no floorboards. And it wasn't so much the noise. He felt drawn to it, as if by an involuntary attraction. Whatever it was, the noise stopped and was eerily replaced by a low guttural moan, prompting him to think an animal was trapped by another animal. One of them hissed. But it didn't just hiss. It groaned and shuffled its claws, giving the effect of dried leaves rustling together. On second thought, maybe it wasn't an animal after all. It seemed to have a human quality, not in any normal sense, but in a pathetic sort of way. Like it was calling. Weakly. Clamoring to be heard. One moment no louder than a whisper. The next, silent.

He could feel a cold sensation knifing up his spine. His hands were perspiring. It reminded him of his childhood fear of darkness when the unknown lurked around every corner, in the attic, basement, beneath his bed. He had the same urge to run from it now as he did then.

He whipped his head around when he heard another sound. The spaniel had his nose in the weeds. His stubby tail was wagging back and forth. Roscoe must have found a mole or a rabbit hole because he started pawing at the ground.

"Roscoe, come here!"

The dog obeyed and came running to him.

David cradled the sticks and branches to his chest with his left hand and with his right he carried the lamp. As he turned the corner of the building, he became aware of a fragrance, something between a perfume and wild flower. At the same time he detected a change in the atmosphere. It felt crisper, charged with an intensity. Roscoe sensed it as well. The cocker spaniel stopped in his tracks, the hair on his neck sticking straight up as he stood facing the barn door. David froze, his eyes drifting from Roscoe to the door.

A latch handle grated against metal. The door began to open, creaking an inch at a time. Roscoe's tail went rigid. The dog whimpered and backed up. David watched, unable to move. The creaking grew louder, the opening larger. The wind was nonexistent. Hinges squeaked with agonizing slowness. Deep within the barn, the interior beckoned. The light barely exposed it. Creeping on its axis, the door swung wide until it was completely open.

"Whoa." *This isn't happening*, David said to himself.

Roscoe tilted his head, stared at nothing, at a black shadow. His entire body was shaking.

From the campfire Elly hollered, "What is it, David?"

He dropped the branches and stood there, unable to answer.

Both women ran to his side, along with Cinders.

"What's wrong?" asked Elly.

"The door..." David caught a case of the nerves, stopping at mid-sentence.

Without hesitating, Alexa marched straight into the barn.

"Uh, I wouldn't..."

Too late.

"Would you two hurry up," she hollered. "I can't see a thing."

Roscoe and Cinders refused to budge. Elly and David matched each other step for step. It was like entering an oversized dungeon—above ground. The lamp cast a faint, lackluster light, dulled by the drabness. The barn stank of rotted, weather-beaten wood. Beams were sagging, cracked in one place or another. Strewn about the dirt floor were heaps of rubbish, lumber, and old discarded farm equipment—horse-driven plows, wagons, buggies, one of them wheel-less, the wheels lying haphazardly by the horse stalls, and every conceivable type of hand tool from the first half of the twentieth century. It was a step back in time, a journey into the mortality of rural architecture, as bleak and foreboding as anything they had ever seen. Every inch of the place was jammed full.

"My God! This place is bigger than I thought!" declared Alexa. Her voice echoed. Even a whisper carried from wall to wall. But her words seemed to shake the very foundation. "It's h-u-g-e! I've never seen a barn this big. Look at all the junk! You could start a museum."

"Well, that was kinda the idea," said David.

Alexa and Elly stepped closer to the light, squinting at the interior posts leading up to the I-beams that supported the roof. The light penetrated the chamber, dying in the distant shadows as if darkness were pushing it back. Every time David moved the lantern the shadows danced...moved like tentacles writhing beneath the sea.

Alexa studied the rugged rooflines as dust fell, trickling down like snowflakes. "Why don't you tear it down?" she wondered.

"Who knows," said Elly." Maybe dad has a warped sense of humor." She coughed and brushed a spider web from her hair. "What's that smell?"

"Mildew," said Alexa.

"No, it's something else."

"It's lavender," said David. There was something in his face. Awareness.

Elly looked at him in shock. They seemed to share a secret.

The two women separated, each exploring a different part of the barn. Alexa disappeared behind a wheel-less buggy, Elly behind a nearby stall. David glanced nervously in one direction, then the other. The lamp flame quivered while shadows crept across the rafters...along the walls even though he was standing still.

"Hey, you two."

One odor dissipated. Another came drifting in, smelling like egg water.

At that point he heard the wind pushing against the roof. Also something else: a low monotonous moan, no louder than a whisper. It sounded more human than animal, calling from far, far away.

"Hey, guys."

It continued in a deep throaty rhythm, as if someone were weeping in agony or torture. It wailed on and on. Then he was conscious of the newer smell, something vaguely familiar. Only once had he smelled death on the battlefield. It smelled of rotting flesh. He looked around and saw shadows crawling in constant motion. It all combined for a chilling uneasiness and the impression that, as far as he could tell, they weren't alone.

"Hey!"

His shout shook the rafters.

Alexa came stumbling from behind the buggy, clutching her heart. "Don't do that!"

From the horse stall Elly yelled, "What?"

David listened. The moaning had stopped. "Did you hear that?"

"Hear what?" both women said.

The fact that they heard nothing no longer mattered.

David waved them closer. "Come on! We're getting out of here!"

No one moved.

"Now, damn it!"

Something at the rear of the barn strained under its own weight or gave in to the ravages of time. It suddenly collapsed, splintering with loud cracks, and came crashing down.

That sent everyone running, sprinting for the door.

* * *

Richard Macklin had just finished his third glass of bourbon and coke. Mostly bourbon. He knew he was drinking too much. He didn't care. One of the few things he enjoyed in life was sitting in the front room with the ceiling light focused on his wife's photograph. This evening was no different than any other, except the visit by their houseguest only reminded him of just how lonely he had become.

Resting on the love seat, he didn't know whether to have another drink or go to bed. He could barely stay awake. He may have fallen asleep. He wasn't sure.

What triggered it, he didn't know. His eyes shot open. He walked to the window and drew back the curtain. What he saw sobered him instantly.

* * *

In the basement, seated at his desk, Caddo was unable to read, unable to write, unable to concentrate. With elbows propped up and head in his hands, he sat brooding over what to do. He pushed the chair from the desk, got up, and paced back and forth. Restlessness for him always seemed to strike a few hours before midnight. He was tempted to call Irene and see if they could get together, but the timing wasn't good. Besides, she deserved his full attention.

Reaching into the cabinet, he pulled out a leather sheath holding a knife and strapped it to his thigh. Ever since a coyote attacked him, he never went outside at night without a weapon. It was almost unheard of for a coyote to attack a human. It merely proved how mad the pack had become. Now it attacked things normally it never would and did so with a viciousness that went beyond hunger. It hunted with a cunning unmatched by its species. In essence, he was dealing with a pack driven to kill, and no man or animal was safe.

As soon as he opened the basement door, his fears were realized.

* * *

The women had no idea why they were running or what they were running from. David seemed to know and that was reason enough. He was acting on impulse. It wasn't just the odor, moans, or boards that had fallen in the barn. He could feel a presence in the night air, like a high voltage wire exposed and dangerous. Once they fled the barn, the atmosphere intensified. The spaniels stood trembling in a light frothy haze that came drifting up from the road.

In the distance, trapped in the cattle yard, cows were mooing. Judging from the sounds, they were ready to bolt at any second.

Roscoe and Cinders didn't move.

Fog had overtaken the hill and field below, accompanied by heavy gusts of wind. Both the wind and fog were now invading the trees to the south.

From the hen house, roosters and chickens clucked as if they were being attacked. Lost in the commotion was another sound. An engine. David was the first to hear it. He listened to a *chug-alug* of an old motor accelerating, sputtering with a whispery *clack-clack-clack* from an exhaust pipe cap.

The tractor! The old John Deere.

Somebody's taking it out for a spin! At nine-thirty at night?

He dropped the lantern and started running. The dogs took off in pursuit, followed by Elly and Alexa. Beyond the hill no one could see a thing. Roscoe raced ahead, a little black orb with legs, swallowed by darkness. A few steps behind, Cinders was barking. David almost tripped, but found his balance as his boots slapped at the ground. He reached the lawn chair, grabbed the pistol, and sprinted down the hill into the freshly plowed field where the fog hung thicker. Not far away the engine hummed. The throttle revved, sputtering and wheezing while the tractor lurched. David thought of his dad, half drunk, slumped over the steering wheel.

He heard Elly behind him, struggling to catch up. Both dogs were barking. The smell of sulfur was so strong it made him gag. It was like inhaling fumes from chloride or a gas.

Ahead, through the clotting mist he could see the dim glow of the headlamps. The lights were wavering up and down.

"Dad, what are you doing?"

The outline of the John Deere rose in the night. It dipped over a mound and stopped. A shadow withdrew as the engine eased into neutral. Headlights probed the field, dying into blackness. The tractor stood still, fumes pouring from the exhaust.

No one got off.

No one was sitting at the steering wheel.

David was five feet from it, staring at a rider-less machine.

Elly halted by his side, breathing hard, staring in disbelief. Roscoe and Cinders were sniffing the tires as Alexa ran up. She was speechless.

"See anyone?" Elly asked.

"Nope," said David.

Caddo came limping across the field, his flushed face beading with sweat. On the other side of the tractor, Richard stumbled forward in a daze.

David looked at the Indian, then at his father. "So if it wasn't you and wasn't dad, who was it?"

Panting and shaking, Caddo whispered, *"Charik waik-ta."*

Chapter 17

"Charik waik-ta."

Caddo's words fell on deaf ears.

Everyone was expecting something else to happen. Nothing did. The first sign that it wouldn't was when the fog receded. Initially, the wind died. Little by little, the air began to clear without any aftereffects from the sulfuric smell.

The first order of business was to remove Alexa from the premises…out of harm's way. As the moon and stars reappeared, everyone went their separate ways. To avoid controversy and any questions, Caddo hopped on the tractor and drove to the barn as fast as he could. Elly and Richard returned to the house while David escorted Alexa to her car. There, the two had a lively discussion about the night's events. Elly watched from a side window. It didn't take much to imagine what they were talking about. She had formed her opinion days ago after inspecting a dead horse. The defining moment came when she measured a wound. The depth was five inches, the width almost eight. That, along with the power outage and collapse of the bridge were perfect examples of occurrences similar to this evening's with regard to peculiarity. She kept her views to herself for fear of what others might think. The idea of expressing your opinion about subjects as farfetched as these was like standing naked in a crowd. By the same token, she felt compelled to share her feelings with someone.

She ruled out the possibilities, one by one. Alexa? Forget it. Can't trust a reporter. Caddo? No way. Extracting information from him was like pulling a tusk loose from a bull elephant—barehanded. Her father? A difficult man to pin down. As irascible as they come. Which left the most logical choice. David. Open minded. And trained to kill.

Elly heard a pair of boots hitting the floor inside her father's bedroom. Richard was preparing to go to sleep. Taking a seat at the kitchen table, she waited for David, expecting the side door to open any second. The door never opened. So she decided to confront her father once and for all.

* * *

He referred to it as the Halting Place, a place where it all began and where it would end. It had many other names, none of them relevant. It belonged to no one really, no land did, for this was sacred ground, once the home of the Mosopelea, the 'Dog People,' for briefer times, the Honniasont, the 'Black Minqua,' the 'Black Badge Wearers.'

For a much briefer period a long time ago, a band from another tribe visited the Hill Country. They were wanderers, nomads, a fierce people who lived a month's journey from here by foot. No one was feared more than the Mohawk, a tribe respected for their aggressiveness in battle. The Mohawk were one of five Iroquois Nations whose domain once extended from the eastern seaboard to the Ohio Valley before the white man came. The history of the Halting Place was both eventful and tragic. These days, however, only a handful of people had any knowledge of that history. After all, no Indian tribe had lived in the region for hundreds of years, whether it was Mohawk, Mosopelea, or Black Minqua.

Caddo's ancestry was Pawnee, descendants of the Caddoan people. Hence, his name. Although he had no direct relation to the Indians who once lived here, he felt responsible for upholding the tradition and honor of those who did. Therefore, the Halting Place had become his own personal sanctuary where he could remain as much of an Indian as his forefathers.

Even late at night without the moon or a light to guide him, he could find his way. Of the many years he had been coming to the Halting Place, he couldn't remember seeing a car or truck on the back roads after dark. Tonight of all nights he was more afraid than surprised for whoever was at the wheel. As the headlights approached, he raised his hands, motioning for the driver to stop.

The men in the white Ford pickup tossed their empty beer cans on the floor of the back seat.

"Jesus, not him again," said Matt. "What's he doing out here this time of night?"

Jack eased his foot on the brake. "I suppose you could say the same for us."

"Keep going. Damn hillbilly Indian. No good can come from us stopping."

"Quiet!" cried Jack. "Let me do the talking. You've had too much to drink." The tires kicked up dust as the truck skidded to a stop. Jack rolled the window down. "Good evening. Need a ride?"

Caddo walked up to the driver's door. "No thank you. Appreciate the offer. Working late I see."

"Picking up blueprints my partner here forgot. Isn't that right, Grady?"

Matt nodded his head.

"How can we help you, Mr. Walker?"

Caddo made a few token inquiries of the golf course. It was strictly a formality. His interests lied elsewhere.

Jack Lorrigan told him how the plans were progressing, then added, "Not to be rude, but there must be a reason you're out so late. Is there a problem?"

"Just concerned is all," said Caddo. "A pack of coyotes have been running loose at night. Haven't seen them, have you?"

"Not me. How about you, Matt?" After Matt shook his head, Jack said, "Why do you ask?"

"Don't want anybody getting hurt. Two deer were found by the river. Nothing left but the carcasses. Health Department says the coyotes are infected, so I'd be careful if I were you."

"If that's the case, I'd worry about yourself. Walking alone. Middle of nowhere."

"Yeah," said Matt. "That knife of yours ain't gonna do much good if a hungry coyote gets hold of you'."

Caddo assured them he could take care of himself.

"I bet you can," said Jack. "You know, it's the oddest thing. Power went out in our trailer again. Third time this week. Always late. Damn near can set your watch by it. And we're using a gas generator. You know what's weirder? Power comes back on the next morning." Jack stroked his chin. "Dog-gone if I can figure it out. If I didn't know better, I'd say someone is playing tricks on us."

"Try using a phone," said Matt. "Sometimes it works. Sometimes it doesn't."

Jack looked daggers at his partner. "I wouldn't worry about us. We're staying at a hotel in town."

Jack slipped the gear into drive.

Caddo motioned for them to wait.

"What?" said Jack.

"How often do you stay after dark?"

The architect considered it an odd question. "Never. We're usually in our rooms by sundown. Or eating dinner somewhere. Why?"

Caddo shrugged. "Just being cautious. Coyotes are probably more afraid of you than you are of them." He looked up and down the road, then put his hands in his back pockets. "Well, have a good evening. Just do me a favor."

"What's that?"

"Promise me you're in and out of that trailer, fast. Find those blueprints and leave."

* * *

David decided it was time to devise some type of strategy. Whether a mission, military exercise, or studies in a classroom, one thing the Navy always did was drill one form of strategy or another into your brain.

Once Caddo parked the tractor, David saw him leave on foot. He was tempted to follow, but tracking an Indian at night was a little like chasing the wind.

With the pistol tucked in his belt and lamp at his side, David sat on the hillside facing the farmhouse, wondering how he was going to proceed. There were three elements he had to deal with. People. Evidence. And the unknown. Of the people, he had already talked to his sister. His father was probably in bed. Caddo was off to who knows where. That left one person he could get some idea of what course of action to take.

When he was a kid, he remembered reading a book written by Henry Purdy. He wondered how Willie would handle the situation. He tried to place himself in Willie's shoes.

Of course!

Why not consult with Willie himself!

Chapter 18

Elly was sitting on the bed beside her father. She could smell bourbon on his breath. Even when he'd been drinking, it was hard to get him to talk.

"So what you're saying is, from last Friday until now, tonight was the first night you experienced anything like this?"

Richard stretched his back, trying to loosen it. "That's right. Man oh man, am I stiff." He glanced at the spaniels lying on the floor. "Now those two, they've been acting up lately."

"Acting up how?"

"Fidgety. Nervous. Growling at little things. Mostly their own shadows."

"And that doesn't worry you?"

"Hell, I've been shot at too many times in my life to worry. They don't growl for long."

She noticed the stress was getting to him. It was beginning to show in his bloodshot eyes, blotchy face, and weight he was losing. Psychologically, it was taking a toll as well. He had no sense of humor anymore. He was moody and often morose—symptoms of a deep depression—until he popped a pill.

Instant happiness. Instant addiction.

She was worried sick.

"All this time and the only thing you've heard is the dogs growling?"

Richard nodded. "I told the deputies the same thing."

"What deputies?"

"Tom Duckett and another guy stopped by Tuesday evening. Like I told them, most of the time I'm in bed by ten o'clock."

"Why didn't you tell me they were here?"

"I didn't think it was important."

"What did they ask you?"

"Usual police stuff. Had I heard anything. What was I doing at such and such time. I honestly believe they think I had something to do with the bridge. Now why I would go and do a thing like that and hurt my own business? I had to walk them through the entire week, mostly between the hours of midnight and daybreak. I said, 'What in the hell do you think I was doing? I was sleeping.'"

"What else did you say?"

He knitted his brows. "What else?"

"Yeah, from the look of your face, doesn't look like you're getting much sleep."

"Can't kid you, can I? Truth is, sleep comes and goes. I'll fall asleep for a few hours, wake up, and drift off again. It's funny. There are times when I've never slept better, strange as that may sound. When my head hits the pillow, I'm out cold. Nothing seems to faze me."

"What's that supposed to mean?"

"Just what I said. When I'm sleeping, I'm in a state of unconsciousness I've never experienced before. It's deeper. I...I can't explain it."

Elly realized she may have touched upon something. She believed these 'deep periods of sleep' were in some way significant.

"Do you dream?" she asked.

Richard seemed troubled by the question. "Of course. Doesn't everybody?"

"What do you dream about?"

He rubbed his brow. "What is this? An inquisition?"

Typical dad response. Avoidance and denial.

"I just don't think you're getting enough rest," said Elly. "I'm trying to find out why. Maybe I can help. So would you please just answer the question."

"Hell, I don't know. I'm like anybody else, I guess. Soon as I wake up I forget what I was dreaming about."

"You must remember something."

He was growing agitated. He wrung his hands and took a few short deep breaths. "Not now, Elly. I have a headache. I just want to go bed." He took off his watch, put it on the night table, rubbed his wrist, and acted like he was ready for bed. "Why don't you and David stay at your place tonight?"

The question implied a concern. Elly jumped on it—

"How come?"

He shrugged. "No reason. Just thought you might sleep better there."

"Why do you think that?"

"Never mind. Forget I mentioned it."

"No, I want to know."

He held a hand against his forehead, grimacing, as if he'd made a slip of the tongue.

"Talk to me, Dad. What are you worried about?"

"Not now, Elly. Please. I don't want you babysitting me, that's all. I can take care of myself."

"Is that what you think I'm doing? Babysitting?"

Anger crept into his voice. "Please. I don't want to talk about it. I don't want to argue."

"Nobody's arguing. We're just...talking."

"Stop it!" Richard yelled. He realized what he'd done, how he was acting. He turned his back and unconsciously laid a trembling hand on his wife's photograph.

The abrupt mood swing was unexpected. Something had snapped. She had touched a nerve. At any moment it looked like he might break into tears.

She had only seen him cry three times. The day he learned his wife had cancer, the day of the funeral, and a week later when the loneliness and suffering became unbearable.

She got up, walked over to him, reached her arms around him, and hugged. They stood that way for a long time, not speaking. Elly was the one who was crying. Not her father. They were silent tears. That's when she realized she never loved him more.

Later, after she left the bedroom, she could hear the haunting, rhythm of Procol Harem echoing through the house, and the words...

> "...One of sixteen vestal virgins
> who were leaving for the coast
> and although my eyes were open
> they might have just as well've been closed..."

Chapter 19

Caddo stopped dead in his tracks. He could smell it from a mile away, that sulfuric odor. He wasn't a mile away. He was much closer. It was like thunder before a storm. The smell of sulfur struck with a suddenness.

With short, choppy strides he started running, hobbling on one good leg. As the moon broke through the clouds, he could see the white Ford pickup parked beside the trailer. The idiots didn't listen. No doubt they were unaware of the danger they were in.

After a hundred yards, his legs began to stiffen, especially the left leg, the gimpy one. Another hundred yards and he began to labor. His muscles were tightening and he had another hundred yards to go.

The smell of sulfur was growing stronger.

Wheezing and gasping, he summoned what little reserves he had. He was running on desperation. His gait was more like a stagger than a trot. He was hopping on one foot while dragging the other. The moon slipped behind a cloud. Fifty yards away stood the trailer. He'd spent every ounce of energy getting to the bottom of the hill.

The atmosphere was changing. An increasing congestion of air was gathering over the Halting Place. Through a window he could see a light inside the trailer. The beam was darting around randomly.

He yelled. He screamed.

He followed the road as it gradually turned into a path. He felt as if he were moving in slow motion, stumbling like a punch-drunk boxer.

Heavy fog began to drift across the field toward the trailer. He yelled as the door swung open. Jack Lorrigan was holding a flashlight. He paused on the porch steps, looking at Caddo. Caddo was waving his arms.

"Get in the truck! Run! Get in the truck!"

A gust of wind came roaring across the valley. The mobile home rocked on its foundation.

Sweat got into Caddo's eyes as he jogged dead-footed. He didn't look behind him, but he could feel something massive forming, gaining intensity. The wind was howling. Sticks and dust came lashing at his back.

Dried leaves whipped around like bats. Maybe they were bats.

Up ahead, the flashlight was waving all over the place. Jack had trouble keeping his balance. The door burst open again. His partner, Matt, stumbled forward and both men went tumbling over the railing. A quake shuddered to the west, from the direction of the park. Lightning struck. The sound of a violent storm erupted, only it seemed to come from a prehistoric beast. The wind was approaching gusts of sixty miles an hour. And increasing.

The air was thick with flying debris.

Jack and Matt panicked and jumped to their feet.

"Into the truck! Get into the truck!" Caddo screamed.

He was hit with swirling dust and wet foamy air. Half-blinded, he watched as the trailer rose off the ground. He heard the sound of a diesel engine starting. Taillights flashed amid the fog. Once more the primeval beast roared. Caddo lost his balance and reached for the tailgate. The truck spun out, recovered, and shot forward. He pulled himself up and over the tailgate, somersaulting across the bed liner. As the truck drove away, he looked back, dazed, his chest heaving in and out from exhaustion.

From inside the truck, Matt slid the back window open. "You all right? What the hell was that?"

Caddo stared into the darkness, into the chaos.

"You tell me," he gasped.

The wind roared once more.

Debris came flying at the pickup, pelting it as hail rained down the size of nickels. Sticks and leaves lashed at his face. He ducked, covering his head, and rolled against the tailgate to keep from being hit.

They could hear the sound of wood snapping, aluminum bending, crunching, followed by a loud crash, like a small aircraft striking the ground.

There was a guttural roar from the *Beast Primeval.*

Caddo braced for an impact, thinking the truck was next. It bounced over a mound as it sped up the dirt road. Tools and surveying equipment clattered against the bed liner. He held his breath and waited. And waited.

* * *

"Caddo, is that you down there?"

The whispered inquiry made him jump.

The stairs creaked as someone walked down.

David looked up. "Jeez almighty, El. You almost gave me a heart attack."

She stood at the bottom of the stairs, hands on hips, staring at a rows of opened boxes. "What are you doing?"

"Looking for a book," said David as he closed the lids. "I found it."

"What book?"

"Which one do you think?"

He tucked a book under his arm and hurried into Caddo's living quarters and laid an arrowhead on the desk.

Elly stood by the door. "Where'd you find that?"

"Amen Corner."

"Huh?"

"Never mind."

"What book are you talking about?"

He stopped at the door, put the lamp on the floor, reached under his arm, and showed her a title—

Musings from Afar,
the Depths of the Eternal Soul
by Henry J. Purdy

He handed her a bookmark with writing on it. He picked up the lamp and continued walking.

"Where are you going?"

"Outside."

"Outside where?"

"Pulling G.D."

"G.D.?"

"Guard duty."

She looked at the bookmark. It read—

Phantom Beast…
Charik waik-ta

The basement went dark the moment David walked upstairs. She whispered hoarsely, "David! Very funny. Turn on the light!"

Her shinbone hit something hard.

"Ouch!"

Boxes tumbled.

"David, I'm going to kill you!" she groaned.

Chapter 20

Two and a half miles away, on a secluded county road Norman "Scootch" McPhee lived alone with a menagerie of cats—twenty-six of them, of various shapes and colors, short-haired, long-haired, Persian, Siamese, mixed breeds, alley cats—in a house full of cat hairs...crammed with junk. Ever since his wife left him and his two kids moved away, Scootch stopped caring. The same lack of attention carried over to the farm. Fields were plowed in slap-dash fashion, rows of tilled soil weaving in and out, the result of drunken binges at the wheel of the tractor. The barn out back was home to a lonely swaybacked horse often neglected and poorly fed.

Norm sat in his armchair, holding a cigarette, wearing a torn undershirt, watching the SyFy Channel on a wide screen TV with the sound off. On the table to his right was a beer bottle, half a bottle of Jim Beam, and an ashtray filled with cigarette butts.

A fat, sandy-haired cat named Ricky-Ticky sat on Scootch's lap. He groaned as Ricky-Ticky's claws scratched at his britches. The cat suddenly jerked her head around, hissed wide-eyed, and bared her teeth as a shadow moved past the front bay window.

From the kitchen, hallway, and back bedrooms of the one-story farmhouse came a chorus of frightened meows. Cats of every descripttion went diving under chairs, under beds, under furniture, into closets, behind draperies.

Normally a passive pet, Ricky-Ticky arched her back. Her hair stood on end as she hissed like the alley cat she was. Panicking, she sprang from his lap.

Norman jumped—"Oww! Damn, girl!—and shot out of the cushions. He looked around nervously, wondering what the commotion was about when he heard a trample of feet outside. Scootch owned two rifles, one for hunting squirrels he called "Betsy," the other "Old Buck," for buckshot, a double-barreled shotgun he used for...well, nothing. He figured the occasion fit Old Buck better than Betsy, so he marched into his bedroom and opened the closet. As he did, he heard a grunt and a shuffling of paws. Out of the corner of his eye he saw something move. A shadow, much too agile for its size, passed by the window.

Three seconds later, at the rear of the house, a horse whinnied. The cats hissed and meowed and shrieked as though the house were on fire.

Soon as Scootch touched Old Buck he could feel his confidence growing. Of course, having drunk five beers and taken six swigs of Jim Beam straight from the bottle helped. But all things considered, his nerves were still rattled—especially when he heard the horse whinny again.

He clicked the barrel open to see if the shotgun was loaded. Yep. Loaded.

"Hurt ole Lester, will ya'?"

Then he snapped the barrel shut, grabbed a handful of shells, and stuffed them in a back pocket. Making as little noise as possible, he tiptoed through the back of the house through a maze of cats who sat curled, quivering balls of fur, ready to jump at a moment's notice. At the back door he stopped to listen.

A trash can fell over. He could hear it rolling across the driveway.

A hush fell the instant it stopped. For some reason the horse had grown quiet. Ten seconds later there was another grunt, a soft plodding of feet. Scootch clicked on the porch light to see if it would scare it away. Pulling a curtain aside, he peeked out a back window and saw the porch light shining and nothing else but fog.

He knew right away he made a mistake by going outside. It seemed like there was no turning back once the screen door creaked shut.

He felt exposed. As if the Thing were waiting, ready to pounce.

He stood fifty feet from the barn, gripping Old Buck tight with white knuckles. A swirling mist hindered his vision, then it went still. There wasn't a sound, except for the distant croaking of frogs and a twitter here and there. He couldn't see the barn at all. He took two small steps. Sweat was pouring from every pore. The silence was unnerving. But Old Buck was the enforcer, the equalizer. It gave Scootch just enough courage to keep going. He took two more steps, bigger steps, when he heard an explosion of wood. It sounded like an entire wall had snapped, beams and all had been broken. It was followed by the bleating of a horse. He could hear the cats meowing from inside the house. His spine went rigid as a light came on inside the barn. The door was open. It had been *smashed* open. Wood was splintered at the hinges and doorframe. The crushed doorway seemed to beckon. He could hear heavy breathing.

Was it Lester? Or the Thing?

Old Buck was pointed at the doorway. The barrels were shaking.

Scootch took two steps, then another, and one more still.

Everything was quiet—except the heavy breathing. It almost sounded like Lester was choking.

The outline of the barn grew more distinct. He could now see inside it. The area between the door and stall revealed nothing. Two more steps and he craned his neck to look. Bile came rising to his throat. It was caused by one thing—

Fear.

He retched. Blinked away the sweat. And the fear. Hard as he tried, the fear remained.

All at once there came a screeching from the horse, baying, whinnying, thud after thud as the walls were being kicked. A roar like thunder. Grunts. A howl of such evil, it could only be made from a creature from Hell.

Then he saw It. Just a glimpse. A hairy rump blocked the stall. The barn rattled as Lester, in the clutches of the Beast, wailed in agony. There were sounds of masticating, chewing, teeth grating against bone. A whimper. A slapping of hoofs. Flesh being torn apart. A growl of satisfaction. Then a thud, this time of a body falling. A roar of pleasure, of evil so sinister it made Norman's skin prickle and nerves go numb. The Beast wasn't intent upon just killing. It wanted Lester to suffer.

Then it abated, the sound of a dying horse.

The end came mercifully.

Now It had its sights set on something else. On Norman.

He pulled the trigger.

The shotgun recoiled violently with a loud boom, scattering buckshot through the open doorway. The howl was deafening. Scootch knew he hit it, knew he struck it dead on, precisely where he aimed. The result was negligible. He heard a plodding of feet, a continuous roar as a huge shadow came running through the fog. The shotgun blast did no harm at all.

He sprinted toward the house.

Amid the crying and screeching of the cats and the charging of heavy paws, he flung the screen door open, dove inside, then opened the second door, shut it, and locked it. He slumped down, gasping, holding the shotgun with one shell remaining.

No time to reload.

The porch screen door was obliterated with one thrust. The crunching of wood sounded like the crunching of bone.

Scootch waited. The barrel of the shotgun never wavered. The second thrust came with a jarring force. The house shook. Hinges were pried loose. The doorframe buckled. In the window, he could see the eye of the Beast.

Norman turned Old Buck around, pointing the barrel at his chin. One more thrust, another lunge at the door, and he would be dead.

The cats went shrieking to the far corners of the house.

He waited, fingers coiled around the trigger. Mouth open.

Not a sound came after that. From the cats. Or the Beast.

Chapter 21

Elly yawned and looked at her watch. "Oh, my God! It's almost one thirty."

She and David had been talking so long they lost track of time. They sat on matching lounge chairs on the driveway with the kerosene lamp balanced on a TV table burning brightly between them. Wind chimes, made of stamped metal, of horses galloping, pinged lightly from the kitchen porch. Insects buzzed the light fixture above the door while traffic along Route 2 had ceased altogether.

An eerie peacefulness had settled over the farm.

David had become obsessed with Henry's book. For the past few minutes he didn't say a word. He kept his eyes focused on the pages in rapt expression.

Elly gazed up at the sky and said, "One more night and the moon will be full. I'm going to bed. I suggest you do the same." When he didn't answer, she reached over and touched his arm. "David, go to bed."

"I will. In a while." With a trace of wonder in his voice, he added, "Did you know Hank once rid a town of a ghost?"

"Good Lord! Would you stop? That's not what I want to hear right now."

His eyes never left the pages. "Sorry."

Curiosity got the better of her. Elly propped her head up, using her forearm like a pillow. "Okay, okay." She waved her hand impetuously.

Without missing a beat, David said, "Plymouth, Massachusetts, 1924. A fisherman named Old Salt George drowned one night when his boat capsized during a storm. Next morning his body washed up on shore, half eaten by sharks. After the funeral, Old Salt haunted the wharf every night. Scared the hell out of everybody for weeks."

"I'm sure he did."

"The townspeople didn't know what to do. After talking to several of his friends, Hank learned that Old Salt hated land. He assumed he hated being buried underground as well. So with a little persuasion from Hank, the townspeople dug up the casket and gave it a proper burial at sea. George was never seen again."

"Brrrrr!" Elly hugged her shoulders. "And a fine story it is. Thanks for sharing that. But what's the point?"

"Time and again, Hank did case studies of survival after death. He believed ghosts existed because their lives were incomplete. They weren't ready to, in his words, 'depart this secular life.'"

"Are you suggesting we're being haunted by ghosts?"

"Sounds crazy, doesn't it? No, I'm not. That I don't have an explanation for. Even if I did, I have no idea what we could do about it."

"Comforting thought. Maybe we should go to my place."

"I don't think that's the answer," said David.

"If there is an answer."

"Okay, bad choice of words. Solution. Outside of the accident, no one's died yet."

"Aren't you're forgetting something?"

"What?"

"Freddie. No one's found him."

The mere mention of Wilfredo Pinoza had a disquieting effect.

Elly realized running away wasn't an option. "You're right. Dad would never leave here, even if the house was on fire. Doesn't it strike you as odd how complacent he is? He's probably in bed right now, passed out from…"

Her eyes suddenly shot wide.

David leapt to his feet as the silence was shattered.

A truck horn blared as an eighteen-wheeler came barreling down the highway. Two more horn blasts followed, each lasting three to four ear-splitting seconds. Cows mooed and chickens clucked.

Elly shook a fist. "You bastard! God, he does that every time he drives by!"

"It's happened before?"

"Always in the middle of the night."

"Have you called the Sheriff? Filed a complaint?"

"And the Highway Patrol. Apparently, they have other priorities. The problem is, I have nothing to go on. No license plate. Nothing to identify the trucking company. And dad's so out of it he's no help at all. Look!" She pointed at his bedroom window. It was still dark. "See what I mean? How could anyone sleep through that?"

David wasn't about to argue. Anyone who could sleep through such a racket had to be comatose. And barbiturates, to a lonely widower, offered a perfect remedy to insomnia.

Elly folded her lounge chair, removed her cell phone from a pocket, and placed it on the table. "Here. In case you need to call 9-1-1. I'm going to bed. Breakfast at seven. I want to get an early start at the library."

"I'll be up in a few minutes," said David. Something about the eighteen-wheeler stuck in his mind. "Hey, El. The truck…did you notice anything?"

She stopped and turned. "It was big. Had a double trailer. That's about it."

He tried to picture the semi as it drove by. There was a logo on the side, a shape all in black. No name. Just a logo. It went by so quickly the image was blurred. But it reminded him of someone, someone he hadn't seen in years. "I thought I saw something. Forget it. It's not important."

"Good night," said Elly.

"Night," said David.

There was a distant call of a coyote, a lonely, protracted cry—*Ooooooo!*

Worried, Elly glanced at her brother, but he was already wrapped up in the pages of Henry Purdy's book.

Chapter 22

Caddo sat by the window with the chair turned, facing the black sky.

"Since you're not comin' to bed..." Irene threw off the bed sheet. Slipped a robe over her nightgown. Walked over to the chair and slid into his lap. "There, that's better. Did you know your friend, David, came to see me?"

"He did? What for?"

"Guess he wanted to check out the goods." She held out her hand and flashed the opal ring. "After all, I am spoken for."

"You certainly are. What did he say?"

She pretended to blush. "Isn't what he said. What he did. One taste of my pie and he was practically on his knees beggin'."

Caddo smiled. "He's a good kid. Has a big heart."

There was a long silence as they stared out the window at the big moon- cabbage perched in the sky.

Bubbles reached around his neck, gave it an affectionate tug. "Wish I could crawl into that head of yours. What are you thinkin' about?"

He was looking at nothing really, a void. Lines of worry crinkled his face. "Oh..."—he reflected for a moment—"how life is, what it should be."

"And how should it be?"

"Good," was all he said.

She laughed. "That's it? Good?" And laughed again. "Caddo Walker, you sure are somethin'! Not long on words, but you get to the point awful quick."

She glanced at him as he looked out the window. He seemed distant. The moment he entered the door she knew something was wrong. He seemed quieter than usual. Pensive. His clothes were dirty and she didn't see that old beat up AMC Pacer of his parked anywhere on the street below. Or the Jeep Cherokee. Caddo never explained how he got there, or why he had come. She was just happy to see him, to give him the comfort he needed and tonight he needed it. She ran her fingers through his freshly shampooed hair and waited for him to speak. Slowly, he grew more relaxed by the gentle strokes of her fingers.

Finally, Caddo said, "Did I ever tell you the story of how the moon came to be?"

She shook her head.

His voice had a contentedness as he spoke—

"To Indians all across this land, the sun and moon were the eyes of the universe, the wells of creation. When people came along, there was only one.

"According to my brothers, the Iroquois, the world was without the second eye then. Only was the eye of the sun. People could not see at night, so they prayed to the *Sky Father* for a light to mark the night trails. It was said *Sky Father* was visible in the young world. He had the body of a mortal. He came to the people and first sought a bow. And they gave him one, a big strong bow of the highest power. *Jawonio*. Then he asked for a burning stick and they gave him one, a big bright burning stick. *Sky Father* looked at the stick and gave it a word. He called it the *moon*. He asked the people where they wanted it and they replied, 'In the Sky, Father.' So he put the moon in his bow and sent it skyward. It struck high against the night and glowed there.

"And softly Sky Father said, 'The moon is my second eye, a part of my face. My face is old and to know what old is, is to understand that life has parts. Ages. *Oxtea*. And to measure those parts I give you another word. The word is *time*, a faceless thing unto itself, yet not faceless when you look at my second eye. So watch the moon and you will see the passing of time as it changes from night to night. It will start full, shrink steadily, and then grow again to full. By watching my face, my second eye, you will be able to count the nights and measure the ages to know what old is.'

"And that is how the moon came to be."

Irene sat there with her mouth open. "It's lovely. What a beautiful story."

He nodded—slow and easy. "My brother told me that story. He called it the '*Miracle of Creation.*' A '*Fable of Life.*'"

"Is that what you're doin'?" she asked. "Waitin' for a miracle?"

He leaned forward, lifted her in one easy motion, arms clasped under her legs and back. "You might say that." He carried her to the bed and laid her down.

She drew him closer. "Promise me, whatever you do, be careful. I'm growin' kinda attached to you."

He grinned.

"Lie down next to me." She patted the pillow and waited for him to crawl into bed. "What you need is a good back rub. Turn around. Take that off." She was referring to his T-shirt. She helped him remove it. Even in the darkness she could see the long purplish scars. One was above the left hip, the other along his thigh reaching to his left knee. "That's it. Now relax. Let yourself go."

She kneaded, rubbed, and stroked his back with her fingers, gently caressing the shoulders, then lightly ran her fingertips around his neck, all the time humming a lullaby. He didn't know what was more soothing. Her voice or her gentle touch.

* * *

The lamp flame had burned to a flicker.

David's attention was solely fixed on the pages. The rest of the world had fallen into oblivion. Henry Purdy's manuscript had taken on an entirely new meaning compared to when he read it years ago. It related experiences from fellow authors and collaborators that delved into deja vu, witchcraft, the occult, mysticism, ghosts, a whole myriad of things, equally mystifying and extraordinary. As David read, he scribbled notes on a yellow legal notepad. His eyelids got heavier and heavier. His head dropped to his chest. His hands went limp as a fragrance filled the night. He drifted off to sleep.

At first everything was black, then a blend of light and gray came rushing at him. He could feel his body rise as images flew by faster and faster. Dark clouds formed. He could see lightning, a frothy turbulence. His body had no weight to it. He was floating, drifting in air through the turbulence as lightning struck. Figures emerged from the clouds—formless, lurching from side to side. He could hear a voice, a chant of some kind. Hands reached out, coiling and uncoiling like a swarm of long tubular bodies—snakes and eels grasping at his arms, his legs. Behind them something dark and evil loomed, hooded, cloaked in a shroud. It drew closer...and closer, then suddenly withdrew into the crevices of night at the sudden appearance of a woman.

Out of the darkness came a long flowing nightgown tufted in white. Her face was veiled in shadow. A scarf streamed from her neck. The gown drifted nearer, fluttering like gossamer. The veil slipped away. Framed in windswept hair was a face without features. Holes opened where the eyes once were—black holes, filled with nothing. A larger hole opened where the mouth was supposed to be.

"It's all right," she whispered.

He panicked. He no longer felt weightless. He was falling. The sensation of flight, of plunging helplessly to death, coursed through his body. It seemed so real—the quickness, velocity of motion, vertigo. He could almost feel the impact, the inevitability of it, of life itself leaving him. Somehow he knew what it was like to die, of having your bones and guts splattered on the ground while watching it about to happen. He could feel a terrible agony welling inside.

A hand touched his shoulder.
"Ahhhh!"
His head jerked up. The hand withdrew.
Somewhere between the drowsiness of sleep and reality, he opened his eyes. He could sense someone or some *thing* moving away, like a cloud of smoke into the wind. When he looked, it was no longer there.

He felt the lounge chair beneath him. The lamp flame had gone out. He jumped to his feet with the notepad still in his hand. A hazy awareness lingered, that of a faceless woman, as did a delicate fragrance. The porch light shined across the side of the house. Every window was dark. He placed the notepad on the railing and noticed some scribbling at the bottom. The handwriting was sloppy, as if a dyslexic child had written it. He looked closer. The letters moved negligibly up and down in an uninterrupted line, like a seismograph. When he realized they were the same words uttered by the faceless woman, something lodged in his throat.

That's when he heard a voice, or voices, coming from inside the house. A door slammed shut, followed by a loud and frantic scratching sound. He reached for the screen door and pulled it open. Cinders and Roscoe whimpered, made a mad dash around his legs, down the stairs, and across the driveway into the lower barn. He wasn't sure if they were being chased or what.

With a silent shuffle, he walked through the kitchen into the hallway and could smell the scent of lavender. It seemed to permeate the house. To his right, his father's bedroom door was closed—a bedroom converted from a living room when grandmother fell ill, unable to climb the stairs. Now it was filled with quiet whispers and dark secrets. There was no doubt the voice, or voices, were coming from there. Maybe Richard was talking in his sleep, but David had a feeling that wasn't the case.

Suddenly, the whisperings stopped. He listened, holding his breath. He felt like a kid again, doing something he wasn't supposed to do, expecting the floorboards to creak any second. He froze and looked at the crack at the bottom of the door. Half a minute passed before the whisperings began again. He backed away, not believing what he had heard, much less what he was thinking.

Quietly, he returned to the kitchen where a cordless phone sat on a countertop. He lifted the receiver, only to find the constant hum of a dial tone. Stunned, he dropped the receiver and sank to the floor, knees against his chest.

He hadn't wept since his mother died seven years ago. There was no shame in it now.

He could feel a wetness in his eyes.

"It's all right," she said.

The hell it was.

Chapter 23

Caddo woke from a deep sleep, the memory of war still fresh, as if it happened yesterday—

"Silent K's down!"

"Sergeant's been hit!"

"VC's advancing!"

"Medic, over here!"

"Charik waik-ta!"

Charik waik-ta—once the battle cry of Pawnee warriors is now the battle cry of the 2nd Platoon, Company B, of the 42nd Infantry, on a hill in the middle of Dead Man's Land near Phong Coa, Vietnam.

M-16's and Russian made AK 47's explode in a din of raging violence. The Vietcong and U.S. Forces are engaged in a strategic struggle.

The prize: Hill 405.

On the ground—rifle fire, machine guns, grenades, and rocket launchers are being exchanged at a maddening rate. Confusion reigns. Above, a three-chopper air strike literally shakes the earth while clouds of smoke, a fiery incandescence, and bomb fragments decimate trees, VC positions, bunkers, and mistakenly some of their own fighting men. The crackle of a walkie-talkie wards off the overhead strike.

"Jay-base-Charlie-one-Bravo, this is Charlie-two Bravo. Christ, you guys. You've got us pinned down. You're killing your own men! Move out! You're short of the mark! I repeat, short of the mark! Move out! Sergeant's been hit. Send in a medic! Do you copy?"

"Roger, Charlie-two-Bravo. Adjusting coordinates. We'll have the choppers make another pass. Have your men dig in. Medic's on the way."

Capt. Richard Macklin releases the button to the walkie-talkie, soaks part of his torn shirt in water, and pats his friend's forehead. "Stay cool," he whispers. "I won't leave you. You said you've never been to Ohio. Here's your chance. Hang in there."

Caddo reaches down with a blood-splattered hand. He's taken two fragments, one in his left side, a glancing wound, the other in his left thigh, tearing through the flesh and muscle and chipping off part of the thighbone. The pain is enough to make any movement unbearable, but he reaches down anyway to feel where he's been hit.

The searing heat of the fragments burns the skin. He can hear it hissing…sizzling. It feels like molten steel is dripping into the tissues.

The pain! Christ, the pain!

He passes out.

When he wakes up, the nightmare is real, only he doesn't know it until Richard reaches out, places a hand over Caddo's mouth while placing a finger over own his lips, warning him to be quiet.

Whether it's smoke, low cloud cover or what, the night is smothered with a dense myopic haze tinged by the scent of lingering gunpowder, napalm, and blood-soaked grass. The voices he once heard, those of his fighting companions are gone, replaced by the Vietcong, ghosts walking through the dead gloom, looking for the wounded.

The ones they find they kill.

Caddo only moves his eyes. He can't see them, but hears them well enough to know they're close by, searching through the fog cover that's his only protection. He closes his eyes and once again finds peace on the edge of the Halting Place.

What was once Silent K's sole protection had become a terror of his own making. Silent K. Silent Killer. The 2nd Platoon's nickname for Sergeant Caddo M. Walker, U.S. Army Infantry, Special Forces, a man who led by example and allowed his M-16 to speak for him, a man who taught fellow soldiers to shout, "Charik waik-ta!" whenever a battle was about to commence.

It didn't take much to trigger memories of those experiences overseas in Southeast Asia. All he had to do was look at the scars on his body and he could recall the day he was wounded. When asked about it, he would probably deny he ever served simply because he wanted to put those memories behind him, impossible as it was. He'd heard other veterans talk about Nam and it still controlled or affected their lives. The best way to cope with it, he believed, was to pretend the war never happened. But all a veteran had to do was look into his eyes and he would know—yes, here was a fighting man, a silent killer, a breed unlike any other.

He regarded himself as a peaceful man. War merely brought out his ability to survive, the warrior instincts, ancestor to the Skidi Pawnee, Stalkers of the Plains, Hunters of Buffaloes. The Indian part of him was always much stronger than the veteran and he believed this was his salvation. It saved him in Vietnam, saved him when he returned home, and he hoped it would save him again.

But Caddo was worried. In the years since the war, nothing threatened him as much as the VC ghosts patrolling Hill 405 near

Phon Cao. Now he was threatened by a new enemy far more dangerous than the Vietcong. He had no idea how to face it, much less defeat it, and for five nights he had tried. He didn't know when it would come or what it would do. Sometimes it taunted. Sometimes it played tricks. Other times it frightened. It had yet to kill, at least anything human, unless Wilfredo Pinoza was the first victim. That's what Caddo feared the most. He knew what it was capable of.

As he leaned up in bed, he had a numbing feeling just like the night near Hill 405 where he and Captain Richard Macklin hid in the jungle waiting for the Vietcong to find them. He looked out the window and saw that it was still dark outside. For some reason he felt a sense of urgency, a sense of dread, that something bad was about to happen. He flipped off the bed sheet and checked the clock. Five-thirty.

"Irene, wake up. Wake up!"

Groggily, she stirred and smiled, then had an expression of concern as she watched him throwing on his pants. "What's wrong, honey?"

"Get up. Get dressed. You have to take me back to the farm."

"Right now?"

"I'll explain when we get in the car. And when I do, you'll think I'm crazy."

"No, I won't," she answered.

"The hell you won't."

* * *

David wasn't sure what he heard first—the dogs barking, the chickens or Elly. She was leaning over his bed, shaking him.

"David, wake up! Wake up!"

He found himself upstairs in his bedroom. How he got there, he couldn't recall. "What time is it?

"Hurry!" said Elly. "The sun's coming up. Something's in the hen house!"

They listened, but couldn't hear a thing. For some reason the dogs and chickens had grown quiet.

"Let's have a look," he said, sleepily.

He threw on some jeans, slipped into boots, grabbed a T-shirt from the doorknob, a baseball bat leaning by a chest of drawers, and the pistol from a night table. They ran down the stairs, down the hallway where, judging from the inactivity in their father's bedroom, Richard was still asleep. As soon as they rushed out the side kitchen door a wet chill embraced them. The farm looked as if it had been swallowed by the shadow of a misplaced sea. To the east the sun was about to rise. A long pinkish sliver of light reached through the fog, stretching across the horizon.

David looked around as they walked across the driveway. "Where are Cinders and Roscoe?"

Elly shook her head. "I don't know. I don't like the feel of this."

He halted and held her arm.

"What is it?"

"Sunup. The roosters...?" He paused to listen.

To his left, inside the cattle yard, the cows were growing restless.

David glanced one way, then the other without moving his head. Ahead, inside a fence, about sixty feet away, was the hen house. Not a sound came from it.

The silence, along with the absence of the roosters, made David and Elly uneasy. But it wasn't just that. The fog had a mustiness about it, a sharpness, all too familiar. What's more, it drifted in dead air like fumes of gas mixed with acidic water, only it was more intense than ever. Tiny specks of light shimmered across the front of the building and to his left, leaving a trail.

"Here. Take this." He held out the baseball bat.

Elly took it in both hands, raised it above her shoulder, ready to swing.

First they heard one cow. Then a second cow. A third. And soon the entire herd was mooing—on the edge of panic, not quite shrieking. Then came the hoof beats. In the beginning only a trample, then it kept building and building, louder and louder, thousands of pounds of Angus beef and one bull, stampeding to the opposite end of the cattle yard. Screaming. Bleating. Running for their lives.

Chapter 24

Irene threw all caution to the wind. She drove her Volkswagen Beetle as if she were racing down the autobahn, reaching speeds in excess of eighty miles an hour. Caddo had complete faith in her. The question was, based on the information he had just given her, did she have faith in him?

In the distance, as the headlights cut through the diminishing darkness, he could see the power substation lit up by a light pole inside a chain-linked fence. After a brief check of the area, he settled back against the seat and studied his fiancé. "Do you believe me?"

Irene kept her eyes straight ahead. The conditions were far different than what he described. She was expecting the worst, something akin to Armageddon, but there were no indications of impending disaster. No wind, no atmospheric changes, no abnormalities of weather, no rain, thunder or lightning, and no fog. Just a simple quiet sunrise, growing brighter by the second.

Just when she thought they were home free, the car thumped as if it had rolled over a bump or object lying in the road. The steering wheel shook as the car shot into the other lane.

"Hold on!" Irene yelled.

The Volkswagen swerved. She lost control. Hitting the brakes, she yanked the steering wheel to the right. Tires screeched. The car leaned, swerved right, veering into the correct lane, the speed falling from eighty to fifty in a matter of seconds.

"I didn't see anything, did you?" she asked incredulously.

"No," said Caddo.

Then it happened again. Something rocked the car. The frame bounced up and over an object, the suspension flexing, groaning, only this time she had a better command of the wheel.

Caddo suddenly realized what lay ahead. He braced himself by putting his hands against the dash. "Slow down! Stop!"

"Oh, my god!" Irene mumbled

As they passed over the crest of a hill they entered a fog bank so thick the car penetrated it like a boat through water. Behind them for miles there were no traces of fog. But here, half a click away from Macklin Farms, a swampy haze drifted across the valley.

Irene slammed on the brakes. The brake pedal pulsated. The car skidded to a stop, grill and bumper pointing at an angle down the road, in the direction of the utility substation. Waves of dense, moist air came rolling in like breakers over a shore, sweeping past the transformer. The power grid exploded. Sparks showered down like fireworks. Voltage crackled, then buzzed, and died amid flashes of ionized vapor. Caddo and Irene watched, stunned, as the substation became engulfed in smoke and a raging inferno.

While the fog kept surging, a peculiar transformation was taking place. A shape began to emerge as it headed straight towards the Volkswagen. Minute crystals of light pulsed against a backdrop of thickening fog, resulting in an extraordinary and startling image, born of air and an ethereal substance, the image of a hooded shadow draped over a body. As the body formed, two winged appendages unfolded and from under the hood something grotesque appeared, almost like a face, only it wasn't a face, but a mere suggestion of a hooded specter wrapped in shadow. In its wake, it left a trail of shimmering particles that soon faded. Beneath it, the power transformer began to spew sparks and small electrical fires everywhere. With a final, feeble explosion, the substation shut down, the lines and grid becoming inoperable, no longer transmitting power.

The lights in the valley went out.

Breathless and confused, Irene turned to Caddo. She was about to say something, but he was already outside the car, running with a limp.

"Go home!" he yelled. "Go home!"

She sat, staring at nothing, but her mind was spinning—
I'll never doubt you again, Caddo Walker.

* * *

Dawn broke with a fiery combustion. David and Elly stopped midway through the cattle yard and watched in awe as footsteps came up behind them. Their father was throwing on a work shirt as he ran. He stopped beside them and all three stood gawking, not believing their eyes. The substation bloomed with flames, and the heat somehow seemed to drive away the fog.

"Un-frickin'-believable," Richard muttered to himself.

From the lower barn Cinders and Roscoe came scampering forward, tails wagging, just happy to be alive.

Elly bent down and petted them as a pair of headlights made a U-turn across Gills Pier Road onto Route 2. In the emerging daylight, she could see a figure hobbling towards them.

At the same time all three heard the cry of an animal somewhere ahead to their left. They saw no traces of the herd, or of Tyson, the prized bull, a long-horned beast of an animal, all gristle, bone, and muscle.

The search didn't take long. The cattle yard was a generous sixty acres, a little more than one acre per head, and while most of the acreage was flat, there was a ravine running along the highway. As they approached, they saw the herd huddled below the branches of a giant oak. The cows were spooked. Richard ran ahead, slid down the embankment, and walked among the herd, touching them, patting their sides.

"E-a-s-y. Don't be scared. Everything's okay." All at once he dropped to his knees and let out a sickened groan. "Oh, no! No!" He sank to his elbows and buried his head in his hands.

Elly and David rushed over and saw why.

Tyson was lying on his side in a patch of weeds, dried and brittle from the lack of rain. Next to him, a young heifer staggered and collapsed. Elly knelt beside her. The calf was wheezing and gasping. Blood and saliva were dripping from her mouth. Elly gently felt along her body, from her neck to her breast, along the ribcage and down her flanks. Elly stood up with a look of concern on her face and examined Tyson next, carefully feeling her way along his neck, chest, and belly while the bull thrashed and mewled in agony.

Caddo, meanwhile, limped to the fence and climbed over it, panting heavily.

"Watch out for the horns!" Richard warned. "Damn fool dogs! Get back!"

Roscoe and Cinders barked and jumped just in time to avoid being kicked by the bull.

After a few soft-spoken words, Tyson quieted down. Elly examined his legs without touching them. The front knees were bent forward, not behind in their normal state. The tendons had become exposed. His right back leg was snapped at the joint, dangling at an angle, tissues and cartilage the only things keeping it attached.

"Well?" said Richard.

Elly wiped a bead of sweat from her brow and replied, "Complete separation of his right rear leg between the flank and hock. A crisp, clean break. Surgery will never repair it. Both front legs fractured just below the hip. I can't imagine how he could sustain injuries like that. Even without damage to the back leg, he'll never walk again."

"You sure?"

"One hundred percent. I've never seen fractures this bad. Poor thing. He's in so much pain he's ready to pass out. Look at his eyes."

Richard rubbed his jaw. It was all he could do to control his anger. "David, go get my shotgun." He looked at Elly, then at the heifer. "What about her? Why is she choking?"

While David went to retrieve the shotgun, Elly did another quick examination. She walked along the fence, inspecting the rails. Two were cracked. The fence post, despite its thickness, was leaning. The base where it met the ground was also cracked.

"Apparently, the herd rushed the fence," she said. "The calf got crushed, pinned against the fence post. Judging from the blood, there's extensive internal damage. She may have a concussion, severely impacted ribs. Could be broken. I don't know." The heifer coughed, vomiting up blood. She attempted to stand, rolled on her side, revealing a pool of blood. "Oh, oh. She's bleeding. Help me turn her over, would you, Caddo?" In the process, Elly glanced at Tyson's right horn, the tip of which was covered in blood. She made the obvious connection. "She was gored during the stampede. The horn penetrated a lung. She's lost a lot of blood. Her eyes are dilated. She won't make it."

Elly remained completely clinical in her assessment. It was a trying moment for all, including Caddo who, on the outside, showed no emotion. Inside, a storm of passion was brewing. He felt a wave of guilt, frustrated by his inability to help.

Tonight, he said to himself. *Tonight comes the reckoning.*

Crippled and in obvious pain, Tyson soon passed out. For the next few minutes, Elly, Richard, and Caddo walked among the herd to see if any more cows were hurt. Fortunately, other than some bruises and unsettled nerves, they seemed to be recovering. David returned with the shotgun, a handful of shells, and gave them to his father.

Once the herd was separated, Richard raised the shotgun to his shoulder.

Elly turned, holding her hands over her ears.

Two shotgun blasts echoed across the valley.

* * *

Seventeen miles from the utility station, a control panel inside the headquarters of a local power company was flashing, signaling a breach in the circuitry. A malfunction in the main transformer and conductor terminals in Sector D, Quadrant 12 had occurred for a second time in one week. The engineer on duty had already called the dispatcher and emergency crews. In record time, with flashers turning and sirens shut off, a fleet of utility company trucks and fire engines arrived on the scene, accompanied by two patrol cars from the Bertram County Sheriff's Department.

Chapter 25

For a two and a half mile stretch, traffic bypassed Route 2. The Sheriff's Department placed roadblocks at opposite ends of the valley, east and west. Damage control units from the power company were hard at work investigating and repairing Substation 12. Firemen had already disassembled the hoses and fire extinguishing equipment. Their job was done.

Elly went to check on the hen house while everyone else assumed the task of burying Tyson. A grave was dug with the aid of a backhoe. A rope was tied to the tractor and both bodies were dragged from the ravine into the hole, leaving a trail of blood. Caddo worked the backhoe, Richard the tractor.

During the burial, a patrol car and a truck from Midwest Electric pulled alongside the highway next to the cattle yard. Deputy Tom Duckett and a utility investigator climbed the fence and approached. Cinders and Roscoe barked and wandered away, sniffing the trail of blood while Caddo cut the engine.

The deputy was the first to speak. "Morning, gentlemen. I suspect you know why we're here. This is Harold Bradshaw with Midwest Electric. What happened to the bull and calf?"

Richard slid from the tractor and removed his gloves. "Freak accident. Tyson broke his legs. Calf gutted herself against a broken fence rail. Couldn't save either one."

"Sorry about that. When?"

"Daybreak. This morning."

"Any idea how...?"

Richard looked at David, then at Caddo. "They were running scared. Something spooked them."

The deputy folded his arms. "Would you care to elaborate?"

Richard shrugged and shook his head. "Sorry. Beats the hell out of me."

"David?"

"They were spooked all right," said David. "By what, I don't know."

Referring to the response time of the emergency crews, Richard remarked, "Didn't take long for you to get here. Did someone call?"

"No," said Tom. "If the system shuts down, an alarm goes off. Least that's how I understand it. Is that right, Harold?"

Bradshaw, a bearded, heavy-set man in his late forties, answered, "Actually, it's a signal, not an alarm."

"Either way," added Tom, "it leads to the next question. The utility station—do any of you know what happened?"

David volunteered, "The place just sort of...erupted. Went up in flames."

"That's it?" The deputy made no attempt to hide his skepticism. "You have no clue as to why?"

"If you're asking for specifics, no."

"Okay, in general then?"

David wanted to cooperate. He just didn't know what to say.

Frustrated, Deputy Duckett turned to Caddo. "Is that how you see it, Caddo? A simple electrical fire?"

"I don't know. I'm not an engineer."

"Well, gentlemen, I am." Anxious to lend his expertise, Harold Bradshaw stepped closer. "I'm afraid it's not that simple. Tom, do you mind?"

"No, go ahead."

"Let me put it this way. Two times this week we had a systems' breakdown, what we call a Level Five, high voltage meltdown, a complete and utter collapse, if you will, of the conductor terminal. Did you see anything late Sunday night? Or anytime from midnight to sunup this morning?"

In one manner or another, they each gave a negative response.

Harold continued, "Amazing how there never seems to be any witnesses. Anyway, the gist of it is, we had a major shutdown again of such magnitude when I say major, I mean catastrophic, like in something I've never seen before. Wires melted. The housing was dented. Energy transfers failed. It's one heck of a mess! Two days ago we applied the latest technology, a systems' breaker, load detectors, and precautionary devises to do a number of things, mostly to regulate the flow of energy, then shut the place down whenever there's a power surge, or whatever. It's ninety-nine-point-nine percent incapable of malfunctioning. What I'm saying is the impossible happened. That, or some freak occurrence of nature went un-detected. Or...or we have an incredibly trained arsonist who happens to be light years ahead of us. All we're asking for is a little help." When no one responded, Bradshaw's voice cracked and veins bulged in his forehead as he pleaded, "Come on! You had to see something!"

Silence.

With jaw and beard thrust forward, Bradshaw was glowering. "We're talking the disintegration of elements! Fusion! These things don't just happen. They're *created*. It's called physics!"

David thought that was a bit of a stretch. "Fusion? It doesn't appear to be life-threatening."

"It isn't. Not by itself. I'm not saying the unit's contaminated. But whatever did the damage could be. Metal doesn't melt like that unless it's exposed to highly volatile materials."

"Look," Richard replied. "The second we woke up, we heard the cattle stampeding. We found them over there, in the ravine, huddled like scared rabbits. First light of day...and fog, that's all we saw, and what happened to the transformer. Looked like the fourth of July. Any more than that, sorry, we can't help you. Now if you'll excuse us, Tom, Mr. Bradshaw, I got a stud bull to bury. Have a nice day."

Tom apologized, "And we're sorry, too. A lot of strange things have been happening lately. Unfortunately, we've had sightings, but no eyewitnesses—check that, maybe one if he's credible—and almost no clues to speak of. If you think you're frustrated, how do you think we feel?"

"Sightings of what?" David inquired.

"Officially, we're calling it *phenomena*. Not much of a description, but that's all we have to go on. By the way, where's Elly?"

"In the house, getting dressed," David lied. He didn't want to drag her into this.

"Tell her to stop by and see me when she goes into town." From his wallet Tom took out a business card and handed it to David. "I'd like to talk to her. Oh, and may I suggest something. Harold and I aren't the bad guys, okay. We didn't come here because we wanted to. We came here to do a job. A little help isn't too much to ask. Just so you understand, I could give you a citation for improper disposal of livestock, but under the circumstances, I don't think that's the appropriate thing to do, so this time I'll let it slide." He glanced from person to person, waiting for someone to speak up. No one did, and this triggered another outburst—

"And the problem with the utility, gentlemen, is only half of it. After two investigations, dozens of man-hours by the best men in the business, we still have no explanation as to why the bridge collapsed. We're sick and tired of the lack of cooperation. And we'll lay the law down hard on anyone—I mean anyone—who withholds information. Understand? If you see or hear anything, let us know. Caddo, I'd like a word with you in private."

Caddo hopped from the backhoe and the two men talked quietly. While Bradshaw said goodbye, Richard slid down into the hole to loosen the rope tied around the heifer's neck. David watched the exchange between the deputy and Caddo. The conversation was short. Caddo kept nodding his head as Tom conveyed a message, followed by a series of questions, which Caddo answered in his customary abbreviated style.

Afterward, when the deputy was gone, David discretely inquired, "What was that about?"

Caddo said, "He asked if I knew anything about a trailer."

"What trailer?"

"The one used by the architect who's designing the golf course."

"What about it?"

"It was destroyed last night."

"Destroyed?"

"That's what he says." Caddo lowered his voice, "He asked one more thing. If I was part owner of the farm. Why would he want to know that?"

"Because, as a partner, you could be named in a lawsuit."

"What lawsuit?"

"The one my uncle's making. It's a nuisance case. He can't win."

"Somebody give me a hand!" Richard cried.

Caddo started to walk away, but David tried to detain him. "The trailer—how was it destroyed?"

But Caddo was already sitting on the backhoe.

A sudden *thump* drew their attention.

While trying to climb out of the hole, Richard slipped and fell against Tyson, almost goring himself in the process, nicking his shirt on one of the horns. The fall drew a trickle of blood below his left shoulder. As he regained his balance, he became agitated. He stood up, kicked at the dirt, and threw his gloves down.

David rushed to the edge of the hole. "You okay, Dad? You're bleeding."

Richard took a deep breath and mumbled, "I'm fine."

Concerned, David jumped into the hole.

"I said I'm okay," Richard insisted. He crawled up the side of the hole, then loosened the rope from the tow harness and got back on the tractor. When he was seated, he turned to his old friend. "Finish up, Caddo. I'll check the generator to see if it's up and running." He looked at his son. Richard's demeanor was such that you could see he was in pain. He did his best to hide it. "David, go help your sister. We need to take an inventory of the chickens. I'm heading into town." Without further delay, Richard fired up the tractor and the John Deere lunged forward.

As he watched his father leave, David wasn't sure what to think but he had a suspicion things weren't what they seemed.

As for Caddo, he quietly maneuvered the backhoe, using the bucket to scrape dirt into the hole. Outwardly he appeared unemotional. Inside, passion was burning so fiercely he could barely contain it. Yet he knew self-discipline and self-control were the cornerstones and foundations for what all *vision seekers* aspire. To survive another night he believed they had to summon all their courage in order to obtain a spiritual reawakening, a state of grace reached by a purity of mind and heart, what the Sioux refer to as *wakonda*, the Iroquois as *orenda*, other Indians as *wakan, mana,* or *manitou*—

The power of the spirit.

A force earned by only a few. By those deserving.

Chapter 26

Tom Duckett parked his patrol car by Substation 12 and punched a frequently called number on his cell phone. After two rings Sheriff Aldrick Pleamons answered, "Hi, Tom. What's the latest?"

"Same M.O. as before. Similar damage. Only more extensive. No witnesses, or should I say, anyone willing to talk. I spoke to an investigator with the utility company and he said there's not a shred of evidence. No tampering whatsoever. The place just went up in flames. It's shut down. Wires, cables, steel…chunks of metal melted everywhere! You should see it. Entire unit looks like it's been blow-torched. Crews are working, but it could take a day or two to repair it. I suggested they post security until we figure this thing out."

"Goddamn! What in the hell is going on? I'm almost tempted to call in the National Guard. How many incidents is it? Eight, nine? I'm losing count."

Tom referred to a notebook lying on his lap. "Eleven incidents since Saturday. This makes twelve. Related or unrelated, I can't say."

"Anything else?"

"Yes. The Department received a call late last night from a guy named Jack Lorrigan, the architect working for the Macklins. I met him shortly before midnight and we talked for an hour. The report's sitting on your desk. He's the first one to step forward and say anything. Incredible what he had to say. Seems like a standup guy, but his story is weird as hell. The trailer he works in was smashed to pieces. I said it had to be a tornado, but he said, no, it wasn't. He claimed there was an element of wind. Also something else. Almost like it was beyond the force of nature. Haunted is the word he used."

"Jesus, let's not get carried away."

"I'm not. Just read the report, then call the guy. I wrote down his number. He's staying at a motel in town—the Alexis. The way he's talking, I doubt the golf course will ever get built. He said he almost had a coronary. One more thing. He told me Caddo just happened to show up when the trailer crashed."

"Crashed?"

"It's in the report. Caddo admitted he was there, but he's not cooperating. I'm tempted to drag the son of a bitch to the station…ask him a few questions."

"Aren't you two friends?"

"So? One way or another I'll get him to talk. First I'm going to drive out to Birch Run. Take a look around."

"Do that. There's something at this end. Got a call from a Mr. McPhee. Some old codger half drunk at seven o'clock in the morning. He said something attacked a horse of his. Chewed it to pieces. Blood all over the barn. Stop on your way back and have a talk with him. Get a feel for what went down. The front desk has the address."

"Yes, sir."

Tom disconnected and looked out over the valley. The morning was beautiful. Not a cloud in the sky. He wondered how long it had been since it rained. A month? Six weeks? Seven? Poor bastards. Farmers have all the bad luck, especially the Macklins.

An old Ford Taurus station wagon drove up to the intersection and the driver argued with a patrolman for half a minute, dropped something at his feet, and disappeared north on Gills Pier Road.

"What was his problem?" Tom yelled as he opened the door.

The patrolman bent down and picked up something wrapped in an orange plastic bag. "He said he had a paper to deliver. Didn't appreciate the road being closed, so he told us to deliver it for him."

"Local paper?"

"Yeah."

"Let me have it."

A minute later, Duckett was sitting in his patrol car with the weekly edition of the *Bertram Sentinel* spread across the steering wheel. After skimming through it, reading the headlines and bits and pieces, he shook his head, wondering why the press had to sensetionalize everything, when they were really just stating facts—facts that on their merit alone were outrageous.

Reaching for the key, Tom turned the ignition. The patrol car crept through the intersection, around the roadblock, down Route 2, heading west.

He kept shaking his head as the car gathered speed.

Haunted—he said to himself.

He was beginning to think maybe the valley was. That or a strange anomaly had entered the earth's atmosphere.

Chapter 27

The patrol car headed west toward Fallen Oaks State Park, the Jeep Cherokee east. Richard Macklin didn't ask about the status of the chicken coop. He just got in his car and drove away like he wanted to run and hide.

As the generator hummed in the background, David and Elly were stuffing dead hens and roosters into plastic trash bags. Something had torn through the hatchery, leaving behind mangled bodies, broken eggs, and crushed birds. A week earlier Elly had taken inventory. The head count was about two hundred. Only a handful survived.

Once David noticed the Jeep Cherokee missing, he went into action. He instructed Elly to go to the hospital or their family physician's office to check on their father while David stayed behind and finished cleaning up.

Elly jumped in her Wrangler, started the engine, rolled down the window and dialed a number on her cell, but no one picked up. "It's out of service. Dad shut the phone off."

They both knew why. Richard was in denial—about everything. A minor wound was no different. There was no sense in discussing therapy now. Time was of the essence.

As Elly was about to leave, David yelled, "Wait! I need your cell phone."

Without asking why, Elly handed it to him, along with a cord and charger.

David stepped back as she put the car in reverse. "Call me when you know something."

"I will," said Elly. "What are you going to do?"

"Once I finish up here, have a little heart to heart with Caddo."

With a wave of goodbye, Elly backed down the driveway and drove away.

David stood between the barn and hatchery. He made two quick calls, one to information, the other to a cleaning service and made an appointment to have the hatchery cleaned as soon as possible. A minute later he was back in the chicken coop stuffing dead hens in a trash bag when a truck pulled up at the gas pump at the end of the driveway. A door opened, then closed. Boots shuffled across the blacktop. A tailgate was lowered. David paused at the door when a man started talking on his cell phone.

"Yeah, what?...Fuckin' power went out again...Who, the daughter? Bet your sweet ass I would...Aw, don't worry about him. I got everything under control...Huh? Haven't fucked anything up yet, have I?...Yeah, yeah. Stop worryin'. Soon as I get some gas I'll be there."

He disconnected.

David felt every muscle tense up.

Oscar Time. He put on his best impression of a hayseed. Hiked up his britches. Started walking. Went out the back door, around the other side of the hen house, whistling the last few steps, and found a man, slender of build, in his mid-thirties, about six-foot-two with dirty blond hair hanging to his shoulders, who was wearing a sleeveless black leather jacket and blue jeans. He was pumping gas into a gas can resting inside the bed liner of a silver, late model Dodge Ram pickup. Another gas can was also sitting in the bed liner.

The stranger watched the gauges spinning at the pump. Once he heard David whistling, he turned, revealing a face that was cold and contemptuous. David said hello. The man released the nozzle, took it out of one can, put it in the second, and squeezed.

"What are you doing?" David asked as nicely as he could.

The man scoffed and shook his head. "What the hell you think I'm doin'? Hear that generator. The power's out."

"Guess it's been out a few times."

"No shit."

"Why is that?"

The stranger nodded in the direction of the hill where the utility crews were working. "Better ask them. They're the ones that can't fix it." He became suspicious. "You a friend of Eileen's?"

David played dumb. "Wouldn't exactly say a friend. Only been here a day."

"Day, huh? No wonder I haven't seen you. You work here?"

"Yes, sir."

"Hit on her yet?"

"Hit on who?"

"Old man's daughter."

"Nah."

"Why not?"

"Boss wouldn't like it."

The man laughed, "Shit. I'd do'er in a heartbeat. You know what I like about country chicks? They like rollin' in the hay as much as the next guy. And his daughter...mmmm...is some kinda tasty."

David walked closer and leaned against the pump. It was all he could do to hold his temper. Until now he hadn't noticed the bloodshot eyes or smell of marijuana. "Probably a good idea to stay away from the daughter. Conflict of interest. The gas there...who should I say is borrowing it?"

The man released the handle, shutting off the pump. "That old man. Shit. He got more money he knows what to do with." He twisted the caps back onto the gas cans, moved around to the side of the truck, inserted the nozzle into the tank, and squeezed. "Why? It bother you...me usin' his gas?"

"Not if you have permission."

"I do."

Somehow that didn't make David feel better. "You must be the sharecropper..." he drawled slowly. "Paul..." He snapped his fingers.

"I ain't no sharecropper. I aim to own a piece of this farm, if the old man and me come to terms."

"You do? Last name's Heidtman, isn't it?"

No reply. Just silence. The sharecropper scowled with a mixture of smug defiance and paranoia. The cannabis effect. The brain exposed to weed.

"If you're not sharecropping, what are you doing?"

"Nosey son-of-a-bitch, ain't ya'?"

"Just curious is all. Boss doesn't seem the type who'd sell property to a sharecropper. "

"I told you I'm not a sharecropper. One day workin' here don't make you an expert 'bout the old man. Besides, everybody's got a price."

"Maybe. Takes a lot of money to buy land."

Heidtman looked as if he'd tolerated just about all he could. "Yeah, well, I wouldn't be workin' here if I didn't think I could afford it."

"Is that so? You don't look like the type who's got money."

"What'd you say?"

"Not many people have access to that kind of money."

"Well, I do."

"Where from? A bank? Rich uncle? What?"

Heidtman fixed him with an icy glare. "You're a laugh a minute. Why don't you crawl back in that hole of yours. What are you lookin' at? I don't like people staring at me."

David was staring on purpose. "Sure you got money?"

Heidtman was more annoyed than amused. "Ever been in the military?"

"Yes, sir."

"In a war?"

"Maybe."

"Well, I have. Desert Storm. One of the perks to bein' a veteran.

We got access to the biggest vault there is. The Federal fuckin' Government. Any veteran worth a shit can get a loan, if he knows where to look."

"Tell me. Why did you come here to work?"

Heidtman grinned that contemptuous grin of his. "Sometimes I wonder about that. Especially lately."

"How come?"

Heidtman laughed a humorless laugh. "Jesus, you don't quit, do you?"

"Hey, if you're having second thoughts about working here, maybe I should, too."

"That ain't it. You'll find out soon enough. After you've slept here a few nights."

"Find out what?"

"Strange shit goes on around here."

"Like what?"

"You don't know? Man, you're either blind or stupid."

Backwash triggered a valve. The gas nozzle shut itself off. The tank was full. Heidtman returned the nozzle to the pump, took out a cigarette, had the presence of mind not to light it.

Oscar Time was coming to an end.

"Aren't you going to tell me?" said David.

Heidtman climbed into his truck, hung an arm out the window, cigarette dangling from his mouth, and said, "Hogs get a little restless at night."

David saw the tattoo on his forearm, a crest with a dagger running through it, and knew it was emblematic of a special Army infantry unit assigned to the Gulf War. "Hogs get restless, but not you."

"That's right."

"And this morning...?"

Heidtman cranked the engine—a big, loud V-8. He removed the cigarette, spit out the window like the conversation was distasteful, and smiled. "My girl and me...well, you know. Man has needs. Bang, bang. Thank you, m'am." As a testament to his manhood, he winked.

"Ah, a romantic," said David. He had a change of attitude. He wasn't acting anymore. He was serious. "Two things before you go."

"What?"

"There's a gas station ten miles up the road. Next time use it."

Heidtman remained perfectly calm. "What did you say you're name was?"

"I didn't. It's David."

"David what?"

He said it slowly, "M-a-c-k-l-i-n."

Heidtman grinned, halfway between a sneer and a smile. "Thought so. You look like a Macklin. Sorry, partner. Hate to tell you...the old man and me...we have an agreement. We share gasoline and machinery."

"Huh-uh. You're not my partner. As far as agreements go, I'm breaking them."

"We'll see." Heidtman pulled out a lighter. Lit his cigarette. Eyed David for a second, then grinned, and blew out the smoke.

"And if you ever talk disrespectfully about my sister again," said David, "be prepared."

"For what?"

"You'll find out."

Heidtman made a face, something between a sneer and a grin, turned up the volume to the radio, and a loud bass drum boomed all the way down the driveway.

The gas generator was still running, but it occurred to David there was one thing he didn't hear—

The backhoe.

It sat unmoving in the middle of the cattle yard with the bucket raised, like a claw of some futuristic beast conceived of metal.

The driver's seat was empty.

Chapter 28

Caddo did another one of his vanishing acts, so David decided to concentrate on the two most immediate concerns. His father's health. And how to keep the farm solvent. Although Elly was in the practice of healing animals, not people, she was certainly far better equipped to handle medical issues. As for solvency, there were no easy solutions. The dynamics were such that David knew he had to take baby steps and giant leaps. First, a baby step. Which began in the basement.

He walked downstairs to Caddo's sleeping quarters. From the bookcase he removed a book titled *Ghost Dance*. He flipped through the pages where passages were highlighted in yellow magic marker and jotted down words on a piece of paper. One particular inscription caught his eye—*Halting Place*.

Once he compiled a list, he raced upstairs and snatched a key and flashlight from a kitchen drawer.

The cell phone hummed and vibrated. There was a text message—

> *using a friend's phone*
> *dad seems to be ok*
> *followed him to the doctor*
> *he's in good hands*
> *off to the library to do research*
> *taking the day off — el*

Less than a minute later, David had the '57 Chevy racing down Route 2. As he drove, he kept thinking about the day he and Caddo met.

He was eight years old when this big, barrel-chested stranger showed up at their doorstep, looking like he hadn't shaved or showered for weeks. The stranger had a pudgy, wrinkled face, long white hair hanging to his shoulders, and a knapsack slung over his back. He wore faded army fatigues, a torn shirt, and shorts that exposed a long purplish scar running to his knee. David gasped like he'd seen a ghost. He didn't overcome his mistrust of the stranger until his mother took the family out shopping one day. She bought Caddo a new wardrobe. Later that evening, Caddo came to the dinner table scrubbed, combed, and clean-shaven, wearing tan khaki pants, white shirt, ponytail, and the biggest gap-toothed grin ever a man could have. After dinner, he took David outside to the porch steps where they sat. There, Caddo revealed a glimpse into his culture by doing what his forefathers did when nightfall came. He told a story.

"Look!" he declared, pointing at the moon. "You can see the eye of Sky Father. It's winking at us. Do you see it?"

David looked up and said with youthful enthusiasm, "Yes."

"Good. Then I will tell you how the world came to be—

"In the beginning there was no land. Water covered everything. Even the Bear and the Wolf lived with the Fish. One day Bear went swimming with Frog. As they swam, they found some mud buried deep under the water. Bear had an idea. He asked Frog if he knew *Someone Powerful* who could dry the mud, so they could walk on dry ground.

"'My friend, the Raven, might know,' answered Frog.

"So Frog talked to Raven, hopped on his back, and they flew into the sky where *Someone Powerful* lived. They told him they were looking for dry ground, a place where they could walk.

"'Is there something you can do?' asked Raven.

"*Someone Powerful* thought for a moment and said, 'This dry ground, where will I find the mud to make it?'

"'My friend, the Frog, knows,' said Raven. 'He will show you.'

"The next day wings were heard beating above the water. An Eagle dove deep, scooped up a claw full of mud, and piled it in one spot. He did it again and again until he formed an island. The Bear and Wolf rejoiced but the Eagle wasn't done yet. He formed valleys and mountains where the water did not flow. But the mud was soft and wet. So he flew back and forth flapping his wings and soon there was dry ground for every four-legged Animal, a home away from the Fish.'

"And that is how the world came to be."

David sat very still, head tilted toward the sky, and said, "Do you think *Someone Powerful* could help me?"

"Depends on the kind of help you need."

"Could he make me a better centerfielder?"

Caddo smiled. "Practice, my young friend. Practice. That will make you a better centerfielder."

"Is that all?"

"Well, ability is important. But let me suggest something, Kiriki. My people have a word. It means power, the power of spirit, the power inside you. It's called *mana*. And *mana* makes you strong. Tomorrow I will take you to the game. Right now I want you to sit there and close your eyes and imagine your *mana* growing, filling you with confidence...with spirit."

David concentrated on thinking positive thoughts that night. The next day Caddo drove them to the game.

On the way David said, "Last night you called me a name. *Kiriki*. I've never heard it before. Is it Indian?"

"Yes," answered Caddo. "You remind me of my nephew. Kirk we call him. *Kiriki* Walker."

"What does *Kiriki* mean?"

"It means you see what others can't see. It means bright eyes, a gift of what you call the *soul*. *Mana*. The Sioux refer to it as *wakan* or *wakonda*, the Iroquois *orenda*, the Algonkin *manitou*, and all other Indians as the *power of spirit*. And today, Kiriki, is a good day to use it.'

David felt honored. He embraced his Indian name with an open heart.

Later, during the baseball game, Caddo shed his passive behavior and became a rowdy spectator who danced and cheered and waved his arms whenever David swung a bat or made a play in the outfield.

Inspired by their newfound friendship, David elevated himself to a star that day, a running, jumping whirlwind of passion, possessed of skills he had only dreamed of until then. Two doubles, a home run, six caught balls, mostly of the acrobatic variety, and a runner thrown out at the plate. He was hoisted off the field on Caddo's shoulders with a dozen screaming eight and nine-year-olds leaping up and down beside them.

As David recalled the boyhood spectacle, he found himself in his truck, not an eight-year old anymore, but a man in his mid-twenties driving along Route 2.

Up ahead he saw a roadblock. A deputy motioned for him to stop. Once the deputy recognized who the driver was, he waved him around the shoulder of the road.

As David drove by, he reached into a shirt pocket and pulled out a piece of paper. He unfolded it and ran his eyes down the page until he came to two words that were underlined—

Halting Place.

Halt. To stop. A place where something stops.

"Ah-ha!"

He realized what it meant.

Chapter 29

Tom Duckett had to see the evidence for himself.

At first glance it appeared as if a tornado had struck. The problem was no high winds had been reported in the county all week. Yet judging from the wreckage, the trailer had been lifted from its foundation and dropped to the ground from a considerable height. The wood, fabric board, and aluminum siding had been deposited in total disarray forty paces from the cement block base.

After sifting through the debris, Tom found no signs of explosives. No burns, no rubble thrown beyond the site itself. It was contained in one small area. Of all the crimes he had witnessed as a peace officer, this was the most puzzling.

Using a digital camera, he took pictures of the damage from several angles. As he did, a bird chirped from far away—just once. A moment later, he heard a high-pitched screech while something dark and swift streaked past his head. Then he felt something crawling up his back *inside* his shirt. He reached behind, trying to swat whatever it was. And whatever it was vanished, leaving him confused and shaken. He knew he didn't imagine it. It clawed at his spine. He had shivers just thinking about it.

He suspected something else—that someone was watching him. He felt vulnerable, like someone had him fixed in the crosshairs of a rifle.

Sweat dripped in nervous anticipation as he retreated to his patrol car. Behind him something slithered through the grass. The underbrush thrashed. He heard a hiss, a snarl, two animals fighting. He panicked. Yanking the pistol from his holster, he pointed the barrel and emptied six rounds into the grass. The area around him erupted. The snarls became vicious, the thrashing more intense. As he reached for the door handle, another screech rang out, followed by a fluttering mass of what, he couldn't tell. It grazed his shoulder, ripping the shirt as it flew by. More bewildered than ever, he examined the torn fabric and winced, impulsively grabbing the shoulder muscle. The penetrated skin reminded him of the sting of a wasp, only it hurt twice as much. After removing his hand, he saw blood on his fingers.

"To hell with this!"

With a last furtive glance at the hill, a gust of wind came blowing from the west, sweeping across his body. His hat flew off. He went scrambling after it.

* * *

Elly hustled through the entrance of the Bertram County Public Library, a monstrosity of a building designed in the late nineteenth century as residence to Clyde Bertram and family, and also as a monument to mankind's greatest fear—

Death.

In one wing, casket makers built and shipped their product. In another, morticians practiced their craft in the embalming rooms next to the death vaults. Viewing rooms lay tucked down long corridors as sanctuaries for the bereaved and departed, where undertakers sermonized like preachers, healers of souls. In a third wing, the residence, the Bertrams lived in gloried splendor, the undertaking business being a gold mine during its heyday—with five bedrooms, ballroom, and winding staircase.

Given the status of an historical landmark, used primarily by students at Ohio Southern and partially funded by the state, Bertram House boasted a collection of books unparalleled for a town its size.

Elly liked the people who worked there, especially Mae, the librarian, a small wisp of a woman who knew more about the library and history of Bertram County than anyone. A longtime fixture at Bertram House, residing in the history section, Mae saw the bouncing strides of a woman traipsing down the hallway with a purpose. The two met and sat at a nearby table.

"I'll tell you why I'm here," said Elly.

Mae held up a finger. "Let me guess. You're doing research on Birch Run. And a fellow by the name of Henry Purdy."

Elly flung her head back. "How did you know?"

Mae let loose a twitter of laughter. "Why, I've worked here for fifty-three years. Interest has never been higher. This week it's Katie bar the door. Just follow me. "

Elly couldn't get her feet moving fast enough. "Hey, where are we going?"

"The Rare Book Section, in the attic."

The next thing Elly knew she was being ushered into what looked like an animal cage, an old elevator with tarnished brass rails, teakwood floor, and folding metal gate. Instead of buttons, Mae shifted a lever. A motor hummed. A gear slipped. The elevator jiggled, dropped a good foot, then lifted. Elly almost tossed her cookies while Mae spoke above the whine—

"Mr. Bertram had this built when he was confined to a wheelchair.

The first privately owned elevator in the state of Ohio. Works amazingly well, don't you think?"

Elly kept very, very still, feeling claustrophobic.

The elevator rattled and clanked until it finally reached the attic. With a jerk of the lever, the gate opened to a corridor, which smelled like old rancid vinegar.

"Come along," said Mae. "Have you been in the attic before?"

Elly covered her nose. "No, ma'm."

Their voices echoed through the corridor. They entered a high-ceilinged room with a marble floor, low-lying stage, oak paneled walls, crystal chandelier, and brass light fixtures with elaborate twists of metal anchored to the walls.

"Too bad," said Mae. "There's so much to learn here. So much to read. It's a shame the public doesn't take more advantage of it."

Elly looked around in wonder. "What is this place?"

"The Grand Ballroom. The Bertrams were ballroom dancers, the elite society of their day. Follow me." Mae hurried down an aisle to a tiny section enclosed in glass. "Here we are. The Rare Book Section, dating back to the Indians before Ohio was a state. We might begin with a document over here..."—she unlocked the glass case and pulled out a tray—"...written by the first-known map-maker."

Elly was looking at a bundle of parchment papers, stained, uneven at the edges, written in longhand with elegant sweeping strokes. Each page was sealed in laminated plastic.

"It's a personal account," said Mae, "of an incident that took place two hundred and fifty years ago. You'll find it quite fascinating. Go ahead. Read it."

Elly lifted the parchment papers from the tray, unable to take her eyes off the first page.

"And I have another article of interest over here." Mae waddled another few feet. "The pride of our collection. Written by Henry J. Purdy. Not for the faint of heart. This, my dear, must be handled *very* delicately. No research would be complete without it."

Mae was gushing from ear to ear, coddling a folder in her arms as she would a baby.

Chapter 30

Traffic restrictions were finally lifted at both roadblocks, east and west.

The Macklins had a visitor. Actually, several visitors.

Coach Ed Kragan, unaware of the unreliability of the phones, was too excited to call. The news had to be delivered person to person.

His high-top conversion van turned onto the driveway alongside an unmarked service van parked by the chicken coop. Two young women were carrying mops, buckets, and brooms into the coop while an older man held the door open.

"Good morning," said Stumpy. "What's with the mops?"

"You the owner?" the man asked.

Ed wanted to say, 'If I was the owner, I wouldn't ask what the mops were for, you idiot.' Instead, he said, "Nope. Just a friend."

The man placed a cement block by the door, propping it open. "Darnedest mess I've ever seen. Come see for yourself."

Half a minute later, with cigar firmly clenched in his mouth, Ed stuck his nose in the hatchery and coughed. "Eeew. It stinks!"

"Look!" the man pointed.

Broken shells littered the floor.

"Eggs?" asked Stumpy.

"Yep. Imagine what it'd smell like in a couple of hours. We got a dozen bags of dead birds to dispose of."

"Dead?"

"Yes, sir. Don't ask. Caller said he didn't know."

Stumpy bit down on the cigar and barely got the words out. "But who...?

"Don't ask me that either," the man interrupted. "Caller couldn't give me an answer no matter what I asked. Just doing my job and gettin' the hell outta here. Awfully damn strange if you ask me."

Stumpy turned without commenting and walked away.

"Hey, where you going?"

"Inside the house. Someone there I have to see."

"Nobody's home. I already knocked."

With his enthusiasm slightly dampened, Stumpy walked to his van, wrote a note on a sticky pad, entered the house through the side kitchen door, and stuck the note to the kitchen counter.

* * *

David approached the front door to the cabin with a key in one hand, a flashlight in the other, when the phone rang. He expected static, poor reception, but the line was clear.

"Hello."

The caller cleared his throat. "Hi…a…who is this?"

"David Macklin. Who's this?"

"Bo Darnell. I own the cleaning service."

"What can I do for you, Mr. Darnell?"

David could hear a muffled chattering noise.

Bo said, "You told me to call this number, so that's what I'm doing. Uh, we got a problem. I'm here in the hen house. And…a…" There was a squawk in the background, followed by more squawks. The hens were making such a racket Bo had to step outside. "Hear that?"

"What's going on?"

"Frickin' birds, that's what. Hey, Laura! Leave 'em alone!" Quieter, Bo said, "Jesus! You'd think we'd thrown in with a bunch of jayhawks. As I was sayin', we got a problem. You told us to scrub the place down, but the hens…holy Mother of Christ! Look at that!"

David tried to speak.

But Bo beat him to it. "Scared outta their wits is what they are."

"Scared of what?"

"Us! Laura, Sue, me! Their own shadows!"

"Do the best you can, Mr. Darnell."

"This is hazard pay, fella. These chickens…they're crazy as shit! Peckerheads won't move. If we go near 'em, they bite. Just what did happen here anyway?"

"We don't know."

"Don't know? Huh. This one's for the books. Psychotic chickens! What do you want us to do with the bill?"

"Could you mail it?"

The connection was beginning to fade.

"Wasn't part of the agreement," said Bo.

"Okay, I'll be there shortly," said David. "We'll settle before you leave."

"Good. We're leavin' in an hour. Don't expect miracles."

David shut the phone off and knocked on the cabin door. "Hello. Anybody home?"

No answer.

He inserted the key, unlocked the door, and turned the doorknob. Light poured into the cabin. He reached in, flicked on a light switch, but the lights didn't come on, so he left the door open, pulled a window curtain aside, flicked on the flashlight, and his jaw fell open.

What impressed him first he didn't know. He was assaulted all at once. He was expecting dust, a barren room, old furniture crammed in a corner, covered with sheets, but not this, not such *clean* orderliness. And definitely not what he was looking at.

It was a tribute to the North American Indian, showcasing a deep and rich culture. A throw rug of Navajo design covered the floor. A five-foot totem comprised of two figures, representative of the Great Pacific Northwest, stood to the right of the sofa. A winged eagle—painted red, yellow, and black—was seated atop a dog or wolf, carved from a trunk of cedar. Hopi kachina dolls, portraying gods and clan ancestors, occupied bookshelves, end tables, and windowsills. Draped on a far wall were two deerskins, one depicting a fierce looking buffalo, the other a splendidly clad Indian in full headdress, mounted on a horse. Both were painted with skill and a beautiful blend of quiet tones and bright colors. Also gracing the walls were Indian shields made of leather with colorful feathers hanging from the sides, rattles, a bow, tomahawk, quiver of arrows, and photographs of Indians in various poses, with a notation at the bottom stating who they were. Even the seat cushions were of Native American design. The room embodied a sense of history, a raw, highly evocative culture—all of it emblematic of a once strong, proud people. And there were stacks and stacks of books, lying on bookshelves, on the floor, piled in the corners. Ninety to a hundred books in all. What held David's attention the most, however, were the deerskin paintings, especially the one of the Indian and horse. The way the rider sat, the decorations of his shirt, his leggings, the magnificence of the stallion, the posture of its body—head raised, mane thrown back as if it were about to launch into stride—it all made for a startlingly real and impressive rendering.

David couldn't take his eyes off it. Then it occurred to him. He knew why for two reasons. First, he realized who the artist was. His mother. Second, was the appearance of the rider. Granted, he was much younger back then, but there was no denying who it was. From the sturdy chin to the cherubic face and deep-set eyes, everything about it, everything throughout the cabin epitomized Caddo. He had created a memorial honoring his heritage, filled with collectibles of the highest quality, and made it comfortable in an almost spiritual way.

And from the looks of things, he'd been living here for years. But the life within these walls seemed to be one of cultural and intellectual pursuit. No television, no radio, no phone. A computer sat on a desk at the back of the room. Otherwise, it was a place used for reference, relaxation, and the contemplative act of study, an escape from the white man's world into the world of the Indian. And the more David looked, the more he noticed.

The books were of a more diverse nature than he originally thought, covering not only every facet of Native American life, from common tribes to the more obscure, it also included Indian culture before the emergence of the white man, religion, winemaking, and present-day civilization of the Indian—much of it steeped in religion and storytelling.

Invariably, David kept coming back to the painting of horse and rider when he realized it wasn't just any horse, but a thoroughbred whose logo was on the sides of every truck owned and operated by a local trucking company—

Fleet Merchant.

David had never placed Caddo and Fleet Merchant together. Nor did he recall his mother ever using deerskin as an art form. He remembered every portrait and landscape she did, but not this, and not the one of the buffalo. In fact, David believed it was the best thing Dora had ever done. Exquisitely well balanced. Full of detail, down to each blade of grass. The richness of the oil-based paints set against the backdrop of an animal skin. It gave it a lifelike exuberance, almost a three-dimensional effect, which jumped off the canvas in a very powerful way.

Below the painting was a framed letter—

> *Dear Caddo,*
> *On behalf of Richard and myself, may I say we are privileged to have you as a friend. It brings me great comfort knowing your prayers are with me at this particular time. Please accept this gift as a token of our appreciation and affection.*
> *Sincerely,*
> *Dora Macklin*

Chapter 31

Even though the prescription said to take one every six hours, Richard Macklin popped three pills and washed them down with bottled water. Taken as prescribed, Vicodin had an almost euphoric effect. When taken in triple dosage, the well-known, potent painkiller came as close to a high as he had ever experienced. A longtime family physician had already cleaned, stitched, and bandaged Richard's shoulder. The cut had penetrated deeper than he realized, but not enough to warrant surgery in a hospital. Just three stitches and a local anesthetic in a doctor's office was all that was required. Now all the Vicodin had to do was kick in.

Richard's Jeep was parked just off Fulton Street in downtown Mistwood, well within sight and walking distance of the county courthouse, business district, and main branch of Farmers First State Bank. He sat in the driver's seat, watching Friday morning shoppers and business people milling along the sidewalks. For an entire week he kept thinking about this moment, dreading it more and more. Antidepressants didn't help. The stress was getting so bad, sometimes he felt an urge to end it once and for all.

It'd be so easy, he thought to himself.

Shotgun's in the back seat. Shells are in the glove box. Just load the damn thing. Hold the barrel to your mouth. And boom!

A coward's way out, he realized, but it was better than living alone.

After seven long years, the memories of Dora still persisted, stronger than ever. There were times at night when he could touch her soft sweet hair, smell her perfume, look into her eyes, and see the pain. But was the pain hers, or the pain she felt for him? That was the dilemma—suffering or pity. Neither of which compelled him to live, nor did they excuse him to take his own life. The more he thought about it, the more disturbing it became.

Get out of the truck, Richard! Get out now! Do what you have to. But don't give up.

He reached for the door handle. Two minutes later he was standing inside Farmers First State Bank, facing a bank teller he'd known for years.

"Hello, Richard. What can I do for you this morning?" she asked.

"Hi, Nancy. I'd like to see Tony, if I could."

"Just a second. I'll let him know you're here." The teller pushed a button, looked to her left at an office where a middle-aged man, bald, wearing glasses and dark blue suit, was seated. The bank executive, aware of the situation, took his eyes off his computer screen and motioned for Richard to come in. "He'll see you now," said Nancy. "Just go right in."

Richard's boots moved quietly across the tiled floor. Nancy could see his left shoulder sagging, his left arm hanging slack, like he was favoring it.

A telephone rang at the counter. She picked it up. "Farmers First State Bank. Nancy speaking." After a few seconds, she said, "Why, hello, David. How are you? What a coincidence! He just walked in..."

Interrupted, she paused and glanced at Richard who was already out of earshot, seated in the office of the bank president, Anthony Drayhill. "Sorry. I don't think he heard me. How can I help you?" She listened for a moment, looked at Richard again, and replied, "No. He looks fine...No, no bleeding...I could go ask...Okay, I won't...What?" She started taking notes, phone tucked between her ear and shoulder, speaking intermittently, "Uh-huh...Okay. Sure. I can do that...When?"

Meanwhile, fifty feet away, Richard pulled a torn envelope from his pocket and placed it on the desk. "Never thought it'd come to this, Tony." He paused to collect his thoughts while the bank president leaned back in his chair. "It's crazy," said Richard. "In a way it feels like I've been violated." There was no anger in his voice. Just mild irritation. "Things sure do change, don't they?" He laughed weakly and sighed, "Oh, how they change."

"Sorry I couldn't return your calls," Tony apologized. "I was out of town. Unfortunately, I have no control over certain things."

"Yeah, I know. Don't have much say-so in bank policy, do you, being chief operating officer?" Richard's sarcasm didn't go unnoticed. Pointing at the envelope, Richard added, "Tell me how would you feel if you got something like that?"

"What is it?"

"A letter from a law firm in Columbus, some fancy collection agency. Read it! Go ahead!"

Trying to be polite, Tony said, "I think I'll pass."

"Go on. Read it!"

"I assume it's about the loan."

"I left you a message."

"I had thirty-two messages on my voice mail...and a stack of notes and callbacks this high when I returned..." Tony held his hand three inches above the desk. "I haven't had a chance to respond to any of them yet."

"Who authorizes a letter like that?"

"No one. A computer generates all the bills."

"Who tells the computer to send them?"

"It's automatic. Bank procedure. You know that. We send out reminders every day to customers whose payments are coming due."

"A reminder I can understand. But there's no need to threaten someone, let alone a long-standing client like me. All my life I've been doing business here. If it wasn't for my grandfather and father, where would this bank be? Hell, there'd be no First Farmers State Bank."

"You know we can't show favoritism."

"You do it every day."

"Not since I became president."

Richard reached into his shirt pocket, pulled out a folded piece of paper, and slid it across the desk. "Okay, fine. I can write you a check for more later. How much, I'm not sure yet. All I'm asking for is an extension."

Tony Drayhill didn't change expression. He looked at the check, saw how much it was written for, and said, "We granted you extensions on the last two loans."

"So. I paid them off, didn't I?"

"Eventually. But you were delinquent, too."

"You got your money, plus interest. Shoot, you should be lickin' your chops over guys like me."

"Look, I know you're doing everything you can, Richard. I'm sympathetic. I appreciate your business. I do. I really do. We loaned you the money in good faith, but this is not what we agreed upon. I can't extend, or issue a second deadline. Not again. It just isn't possible. Preferential treatment is something we're trying to avoid. Fair, consistent treatment for everyone, that's our goal."

"Jesus, you sound like a commercial."

"Let's just stick to the facts, Richard. Don't personalize it."

"Okay, I owe sixteen-five, right? The loan before that twenty grand. Paid it all back in the winter when you can't plant a thing."

Tony nodded.

"And you know my credit history," said Richard, "down to the penny. I've never defaulted or reneged on anything."

Another nod.

"With all the things my family has done for you and this bank, you can't give me a couple of months? Two lousy months?"

Tony sat still, doing all he could to suppress his anger. "Richard..."

"Do you think my father would do such a thing, have an

anonymous letter written by some badass lawyer who's all too happy to put the squeeze on somebody, whether it's deserved or not...and not show any respect? Do you think he'd stoop to that?" Richard paused. When there was no reply, he said, "Okay, how about one month then? Four weeks. That isn't too much to ask."

Tony put his elbows on the desk. "I'm sorry. I have a board of directors to answer to."

"Board of directors?" Richard's face turned bright red. "My father-in-law, Drew Treshler, you mean. And that good-for-nothing son of his! Whatever happened to the old way of doing business? A little courtesy?"

"I approved the two previous loans when no one else would. I did it as a courtesy to you and your family. Me! No one else. As you say, things have changed. The restrictions I'm conveying to you come from the last board meeting. So I suggest you talk to them."

Richard quieted down and became more composed. "Okay. Maybe I will. What about the golf course? What if I told you I could deposit two hundred thousand in cash in two months? Think about what you could do with it. Make loans, build interest, raise profit, create growth. Hell, you could make a bundle, probably a third of that again in less than a year."

Tony held up his hand. "I hate to tell you this, Richard. That money is a pipe dream. Complete fantasy. It won't happen."

The color drained from Richard's face. "What do you mean—won't happen?"

"The corporation, Golf Design, it's pulling out."

"How do you know that?"

"We're one of the principal partners. The architect, Jack Lorrigan, was here this morning when we opened the doors. I just got off the phone with the corporation president. We found another location."

Richard practically jumped out of his seat. "Another location? You can't do that! I have a signed note in writing that Golf Design will not under any condition, under any circumstances...*will not* build another golf course in this county or surrounding counties to...and I quote, 'compete with the location of said property known as Macklin Farms!' It's in the contract!"

"Non-binding. It can easily be voided. Or so our lawyers tell us. The competitive aspect is a non-issue, especially when nothing's been done yet. You haven't even agreed on a price."

"So, I'm screwed is what you're saying. Humped by a bunch of sons'-a-bitches who don't have a lick of guilt."

"Richard, calm down! The ladies can hear you. I do what the board tells me to do."

"The board. Christ, they're humpin' you."

Tony stood up. "Okay. That's enough!" He looked past Richard and saw Nancy, the bank teller, holding a note, trying to get his attention.

Richard was fuming. "Don't tell me. The other location, it's on Treshler property. So now Mark wants mine and he's using you to get it. Is that it?"

The teller was pointing a finger at Richard, mouthing the words. Tony walked out of the office. The teller met him half way. They talked. Tony's attitude changed as he listened, his body language changed. He was evidently surprised by what the teller was saying. Tony looked at Richard and Richard looked at Tony. Soon they were standing face to face.

"Seems you have a benefactor."

"Benefactor?"

"Yes. It appears your loan will be paid later today. In full."

"By who?"

"I'm not at liberty to say."

"Why not?"

"Because the party or parties wish to remain anonymous."

The news hadn't sunken in yet. Richard thought for a moment, then asked, "It's not coming from Elly's or David's trust, is it?"

"Again, I'm not at liberty to say. It's confidential."

"The executors would have to be notified, right?"

"Correct."

"Then who..." Allowing the question to linger, Richard looked at the bank president, awestruck.

Tony countered with a shrug of his shoulders.

"This transfer," said Richard, "how is it supposed to be done? In person, by phone, carrier pigeon, what?"

"The procedure is simple. Wire to wire. Bank to bank. We do it all the time. The transaction will be made by three o'clock."

Richard raised a hand to his mouth, suppressing a giggle. "Bet that brings a tear to your eye, eh Tony? Benefactor. Ain't that a lump in your throat. Sure beats being corn-holed by your board of directors. Now that Lorrigan guy, maybe I'll be giving him a call sometime soon." Tongue-in-cheek, he quipped, "What do you say there, Tony-boy? Maybe that benefactor could be pulling more strings...on the phone talking to my lawyer maybe. Guess we'll have to wait an' see. Good talking to you. Give my regards to Mark and Drew if you happen to see 'em. Oh, yeah. And tell them that golf course, if it ever gets built, it'll be on my property. Not theirs."

Encouraged by the sudden turn of events and heavy dose of pain-killers, Richard stood up, smiled, reached across the desk, took the envelope, and ripped it in half. "Do me a favor. Throw that away."

"What about the check?"

Richard reached out. "Guess you won't be needing that either." He grabbed the check and left a new man.

Anthony Drayhill, meanwhile, picked up the phone, and dialed a frequently called number to one of the bank's board of directors—

"Hello, Janice. Is Mark there?" He listened and then replied, "Have him give me a call as soon as he can. It's important. Thanks."

Chapter 32

Alexa Wilde was waiting inside the offices of the Fleet Merchant Trucking Company, facing the company logo, a life-sized depiction of a black thoroughbred, its mane streaming from its neck as it galloped toward the finish line. No rider. Just the horse. It was beautifully done, cut from plywood, and hung a few inches from the wall, giving it a three-dimensional effect. The logo was on every truck in the fleet.

A receptionist opened a door and said to Alexa, "He can see you now. No more than fifteen minutes. His schedule is very tight."

Alexa was led down a hall filled with photos of famous racetracks and famous horses into an office with plush beige carpet, teakwood walls, and giant mahogany desk where Mark Treshler sat. He was on the phone, but acknowledged his visitor and gestured she have a seat. His eyes widened when he saw Alexa, flashing like two tiny light bulbs at the sight of a woman, stunning in appearance, trim in the right places, curvaceous in others.

The receptionist handed Mark a note and whispered, "He wants you to call right away. It's important."

He nodded. She exited.

Alexa had time to examine the room. The back wall facing the visitor was covered with photographs, plaques, and honorariums, including the Rotary Club's Man of the Year, the centerpiece being a large picture of Mark and an older gentleman with thinning grayish hair and pencil-thin mustache. Both were holding a trophy and smiling as they stood beside a horse with a wreath draped over its neck. To her left was a trophy case filled with silver goblets, crystal vases, cups, medals, ribbons, and other assorted trophies. She was caught staring at the photograph of the horse and two men flanking the wreath.

"That was a great day for our family," declared Mark as he hung up the phone. "Not bad for Ohio farm boys. Fleet Merchant won seven races in two years. Getting a little long in the tooth, but we still use him for stud once in a while. So...I understand you're interested in our community, Miss..."

"Alexa Wilde."

He reached across the desk. They shook hands. "Mark Treshler."

She looked around. "Very impressive."

"A bit excessive, I admit. Most of the time I'm the only one who sees it. Hard to believe, but I've got twice as many trophies at home."

Overindulgent. Compulsive. Obsessive, she thought to herself. *Egotistical. Fixated on himself.*

"My secretary tells me you're doing research, I believe, about the history of Bertram County. Is that correct?"

"Yes, I am."

"Hope you don't mind me asking...why? For what purpose?"

"Why not? Why the history of anything? Sometimes it's more interesting than fiction."

"I suppose you're right. You're not from around here, are you?"

Alexa laid the accent on thick. Like molasses on cornbread. "Born and bred in the South. Butter-beans-and-grits country. Army brat. Georgia or Alabama I call home, depending on who's winning in football."

"Ohio State isn't too shabby. Why our neck of the woods? What brought you here?"

"A scholarship. Ohio Southern has one of the better journalism schools in the country."

Mark nodded. "Hate to keep harping back to it, but why the interest in our little community? What approach are you taking?"

"I'm focusing on three families mostly," replied Alexa. "The Bertrams, Treshlers, and the Macklins." She quickly gave a brief synopsis of each, portraying the Bertrams as philanthropists, tycoons who parlayed millions from the mortician business, the Treshlers as rich conservative magnates, modern-day barons of the county, and the Macklins as hard-working farmers, a once-thriving family whose fortune was now on the decline.

When done, Mark said, "Well...that pretty much sums it up. One thing before we get started. I'd like to ask a question."

"Certainly. I'm game if you are."

"The editorial the paper did a few weeks ago...about our charity golf event, the one upcoming in May, who wrote that?"

"It was a collaboration...from the entire staff. Why?"

He chuckled, "Guess I have trouble with people who bash something when all you're trying to do is raise money for a good cause."

Alexa sat up, back straight, perfect posture. "It's not the cause. Raising money for foster homes is very admirable. With all due respect, Mr. Treshler, it's the distribution of charitable cash, the amount, that your critics find fault with. Forty percent of a hundred thousand dollars isn't much to pass along. Some say you're using tax loopholes to fund a big party."

"So what's wrong with tax loopholes? The government is a big insatiable, money-gobbling machine. When it comes to taxes, it's a sieve. And the waste. Oh, my God. Don't get me started. Besides, forty percent is incorrect. It's more like sixty. And we pay for foster home care and administrative costs."

"Not as much as you could. Administrative costs could mean anything. And, frankly, Mr. Treshler, if you ran your golf tournament like your businesses, a lot more money would be poured into it."

Humored, Mark slapped the desk. "You know what? You're right. I should have my people look into it. We'll just do away with gifts and after dinner expenses. Go ahead. Getting back to the interview, what do you want to know?"

Alexa referred to her notebook. Pages were dog-eared, either folded at the corners or identified with paper clips. "The Treshler businesses are very diversified. Trucking, insurance, cars, used and new. Two dealerships..."

"Two?"

"Yes, the one here. The other in Jesup. You own sixty percent of the Ford franchise. The rest is split between your son and daughter."

Mark blinked. He was caught off guard. "How did you know that?"

"I have my sources. You also have interests in investments, farming, cattle, banking..."

"Banking?"

"Well, you and your father are on the board of directors of Farmers First State Bank. The two of you own more shares than anyone else."

Mark smiled. It wasn't a happy smile, more of an amused sneer. "Very good. You've done your homework. What else?"

"Real estate, construction, farm supplies and equipment, horse breeding, racing. That's quite a list."

"Sure is. But I owe it all to that guy..." He jerked a thumb at the largest photograph, the centerpiece, hanging behind him. "My father, Andrew. He got the ball rolling, along with his father."

"With a little help from the Bertrams. It was their money that got you started."

The President of Fleet Merchant twisted in his chair. He let loose another chuckle. "Wow, you're no shrinking violet, are you? Okay, I'm not bashful either. In a sense you could say that's true. It was a simple loan, a modest amount. But let me lay the ground rules. If you're here to talk about finances concerning any of my companies, I'd rather you talk to my accountants. I was told the interview would be on a much broader basis."

"I never put limitations on anything, regarding this or any story I do."

"Just as long as you understand. I'm a little cautious when it comes to reporters."

"Most people are. I can assure you, my intentions are fair."

"Good. The less personal, the better."

Alexa clicked her pen and held it against her notepad, poised to write. "Generally speaking, with an empire so vast..."

"Hold it!" he interrupted. "*Empire*? That's a bit much. I'm no king sitting on a throne."

"All right. Having so many businesses..."

"That's better."

"How do you keep track of it all?"

"Sometimes I'm not sure myself. Seriously, it takes good people. Put them in the right places, make them accountable, and you have a pretty good recipe for success, as long as what you offer has value."

"Did you know you're the biggest employer in this part of the state, by far?"

"I'm aware of my responsibilities, if that's what you mean."

"Plus, you own more land than anyone else, except for maybe Richard Macklin. Square-footage-wise, he's bigger, but not by much. Value-wise you're the *king*."

Mark sat back with a knuckle pressed against clenched teeth. "Enlighten me. Where are you going with this?"

"Nowhere. Just stating a fact. It's all there written in the various county records, the treasurers' offices. The Lake Russell Project for example. Half of the lake front property is owned by *Westgate Management* and *Treshler & Hopwell Realty*. If I'm not mistaken, the last company has your name on it."

Mark could do nothing but shake his head.

Alexa was just warming up. She could hear this little voice chirping in her ear. *Go girl!*

"Since it's a manmade lake," she continued, "I was just wondering when you got wind of it, and how you came to own most of it."

"Simple. Bids. We outbid everyone. And we watch the market very closely. We know when to buy, when to sell As to how we got '*wind of it*,' my father helped push the project through the state legislature. Understand, a lot of the land we own is under water, has no value whatsoever."

"A small price to pay. Lose some. Win some."

Mark sat up, grinning. "I like you. You got spunk. Is there a recorder in that purse of yours?"

"You saw me when I came in. I wasn't carrying a purse. You're more observant than that."

"You're pretty damn observant yourself. And not a bad looker."

Alexa stiffened, a common reflex when flattery was unwanted. Blushing, she referred to her notebook again. "Let's see. Bridgestone Construction. I believe they built the marina and restaurant at a cost of three-point-five million. The property on both sides escalated, shot way up to hundreds of dollars per square foot, facing the lake. You own the developments—condos, upscale homes—north and south of the marina, probably a portion of Bridgestone, too. I haven't been able to trace the latter back to you."

"Hold on a second, Miss…Miss…"

"Alexa. Alexa Wilde."

"Okay, Miss Wilde," Mark said irritably. "If you're trying to impress me, you have. There's no story there. The state has already conducted an investigation—back in November. No law was broken."

"I was just trying to establish..."

"No. We're not establishing anything. Next question. Lake Russell is old news. Everything I've done, all my businesses associated with it, has been exonerated. Let's move on."

"Okay then. Considering all your enterprises, which one do you enjoy the most?"

That's harmless enough, Mark thought. "No doubt, the horse business. Breeding and racing are in my blood."

"What about it do you enjoy?"

"Everything. Watching a young foal being born. The sleekness of the animal. The amazing maturity it has just after two years. The strength, obedience, and grace of all that God-given muscle trained for speed. Watching champions develop. The atmosphere of great racing venues. The excitement you feel when thousands of people are watching your thoroughbred compete in one of the majors. I could spend all day talking about it."

"I can tell. Have you always been interested in horses?"

"Heck, no! Now women…I've always been a man who enjoys the fairer sex. Also love to hunt. My dad always said, tracking wild game is like seducing a woman. The excitement's in the chase."

"Interesting you would make that analogy."

"Believe you me, when you have money, women do the hunting. Hope that doesn't offend you, but it's true."

Alexa felt her heart beating faster, not because of his advances and lustful stares, but because of the direction the interview was going. She couldn't wait to ask the next question. "So, how did you get started in the horse business?"

"I bought a horse."

"You bought it?"

"Yes."

"What was the horse's name?"

"You're looking at him. Up there. Fleet Merchant."

"You've made a lot of money off it."

"Depends on what you mean by 'a lot.' Guess that's one area I don't mind talking about. Profits. Most of it is public record anyway. The paper reports the prize money. Win, place or show. I'm surprised you don't know how much."

"As a matter of fact..." Alexa flipped through her notebook, glancing at the pages, but most of the pages were blank. "From what I could gather...during a two year period, when he was in top form, Fleet Merchant grossed more than a million-four conservatively, excluding stud fees."

"You're guessing, I can tell."

"Pretty accurate guess."

Mark burst out laughing. "Damn, lady! You have nerves of steel! I should hire you. You're as coldblooded as they come. I bet you're the type, if you want something, you go after it."

Alexa gave her best impression of a steely-eyed, coldhearted reporter. "Absolutely."

"Does that include men?"

"Maybe. Aren't you married?"

"When it's convenient. My wife and I have an arrangement."

"How's this for an arrangement? I figure, combining all the money Fleet Merchant has made, you've grossed about two million. Give or take half a million for travel, salaries, upkeep, what have you, and you've still made a killing."

"Handcuff me! Take me in, officer! I committed a crime. I like money! You make it sound dirty."

"I never meant to insinuate anything. Money's not dirty. How you earn it can be. Who did you buy Fleet Merchant from?"

"My brother-in-law."

"Richard Macklin?"

"Yes. Do you know him?"

Alexa took a deep breath. *Here goes*, she said to herself. "Not really. Since you don't mind talking about the financial side of the horse business, how much did you pay for the thoroughbred? Or would you rather I call him a stud?"

"Amazing. Truly Amazing." Mark settled back, fingers interlocked, giving her a stare that could poke holes in a wall. "You didn't come here to talk about the history of Bertram County."

"Guess what, Mr. Treshler, you didn't pay a penny for that stud horse of yours. Seems we're both guilty of something."

Suddenly reserved and calm, Mark tried to ignore the remark. "I suppose I should be angry, throwing a fit, but somehow I think you'd like that. Tell me. Why did you come here?"

"I wanted to see if you'd own up to your transgression, the ethics of what you did."

"Ethics? Christ all Friday! I can't believe this. By the way, this interview is over. I want you out of here." For a moment they just looked at each other. As Alexa got up, Mark said, "Just humor me. What did you really hope to accomplish? You certainly didn't expect me to pay the son-of-a-bitch anything, did you?"

"Wouldn't hurt. That would be the right thing to do." She walked to the door. "No, Mr. Treshler, I suspect the only right thing you do is what you do for yourself. What did I hope to accomplish? I wanted you to know, morally and ethically, you did commit a crime. You stole someone else's property. Also to see if you're as big an asshole as everyone says you are. And you know what? You're the King Kong of assholes!"

Chapter 33

Tom Duckett had amassed enough information to hazard more than a wild guess. He built a scenario that was indeed wild, but also preposterous. From the incidents listed in the reports and his experience this morning at Birch Run, he was able to put together a case strong enough to present to his boss, Sheriff Aldrick Pleamons. Yet in view of the fact that he didn't know what to do with this incredible information, not exacting the relevancy of it or knowing specifically what was doing these things, channeling it into some cohesive, constructive course of action seemed not only implausible, but crazy.

He could hear his boss now. "Duckett, I'm sending you to the nut-house!"

A trip to his family physician to have his shoulder looked at didn't help. The doctor said he wouldn't need stitches. Ointment, an antibiotic—yes. "It's a bite of some kind, infected I might add…like you were bitten by a bat. How did you get it?"

Tom answered, "Jogging."

"Well, jog someplace else. There's going to be some swelling and inflammation. Some irritation, too. I'll give you a prescription. Take three pills a day, then come back and see me on Monday."

With his wound now gauzed and bandaged, the medication administered, Tom was ready to seek someone out, someone who knew the Macklins and Caddo, who had a relationship with him, and in their intimate dealings things were said that could shed new light on the subject—because Tom believed Caddo knew more than anyone else. He was the clue, the key figure in the crisis. And who knew him best? The waitress, Irene Vernath.

After the doctor's office, the deputy drove straight to Jake's Country Cafe. It was ten-thirty when he arrived. The breakfast crowd had thinned out. Most of the tables were empty. Bubbles was wiping down a countertop. Once she saw Tom, she had a cup of coffee waiting. Tom didn't like mulatto coffee. He liked it black.

He led her to a booth, so they could talk in private. Out of the corner of his eye he saw Jake watching from the serving station. "Everything's cool, Jake. Official business. Only need her for a few minutes."

Irene slid into the booth first. "What did I do? Rob a bank?"

Tom placed the cup of coffee on the table, his hat on the seat. "I don't know. Did you?"

"Honey, I've thought of doin' lots of things. Robbin' banks. Beggin' on a street corner. Shoot, it would probably pay better than workin' here."

Tom didn't crack a smile.

Despite her glibness, Irene sat unsmiling, a little apprehensive. "What's up? Those handcuffs ain't for me, are they?"

"No," said Tom. He took out a pen and notepad to keep track of what he termed *'culpable responses.'* Body language, lies, guilt, suspicion, nervousness, anything that could be regarded in a negative way, he wrote down. When the points added up to five, it spelled trouble for the person being questioned.

With pen in hand, Tom observed Irene's every move, her eyes, her facial expression. She was notorious for being an easy read. "Actually, I came here to talk about Caddo."

"He's all right, I hope."

The statement alone, by its mere suggestion, earned her a culpable response straight out of the gate.

"Far as I know," replied Tom. "Are you worried?"

Both of her eyes twitched. "No. Not at all."

"You make it sound like you are."

"Well, I'm not. Seein' as how you're so dag-gum worried yourself, I might as well break the news. We're engaged." She fiddled with an diamond-studded opal ring. She kept twirling it, twisting it around her finger. "Just so you know," she said, "what concerns him, concerns me."

"I understand. Congratulations. When was the last time you saw Caddo?"

She folded her arms. "Last night."

"Until what time?"

"Better not drink that coffee. Arsenic might be in it."

"Stop kidding around, Irene. This is serious. Did you spend the night together?"

"Maybe. What does that have to do with anything?"

"Where?"

She got a little defensive. "At my apartment. Before you go snoopin' any further, I'm tellin' you right now. What happens in my apartment, stays in my apartment."

Tom couldn't help himself. He smiled, but quickly wiped the smile from his face. "I can assure you. What you do in private is no concern of mine. Where is he now?"

"I don't know. Haven't seen him since I took him home."

The deputy leaned his elbows on the table. "What time was that?"

"Early this morning. Before sunup."

"What did you see...on the way there?"

"Road mostly. What was I supposed to see? It was still dark."

"Was there anything you would consider...unusual?"

She glanced at her ring and started playing with it again. "No."

"You're absolutely positive...you saw nothing at all?"

She thought about the drive to the farm and what Caddo had said, how vital it was that what he had to say was confidential. He made it clear that if word got out and he was detained by the authorities and couldn't perform a certain task, people would be put at risk. He made her give her word. She gave it unconditionally. "If you tell anyone," he said, "you'll never see me again. I'll be dead."

She wasn't about to jeopardize his life, or anyone else's. It was at that moment, sitting across from Tom, she realized how much she loved Caddo. She would even lie for him.

As sincerely as she could, she answered, "I'm positive. I dropped him off and drove straight to work."

"You're not holding back anything, are you? Because if you are, you're only making it more difficult on yourself."

"I have no reason to lie to you. Is Caddo in some kind of trouble?"

"I don't know yet." Tom looked deep into her eyes to see if she would fold under pressure. Years ago he learned that silence was sometimes more effective than a question. Unfortunately, this time it didn't work. Disappointed, he leaned back. "I don't believe you. You know what gave it away? The ring."

They sat, staring at each other, not speaking—Irene resolute, Tom unsure if he should be mad or envious of her loyalty.

"I could take you in, you know," he said, finally. "The sheriff would make your life miserable. He'd break you."

For a split second, Bubbles showed a tiny crack in her armor. She blinked. After that, her facial expression remained implacable.

Tom was persistent. "The conditions," he said, "other than it being dark, could you describe them?"

"Conditions?"

"The weather."

"Um, overcast. A bit...cool."

He repeated it slowly, "...a bit cool," a hint of doubt in his voice. "No wind? No...fog?"

She chose her words carefully. "If there was, I wasn't payin' attention."

Tom's reaction was unhurried, a pace he often used when trying to build tension during an interview. He read the culpable responses he wrote down and counted the points as he went. Her opening comment, what it suggested, earned her one point. Nervousness another. Anxiety a third. Her posture, general attitude, defiant nature, having a tendency to be disrespectful earned a fourth. And the last, harshest, most egregious offense of all, she was lying.

Five points total.

"Pitiful. Truly pitiful," said Tom. He eyed the cup of coffee for a second, then inched forward, leaning on the table, and stared at her. "I'll give you one last chance. But before you answer, let me paint you a little picture." He spoke with a severity that, by necessity, was out of character. "Your refusal to help could put you in jail. If anyone dies as a result of your or Caddo's unwillingness to cooperate, if either of you are obstructing the duties of my office, you'll see a side of me you've never seen before. Do you understand? That's my message to you, as sure as I've given oath to this badge. What's your answer?"

Irene was no longer Bubbles. She was a rock. She refused to be intimidated. She returned his stare and sat in defiance of an enforcer of the law, her pledge to Caddo much stronger than any oath to office.

Tom sighed and slowly picked up his hat. "Oh, well..." Quietly, he shuffled away.

* * *

Caddo used it as a refuge whenever he wanted to be alone. Weather permitting, sometimes he slept in the hayloft close to the *wakan*, the *orenda*. To him, the barn was a sacred place, possessed of immense power, or, as the Pawnees called it—*jawonio*.

He liked the tall rooflines, the smell of aged wood, the old discarded farm equipment, and brick-a-brack lying everywhere. What some people considered trash, he viewed as museum pieces. But most of all, he liked it because it was abandoned. Today he couldn't be bothered. He had preparations to make. Inside these venerable walls he could work, move about, and not be seen. The preparations began five days ago when he bought an old painter's tarp from a farmer. The rest he bought at the hardware store or found lying around somewhere.

Now everything was ready. The project which he had carefully planned was about to take shape. In the center of the tarp he cut a hole and through it he slipped some poles fastened at one end. Using a pulley and rope, he was able to raise the contraption, suspend it in air as he spread the poles wide and anchored them to stakes. He stepped back. From a distance it looked like a tepee. For a final touch, he cut a slit at the base for a doorway.

From the moment he first entered the barn, he kept hearing tired sighs, what may have been construed as weeping and moaning. To counteract it he hummed an old Pawnee song. He'd forgotten the words, not the melody. It was more of a chant than anything else, each note repetitious, rhythmic yet lyrical, wavering up and down an octave at a time. He never stopped humming or dancing. Caddo mimicked his grandfather by doing the Eagle Dance and making his body glide. Arms outstretched, he circled like a bird in flight, his legs and feet lightly pumping up and down, hopping and skipping. Even standing still, he would move his legs to the rhythm in his head, and, as he got closer to the completion of the project, his humming grew louder, his feet moved quicker, and body swayed with more enthusiasm. Even while he carried logs and rocks inside the tepee, he would dance and sing until, finally, everything was done and he was satisfied.

There were a few minor details, however, he had to do outside the barn before he could begin a larger task, something he had never done or felt capable of doing. But for the sake of everyone he knew and loved, he had to try. With every fiber of his being, he had to devote himself…commit himself to *jawonio* and reach a state of mind seldom achieved by the most devout of Indian priests.

Would it be enough?

He looked at his watch. It was approaching eleven o'clock in the morning.

He feared maybe it was already too late.

Chapter 34

Elly's patience was wearing thin. After several attempts at making a call, she'd just about given up. "Come on, David. Pick it up! Pick it up!"

Three rings…four… "Please leave a message after the dial tone…"

"Hello," said a winded voice.

"Finally! What have you been doing, David? I've been calling and calling."

He detected a note of irritation in her voice. "Taking care of business."

"Who were you talking to?"

"Various people. Our lawyer. The bank. Have any luck?"

"Boy, did I ever. Did you know you're in today's paper?"

"I am?"

"The accident is big news. There's a story about us on every single page. The family's got the paper covered, front to back. I suggest you read it."

"Maybe later. What did you come up with?"

"Do it as soon as you can."

"Why?"

"There's an article in the Business Section about a fifty-two-million dollar project. Developed by—*ta-da!*—none other than good ol' Uncle Mark! Marina, yacht club, upscale homes, condos, golf course. Everything! And it's on our old property. The paper didn't mention a word about our course. Guess who he's trying to hire as the architect?"

"Jack Lorrigan."

"Are you telepathic?"

"The paper's not high on my list of priorities. If you don't mind, I'm kinda in a hurry. What did you find out?"

"Plenty. The stuff Mae knows is incredible. Want a quick run-down now, or when I get home?"

"Just the basics for now."

"We could find only two references to a burial ground. And there wasn't one tribe living in the area. There were *three*."

"Who besides the Mosopelea?"

"A tribe called the Black Minqua. And the most feared of the eastern tribes. Take a guess."

"Iroquois?"

"Getting warm. Who shaved their heads?"

"Mohawk?"

"Right here on the banks of Little Bass River. And get this. The Mohawks supposedly attacked a wagon train and fought a battle against a group of militia and British soldiers."

"Good work. Make copies of everything you can. Is that it?"

"Not quite. Historians called it the *War of Blood*. Only a few Indians survived. And they didn't *bury* the dead. Not underground anyway. Not like we do. They placed them on burial platforms. Scaffolds."

"Did you find out where?"

"Not exactly. Not far from a river is all the source said." Elly could hear him rummaging around in a confined space. "There's something else you should know. Caddo borrowed some masks from the library for cultural studies."

"So?"

"The masks were used for healing rituals...to chase evil spirits away."

"Interesting."

"I thought so." She heard something go *ka-thunk*. "David?"

When he spoke, his voice sounded hollow, like he was in an echo chamber. "Hate to change the subject, El. You know where I could find Jack Lorrigan's cell number?"

"Don't you want to hear the rest of it?"

"The number..."

"Try the Rolodex in dad's office."

"Thanks." There was a long pause. David did more rummaging around and said, "I might not be here when you get home. I'm going to pay someone a visit. If he's home."

"Who?"

"Grandpa."

Elly looked at the phone, scrunched up her face, and put the phone back to her ear. "Why? You haven't seen him in years."

"Leverage. Sorry. I have to cut this short."

"Wait!" she cried. "I've saved the best for last. Henry Purdy...he claims he was there."

"Where?"

"The War of Blood."

Dead air. David didn't know what to think. "Where did you read that?"

"Here. In the library. Hank's autobiography."

"You mean he claims to have lived for two hundred and fifty years?"

"No. He died at age seventy-four."

"You lost me. We'll talk about it later."

Elly let one word drop. It dropped like a bomb. She said, "*Reincarnation.*"

There was total confusion at the other end. David was clueless. "Reincarnation?"

"Hank believed he lived multiple lives."

"He what?"

"You heard me." The sound of shoes thumped against the floor. "David. What are you doing?"

"Going through your closet. Ah-ha! Found it."

"Found what? Why are you doing in my closet?"

"Got to go, El."

"Wait! One last thing!"

"Make it quick."

"The word I mentioned last night. *Revenant.* I looked it up. Guess what it means." She paused to dramatize the point. "It means *ghost.*"

She heard the phone click, then buzz with a dial tone.

* * *

David entered the office on the second floor, sat down, flipped through the Rolodex, found the number, and dialed.

After three rings, a man answered, "This is Jack."

"Mr. Lorrigan. David Macklin. We talked yesterday."

"Yes." Jack wasn't in the friendliest of moods. "What can I do for you, David?"

"I understand there's an article in today's paper about you and my uncle building a golf course. Is that true?"

After a long pause, Jack replied, "Yes, it is."

"What changed?"

"Ah...hold on a second." Jack must have cupped his hand over the mouthpiece because the sound was muffled. There was mumbling in the background, whispers. "What changed? The price."

"But you said price wouldn't be a determining factor."

"I did. But I have partners. It was a business decision. Mr. Treshler changed his bid. Made it more attractive. It was in our best interest to reconsider."

"How close were the bids?"

"You know I can't divulge that. Let's just say the difference was substantial."

David felt his muscles tighten. "Okay. For the sake of discussion, if all things were equal, where would you build the golf course?"

Again, another pause. When Jack answered, he sounded like he was being placed in an awkward situation. "Can't say right now."

"Why not? Because you don't know? Or because someone's listening? Say *yes* if someone's listening."

"Yes."

"Are there extenuating circumstances?"

"You might say that."

"Yesterday you said you preferred our property, the way the land was contoured, the proximity of the river. You compared it to the Masters. Amen Corner. High praise for a lot of dirt, weeds, and a few trees. If you can't talk, say *that's right*."

"That's right."

"Despite whoever's listening, and I'll make it quick so they won't get suspicious, despite everything else, if cost wasn't a factor and these extenuating circumstances were eliminated, what site would you choose?"

"Sorry, David. I'm not the one who decides."

"But you recommend, don't you? Make recommendations?"

The line remained quiet.

David asked the question again.

"Yes," Jack replied.

David was clinging to a thread of hope. "One last question. When we talked, you said a decision might be made soon. How soon?"

"Very soon."

"What? A day, two days, a week, a month?"

"Possibly by Monday."

David clenched his jaw. "Do yourself and me a favor, Mr. Lorrigan. Delay your recommendation. If you truly believe our property is as good as you think it is, don't sign anything."

"Sorry, but there's nothing you can do, David. Basically, the decision's already been made."

"Because of what happened last night?"

Jack hesitated. "Partly."

David felt sick. He wanted to scream. Quietly, he said, "I understand. If you change your mind, let me know."

They exchanged goodbyes.

David's stress level went up. He realized he had to rearrange his priorities.

He removed a piece of paper from his pocket and on the back of it he wrote a list of one and two-word reminders of things he had to do—

read newspaper
see Drew
talk to Caddo

make money transfer
Revenant/Ghost
War of Blood
Halting Place
Phantom Beast
Charik waik-ta

By Caddo's name he put an asterisk. He folded the paper. Put it in his pocket. Ran downstairs, then outside to the chicken coop where Bo Darnell and the cleaning crew were hard at work. He told Bo to send him a bill and enticed it by padding it an extra fifty bucks. After that, David marched away like a man on a mission. A quick look around the base of the driveway came up empty. The newspaper wasn't there. It wasn't in the mailbox either.

He looked at his watch, an underwater timepiece awarded him when he became a member of a select Navy Seal team.

1:27 pm.

His internal clock was ticking.

Time for a giant leap toward solvency.

Chapter 35

The last time David visited the Treshlers' estate was a Fourth of July picnic. He was ten years old. Two hundred people attended. The air smelled of roasted pig barbecue, slowly smoked underground in a pit.

The celebration started on the wrong foot and trickled downhill from there—initiated by cousin Rex, Mark's boy, during a baseball game, with a smidgeon of help from his twin sister, Horrible Helen, both of whom attended prep school for the rich and spoiled. Rex was eleven. Not exactly a bully, Rex was the type who weaseled and whined until he got his way. Right off, he wouldn't let David bat or touch a baseball. On top of that, he and Helen told lies to other kids about David, whispering scurrilous, secretive things while gloating mockingly. Then Rex had the misfortune of calling David something to his face. A Macklin! Rex made it sound like a piece of dog scum. That did it. David whipped into him like lightning. Broke Rex's front tooth. It wasn't even a fight. But the blame fell squarely on the shoulders of Richard's son. For the remainder of the afternoon David was an outcast, banished from any further activity.

The first change he noticed about the estate was the entrance. At one time there was nothing but a road, fences, and a few trees. Now there was a wrought-iron gate with an English T centered above it, connected by two brick stanchions, and thick clusters of bushes and trees to hide the property. Once David got out of the truck, he peeked through the gate and saw not one house but three opulent country mansions encircling an oval driveway where a six-foot-tall fountain of a bronze horse in mid-stride spewed water from a sculpted base.

"Wow!"

Standing before a box, he pressed a button.

A voice said, "Yes?"

David cleared his throat. "I'm David Macklin and I'm here to see my grandfather."

"For what purpose?"

"To see him. Do I need a reason?"

Five minutes later, he was buzzed inside and told to park in the guest lot. David drove around a winding driveway, parked in front of the biggest house, and reached for a sketchpad lying in the passenger's seat.

A tall, dark-haired man opened the front door. "I told you to park..."

David brushed past him. "Look, I don't know who you are, but I'm family. I come visit every seventeen years if it kills me."

The man ushered him through a house that could be featured in *Architectural Digest* and then outside to a pool where a very attractive woman about David's age, wearing a very revealing bikini, was sipping a drink.

"Who's that, Ben?" she asked, as if David weren't there.

"David Macklin."

"My God!" Her eyes bulged. Her body started jiggling. Seductively, she moved closer, smiling, holding out a hand. "It's Katie."

"Katie?"

"Helen Katherine, your cousin."

He had to admit Horrible Helen never looked so good.

After a minute of small talk in which he could smell tequila on her breath, at noon no less, he learned that she was married, had a summer home at Hilton Head, was desperate for attention, enjoyed tennis, vacationing in France, and flirted way too much.

"And you, what do you have there?" she asked, pointing at the sketchpad.

"Oh, this? Nothing." He stated his name, rank, and the base where he was stationed, barking them off as if he were addressing an officer, then politely excused himself. The only thing he didn't do was salute.

Behind the pool, a terrace led to a magnificent view of white painted fences, racing track, and rolling fields where horses ran free for hundreds of acres. To his right, down a brick pathway was a garden about to bloom and a one-story structure.

"You'll find him in his work studio," said Ben. "No need to knock."

David walked down the steps, having no idea what he was going to say. With a firm grip on the sketchpad, he turned the doorknob and walked in. The studio served one purpose—the making of furniture. From the storage of raw lumber, rare and expensive judging from the colors and textures, to the machines that carved, shaped, and sanded the wood, it appeared to be more than just a hobby.

Andrew Treshler took a dust cloth and wiped a table leg he'd just spun on a carpenter's wheel. Eighty years old, Drew looked to be in excellent health. Gray-haired. Trim and fit. He had a modest mustache cropped close, which gave him a distinguished appearance.

"I understand you're in the Navy," said Drew.

"Yes, sir. Seven years."

"As you can see, I'm retired now. Just an old coot, tinkering his life away. Sometimes I'll spend twelve hours a day messing around here, now that your grandmother's gone. Hungry? Want something to drink?"

"No, sir."

"Last time I saw you was at your mother's funeral. You've filled out quite a bit. Taller, too. What did you do to your head?"

"Car accident."

"The one in the newspaper?"

"Yes, sir."

"Yes, sir. No, sir. I suggest we dispense with formality. Judging from the pictures, I'd say you're lucky to be alive. What's that under your arm?"

"Oh, nothing."

After screwing the top to a can of linseed oil, Drew wiped his hands on a rag. David felt like a lawyer ready to plead his case before a judge.

Finally, Drew said, "I doubt you came here for a lesson in cabinet making."

"I bet you're wondering why."

"Has crossed my mind."

David placed the sketchpad on a workbench and put his hands in his pockets. "Since I've been home, I've been doing some thinking. And one of the issues I have concerns our families. As you and I both know we're not exactly close."

"Ha!" Drew shook his head, as if it were an understatement.

"Lately, I think our relationship has gotten worse."

"What makes you say that?"

David realized there was no delicate way to put it. "Do you know about an injunction filed by the state against my father?"

"Injunction to do what?"

"It's a temporary restraining order. The State Environmental Protection Agency and Ohio Department of Natural Resources have filed a joint claim, stopping development of properties 'deemed as wetlands' on our farm."

"So?"

"It's the timing, sir. Why would the state...excuse me, why would two state agencies issue an injunction? My father hasn't applied for any permits."

"I'm afraid you're talking to the wrong person. The case has no bearing on me."

"Sir, forgive me. I happen to know your son is behind it. I also know it's a bluff. I called our lawyer this morning and he said it won't hold up in court."

"Then what's the problem?"

"It's the principle. It costs money to hire a lawyer."

"Principle, huh?" Drew walked a few paces, head bent in thought. "Interesting word—*principle*. Sometimes it depends on which side of the fence you're on."

"Sorry. I don't understand."

"Principles. Depends which way you look at it."

"Mostly I just know what's right and what's wrong, sir."

"I told you not to call me 'sir.'"

"It's the Navy. How we're conditioned. I'll try to refrain from it... sir."

Drew grinned. "Sarcastic. That's what I remember about you. What is it you want?"

"Breathing room. I'd like you to talk to your son. Tell him to leave my father alone."

"Why me?"

"Because I don't know him very well. Besides, I think you'd have more influence than I would."

"I see. You come here, into my house, asking me to take issue with things I know nothing about. Against my own son."

"No, sir. All I want is what's fair."

"After all these years, you expect our families to throw aside the bad blood and embrace each other, is that it?"

David could see he was being manipulated into saying something he would regret. "Whatever differences we have, I want them to end."

"Reasonable enough. Other than this injunction, how has Mark taken advantage of your father?"

"You sure you want me to get into that?"

"Please. If we're going to air things out, air 'em out!"

"You know about the golf course, right?"

"Which one?"

"The one at Birch Run. It's dad's way out of debt. I understand Mark has put in a bid for another site—on Treshler property. He doesn't need the money, but he thinks by outbidding us, he'll be able to position himself to..."

The words seemed to hang in the air.

"To what?" prompted Drew.

"Take over Macklin Farms."

The allegation was like a slap in the face.

Drew took it calmly. Inside, it was a different story. "That's a pretty serious accusation. You're presuming an awful lot."

"Am I?"

"Commerce. Politics. That's what's made this country great."

"We're talking about relatives. Going out of your way to hurt a brother-in-law."

"So far you haven't convinced me of anything."

"What about Lake Russell?"

Drew raised his eyes slowly. "Maybe you'd like to spell it out."

"No problem. About fifteen years ago Mark approached my dad. We had a nice piece of property, about eight hundred acres at the north end of the lake, which we planned to give to Ohio Southern. The university was going to use it in their agricultural studies—for trees, experimental crops, that sort of thing. Do you remember any of this?"

"Vaguely."

"Well, your son offered to buy all eight hundred acres. Above market value, he claimed. Dad thought, what the heck. That's a generous offer. We had other properties we could donate, which eventually we did. Huh-uh. Huge mistake. Three months later. Big headlines! *State announces plans for expansion of Lake Russell,' making it the fourth largest manmade lake in the United States!* Property values skyrocketed. Now they're turning our old property into a multi-million dollar development. Uncle Mark made a killing at our expense. Yeah, commerce and politics. That's what makes this country great."

Drew made no comment. He rearranged a few cans. Picked up a block of wood. Ran his fingers over it.

"Should I go on?" David asked.

"You seem to know quite a bit. Don't let me stop you."

"I think you may remember a horse named Fleet Merchant. If you like stories, I'd be glad to fill you in."

Drew started to pace, then stopped. "I'm somewhat familiar with the subject. Are you?"

"I think so."

"Tell me. Do you know how your father got that horse? Do you know the circumstances? Who was involved?"

"Not everything, no. I think he bought it from somebody in Kentucky."

Drew let loose a rumble of laughter. "Bought it? Do you have any idea how much a horse like that costs?"

"I don't know. Fifteen...twenty thousand."

More laughter. Drew was practically beside himself. "Try dozens of times that. How about, conservatively...a quarter of a million dollars."

David didn't know what to say. "But dad..."

"Couldn't afford it!" cried Drew. "Believe me, I know. Before we continue, there are some things you may not want to hear."

"Go ahead. I started it."

Quietly, Drew said, "A few years after you were born, your father stopped by my office. He asked to borrow a large amount of money for what he called 'improvements' to cover an extension of a farm loan. I never questioned it. Later, I found out through a friend, purely by accident, your father was gambling heavily on horses. Had been since he returned from Vietnam. He also had a substance abuse problem. Marijuana. Did you know that?"

David never changed expression. "No."

"Thank God he quit. Anyway, he lied to me about the loan. Using my money, he won a horse on a bet, a foal from a filly named Star's Promenade, a retired thoroughbred that once came in second the Kentucky Derby. The owner helped Mark and myself get started in the horse business. Not a very good way to treat family, to lie like that. It left a very bad taste. Your father was lucky he didn't lose the farm."

"How much did he borrow?"

"I suggest you ask him."

"Did he pay you back?"

"Let's just say the debt's been settled."

David didn't expect a direct answer. After all, the bad feelings between the families centered on this very issue. The horse became a bartering tool, used to negotiate. In more blunt terms—blackmail. Blackmail instigated not by Drew, but by his son, Mark. Richard agreed to lend his horse for breeding purposes if nothing was said to his wife about a "certain indiscretion." Meaning, of course, gambling. The rift grew proportionally, as did the allegations. It became a private war—between Richard and Mark. In the end confidentiality was guaranteed. The Treshlers made a fortune on the stud services and a marriage had been saved. For a price.

"A quarter of a million dollar horse," David said at last. "Dad must have borrowed quite a bit."

"It wasn't the money." For the first time bitterness crept into Drew's voice.

"What was it then?"

There was no reply.

David repeated the question, then answered it by saying. "It's my dad. You don't like him. You never did, did you?"

"He's irresponsible. Weak and irresponsible."

"Weak? Because he gambled? Smoked marijuana? He was young. Just back from Vietnam. He made mistakes. He quit both, didn't he? He was decorated twice during the war. Anyone willing to risk his life for his country I wouldn't consider weak."

Drew was so upset he was shaking. "He dated my daughter without my permission! They eloped! What did he ever do for her?"

A word popped into David's head. "Do? You mean—*deprive!* Why did he deprive you of your daughter? You considered it a marriage where love was taken from you, not a marriage where two people loved each other."

"He had no ambition!"

David almost laughed. "Yes, he did! All he ever wanted, the only thing, his sole ambition, was to make your daughter happy. It's too bad you never had a chance to see that...to realize what they meant to each other."

"I invited them to my house many times."

"No. You invited mom. There's a difference. How often did you visit us? I can't think of once. Not one time."

"So, it's my fault. I'm responsible, is that it?"

Drew was becoming defensive and David could sense it.

"I'm not saying it's your fault," said David. "No one's responsible. Not one person anyway. We all are. We're guilty of neglect, and if you can't see that, I'm sorry. Dad should have tried to patch things up. He even said so himself. But he kept putting it off, putting it off until it was too late. To this day I don't think he holds a grudge against you. Mark, maybe. But not you."

A door opened and the man who escorted David to the work studio stepped inside. "Everything all right, Mr. Treshler? I heard you two arguing. You want me to see him to his truck?"

"No, Ben. We're okay. A slight disagreement."

"Sorry to bother you, sir." Just before he shut the door, Ben stared at David with a look of contempt.

After the interruption, neither Drew nor his grandson knew what to say. They had reached an impasse, with little hope of reconciliation.

Finally, in a less adversarial tone, David said, "For just a second, forget about me. And forget about my father. There's something you're losing sight of. We were all privileged to know your daughter. We all lost something when she died, but we can gain a part of it back by remembering who she was."

"Leave her out of this. If she'd married anyone else, she'd still be alive."

"How? She died of cancer!"

Drew raised his voice, "It could have been detected through regular checkups."

"Every six months she saw a doctor. Every six months! She had pancreatic cancer. It was in her blood!"

"Your father didn't do enough!" Drew was practically shouting. "There were clinics, places where he could have taken her, places where she could've gotten better treatment. Cleveland Clinic. Mayo Clinic. Not a county hospital."

David tried to control his anger, but failed. He pounded his fist on the workbench. "Don't blame him! It was her choice. She didn't want to go anywhere else. What about you? If anyone could afford clinics…"

"I wasn't here when she was diagnosed. I was out of the country."

"Does that mean it was your fault? Hell no! It was just the way it was."

The room was heavily charged. Drew turned his back and lowered his head.

David was mad at himself for coming here. He took a deep breath and exhaled, trying to ease the tension. "Sorry. I…I didn't mean to upset you."

Turning, Drew said, "Was it you who sent the reporter to see Mark?"

"What reporter?"

"The young lady. This morning."

"No. I had nothing to do with it."

"Don't lie to me."

"I said, I had nothing to do with it. Why do you ask?"

"Because we've been talking about the exact same things."

"Like what?"

"Lake Russell. Fleet Merchant. It's almost like the two conversations were scripted."

"Coincidence." David put his hand on the sketchpad. He was ready to leave, but something held him back. "I want you to look at something." He held out the sketchpad. "Here. Take it. Come on. Take it."

His grandfather reached out reluctantly, shaking his head.

"Open it," said David. "Fourth page. Who do you see?"

Drew opened the sketchpad and was immediately taken by the renderings of people and places, all done in colored pencil and charcoal.

"That's you," said David. "The next page…grandma."

Drew turned the page and something caught in his throat. "What's the point? I know how talented she was. Every day I see it. In my office, the library, dining room. I have several of her paintings."

"You do?"

Drew stared at David. "Yes."

"Keep looking. Describe what you see, the artist, anything that comes to mind."

Growing more puzzled, Drew leafed through the pages. "What do you want me to say? She had an amazing gift. Caricatures, serious paintings, portraits, still lifes. Depth, contrast, detail, lightness, shade. It's all here."

"What does that tell you about her?"

Again, Drew had a puzzled look on his face. "Why?"

"Just humor me."

"She enjoyed life. Had spirit...a vitality that translated to canvas. She could capture a moment, a setting perfectly. Obviously, she loved people. Loved her family very much, especially her mother. I never understood how she could turn a simple stroke of the brush into such beauty. It's a talent, I'm afraid to say, she didn't inherit from me."

Drew continued to turn the pages. His eyes grew softer, almost reverential in his appreciation of the artist. Instead of the contempt he'd shown just moments ago, his eyes glowed with rapture as he discovered sketch after sketch. He became lost in the moment, immersed in the style and subject matter, and also by the humor and multiplicity of feelings they inspired—

Cinders—with her long drooping tongue. Of course, dogs don't laugh, but Cinders was laughing. The splendid Victorian house where the Macklins grew up. Caricatures of old cartoon characters—Mickey, Goofy, Betty Boop, Koko, the clown—doing a high wire act in a circus.

A view of the Eiffel Tower in Paris, made it look as if Paul Klee, the Swiss artist, had painted it. A more realistic depiction of a teenage boy sitting on a dock, fishing, straw hat on his head, pant legs rolled up, feet dangling in the water—David. Done in the style of Norman Rockwell.

A scene from the Wizard of Oz. Going down the yellow brick road. Caddo was the Cowardly Lion, Richard the Tinman, David the Scarecrow, Eileen was Dorothy, and either Cinders or Roscoe did a stand-in for Toto. The range of talent was extraordinary, the skill amazing. The artist displayed a rare combination of style, ability, imagination, and interest.

And Drew was responding to it.

"Is that it?" asked David.

"I'm sorry." Shaken, Drew closed the pad. "What was the question?"

"The drawings. I was wondering what your impression was."

"Remarkable. I've seen a lot of her sketches, but I don't remember any of these." Drew handed the sketchpad back.

David opened it, turned to a specific page, and carefully ripped it out.

"Wait! What are you doing?" cried Drew.

"Here." David offered the torn page.

Drew was confused, filled with conflicting emotions.

"Here. Take it," David insisted. "She'd want you to have it."

"I don't know what to say." Drew looked at it. It was a picture of a woman in a long flowing sundress, standing in a field of flowers, one hand on her hip, the other on a sunbonnet. She was facing the viewer and smiling. It was Dora, his daughter. Her expression, the way the portrait was presented, sucked Drew's breath away. He was genuinely touched. "Thank you. I..a..." He had trouble speaking. He was fighting back the tears. "I'll have it framed." He pointed at the sketchpad, choking on emotion. "Where...where did you find it? Was it lost?"

"No. Maybe we're talking about two different people. Whose sketches do you think these are?"

"Dora's, of course. "

"No. Try your granddaughter's." David waited for a reaction. It was slow in coming. "You know," said David, "the really sad thing is, is how much Eileen is like her mother. The way she looks, her sense of humor, the talent she has, but never uses...because it's too painful. The drawings, the sketches—they're the only ones she's ever done. Hard to tell these from your daughter's."

"I had no idea..."

"It surprises me, too. More than I care to think. Sometimes when Elly plays the piano, I'll see mom sitting there and damned if I don't feel...I don't know...not as *empty* as I used to. That's what you've been missing—a granddaughter. "

David couldn't continue. Too many memories, too many feelings had surfaced. It wasn't maudlin sentimentality, but a true sense of love for his family that made him say what he did. He eased from the workbench and walked to the door, afraid to look at his grandfather. When he did, he saw Drew's face buried in his hands.

David knew it was cold thing to say, but he had to say it.

"Just tell Mark to leave us alone."

Chapter 36

Music didn't do much for Richard Macklin any more. He listened, but the deep stirrings once generated by jazz, classical, and rock n' roll now left him hollow, with a vacuum of feelings. His passion came from his wife's passion and died when she passed away.

He kept the radio tuned to a local station that played rock n' roll oldies, songs with lyrics he could still remember. As the Rolling Stones sang *Gimme Shelter,* "*Ooo, I want to fade away...*" he sang along not because he was moved by the music, but because he was tired, reacting to the mild euphoria created by the Vicodin. Singing kept him awake. Twice he almost pulled off to the side of the road, but he was almost home. After the Stones ended their rhapsody about "*stormy weather*" a voice cut in—

"This is your meteorologist, Rollie Peterson. Today's forecast, brought to you by Farmers First State Bank, calls for sunny skies and temperatures…"

Click.

Richard turned the radio off. As he pulled into the driveway, he saw two young women with mops and brooms hop into the back of a white van parked by the hen house. Halfway down the driveway the van and Jeep stopped side by side, pointing in opposite directions.

"Are you…"—the driver glanced at a piece of paper—"Mr. Macklin?"

Richard nodded.

"Your son wanted me to mail this, but if you don't mind, it'll save me the trouble."

"Mail what?"

"The bill—for cleaning the hen house. Here. Sign at the bottom. The yellow copy is yours."

A clipboard was handed from window to window.

Richard looked at the bill. "I didn't okay this. Why so much?"

"Your son said he was paying for it. Two hours of work and three people? That's cheap. And we have to get rid of eighteen bags of dead chickens."

Richard dropped the clipboard, hit the gas pedal, and the Jeep shot forward.

"Hey, where you goin'?"

Within seconds, Richard was standing in the doorway of the

chicken coop, staring inside, scowling angrily.

Bo came running up, holding the clipboard. "What? You didn't know? Don't you own this place?"

Richard wasn't listening. He kept staring in disbelief as a few chickens clucked. The hatchery was pretty much deserted, except for a handful of hens in a place that a few years ago housed seven hundred hatchlings and fryers.

Bo handed him the clipboard. "Sign at the bottom where the **X** is." Richard quietly scribbled his name and handed the clipboard back.

"If you don't mind me sayin'," said Bo, "I'd put a lock on the door if I were you."

Richard didn't say a word. He just walked away in a daze.

Bo called out, "You wouldn't reconsider and write me a check right now, would you?" When he saw the look on Richard's face, he knew he was pushing his luck. "Nah, suppose not. Thanks for your business." He waited a moment and said, "Well, I guess what happened in the coop proves it."

Richard stopped and turned. "Proves what?"

"This place...they say it's cursed." Bo tipped his cap, waved goodbye, and went on his merry way.

Richard watched in disgust as the van pulled out of the driveway.

He was ready for a nap, but didn't feel like crawling into bed. Beds were for serious sleep. Naps, for recharging the battery. This past week, however, he approached sleep with a certain amount of anxiety. He didn't want to face up to the fact that his dreams were unlike any he'd had before and were often drawn from experiences he wanted to forget.

Cursed?

For him, sleep was indeed a curse.

Right now the need outweighed everything else. He ached for sleep.

Instead of entering the house, he found a chaise longue chair lying inside the barn. He placed it by the door. Unfolded it. Stretched out. Relaxed. Laid his head back. And could feel the lure of slumber begin to take hold. The moment he closed his eyes he heard a distant clap of thunder. Sedated by Vicodin, captivated by thunder, he no longer fought the urge.

Seconds later, he was sound asleep.

* * *

It wasn't hunting season. Far from it. Caddo wasn't sure what the punishment would be if caught. A fine probably. A few days in jail.

Hunting out of season in Ohio was a pretty serious offense.

Without a license it was downright criminal. But right now that was the least of his concerns. His weapon of choice was bow and arrow, handmade by a Navajo and bought from a catalogue selling authentic Indian crafts. With a weapon in his hands, Caddo was transformed—no longer a quiet, unassuming farmhand, but a tracker, killer of game. And as most hunters know, during dry seasons animals tend to gather where there's water. That's why he chose the river for his stalking ground. Given enough time, he knew he would find a beaver or muskrat nesting along the shallows of Little Bass River, or better yet, a deer feeding on leaves and acorns in the woods nearby. He also knew if he were to have any success that evening, he had to ignore the law.

Standing on the riverbank with both spaniels at his side, he watched as a blanket of dark clouds began to form. The impression was both immediate and troubling. For one thing, according to recent radio broadcasts, the forecast called for sunny skies, not rain. Worse yet, the weather conditions and wreckage of the bridge reminded him of another bridge deep in the jungles of Southeast Asia near the Cambodian border once used by the North Vietnamese as a main supply route for food, supplies, and troops—a bridge American forces regarded as a strategic target. It was almost forty years ago when he and ten others were flown in behind enemy lines to blow up the bridge. The next day when a monsoon struck, he realized he had a special gift, something usually associated with a shaman, believer of *jawonio*, but by no means was he a shaman. Now he knew he had to exercise that gift again. This time he had to summon it, will it into being. That was the problem. The question was how.

Half a click downriver he wandered, looking for animal tracks. The storm was approaching from the northwest, closing fast. That was the thing about living in the country. A storm can't sneak up on you like it can in the city. And the clouds were moving southeasterly at an accelerated pace—so much so, they seemed to be driven by some perverse force of nature. He could feel a change in temperature. It was ten degrees cooler than it was just moments ago.

Once he crossed a cornfield, Caddo reached a thicket of trees along the north side of the river. It was just as nature preserved it— untouched by man, filled with hundred-year-old trees. He was very much at home in his element, alone with two spaniels and creatures living in the wild.

Here he conducted his search. He was looking for an animal to be sacrificed later as part of a ritual. As he entered the woods, the air began to thicken and churn with the wind. The storm appeared to come out of nowhere. He didn't know what to do. The dogs stood at his side, anxiously waiting for him to make a move. Trees were bending and branches swaying while the dark clouds kept rolling in. He could tell by the wind the worst was yet to come. Exposed to the elements, he was trapped with nowhere to go.

Suddenly, lightning struck a tree. Thunder exploded with a deafening boom. A branch snapped, shuddering violently, and came crashing down at his feet. He barely had time to recover when there was another flash of lightening, followed by a crack of thunder. The lightning smote the treetops with a blinding brilliance. He could feel the power of it as it struck a second tree. He was knocked backwards on impact. The smell tinged the air like acrid bolts of electricity.

Roscoe and Cinders panicked and went running through the woods, howling. Caddo knew this was no chance occurrence. Although he hadn't slept much or eaten in days, he was convinced of one thing—

He was under attack.

Chapter 37

Elly was sitting in her Jeep, watching the lightning when the first raindrops pattered against the windshield. She gathered a stack of papers from the passenger seat, opened the door, and rushed across the driveway into the lower barn, running hunched over to keep the papers from getting wet. Just as she made it, the rain started coming down in buckets.

She placed the papers on a workbench and walked over to the chaise longue where her father was sleeping. She watched him fidgeting in the chair and noticed for every roll of thunder he would react with a slight shake of the head or twist of the shoulders. His eyes twitched, rolling in their sockets, and cheeks puffed lightly while he made a series of grumbling sounds, sort of like a dog barking in its sleep.

Outside, lightning struck, followed by thunder. The rain was coming down hard and heavy, beating against the roof.

Roscoe and Cinders came sprinting into the barn, drenched. Starting from the neck down, they gave their bodies a lusty shake, shedding water as affectively as a spin cycle in a washing machine. Once they saw Elly, their cropped tails started jiggling.

"Where have you two been?" she whispered. A mere touch of her hand sent them shaking into fits of convulsive joy. "Huh? Where have you been?"

She turned at the sound of a sleep-uttered groan and studied her father. As a trained veterinarian, she'd seen hundreds of animals asleep and could tell from their breathing and subtlety of movements whether they were having a good dream or a bad one. From the looks of it, Richard was having a bad dream. Again and again his body trembled as though he were having a seizure or spasm attack. He uttered a stifled scream, then mumbled, "No, no..." his cheeks puffing out, then slackening.

Elly nudged his shoulder. "Dad, wake up. Wake up."

He stirred like a bear from hibernation.

She leaned over him and shook her hair playfully, letting droplets of water fall on his face. "Rise and shine, soldier."

He sat up and messaged his neck, then looked around and blinked, as if he had no idea where he was. "Um. Oh, boy. I was out cold."

Elly touched his cheek. "How's your shoulder? What did the

doctor say?"

"I'm okay."

"Dad..."

He shrugged it off. "I'm okay. Don't worry about me."

"You need to get more rest."

Just then she realized the rain had stopped. No thunder. No lightning.

What an eerie coincidence, she thought to herself.

* * *

Caddo couldn't believe it. The last thing he remembered seeing were bolts of lightning coming together, hitting the base of a tree, and the trunk falling straight towards him. Once he opened his eyes, he realized why he hadn't been crushed. The upper part of the trunk had collapsed against a young oak, acting as a brace against the fall. Sprawled on his back, soaked with rain, he glanced at the tree leaning above him. The base was teetering. A patch of bark was still smoldering where the lightning had struck. Branches extended like gnarled appendages, serving to buoy the weight of the tree. Wood was splintering, making buckling sounds, cracking as the trunk slipped down closer inch by inch. Caddo rolled to his left. The trunk gave way, thumping heavily against the ground, limbs recoiling from the force of the fall, mud splattering as it hit. Five feet closer or three seconds earlier, he would have been dead, squashed like a bug. He rolled to his knees, panting—clothes, hair, and face covered in rain. He scraped the mud from his hands, reached down, picked up his bow and was about to walk away when, somewhere above to his right, he heard a flock of crows cawing. With a thrust of wings, they leapt into the air. He watched as they swooped above the treetops, flapping wildly, as if spooked.

A sudden change of wind made him aware of an odor. Something disgusting was rotting and judging from the smell, it had to be a dead animal at least the size of an adult deer. Smaller animals wouldn't have the same intensity. Based on that alone, a decaying body had to be close by. A quick search of the underbrush came up empty. He raised his sight lines and did a fast sweep with his eyes and something caught his attention. It was almost subliminal in a way. It seemed out of place. It wasn't a broken tree limb, dead tree, or anything like that. What he saw wasn't part of the forest. He turned and looked again and saw nothing of any distinguishing size, shape, or color. He was absolutely certain he saw something and this time with the keen eye of a hunter he scanned the upper part of the trees. And there it was—a flash of orange hidden among the foliage. A piece of clothing was clinging to a branch where the trunk had split. As he walked closer, he could see something fleshy and pale next to it. Thirty feet in the air, it was hard to make out the shape until he stood at the base of the tree and looked up.

He'd seen death hundreds of times, both as a soldier and patient, spending weeks in hospitals on two different occasions, and no matter how conditioned he thought he was to death, he was never immune to the physical and psychological side effects of it. He felt a gag reflex in his throat. After repeated gasps, he fought to keep it down.

A friend and working companion was stuck *to* a tree—among a swarm of insects. One arm was curled around his neck, the other dangled loose from his shoulder. Blood was clotted to the branches below. He was wearing an orange T-shirt with OSU written across the front. It was Wilfredo Pinoza, the missing person. His corpse was barely recognizable. The stub of a broken branch protruded from his belly. He was impaled. It looked as if he'd been thrown against the tree. The absence of blood, plus a week of exposure and decomposition left him jaundiced, his skin a sickly yellowish-brown, the flesh sagging from his face. It was the expression, however, that alarmed Caddo the most, an expression of a man who died not from any wound to his body, but from sheer, extreme fright. Caddo also realized something else. The position of the body, the arms and legs, and how Freddie was impaled—he'd seen once before during a patrol in Vietnam when he and fellow platoon members saw the jaundiced body of a soldier who'd been tortured and hung up in a tree as a warning to other American soldiers. The image, both then and now, was eerily and gruesomely the same, so much so he knew it couldn't be coincidence.

Chapter 38

"Lunch is ready."

Cinders and Roscoe were already munching on dog food.

Elly placed two bowls of clam chowder on the kitchen table alongside ham and cheese sandwiches. Richard shut off the faucet in his bathroom, entered the kitchen a few seconds later, wringing his hands, and sat down.

Elly took a nibble of her sandwich, rinsed it down with coffee, and watched her father sip a spoonful of soup. His dark eyes were staring at nothing from a drained, expressionless face.

After pouring more cream into her coffee, she remarked, "I hate to keep bringing this up, Dad, but you're not getting enough sleep."

"Look that bad, do I?"

"No, just..."

Richard glanced up from his bowl, eyes glazed, a bit unfocused.

"...Tired," she said. "Maybe you have a sleep disorder and don't know it." She stopped eating and put both elbows on the table. "How much sleep do you get?"

"Don't need much."

"Do you sleep without interruption?"

"What do you mean?"

"Do you sleep from the moment you go to bed until morning, or do you wake up periodically?"

"Mostly until morning."

"Five, six hours? How long?"

"About six. Why?"

"I care about your health."

"Me too."

They ate in silence until Elly brought the subject up again. "You've been dreaming a lot lately, haven't you?"

Richard ate a spoonful of chowder and followed it with a bite of sandwich, answering with a nod.

"The dream you had earlier," said Elly, "what was it about?"

He stopped chewing. "Earlier?"

"Yeah. When you were sleeping in the barn, you were dreaming. I watched you. You *were* dreaming, weren't you?"

"I guess so."

"Is it something you care to talk about?"

"Not really. More like something I'd like to forget." He yawned and sipped another spoonful of soup.

He seemed lethargic, slow. He had a distant look in his eyes.

"I think you should talk about it," said Elly.

"Why?"

"Because I think it's important."

"Important how?"

She suspected his grogginess wasn't from the lack of sleep. "I don't know," she replied. "Maybe there's a connection to how you feel. If there's a problem, I'd like to help."

"Yeah, well...you can't change a person's past."

Leaning across the table, she placed a hand over his. "The dream. When I watched you, you were talking in your sleep. Mumbling. You kept saying, 'No, no,'"

He pulled his hand away and took a bite of ham and cheese.

"Was it about the farm?" she asked.

He shook his head.

"Mom?"

He shook it again.

"If you remember, then tell me."

He put the sandwich down and stared at the plate, his eyes liquid gray marbles, lifeless, cold. "For some reason I've been dreaming about the war."

"For how long?"

He shrugged. "Not long."

"A couple of weeks, months, days...?"

"A week. Maybe less."

"How often did you dream about it before that?"

"I didn't."

Elly slid to the edge of her seat. "Was it about a specific place? A specific thing?"

He didn't react. There was something about his face that suggested he knew exactly what it was.

"Where?" she asked.

"Vietnam. Near Laos."

"During combat?"

He hesitated and nodded again.

"Can you describe what happened?"

"Describe it?"

"What I'm asking is, was it like most dreams? Or realistic?"

"Oh, it was real all right. You can't imagine something like that." Richard was trying to come to grips with it, whatever it was. Induced by drugs or a sense of psychological release, he was more candid than usual. "We were given orders to blow up a bridge behind enemy lines. Flew in during the night. Eleven men. Special Forces. Two helicopters. No one expected a monsoon the next day. Lucky for us it rained as hard as it did. The mission would have been suicide if it hadn't."

"That's what the dream was about? A bridge?"

He nodded.

"What happened to it?"

"We blew it up."

"Was it raining?"

"No."

"So the rain came *after* you blew it up?"

"Yes."

She looked out the window and saw a gray patch of clouds drifting away. "Did you ever dream about the bridge before? Blowing it up I mean?"

He sighed.

Elly leaned closer and looked into his eyes. "You did, didn't you? When?"

He had to think about it. "Earlier in the week."

"What day?"

"I don't know. Five, six days ago."

"Sunday night?"

"Maybe. Yeah, it mighta been Sunday."

A thought suddenly struck her. Sunday night was the night the railroad bridge collapsed into the river. "What else have you been dreaming about?"

A car pulled up on the driveway. They could see an old dust-gray two-door Buick through the kitchen window.

Richard turned his head to look. Cinders and Roscoe barked, ran to the kitchen door, and put their front paws up on the screen, wagging their tails.

Elly reached out and squeezed Richard's hand. "What else?"

A car door opened, then closed. Richard became distracted. She was beginning to think he was avoiding eye contact.

Both dogs went racing down the hall, barking.

Elly squeezed his hand harder. "Mom—ever dream about her? Look at me! Do you ever dream about Mom?"

He didn't speak. Whatever delusions he had, whether he was drugged, strung out on barbiturates, painkillers, or tired, the look on his face confirmed her suspicion, that he was taking some form of mood-altering medication.

"How often?" she asked.

The front doorbell rang.

Elly was growing impatient. "I need to know."

"Every night," he whispered.
"For how long?"
He slid the chair back and stood up.
The doorbell rang again.
"How long?" she repeated.
He muttered something. She thought she heard him say, "A week."
"Mom's been visiting you...in a dream?"
His body sagged at the shoulders.
"For a week?"
Once more he didn't speak. He had a nervous twitch in his eye. He rubbed the back of his neck. His hand was shaking.
"That's why you're reading that book, isn't it?" Elly was sorry as soon as she said it. She could see him tense up, like she'd touched a nerve. The subject, it appeared, was too sensitive. She didn't have the heart to question him anymore. Besides, she had a hard time convincing herself such a thing existed.
Richard walked down the hall like a condemned man to his execution. He opened the front door. Standing on the porch step was Ryan Cooper, manager of the grain elevators. Elly didn't have to hear the conversation to know the gist of it. It concerned the shutdown of the operations, the resignation of the employees, Cooper the last to quit. Their body language said it all. He handed over a ring of keys and the two men shook hands.
It was sad to see.
Elly turned and for the first time noticed a note sitting on the kitchen counter—

David,
Call me. It's important.
Coach K

She heard the front door close.
Richard followed Cooper down the front steps.
A few minutes later, two gray sedans pulled up on the driveway. Five men, wearing dark blue suits, got out, waited for Cooper to leave, then approached Richard. One of them flashed a badge. The others stared at him as if he were a criminal.

Chapter 39

Richard climbed into the back seat of a sedan at the request of the lead investigator for the Ohio Bureau of Investigation, a man named Kenneth Frost. Agent Frost and his top assistant who he introduced as Brian then entered the front seat and sat down while two of the three remaining agents separated to inspect the property. The third agent jumped into a sedan and drove away.

Richard heard a click as the doors locked. "I did this the other day, you know. I gave a statement to the Bertram County Sheriff's Department."

Agent Frost put his glasses on, arranged a few pages of notes on his clipboard, and turned sideways to begin the questioning. "A lot has happened since then, Mr. Macklin. We'd like to go over it again."

"Fine. Go ahead."

"According to our records, you were decorated twice during the Vietnam war. Captain, Special Forces. Were up for review for a higher rank. Served three consecutive tours of duty in combat intelligence, then came home. Very commendable."

"I had to go. I was drafted…right after college."

"Just the same, your service record is quite impressive."

"We're not here to discuss my service record."

Agent Frost peered over the rim of his glasses. "Like I said, all we want to do is ask a few questions. Let me be the judge as to what's relevant and what's not." He paused to refer to his notes. "Last Sunday, could you explain what you were doing that night?"

"Sitting at my computer, arranging my budget for next month. I went to bed about ten-thirty as I do every night. Slept 'til morning."

"Can anyone back you up on that?" said Brian.

"'Fraid not. Unless my dogs count."

Agent Frost pulled a pen from his pocket and wrote something down. "Could you tell us a little more about your military background?"

"Isn't it on that sheet you have there?"

"Just answer the question," said the other agent, Brian.

Out of the corner of his eye, Richard watched an agent inspect the lower barn. Elly walked up to him and started talking.

Brian said impatiently, "Our time is limited, Mr. Macklin."

Richard had to think about the question. "Background? I was trained in communications at Fort Gordon. Transferred to Fort Holabird, then Fort Stewart. Small arms, explosives, combat. Started out with a little training as a MP. Kicked around a lot. What else do you want to know?"

Agent Frost resumed, "Very extensive. You were on a fast track to Colonel. Did you ever have training as a specialist in engineering, electrical energy, that sort of thing, aside from explosives?"

"Some engineering. Enough to pull a pin on a grenade."

"Any technology that's not on our records?" asked Brian.

"No, sir."

"Tuesday night, April the 23rd," continued Agent Frost, "after nine pm, what were you doing?"

"The truth?"

"No, we want you to lie," said Brian.

Richard looked at both men, then directed his answer at Agent Frost. "Unfortunately, I had a little too much to drink. I went to bed early. My daughter stayed with me that night. She's my alibi if you need one."

"We don't need an alibi," replied Brian. "You do."

Richard let the remark pass. He waited and said quietly, "What exactly am I accused of?"

"Nobody's accusing you of anything," assured Agent Frost. "As I told you earlier, we don't have much to go on. Here." He reached down, grabbed a newspaper. Referring to the front page, he said, "Have you seen this?"

Richard looked at the photographs. First, of the fallen bridge. Next, the crumpled wrecks of two automobiles. He opened the paper to a second page and saw a picture of his son in uniform with a caption beneath, stating how David had 'miraculously walked away' with only a minor concussion.

"Did you discuss the accident with your son?" said agent Frost.

"Yes."

"What did he say?"

"Not a lot. He doesn't remember much."

"Doesn't remember?" exclaimed Brian. "Come on!"

Agent Frost leaned over the seat, folded a corner of the paper and pointed to the front page. "Look at it, Mr. Macklin! He walked away from *that!*"

Richard stared at the photograph. "Sorry. there's not much to say."

"It would help if you try."

"Didn't the Sheriff's Department file an accident report?"

"Yes. But sometimes details can be overlooked."

Richard handed the newspaper back. "Wish I could help, but I can't."

"Did your son say anything about the cab driver?"

"Only that he died."

"Anything else?"

"No."

"You sure?" said Brian.

Richard nodded. "Yes, I'm sure."

Agent Frost removed his glasses and indicated somewhere up the road. "The accident occurred about a mile from here. A sound like that travels far. Did you hear anything?"

"Or did you have too much to drink?" asked Brian.

Richard darted a look at Brian and said calmly, "No. My daughter stayed with me that night as well. She didn't hear anything either."

Agent Frost was mildly surprised. "But she was the first to visit your son at the hospital. How did she know he was there?"

Richard glanced to his left, at the agent talking to Elly. "She got a call from somebody at the hospital. I didn't know about the accident until my son mentioned it later."

"Is your son available for us to talk to?" asked Brian.

"At this moment I don't know where he is."

Agent Frost referred to his notes again. "Tell me about Mr. Walker. I understand you two served in Vietnam together."

"All three tours. Saved each other's hide many a time."

"You get to know somebody pretty well, fighting side by side."

"Yes, you do."

Agent Frost flipped to a page in his clipboard. "Sergeant Caddo M. Walker, Company B, 502nd Infantry Battalion, Special Forces. Also decorated twice. Heroism beyond the call of duty. Wounded in Combat. Purple Heart. Nicknamed Silent K. Why is that?"

"Paid killers. That's what we were. Paid assassins. Caddo did it a little quieter than everybody else."

"Silent K—Silent Killer," Brian commented.

Richard grinned. "There's hope for you yet."

Agent Frost ignored the animosity between the two. "Regardless of what we know, with respect to your friend, how would you characterize Mr. Walker?"

"How much time you got?"

"Cut the bullshit!" grumbled Brian. "Just answer the goddamn question!"

Agent Frost tried to be a steadying influence. "Take as much time as you need, Mr. Macklin."

"Um, I'd say tough. Loyal. A bit sensitive at times. Intelligent. Quiet. A good friend."

"Is he violent?"

"Not at all."

"Have a temper?"

"Only when he's crossed."

Agent Frost pulled a sheet of paper from his clipboard and held it up. "Are you aware Mr. Walker has an arrest record? Jailed twice for being drunk and disorderly. Again for possession of marijuana."

"That was a long time ago. Before he worked for me."

Brian added, "Did you know he almost did time for manslaughter?"

"You don't *almost do time* for anything. Either you do or you don't. He told me about a situation once where he had to defend himself. A back alley brawl somewhere. Behind a bar. Two men attacked him. One of them didn't walk away. If that's what you're referring to, yes, I know."

Agent Frost jotted down more notes. "What can you tell me about his training as a soldier?"

"Top notch. There's none better. He shoulda been captain, not me."

"We're referring to explosives," informed Brian. "The engineering aspects of war."

"Engineering aspects of war? Never heard a term like that."

"Technology," said Agent Frost. "Electrical engineering, incendiary devices, bombs, explosives, things of that nature."

"Caddo? He can barely put a plug in a wall socket. Technology he hates. Grit, dirt—he loves that."

"What about chemical weapons?"

"Now you're reaching. Where are you guys going with this stuff anyway?"

"We're asking the questions," said Brian, testily. "Not you."

"Listen, pal," Richard replied, "this is my property. Guilt, suspicion—there's none of that here. If you're trying to insinuate that Caddo or I have any involvement with what's going on, forget it. Let me out of this car right now!"

Brian rose from his seat. "Who in the hell do you think you are?"

Agent Frost, in trying to restrain him, put a hand on Brian's shoulder. "Easy, Brian. Go wait outside."

Nostrils flaring, Brian pushed the door open and got out.

Agent Frost turned with an apologetic look on his face. "Sorry about that."

"Where'd you recruit that guy?" Richard wondered. "San Quentin?"

"I admit he's a bit overbearing at times."

"You know what surprises me about all this? I would expect the FBI or Federal Government to have files on soldiers like us, but not a state agency."

"Ohio's one of the more progressive states when it comes to matters of security. Terrorism exits everywhere these days. Networking is the future of our business."

"To be honest, I've never heard of the Ohio Bureau of Investigation until a few days ago."

"Most people haven't." Agent Frost rubbed his chin, thinking. "I'll tell you what. Let's cut to the chase. One simple question. What do you suppose we're dealing with here?"

Richard looked out both windows, left and right, down at the floor, sighed, then back at Agent Frost. "Damned if I know. How about you?"

Agent Frost mimicked him move for move and replied, "That makes two of us."

Chapter 40

The surveillance team parked on the shoulder of the road in an unmarked van similar to one used by a television crew when transmitting a live newscast. Three satellite dishes, a camera, and a retractable antennae protruded from the roof.

The driver, a woman in her mid-thirties wearing a blue uniform, looked at the one-floor farmhouse nearby with its dingy white aluminum siding and front porch cluttered with junk and said, "I wonder what the neighbors will think."

Her partner, a man in his late forties, attired in matching uniform, sporting a mustache and goatee, unbuckled his seat belt, unlatched the door to the rear compartment, and muttered, "Quit worrying. Give me a few seconds." He ducked through the latch-door and left it open.

She could hear switches clicking on in the back of the van, the hum of a generator, antennae rising from the roof as a reflection from a bank of monitors and overhead light spilled into the cabin. They were in the process of testing various pieces of equipment when a cell phone rang.

The driver picked it up from the center console. "This is Liz." She listened, gave directions, hung up, sat up straight, and ran down a checklist of procedures much like a pilot would in preparation for takeoff. Two minutes later, she perked up. "Pete, we have a visitor."

"The agent from the Bureau?"

"No. Some old codger. Looks like a Homer. Homer McFudd. Must be the guy who owns the house over there."

Shuffling towards the van in overalls, skinny and withered, with barely a thread of hair on his head, was a sharp-jawed, tight-lipped farmer with beady eyes that looked perpetually angry. He seemed to be chewing on his tongue as he walked. Liz didn't bother getting out of the van. She waited for the old codger to come to her. Which took forever. Finally, she rolled the window down as he shuffled to the driver's door.

"Hi, there," said Liz.

"What'cha doing on my property?" the farmer squawked.

"Sorry. This is a county road."

"No, ma'm. This here is *my* road."

"Isn't this County Road 156?"

"No, ma'm. This here is *my* road."

"And your name is…?"

"Don't matter who I am. Who are *you*?"

"Maybe this will help." Liz pulled an identification card from the center console and held it up for him to see.

He squinted…stretched his skinny, little neck. "Don't have my glasses. What's that supposed to be?"

"Can you read?"

He made two fists and shook them. "Course I can read. What is it?"

"My I.D. Gives me permission to park here."

"Like flying hog shit, it does!"

Liz decided enough was enough. "Okay, buddy, I tried to be nice. This is a state-run operation. Your property is being used temporarily by the state of Ohio, okay? Now go back to your house and stay there."

"State-run, is it?" The farmer leaned to the side and twisted his puny neck around. "What do you have back there?"

"Hey! We're a licensed state-agency on assignment, okay. Our job is security. We're here to protect you."

"Get this contraption outta here!"

The old man turned as a gray sedan came speeding down the road toward them. The driver of the oncoming car had the window down as he drew alongside the van. He was chewing on a wad of gum, working it hard. "Hi. You must be Liz. I'm Agent Roy Segedi. Who's your friend?"

"Hi, Roy. This…"

"This here is *my* road!" wailed the old farmer. "I want all of you people gone! Outta here!"

"Hold on, old timer! Don't bust a blood vessel."

"I'll bust you, you good for nothin'! Don't you city people respect what ain't yours! This here is my road. My land, by God! And you pieces of flyin' hog shit better be leavin', you hear!"

"No reason to get excited, old fella," said Roy.

"Excited?" snapped the farmer. "Where were you last night when Lester got killed?"

"Lester?" said Segedi.

"My horse. Something attacked it. Chewed it to pieces. Spilt blood all over the barn. I shot it. Didn't even slow it down. That deputy— he was no help neither. I want you people off my property!"

"This *thing* that attacked Lester," said Segedi, "did you see it?"

"See it? With all that fog?" replied the farmer. "*Sheee-it!*" The mere thought seemed to trigger his anger. "Now pack up and git outta here!"

Pete the technician unlocked the swinging doors to the back of the van and walked forward. "I'll take care of this." Without missing a step, he took the old man by the arm and kept walking. "Okay, Homer. You're coming with me."

"Le'me go!" the old codger wailed. "Le'me go!" As he left, squirming and pitching a fit, he let loose a tirade of obscenities only a mean-spirited old farmer could vent.

Shaking his head, Agent Segedi got out of his car. "Nice old fella. Reminds me of an uncle of mine. Looks like you picked a good spot. How long before you're set up?"

"Two hours at least," said Liz. "We're getting a late start because of the cameras. Other than that, we'll be ready. How many headsets do you need?"

"Five or six. Better make it six."

When Liz stepped out of the van, her six-foot-four frame towered over him.

"Man, you're tall!" Roy exclaimed. "You play basketball?"

"Back in the day." Smiling, she sang two bars of *'Hail, hail! to Michigan!'*

They walked to the rear of the van where Liz opened the swinging doors. Inside, it looked like Space Command Headquarters at NASA with monitors, computer screens, and control panels everywhere and two high-backed chairs with metal swing rods bolted to the floor.

"Holy smoke!" cried Roy. "This thing have rocket boosters, too?"

"This *thing*," replied Liz proudly, "can pretty much do anything but fly."

"And I thought surveillance was a hidden camera and microphone."

"Not anymore," said Liz. She pointed at a bank of monitors. "The big screen to your left is a thermal-imaging system. The row of monitors straight ahead are the cameras. They're wireless, self-powered with both solar and battery-operated generators along with an infrared setting we can switch to at night."

"My, oh, my!"

"That's only half of it," said Liz. She went into great detail explaining how the various aspects of the van worked. After five minutes of boring technicalities, which included field tracking systems and satellite dishes, she said, "There isn't much we can't see or hear."

"Hear? Are you serious? You actually listen? To what?"

"The entire valley. We usually concentrate on one fixed location, so it'll be interesting to see how the computer handles such a wide area."

"How can you listen to everything?"

"The computer does it for us. We use audio sensors, 'sound bugs,' ultra-sensitive microphones that can hear a pin drop within a mile or two of the area under surveillance, a *Micro-Electronic-Audio-Projection-System*, or *M.A.P.S.* as we refer to it. It has a sound filtering system that can identify, sort, and..."

"Hold it! Hold it!" cried Roy. He held up his hands. "Just give me six headsets and tell me what to do."

As she explained how the headsets worked, Pete the technician trotted to the rear of the van, shaking his head—

"You should see the inside of that old guy's house. Cats everywhere. Junk all over the floor. And the smell? Whew! By the way his name's not Homer. It's Scootch. Norman Scootch McPhee. And from the smell of it he's been hitting the bottle hard."

"Did you check out the horse?" asked Segedi.

"I did. Blood everywhere. The body was torn in pieces. I told him not to touch anything until our people had a chance to look things over."

"I'll call it in," said Segedi. He gestured to the gadgets inside the van. "Pretty impressive setup, Pete. Is it legal?"

"There's no law against it as far as I know," said Pete. "It's what we do with the information that gets a little tricky. Essentially privacy as we know it is a thing of the past. Imagine the possibilities...what the future will bring. We can listen to any conversation we want. Any time. Anywhere. There isn't a criminal or Third World thug who can hide."

Pete waited for the impact of the statement to sink in, then turned to the agent and said, "What killed that horse worries me. Have any idea what it is?"

"No. Wish I did," replied Segedi, still chewing a wad of gum.

Pete removed his glasses and wiped them on a shirtsleeve. "What exactly are we looking for? Or should I say, what are you expecting?"

Roy laughed weakly. "I was afraid you'd ask me that. The explanation, what little there is, I'll leave to Agent Frost."

"Can't you tell us anything?" said Liz.

"That's just it. There isn't much to tell."

Chapter 41

David was eating a late afternoon brunch in a Mexican restaurant, reading the latest edition of the *Bertram County Sentinel*. On the second page, there he was—mug in hat and uniform.

As he thumbed through the pages, headlines, captions, and phrases kept jumping out at him. Words like—*"unidentified source... mystifies authorities...cause of damage unknown*—no doubt sold a lot of newspapers.

The stories must have created quite a stir because an older couple seated in the next booth kept staring at him and whispering. David was too occupied to notice. Ordinarily, the *Sentinel* was eight pages long, most of it dealing with events or stories involving the university, agricultural news, or the usual stuff of a small town newspaper. Not this week. A special edition had been expanded to ten pages and there was a drastic departure not only in the content but where the news originated. David counted no less than eleven stories or references made to Macklin Farms and the area in question.

Alexa promised a soft, gloves-on approach, but based on the amount of news and the nature of the subject matter, she landed a bare-knuckle uppercut to the chin.

The only real news David didn't know had to with the power outages. In both cases the causes were attributed to a "transformer malfunction" and "electrical surge overloads" estimated at a cost of $107,000. An unnamed source claimed arson was suspected and Midwest Electric was offering a $2,500 reward to anyone giving information leading to an arrest.

The story concerning the slaughter of livestock was very sketchy. No details were given as to what killed them, but according to an unidentified source with the Ohio Bureau of Investigation, tracks were found, considered by many to be those of a bear, which was shocking since no bear had been seen in the area since the late 1800's.

The big news was an announcement of a high-scale development, boat and golf club called *Arcadia Hills*. The project, bordering a manmade lake named Lake Russell, boasted 36 holes of tournament-caliber golf, clubhouse, marina, pool, restaurant, possible casino, and dozens of condominiums and homes at a cost of fifty-two million dollars, the single most ambitious project of its kind ever undertaken in the tri-county area.

The paper closed with two stories on the editorial page—the first about a scandal involving "unethical legislative leaks" and "questionable business practices" that paved the way to the expansion of Lake Russell. The second, from a column called *History Today*, praised the founders of Farmers First State Bank for their "generosity" and "civic responsibility" in helping customers when the stock market crashed on Black Monday, October the 29th, 1929.

No name was mentioned in an eventual takeover by William Treshler who was spared ridicule years after his death. But the writer intimated no one had run the bank more efficiently, fairly and with "more civic pride and care" than its two founders, father and son, Robert and Wil Macklin.

David laughed and slapped the table, "That a girl!"

Considering the paper as a whole, the clout of eleven stories in one edition involving one family had to generate a firestorm of public opinion. And nine of those were clouded in mystery and unknown circumstances.

Eleven stories! In one edition?

David shook his head. Folded the paper. Ate the rest of his enchiladas and chiles relleno. Stepped outside to his truck. Picked up Elly's cell phone. Went down the list of frequently called numbers and dialed.

The phone rang once, twice, an operator picked up, and directed the call to the newsroom.

A man with a deep baritone voice answered, "News desk."

"Alexa Wilde please?"

"I'm sorry. She's not here. Would you like to leave a message?"

"I'll call back later. Thanks."

"May I ask who's calling?"

"David Macklin."

There was a lengthy pause. With measured politeness the man said, "Well, hello, David. I'm the editor, Sam Tully. We met briefly a few years ago at a baseball game. I did a story about you. Do you remember?"

"Yes, sir. I do. It was very kind of you."

"Kind? You were good. Damn good."

David blushed. True or not, it was nice to hear. He anticipated, however, the conversation was about to take a turn in another direction. And it did.

"Say, listen, David, this call, it…a…wouldn't be about today's edition of the newspaper, would it?"

"Possibly."

"I'm assuming you read it. Any comments?"

"Concerning...?"

"Anything."

"Not really."

"I'm a little surprised. After all, the Macklin name comes up a few times. If you don't mind, I'd like to ask you a couple of questions."

"No disrespect, sir, I'd rather talk to Alexa. It's kinda personal."

"At your discretion then. If I keep it off the record?"

The line went quiet.

"Hello. You there, David?"

"I'm here."

Sam dropped all pretenses. All right. Forget that I'm a reporter for a second. Do you have any idea why the power went out twice in one week?"

"No, sir."

"Nothing. No guess? No clue?"

"Sir, if it's okay with you..."

"How about the livestock?" said Sam. "Several were killed, you know. Very strange, the circumstances. Mutilation. Blood all over the place. Any idea what kind of animal would do a thing like that?"

"Sir. I'd rather talk to Alexa. Do you have her number?"

There was a sigh of disappointment. "Sorry. We don't give out personal numbers of the staff. I could have her call you. What's the number there?"

"That's okay," said David. "I don't give out personal numbers either."

He hung up.

A second later Sam was calling his best and most trusted reporter.

After three rings, Alexa answered, "Hi, Sam."

Sam couldn't contain his excitement. "Things are heating up, kiddo. Where are you?"

"In my car. On the way to the gym."

"Guess who just called?"

"Mark Treshler."

"No. The object of your affection. David Macklin."

"Of my what?"

"Be honest. When it comes to objectivity, you've lost it."

"I have not! What did he want?"

"I don't know. He said it was personal. I think it had to do with the articles in today's paper. The phone's been ringing off the hook. Incidentally, Mark Treshler did call. Or his secretary did. It appears you've upset the apple cart..."

"Sam."

"What?"

"I think I'm being followed."

Chapter 42

Agent Frost and three of his associates drove to a remote corner of the valley and parked. All four men clipped battery packs to their belts, switched on the microphones, and inserted the earpieces.

The first thing Agent Frost did was address a concern. "All set, Pete. I understand it may be an hour or two before we're fully operational."

"We ran into a few glitches. We're waiting for the satellite link. And the cameras still have to be set up."

"Any way of speeding things up?"

"I'll try, but everything has to be tested and programmed and that, my friend, takes time."

"Any visuals at all?" asked the agent.

"The one anchored here to the van is operational. The technician responsible for the remote cameras is running late. We'll be good to go soon, definitely before nightfall."

"What about audio?"

"Working on it. The computer's doing a full sweep."

"Make sure you give priority to the Macklin residence."

The line remained silent.

"Pete, did you hear me? Make sure you give priority to the house."

"Uh, that's where we have a slight problem. Just beyond the farmhouse to the park, I'm getting interference."

"Damn," Agent Frost snapped. "A second ago they were glitches. Now interference?"

Pete responded with a bit of an attitude, "Hey, I'm doing everything I can. Give me a while. I'll correct it. While I have you on the line…I still haven't been briefed. I need to know what to look for. The other agent said I should ask you."

Agent Frost didn't know what to say. The entire matter was very embarrassing. An eighteen-year veteran of the FBI and state law enforcement and he had never been so inadequately prepared for an assignment.

"Well…?" said Pete.

"You weren't briefed because there isn't much in the way of background. Are you and your partner carrying weapons?"

Pete gave his partner, Liz, a worried look. "Yeah. We both are."

"Good. Keep them close at all times. All we have to go on is a few sets of tracks...and a bloody mess at the each of the scenes. Whatever it is, it attacks at night."

"So," whispered Pete, "we're dealing with two separate issues. Whoever blew up the bridge. And whatever's attacking the livestock."

"Looks that way. We haven't ruled anything out."

"Anything?"

"You heard me."

Pete didn't like the sound of that. It left the door wide open. He typed in his computer log: *phenomena unknown*.

On one of the monitors, something caught his eye. "Gentlemen I'm tracking a vehicle clocking well over the speed limit. Someone's in an awfully big hurry. Doing eighty. Just now entering the Watch Zone."

"Not our responsibility," said Frost, "but keep us posted if anything develops."

"Will do," said Pete. "Just to let you know. I have some feedback. The computer's making a list."

"Anything interesting?"

"Other than the speeder? Not so far. Lots of animals, the usual traffic, that's pretty much it. Except..."

"What?"

"A door just closed."

"What's so interesting about that?"

"The location."

"What about it?"

"It's near the river. Must be a house there. I hear someone. I think it's the Indian. I was told he's a priority."

Agent Frost motioned to the driver, Brian, to get moving. "What makes you think it's Walker, Pete?"

"He's singing. Or chanting...some sort of Indian song."

"What road is it on?"

"Gills Pier. If you wait a second, I'll check." After a short delay, Pete said, "It's listed as a grade B residence. Must be a trailer or mobile home."

Agent Frost referred to a map of the area. "Stay with it, Pete. Segedi, you listening? Where are you?"

Segedi was still working a piece of gum. "Just left the Sheriff's office. Ten minutes away."

"What did he say?"

"He'll cooperate any way he can. He's sending three of his deputies to work with us as part of the surveillance team."

"Great," Frost muttered. "All we need is two more guys to screw things up. Stop chewing so loud, Roy! You sound like a horse chompin' on the bit. The mobile home shouldn't be hard to find. Meet us there."

"Will do. Can't help it. I quit smoking two days ago."

The earpiece beeped. "Yes, Pete."

"The speeder," said Pete, "I have an identification."

"Who is it?"

"David Macklin."

"How in the hell do you know that?"

"Voice recognition. He's singing a Moody Blues song. Matches a recording from a previous call."

"Previous call? How can you record anything when you're not set up?"

"Trust me. You don't want to know."

"Ah, but I do."

"We have a recording on file from the Navy. Matches just like a fingerprint. We have voice tracks on more people than you can imagine."

Jesus, Frost thought to himself. *Is nothing sacred anymore?*

Chapter 43

The way Caddo saw it he had four choices. Alert the authorities and bring unwanted attention to himself. Do nothing and allow the body to rot. Remove the body from the tree and give it an informal burial. Or none of the above.

Circumstances dictated his decision.

He figured if there was a ladder tall enough to do the job, he'd find it in Freddie's carport next to the trailer. No such luck.

When Caddo returned to the tree, he found a raccoon balanced on a limb, sniffing Freddie's flesh. He tried to scare it away by hissing, throwing rocks, sticks, or anything he could get his hands on, none of which did any good. So he resorted to the only weapon he had and shot it down, using his bow and arrow.

Glancing up at Freddie, he said, "Sorry, my friend. Can't help you right now." He walked over to the raccoon. Apologized for taking its life. Knelt down and said a prayer for Freddie. Then picked up the raccoon by its feet and walked away.

* * *

Two and a quarter miles away, the technician glanced at a screen that monitored a thermal imaging system. It identified a life form as human. Another screen displaying audio surveillance issued a red alert. A blinking asterisk marked the location.

Since the camera covering that area wasn't working yet, Pete froze the audio screen. He highlighted and clicked on the location. By digitally remixing and amplifying, he was able to isolate, record, and get a fix on a specific time and place, about five minutes in length. He listened as an animal howled briefly and what transpired after it. "Sorry, my friend. Can't help you right now." He distinctly heard the man say, "Sorry, Mr. Raccoon." He was particularly interested when the man whispered what appeared to be a eulogy. "Go in peace, my friend. May you rest as you sleep in our heart."

After that, there was a long silence, followed by footsteps so quiet the audio sensors lost them as they moved away, as did the thermal sensors. It was like the man suddenly disappeared down a hole.

Pete pounded his fist on the arm of the chair in disappointment. A second later his earpiece beeped.

"Okay, Pete," said Agent Frost, "we're approaching the trailer. About a half-mile away."

"Perfect timing. Our friend, the Indian—I think he's onto something."

"Okay…"

"Listen. I'll replay a recording." Pete pressed a button on the control panel. He leaned forward, tilting the microphone closer to a speaker. The recording replayed the episode, condensing it to a mere thirty seconds. "That's it," said Pete.

"Are you still tracking him?" Agent Frost asked.

Pete regretted what he had to say next. "Unfortunately, no. We still have a slight problem."

"I don't want to hear it, Pete. Just fix it."

"I can't."

"Why can't you?"

"The interference. The area I mentioned before—it's still blank. It covers a three-quarter-mile area, from the park just shy of the farmhouse. When Walker was outside the circle, there was no interference. He's inside the circle now. Coverage inside is erratic. We can't penetrate it."

"Why not?"

"The computer can't come up with a reason. It's very unstable."

"You mean, dangerous?"

"No, no. I mean it can't be penetrated. Whenever the computer hears a sound, it identifies, color codes it, and puts it on screen like one of those weather radar scanners you see on TV. Right in the middle there's a dead spot. Completely blank. Not a single noise is registering. The only thing I can compare it to is a Black Hole in space, which if I understand correctly, has an absence of energy. This is the antithesis, the exact opposite. I'm having the same problem with the heat sensors. Unfortunately, there's something else."

"Great. What is it?"

"The Black Hole, it keeps changing. By that, I mean shape. There's a band around it where the computer is able to penetrate it, only at certain times and with limited success. The outer edges of the Black Hole keep moving, narrowing…expanding like a heart-beat. There's a rhythm to it, sort of like a pulse, only it's slow. Not very noticeable."

"You're getting too technical, Pete. Forget about that for now. The recording—what do you make of it?"

"I think Walker killed a raccoon. No rifle or handgun was fired, though. At least that's what it sounded like to me. Shot it down from a tree or roof of a building. If that isn't a body hitting the ground, I don't know what it is."

"The weapon—what do you think was used?"

"Something that doesn't shoot bullets. Only thing I can think of is a bow and arrow."

Several voices spoke at once.

"Quiet!" Agent Frost cried. "What's your take on Walker, Pete?"

"Hold on a second. I'm running a trace on the residence. The computer lists only one address in the area." Pete typed a message into the computer, waited, and mumbled, "Your question...what did you ask?"

"I said..."

"Oh, my God!" Pete interrupted. Voices chattered. Pete wasn't listening. His eyes were locked on the computer screen where a name and address were written. "It's a mobile home. 6766 Gills Pier Road. The occupant is listed as Wilfredo Pinoza. The missing person!"

* * *

Alexa Wilde checked out the parking lot, looking for what, she wasn't sure. She had no visual evidence to prove she was being followed, but something in the back of her mind told her she was. She hadn't worked out in weeks and that's just what she needed. One hour of sweat not only did wonders for the body, it unwound weeks of tension. As she entered the university's exercise facilities, her cell phone rang. She was tempted not to answer it.

"Okay, Sam. What now?"

"This might be the break we've been looking for, kiddo. Remember the conversations you overheard at the compound earlier today? Sources in the Federal Building have confirmed it. A task force from the Ohio Bureau of Investigation set up headquarters at the Law Enforcement Center. And a surveillance team just arrived. Lab technicians are at the compound right now, also at the site where the accident occurred. You cover one. I'll cover the other. What do you say?"

"Just one hour, Sam. Give me one hour to myself."

"You're joking, right? You can't be serious."

"You know as well as I do lab technicians aren't going to say anything."

"You're killing me. I can't believe this."

"Sorry."

Sam's cheerful disposition suddenly vanished. "What's wrong?"

"Nothing."

"Two years...two years I've known you," said Sam. "Enough to know when something's bothering you. What is it?"

Alexa didn't want to say it. It made her sound weak, and she was anything but weak. Another glimpse through the window prompted her to utter the unspeakable. "I don't think I'm being followed, Sam. I know it."

"How do you know?"

"A white Mercedes..."

"Yeah?"

"I'm looking at it."

A two-door white Mercedes with rusted wheels drove slowly through the parking lot.

"How long has it been following you?" Sam asked.

"I don't know. I didn't realize it until today."

"Get the license number."

"What?"

"License number. Get it!"

Alexa dropped her workout bag, hit the front door running with the phone to her ear, and said as the Mercedes accelerated out of the parking lot, "Shoot! It got away."

"Did you get the number?"

"No."

"Anything about the plate you can tell me?"

"Two things. It's blue and out of state."

"Michigan or Pennsylvania is my guess."

"What do we do now?" she wondered.

"You have one hour, kiddo," said Sam. "It shouldn't be hard to trace a white Mercedes with a blue license plate in this town."

Chapter 44

Whether it was physical pain or mental anguish, it didn't really matter. Richard looked at the haggard face in the mirror, swallowed another pain pill, a second, a third, and rinsed them down with a shot of bourbon to intensify the effect. All he wanted was to be left alone, to deal with his personal demons in private. No questions. No explanations. No hassles. It was the easiest way to cope.

He walked into the hallway and paused to listen. He could hear Elly in the front room. She was sitting at a baby Grand piano, turning pages of sheet music, looking for a song to play. Cinders and Roscoe stood at the end of the hallway, waiting to follow. When the first chord was struck, Richard crept into the kitchen. Accompanied by both spaniels, he walked outside, removed the shotgun from the back seat of his Jeep, a handful of shotgun shells from the glove box, and disappeared into the field across the highway.

Meanwhile, echoing through the house was a longtime favorite of the Macklins, George Gershwin's *Rhapsody in Blue*. Elly played it slowly at first, barely touching the keys. She played it to soothe her father, also to soothe herself, swaying in time to a melody that quickly evolved into a jarring resonance, a sharp contrast of shifting accents and cross rhythms derived from jazz and '*metropolitan madness*,' all of which produced a strong internal dynamic. Up the emotional stairway the *Rhapsody* carried you, a movement intended to, as one music critic once put it, "*hitch the rhythm of the body to the sentiments of the mind and heart*." Elly lost herself in the mood of it, creating gentle tones one moment and bold, seductive scores the next.

Given the complexity of the piece, or because of it, she found herself inspired in ways she hadn't experienced before. Her feelings seemed to ebb and flow with the tides of music. She could feel something inside her influencing every stroke of the keys. The last bar reverberated like a persistent storm, rumbling through the house, a long protracted, musical crack of thunder. She held her foot on the damper pedal to sustain the echo, and as it went pulsating from the baby Grand, she could feel someone watching her.

Slowly, she looked up.

The last chord faded as she lifted her hands.

A fragrance lingered, that of wild flowers. A bittersweet smell.

Like jasmine. Or lavender.

"Dad?"

She rose from the piano bench. Across the hall, inside the converted porch, a curtain fluttered, a movement so slight it was scarcely noticeable. She walked into the room. The porch windows were shut.

"Dad, where are you?"

No answer.

The fragrance was growing stronger. A draft swept through the hallway. Chill bumps crept up and down her forearms. It wasn't fear she felt, more a pang of anxiety. With a heightened sense of awareness, she searched the rest of the house, calling to her father as she went. The house was cold, quiet, lacking of life. Every time she walked into a room, she had a feeling someone just left. A draft followed wherever she went. Not knowing what to do, she paused by her father's bedroom, knocked on the door, then pushed it open. Through the window, she could see his Jeep parked at the end of the driveway.

Where did he go?

She heard the sound of tire tread on pavement and saw the '57 Chevy pull up behind the Jeep. Half a minute later, she greeted David as he entered the house.

When she saw what was in his hand, she remarked, "So that's why you went through my closet. What were you doing with my sketchpad?"

"I told you. Leverage." He laid the pad on the kitchen counter, opened it to the missing page, and told her about the conversation he had with their grandfather. "He's now proud owner of one of your sketches."

"How generous of you."

"Where's dad?"

"I don't know. He must've slipped out a few minutes ago."

"Is he okay?"

"I guess so. He favors the shoulder a little."

"And the papers from the library...?"

She pointed at a stack resting on the kitchen table.

He sat down and scanned the first few pages while Elly opened the kitchen closet. She removed a key ring hanging on the door and placed the ring on the table. David looked at it, not sure what to make of it.

"Ryan Cooper's keys," she explained. "He quit two hours ago."

They both knew what that meant. The final nail in the coffin.

"And agents from the state were here, talking to dad," she said. "They treated him like he was suspect." Without further comment, she slipped down the hall, was gone for about twenty seconds or so, and returned with a book, which she dropped on the kitchen table.

"What's this?" David asked.

"*Revenants*...ghosts. Remember? I told you he keeps it in his nightstand. He's been having dreams about the war...and mom."

David looked up in surprise. He tried to keep his emotions in check.

"He says she visits every night while he's asleep."

A look of bewilderment clouded his face. "How long has this been going on?"

"About a week."

"How do you know?"

"He told me. At lunch today. When I came home, he was asleep in the barn. I watched him. His eyes were twitching. I see it every day at work—body spasms, movement of the eyes, the sounds animals make when sleeping. Dogs dream just as much as people. Something about the rain reminded dad of the war."

David's eyes drifted to the window. The rain clouds were slowly receding.

"Call it coincidence if you want, but dad told me something else. He said his platoon blew up an enemy bridge near Laos almost forty years ago. If it hadn't rained the next day, he says they wouldn't have survived. Sunday night he had a dream...the same night the railroad bridge collapsed." She pointed at the book. "Open it to the first page. Read the first paragraph."

He opened the book and leaned over the table—

"*All of us at one time or another have experienced situations which cannot be explained. Some call them mysteries, others paranormal occurrences. Regardless of how you view them, there have been occasions where I have seen images, heard and felt things that defy all logic, all rationale...*"

Elly commented. "I think it was Freud who said, 'dreams allow us to be safely insane.'"

David wasn't listening. "Huh? What did you say?"

"Nothing. Forget it." She stood up and walked across the kitchen.

David glanced over his shoulder. "Hey, El. Last night, inside the barn, did you hear anything?"

"Like what?"

"Voices. Somebody crying."

"No."

"Later, after you went to bed, did you hear or feel anything?"

"Last night?"

"Yes."

"Huh-uh. Why? Did you?"

He didn't answer. He glanced at the stack of papers and started reading.

Elly said to herself, *No, not last night, David. Today. Just a few minutes ago.*

* * *

Caddo closed the barn door and inserted a board in the latch-jamb. Dust rained down from the ceiling as a gust of wind blew. The wallboards creaked. It felt like the place was teetering.

He found a burlap sack and stuffed the dead raccoon inside it. He hung the sack on a hook by the doorway and walked around the farm equipment, sidestepping puddles of water on the floor. What impressions he had about the barn seemed to be growing. The feeling of solitude, of aloneness, had never existed before. But now it was almost palpable—this feeling that he was *not* alone.

In spite of it, he went about his work and raised the flap to the tepee. Inside was a fire pit with rocks laid end to end in a four-foot circle. At the center of the circle, kindling and logs were piled. Instead of using a match or lighter, he made a fire the old fashioned way by rubbing two sticks together, then set fire to the kindling. As the flames spread, he removed his moccasins, placed them on the rocks to dry, and began to undress in preparation for—

A Night of Reckoning.

Chapter 45

The agents had changed into weather resistant gear, blue polyester jackets with OBI stitched on the back, and rubber-soled hunting boots. They were following footprints through a field—footprints made not by shoes or boots, but a pliable, smooth material. Agent Segedi hazarded a guess. "Moccasins?" Spread out fifty paces apart, the team of agents was approaching a stand of trees alongside Little Bass River.

"How far, Pete?" Agent Frost asked.

"Almost there. Less than a hundred yards."

They followed Agent Roy Segedi's lead. Heavy breathing was heard through the earpieces. They plodded through a field, which until today hadn't had rain for weeks. The mud was half an inch thick. They walked around a swampy depression filled with cattails.

"Sixty yards," said Pete. "You should be entering some trees any second."

"How do you know that?" said an agent named Dennis. Everyone called him G because of his last name—Glowacki.

"The raccoon," said Pete. "It fell from a height. No buildings out there, so it had to be a tree."

Segedi coughed and said, "Catching a whiff of…man, oh, man…it's bad, whatever it is."

All five agents removed their pistols—Glocks, Berettas, Police Specials—and crept forward another thirty yards when Pete warned—

"You're almost there. The Black Hole is just beyond the trees."

They began to notice an odor, sour and unpleasant, which smelled like skunk. For the first time they heard static through the headsets, just loud enough to be annoying. Everything else was quiet, except for the rustle of polyester. The breathing became louder as their anticipation grew. Once they entered the trees, the static began to worsen while the odor intensified.

Agent Frost broke the silence. "Segedi, can you hear me?"

Segedi's voice crackled. "Barely."

The odor was becoming stronger, rank like feces.

"Jesus, what died?" said G.

Everyone suddenly heard a gasp through the headsets.

"What is it?" cried Agent Frost.

Segedi coughed and wheezed, "Come here!"

Everyone started running. Agent Segedi stood at the base of a tree with a sick look on his face. They gathered around him, breathing through their mouths. Agent Brian Riddick reached for a handkerchief and held it over his nose. The rest of them stood there, trying not to gag, staring up at the tree, at a body impaled against a broken branch.

Agent Frost stopped and caught his breath. "What the hell..."

"Would somebody tell me what's going on?" said Pete.

"The missing person," said Agent Frost. "We think we found him. Brian and Roy, see if you can pick up any tracks on the other side of those trees."

While the agents hurried away, Agent G motioned to Agent Frost. A few feet from the base of the tree there was blood on the ground. Wet blood. Fresh Blood. G fished through his pockets, pulled out a vile and rubber gloves, and took a sample of blood.

The earpieces were crackling with static now. Pretty much useless.

Agent Frost shouted, "Talk to me, Brian."

Whatever Brian said, it was fragmented.

"If...go...farth...lose you," said Pete, his voice fading in and out.

Agent Frost backtracked. Once he reached the base of the tree where the body was, communication returned except for an occasional interruption. "Pete, what's happening?" he said while waving everyone closer.

"It's that damn Black Hole," said Pete. "The equipment can't function. It's like there's a...a barrier or something. I can't figure it out."

"We'll worry about that later. Notify the coroner. And the lab techs. And the Sheriff's office." As Agent Frost looked at the body hanging above him, he said to the others, "What I want to know is, how a full grown man could be thrown thirty feet in the air."

* * *

David read three stories, each dealing with local history, including a clash between Indians and Whites termed *"The War of Blood,"* a war *"fraught with such carnage no man should ever see or be the victim of..."*

But it was an explorer's description of a Mohawk chief that enthralled David the most: *"So wicked was this Presence, to look upon him was the most frightening experience of our lives. What we saw was a dead man rising with a spear through his back, hooded by bearskin & bear's head, evoking such Unholiness even God would fear him. Upon sight of him, our horses took fright & we were driven away!"*

Of the papers Elly had copied, there was a manuscript by an archeologist written a few months after the War of Blood. In it he claimed to have stumbled upon an Indian burial site mounted on platforms…*"cluttered with bones, war clubs, tomahawks, knives and scaffolding perilously close to falling down…about to be claimed by the hazards of time…clearly belonging to an indigenous race…"*

David saved Hank's manuscript for last. Holding the papers in his hand, he got up, hurried into the front room, and sat on the love seat opposite the portrait of Hank the Willie. The look of amusement on Hank's face seemed more noticeable now.

David felt oddly self-conscious sitting there as he began to read.

Chapter 46

*S*ome of my contemporaries think I am a victim of my own imagination. I, on the other hand, believe I am an observer, a sufferer of something that happened many lifetimes ago. Rebirth, reincarnation, call it what you will, these events of which I am about to describe to you are gathered from experience, one unfortunately I remember all too well. It happened during another life, one that in retrospect has been cast in shadows so deep I cannot sleep without being reminded of that dreadful time when I had to hide alone in the midst of peril and run for my safety.

There was no precise moment when I became aware of this 'other life.' It came upon me slowly and progressed in stages, resulting in flashes of images asleep and awake. 'Psychic images' as I refer to them. I refuse to call them dreams because they were more vivid than any dream, and there was a physical sense about them. If they occurred during sleep, I would awaken with a clear conscious and memories so detailed there was no doubting their existence, memories I could summon whenever I wanted to, one day, two days, weeks, months, even years later, and those memories unleashed other memories until finally I could recreate events as a whole.

Not by chance, words unlike any I had ever spoken began to creep into my vocabulary, words like 'papou" and "yinglee,' Indian words from tribes I had no association with, at least that I knew of. As a young man I had enrolled in a university recognized as one of the leading institutions in Native American studies. There I began to read about native customs and cultures. I examined many Indian dialects and without prior research or prior knowledge understood certain words and certain passages.

To illustrate, a colleague once asked me if I knew what an Indian Ghost Dance was. I told him I believed it had little to do with what it implied, but was intended to chase white men away from Indian lands by whatever means necessary, in this case through the influences of ghosts. He argued the Ghost Dance had not been initiated until the late 1880's by a man named Wovoka, a Pah-Ute. I countered without any proof I had witnessed a similar dance long before that, performed not by any Pah-Ute, but by a Mohawk, a warrior named Standing Bear who ruled by intimidation and made brave men cower in his presence. It is of this person and time I now *speak. I cannot recall the year, the place, or specifics of where or when, only the reality of the misfortune I was in...*

It was a warm summer's day. My mother, father, sister, and I were traveling in a caravan of wagons, embarking upon a new frontier. A man saddled on a beautiful, brown-haired horse led us. I do not remember his name, but the impression he made—clothed in buckskin, rifle slung over his arm, ruggedness of his body, and 'coonskin cap—kept us in good faith. It instilled confidence in us, a feeling that we were safe. Alongside him rode two scouts, men of different persuasions whose complexion was darker, hair longer, and garments more basic. Of these so-called 'Indians,' a reference I do not like but must employ since I know of no acceptable word to use, I was intrigued. In fact, to one of them I became indebted. This fellow who I called 'Jim' later saved my life.

We were traveling in an unfamiliar land inhabited by creatures that made the most dreadful noises at night. It surprised me to see no farms at all, no houses, no buildings, nothing to which I was accustomed. On each side of our path grew an endless parade of forest and wilderness grass. If we had difficulties, I do not recall, for we moved at a steady pace through a terrain that consisted of easy, rolling hills. Plough horses, a few mules, pulled our wagons. Mothers held the reins and fathers sat in protective custody of the children.

We had one common purpose: To find a new home and live our lives in peace. But that was about to change.

It started when the dogs became nervous. They growled and barked for no apparent reason, then the horses and mules became nervous as well. Our leader gestured for us to stop and the wagons came to a halt over the untrodden path. A sense of anticipation gripped us. I noticed our leader was no longer cradling his rifle over his arm. He held it with his finger curled around the trigger. He motioned for us to move on and slowly we passed through a ravine, one of the few times it was open, not hemmed in by the trees.

During this passage, a strange and unexpected sight caught our attention. A man hooded in bear's head, cloaked in bearskin, stood atop a hill to our right. Apart from his size and daunting physical presence, I was struck, or I should say awed, by the fierceness with which he conveyed himself. He appeared to be much larger than our two scouts who, I believed, were of the same race. No one or nothing I had ever experienced before inspired such alarm. His face remained in shadow. Streaks of red and yellow paint underlined his eyes—eyes that were cold and sharp, like a bird's or predatory animal that lives by cunning and instinct. He watched us as an eagle would its prey.

If he disappeared, he would return minutes later, as if by magic, standing beside a tree or opposite a stream, watchful, waiting with a patience given to someone contemplating a plan, and we knew that plan somehow involved us. At night when we camped, we would hear strange utterances, the cries of wolves, the calls of creatures hostile and hungry. But we suspected these sounds were made by men, Indians, not unlike the dark-skinned man stalking us.

The next day, just when we thought we were free of this torment, we were attacked. It came with a suddenness that still haunts me to this day. First, it was arrows, aimed with precision. Some were on fire. They came flying at us from every direction. I saw one of our scouts fall from his horse, choking and gagging, an arrow through his neck. My mother tried to incite the team of horses by whipping them and snapping the reins, but the lead horse was fatally shot. It collapsed at the feet of the others who were unable to move. I remember my father shouting, pushing my sister and me to the rear of the wagon, the awful look in his eyes when the arrow pierced his back and the shock of it as he slumped against the seat.

All around me gunshots rang out. People were screaming. Fires spread from carriage to carriage, sending up thick clouds of smoke. A wagon carrying gunpowder exploded, scattering pieces of wood and debris everywhere, knocking me to the ground. Stunned, I glanced up at my sister. She had this growing look of fear in her eyes.

Indians wearing animal skins, the heads of panthers and wolves, came running from the trees, brandishing knives, war clubs, and tomahawks. One of them chased after me, but I eluded him by ducking into the underbrush. My sister was not as fortunate. She was swept up in the arms of an attacker and carried away. The speed and decisiveness with which the ambush came and the way it was executed compelled me to run. And run I did. Only once did I look back. By then the Indians had overtaken the wagon train. Most of the wagons were engulfed in flames. A team of horses panicked and bolted with a wagon still in tow. Just before I entered the woods, I saw my mother attempt to come to my sister's rescue, but she was overcome not by one, but several Indians, a scene I cannot put into words, nor do I have the desire to do so. The horror I felt was indescribable.

Not knowing what to do, I escaped into the forest. By darkness I was alone, tired, hungry, and scared, lost in a dangerous land. With no previous experience in the art of survival, I endeavored to last the night. With great discomfort, I slept for short periods of time and somehow made it through the bleakest, most disturbing hours of my existence despite the constant cry of predators and those they preyed upon.

When morning broke, I was afraid to move, worried that I might awaken a bear or wolf. I went all day without food and water. I had no skill as a hunter...no idea how to make a fire. Had I killed a rabbit, I didn't know how to skin it. Nor did I have a weapon to do it. I ate berries, roots, but only managed to get myself sick. I lived in constant fear of being attacked by an animal or Indian hiding in the bushes.

It occurred to me I might return to the wagon train, but I was far too lost by then. The landscape was luxuriant, yet also very repetitious. Hills, streams, grasses, trees—it all looked the same to me. I was in a continuous state of confusion as I wandered aimlessly—in a daze from sickness and malnutrition.

Then one afternoon I stumbled across a set of tracks, those of a wagon wheel and horse. I rejoiced at my good fortune, believing the tracks might lead to a house, a town, or perhaps civilization. Gradually, I adapted to the rigors of the trail and grew bolder, wiser, more acute to my surroundings. To compare the child I was before the ambush to the one after was like comparing two different people, a transformation necessitated by my environment. If not for the living in the wild and existing off nature with little more than my bare hands, I would never have acquitted myself of the series of events to follow, for indeed the tracks did end and I met up with those who had taken my sister captive.

It occurred soon after I came to a forest that grew upon a succession of hills. I saw smoke rising beside a river. What particularly drew my attention was the smell of roasting meat. Driven by a ravenous hunger, I crept closer when, on the path I was walking, I happened upon some Indians. As I turned to run, I was seized by the neck in a grip so strong it could easily have snapped my neck in half. In an effort to break free, I was struck on the head with something hard and knocked unconscious.

I awoke tied to a post in an Indian village, surrounded by people of two distinctly different tribes, one that would come to know as 'Dog People,' the other, a much smaller party, called Mohawk. It was the sting of a horsewhip that woke me, the same whip used by my mother to urge her team of horses.

As I was lying there, sights I had never seen before assaulted my senses. Dogs came sniffing at my feet, as if to judge them suitable to eat. Slabs of deer meat were roasting over fire pits. Lodges built of mud, bark, and thatch stretched from the forest to the banks of a river. Women cooked while men sat in a circle, talking, some of whom still bore the heads of animals. Of particular interest were two men, the scout I referred to as Jim who appeared to be acting as translator, and the wearer of the bear's head whose name I later learned was Standing Bear.

Clutching a spear in one hand and horsewhip in the other, he spoke with passion and indignation, shouting incomprehensible words one moment, whispering them the next. He kept stalking around, thrusting his spear, screaming, "Yinglee, yinglee!" and "papou," over and over as he pointed at me, terms which I knew were derogatory, the first a derivation of the word 'Yankee,' the latter meaning 'baby,' inferring I was acting like a child.

That evening a feast was celebrated in honor of the taking of the wagon train. At the height of the festivities, a young white woman was retrieved from one of the lodges. A leather sack covered her head and she was dragged to the campgrounds where Standing Bear ridiculed and taunted her with a spear. With much to-do, he thrust the sack from her head and everyone groaned in derision.

It was, of course, my sister.

My heart sank as I watched her. She displayed remarkable courage, neither crying nor whimpering. She sat with head bowed and eyes closed as Standing Bear paced around her, mocking her, subjecting her to repeated acts of humiliation. The Dog People seemed as much afraid of him as me. Why? Why did they cower to him so willingly when they outnumbered the Mohawk? Who were these strangers who dressed in animal skins? And why had the two tribes come together?

The answers were about to be revealed.

Standing Bear made a display of his powers. He spoke in a slow, deliberate manner, almost whispering as he put his hand over a fire, then immersed it in flame and held it there, smiling. The men stared in disbelief. All we could hear was a crackle of flame and juices from the deer meat dripping into the fire. And then he laughed. It was a roar of laughter only a madman could make. We all realized then he was no ordinary man, but a man to be feared and obeyed.

That night I was thrown into a lodge with my sister. We held each other, afraid to let go. To his credit, one of the Dog People along with Jim, snuck into our lodge and gave us food and water. I took great comfort in my sister's arms and she in mine. The next morning I was taken from her arms and put to work—work even a pack mule couldn't endure. I carried animal skins filled with water and watered a field of corn, beans and squash, walking back and forth all day from the river. And accompanying me every step of the way was Standing Bear, cursing and hitting me with a stick if I fell or displeased him in any way. One wrong look and I was beaten. Indecisiveness was met with the tail end of a switch. And if I *protested, I received a thrashing worse than the one before.*

At great risk to himself, Jim brought a bowl of grease to our lodge and my sister gently applied a salve to sooth the wounds to my back. Deep into the night we talked—mostly about Standing Bear. I asked Jim why I was despised so much and he explained in broken English the Mohawks considered white people the enemy. White civilization, he said, had forced itself upon the Indian and it was Standing Bear's intention to unite all Indian nations together to prevent the proliferation of the white race. Jim claimed the Mohawk chief was a priest capable of performing feats far beyond the abilities of ordinary men. He could make fire just by a mere flick of his hand. He also had strange manipulative powers and could exert his influence on psychic images or dreams. Provided there was a basis in thought, he could expound upon those dreams and control and shape them as he desired. Many times I was a victim. One of my greatest fears was being attacked by a bear or wolf. Not a night went by where I wasn't chased by one or the other and invariably caught.

Jim claimed Standing Bear's powers extended to the Spirit World as well. He was known as a 'Shape Changer,' a conjurer, and mystic.

Nighttime proved to be what Jim called "fearing time" and late one evening I experienced a time to be feared like no other. Masks carved from wood were hung from poles throughout the village—masks exaggerated and provocative by design, misshapen with bulging eyes and down-turned mouths, intended to, I gathered, represent some bizarre function during a ceremony. At sunset I was taken outside and tied to a tree. Behind me, Standing Bear and his men danced around a fire and sang until their throats were raw. As night wore on, the singing grew louder, the dancing more intense. Then mysteriously everything grew quiet and the shadows disappeared despite the glow of the fire.

I heard a commotion in the trees, heavy breathing, a grunt of some kind. Jim came running to me, knife in hand, and hurried to cut the bindings loose. From the look of his eyes I knew we were in danger. Branches shook and grasses rustled. I heard another grunt as something large stalked through the forest. When my hands and feet were cut free, Jim told me to run. At the same time an animal pounced into the clearing, but instead of leaping at me, it leapt at Jim. I heard him scream as his body was being dragged into the bushes. I stopped and saw him struggling...lashing out with his knife. I saw teeth, a long snout—the eyes of what, I was not sure. It clawed at Jim and buried its fangs upon his writhing body. The knife fell. The next thing I knew I was holding it, running toward the Beast. In the heat of the moment I threw all caution aside and stabbed, not once, but again and again, *sinking the blade deeper and deeper. Stunned, the Beast howled. A paw struck my face. I heard a whimper, growls of pain, and plodding feet retreating into the underbrush while I was lying on the ground, dazed. When I looked at Jim, he was bleeding badly, attempting to stand. I saw shadows dance across the treetops in shapes distinctly human, but the manner in which they departed was not. The shadows drew upward like cloaks blown by the wind. The trouble was, there was no wind, only a loud rushing sound and fading cries that died away like voices down a hole.*

My heart leapt at this odd and disturbing occurrence. I had witnessed something that, except for Jim, none of us could comprehend. The Mohawks had disappeared as quietly as a wisp of smoke.

My sister and I did all we could to wrap Jim's wounds and stop the bleeding. We applied tourniquets and bandages, but there was little more we could do. As Jim lay dying, he told us about the dance that night. He called it a 'Ghost Dance,' meaning ghosts had been invited to participate. Why? To quote Jim: "Chase enemy...away." What enemy he was referring to, he would not say. We were not under attack. The only aggressions I knew of were those being imposed upon us by the Mohawks. Confused, I let the matter drop.

At dawn Jim died. A great sadness came to my sister and I as we knelt by his side and said a prayer.

That very same day a sight I hoped I would never see again reappeared from the forest. The Mohawks arrived in need of assistance, especially their leader who staggered from an injury he sustained while away. He limped and glanced in my direction with such hatred, if not for his incapacity, I know he would have killed me. But one thing held him back. A coat. A bright red coat. He made a big show of it while holding it on the tip of his spear. "Yinglee! Yinglee!" he shouted. And the Mohawks raised their weapons and shouted as he held the coat over a fire and watched it burn.

In due course, I knew my unbearable life was about to take a turn for the worse. For the time being the Mohawks appeared to be preoccupied with matters far more urgent than those pertaining to me. Standing Bear leaned on his spear, shouting orders, and had both his men and the Dog People running around, collecting weapons and preparing for battle. The dogs, sensing the excitement, barked and ran about the village in a state of alarm. And soon this life as I knew it would come to a swift and violent end.

Gunshots rang out, echoing so loudly I flinched. I could see puffs of smoke being discharged and a slight delay in the firing of muskets and pistols. Indians of all ages, men and women, Mohawk and native, were falling around me and the casualties were mounting by the second. I had no idea who was shooting at us, or why. After recovering from the initial shock, I became aware of men in Red Coats advancing upon us.

Among them was a rider of a brown-haired horse. Dressed in buckskin, wearing a coonskin cap, I realized at once it was the leader of the wagon train. By then I had enough wits about me to crawl next to a dead body and pretend I, too, was dead. Lying there, I agonized over what to do when suddenly it struck me—what I had once considered my retribution was now the retribution of a race. Sadly, it involved the Dog People whose innocence was evidenced by the way they reacted. Gunfire was not something they had heard before and after each blast, which they mistook for thunder, they would stop and look about in confusion.

Having seen enough of this madness, I ran for safety. Hiding behind a tree, I watched the slaughter of men, women, and children. Thinking only of myself, I abandoned my sister and escaped into the forest. In a matter of hours the guilt began to weigh heavily on me, so I decided to come to her rescue, not knowing if she was alive or dead. Later that afternoon I returned to the village, only to find bodies lying everywhere and packs of dogs chewing on human flesh. Since they posed a major threat, I armed myself with bow and arrows and shot as many of them as I could, picked up a tomahawk and proceeded with caution.

As I walked among the dead I saw no Mohawks. Leading up a hill, however, were tracks made by drag poles, devices used for hauling, so I followed the tracks into the forest and happened upon two Indian boys pulling a sled with a dead Mohawk lying on it. A few feet in front of them was a white girl dressed in tattered clothes, pulling a sled carrying another dead Mohawk. You can imagine the joy I felt in seeing my sister. After watching her, I could see she was obsessed with dragging the body up the hill. I wanted to run to her, but instead followed at a distance until I came to the edge of a clearing.

I trembled at the sight.

Graves were being built on platforms cradling the dead. And who should preside over them? My hated foe, Standing Bear!

I watched, dismayed, as work continued into darkness. Masks were hung on poles at the base of the gravesite. Standing Bear stood with whip in hand, snapping it, shouting at the children as they lifted and placed the bodies on the platforms. Boy, girl, Indian and white child, each was subjected to the sting of the whip and berated constantly until they collapsed from exhaustion.

What a tyrant Standing Bear was! In all likelihood he was crazy before this, but the grief and loss of his fellow Mohawks made him stark raving mad.

At dusk he made a fire and hobbled around it. For the rest of the night all I heard was his tireless grumbling and an occasional cry of some beast lurking in the forest.

Doomed to ignominy, I cried. I cried not knowing the end was near and once again found solace in the forest, not caring if I lived or not.

I was awakened later by the sound of children begging and pleading for forgiveness. It was daybreak, but a heavy fog had settled over the valley. Quietly, I snuck into the village and there I saw my sister and rest of the children dragging the dead bodies of the Red Coats into the campground, under the supervision of Standing Bear, of course. Once the bodies were stacked and covered with wood, he set fire to the logs by a mere flick of his hand. I watched in awe as these acts were repeated time and again.

My poor sister was lying on the ground, too exhausted to move, which infuriated Standing Bear all the more. He dropped his spear and kicked her, then lifted her by the neck and shoulder. She put up a fight, flailing and thrashing wildly, but he was too strong. He lifted her over his head and staggered toward one of the fires. I had to do something, so I ran and picked up his spear. As he was about to throw her into the flames, I drove the spear as hard and deep as I could.

It was not the roar of a man I heard, but the roar of an animal—impaled through the back!

A gust of wind came blowing across the village, sending sparks into the air. Flames went dancing like moths, fluttering into the trees. A few trees caught fire. Then a few more. The flames began to spread, crawling from branch to branch, tree to tree. Fires raged. Walls of flame ate giant swaths through the forest.

I heard horses.

Deep amid the smoke and fog, beyond the burning trees, I could barely make out a group of riders. If they were yinglee I could not say since the forest was now a raging inferno.

From this point on everything became a blur. I remember taking my sister's hand, seeing the spear sticking through Standing Bear's back, the crazed look hooded beneath the bear's head as he watched us run away. It was the same look as that of the Beast that attacked Jim the night before. Once my sister and I reached the trees, we felt the heat of the fires. A final roar came from below. It was the last thing I remember...

Sleep is now my enemy.

Dreams, nightmares, psychic images—these are the consequences of my former life. I have spent countless years traveling, reading, investigating, and consulting with others who adhere to views *similar to mine. We all share a passion for things that seem outside our grasp, things that defy all logic. Many times in articles, newspapers or magazines, and at speaking engagements at universities that allow me the privilege, I have put forth the supposition that there are worlds outside our own, phenomena that exist outside our awareness.*

Psychologists, theologians, and psychical researchers have long since been involved in this field of study and there are libraries filled with thousands of books and materials professing the same. I have attended institutions whose sole purpose is the legitimate study of things mysterious, psychical in nature, or beyond the realm of objectivity—Institutions such as the American Society of Psychical Research, the London Institute of Paranormal Study, Institut Metapsychique International in Paris. I have met people in all walks of life, of all ages, and the stories they tell mirror the supposition as a whole.

My experience you just read was the result of extensive research. It began, however, by accident. I was visiting the Museum of Natural History in New York City when I came across a collection of Indian masks. The Mohawks used them in ceremonies and called them False Faces. Once I stepped into the Great Hall, my heart stopped. I had seen the masks before. Authorities told me a few masks were found by an explorer in the hills of southern Ohio. I retraced his tracks to a county called Bertram to a farm owned by Robert and Vera Macklin, whose son, Wil, I befriended. It is on their property that, in a manner of speaking, I discovered myself. By simply being near the village I once lived in as a prisoner unleashed a whole host of memories.

But the one true, undeniable proof of my former existence was the land itself. I remember the first time I walked through the hills. The forest was gone, but the feeling the land evoked was overpowering. As I approached a particular hill, I was overcome with emotion. I had visions before, but now I was actually reliving my past, each miserable moment of it. They were not just flashbacks or bouts of delirium. I was experiencing events as they were unfolding and found myself trapped in situations from which I had escaped centuries ago.

From that day forward I had a clear understanding of my former life and knew it was not imagined. It was something no child should ever be subjected to with eyes open or closed.

As a friend and scholar once said, "Man is not the only creature who resides in dark places. There are those that shadow, provoke, haunt, and protect us from dimensions outside our own."

I write this because it is my hope that one day we all find pro-

tection and never suffer from the provocation and haunting of our souls. And dare I say there are those who lie in waiting, ready to prey upon our soulless spirit.

I know. I speak from experience.

As God is my witness,
Henry J. Purdy

Chapter 47

David placed the papers on the love seat and stared at the portrait of Willie. He remembered reading from a personal journal where Henry had been born a Gemini on May 24th. Although he gave little credence to astrology, David thought it intriguing that the writer believed he possessed dual personalities. Like the antithesis of Dr. Jekyll's Mr. Hyde. Henry Purdy versus Hank the Willie. True opposites living in one body. Whichever one he was—Hank or Henry—David found his story to be a paradox, a notion so absurd that maybe there was some validity to it.

"Well, what do you think?" Elly stood in the hallway, arms folded, leaning against the wall.

"He's either a good storyteller or I'm crazy."

"Which is it?"

"A little of both."

"So what do we do now?" she asked.

David thought about it for a moment, unable to come up with a satisfactory answer. "Not sure. There is one thing I do know, however. We have to assume what Hank wrote is true."

"Why?"

"If we don't, where does that leave us?"

"We can't just sit around and do nothing."

"You're right." He stood up and started walking. "Come with me."

* * *

After more than half an hour on the jogging machine, Alexa could feel the sweat dripping from her face. Her leg muscles ached, but it was a good ache.

"Alex, phone call," a trainer shouted. He pointed at the front desk.

Grabbing a towel, she jumped off the machine, wiped her face, and ran to the phone. "Hello, this is Alex."

"Hate to cut short your workout, kiddo," said her boss, Sam Tully, "but something's happening down the street at the Sheriff's office. I just saw a patrol car drive away in a big hurry. Haven't heard a word on the scanner, but I have a sneaky suspicion something's going on."

Alexa could feel her adrenalin kicking in. "Which direction did it go?"

"West."

"I'm on my way."

She hung up, ran into the locker room, collected her gear, and was outside throwing a coat over her workout attire as she ran to her car. The Saab convertible left fifty dollars of rubber on the parking lot pavement. Twenty seconds later, she was fumbling through her workout bag for her cell phone. Once she found it, she pressed a number.

"Hold on, Alex," Sam declared. "I'm talking to the desk sergeant on the other line."

While she waited, her instincts told her to follow Route 2. Once she made the turn, she was outside the city and the Saab shifted into turbo-charge, navigating the road at twenty miles an hour over the speed limit. She slowed down only when she saw flashers in the rearview mirror. A Bertram County patrol car passed her as she pulled over.

At the same time Sam came back on line. "Sorry, Alex. Nobody's talking. Whatever you do, you're on your own."

"No problem," she said, grinning to herself. She turned on the emergency blinkers and pressed the accelerator to the floor. The engine roared as she ran through the gears. "I'll call when I know something, Sam. See ya'. Bye."

* * *

Caddo sat in a blackened tomb, wet with steam and hot from burning wood. The Cleansing Lodge. He was undergoing a purification of spirit and flesh, sitting naked where no sunlight could reach.

Normally the purification process took a day at least, sometimes two or three, but Caddo had only a few hours before he would undertake another ritual more important than the one he was taking now. Cleansing was only the preliminary stage and he sat in stoic silence, contemplating what to do while praying for guidance and assistance from those much more significant than his lowly self.

He opened his eyes and watched the smoke escape through the hole at the top of the lodge, then reached down and unfolded a small sheet of waxed paper lying by his knee. Inside there was what looked like the cap of a mushroom about the size of a coat button, only this was edible, taken from a cactus. He ate a piece of it, inserted the rest into a pipe, lit it, took several puffs, and waited for the smoke to take effect.

At the fire pit in front of him a pan of boiling water rested over a metal grill balanced between two rocks. Taking a wide, prong-shaped utensil, he dipped a handful of grass into the water and laid the wet grass over the heated rocks, creating a gust of steam so intense it practically scalded his face. With sweat dripping from every pore, he picked up an eagle claw, and immersed that too. Once it was hot, he made a sacrificial gesture by raking the claw down both shoulders and across his chest. The sharp talons dug in, drawing beads of blood.

Arms extended, he prayed to his Guardian Spirit. Rocking back and forth on his knees, he began to chant in the Caddoan tongue, language of the Skidi Pawnee, his ancestral clan. But it wasn't his Guardian Spirit he heard. He heard a slight whimper. It sounded like someone was crying. And it came from just outside the Cleansing Lodge, somewhere in the back of the barn.

Chapter 48

David pushed the door open and held the lamp high to shed more light in the room. "Okay, you can open them now."

"Oh, my!" Elly cried as she opened her eyes. She walked inside the cabin and looked around in awe. The first thing she noticed was the painting of Caddo seated on a horse. "Oh, look—Fleet Merchant. Did you know this was here?"

"No."

"Look at all the books!" She paused by a stack of books and read several titles. *Black Elk Speaks. Religions of the North American Indian. A Winemaker's Guide.* "I didn't know Caddo was interested in wine."

"So much he's been taking soil samples." David glanced at a shoebox resting on the table. He pulled it closer, opened it, and flinched. "Well, well. What do we have here? Interesting. That must be how he found this. I'm not an anthropologist, but it looks like a human jawbone, and if I had to guess it's probably two hundred and fifty years old. If that's true, there's only one thing to conclude. He found a burial ground."

Elly studied the bone. "I thought Indians believed a burial ground was sacred. Why would he keep a bone here?"

"Good question. Maybe we should ask Caddo."

On a shelf beside the computer was another stack of books—*Indian Mythologies, Cultural Distinctions among Native American Societies*, a book of Navajo poetry, and one titled *Rain Dance, the Rituals, Customs, and Ceremonies of the Native American Indian*, written by Aaron Caldwell. Inside the book jacket were several pieces of stationery. David removed them and opened the first—

Ma' heo o (Cheyenne)	god
mat'aho (Cheyenne)	peyote
Woyusinyaye (Delaware)	ghost
Woniya, nagi, oniga (Delaware)	spirit
Ga' gwa' (Cayuga)	sun
Eni' ta (Seneca)	moon
Pauwaw (Algonquin)	he dreams
Sachem (Algonquin)	tribal chief
poko, po'co (Hopi)	dog

Okton (origin unknown).......................... malevolent demon
Oyaron (origin unknown)....................... *guardian spirit*

The last two words held his attention. Okton. Oyaron. He kept repeating them over and over in his head. At the bottom of the page Okton and Charik were written in parenthesis. Suggesting what? Were they the same? On the next page were notes taken from reference books—

> *metaphysics* - beyond the laws of nature
> *telepathy, clairvoyance* - not qualified by physical laws
> *psychokinesis* - mind over matter
> *eternal wandering* - ghost
> *crytomnesia* - ability to recall mental images
>   buried in the subconscious
> *host possession*
> *animism* - system of beliefs in souls and spirits
>   among tribal societies
> *automatism* - spiritual guidance, inspirational activity
> *abode of spirits* - graveyard, cemetery, burial ground,
>   Halting Place
> *Shape Changer*
> *shamanism* - feats of the supernatural

What manner of things was Caddo reading?
The next page had to do with—

DREAMS

> *Stairways, windows, portals into other worlds*
> *water – symbolic of emotions*
> *rain – evocative of an emotional state*
> *gray skies – subconscious working with feelings of*
>   *depression*
> *blizzards, avalanches – overwhelming emotions, out of*
>   *control*
> *storms, thunder – charged emotional content, passion,*
>   *anger*
> *fog – uncertainty, state of denial*
> *fire – intimacy, unpredictability, danger, trauma*
> *falling – fear of height, vertigo*

Animism? Ghosts? Spirits? Dreams?

It appeared Caddo was studying a number of subjects from a linguistic, spiritual, psychological, as well as analytical basis, approaching them as an academic would. David tried to sift through what was meaningful before he opened a correspondence from a fellow Indian—

> *Greetings from the Land of the Silver Lakes.*
>
> *In response to your letter, there is no shame in not knowing, only in refusing to learn. Belief in occurrences which you have described to me are beyond the comprehension of most men, except for the gifted few who are blessed at birth or in the wisdom gained afterward. In my opinion you have gained sufficient understanding to proceed. Therefore, I am offering you what little knowledge I possess, from basic cleansing techniques, to fasting, thirsting, sacrifices you must make, and prayers you must follow to attain success.*
>
> *The process is unconditional, demanding, and very risky, and often takes days, if not weeks of preparation. If for any reason you stray from the objective, you will fail. I cannot make it any clearer. Lack of faith, not adhering to doctrine, weakness of character, of will, not sound of body or mind and surely you will fall short of what you are attempting to do.*
>
> *Enclosed is the information needed for men such as youself who understand the Indian way, men of the Indian race, of all nations, tribes everywhere loyal to one belief, who share in a common faith in all things relating to our world and culture.*
>
> *I wish you well, not luck. You must rely on something more than mere chance. It is a feeling, a thought, a state of mind and heart. Most of all, my friend, you must earn it.*
>
> *Just remember — in a dream, anything is possible.*
>
> Sincerely,
Aaron
Caldwell
>
> *One last thing. Whatever you do, it must be done in the strictest of confidence.*

Of course!—David thought.

It was beginning to make sense.

He put the letters back in the book, placed the book on the table, and walked to the door.

"Where are you going?" asked Elly.

"Home. Come on. I have one more thing for you to do."

Chapter 49

Alexa counted no less than a dozen vehicles parked near the trailer when she arrived. A deputy waved the patrol car through the narrow lane between cars, but stood in the way of the Saab convertible, hand raised, denying entry. She pulled up short and shut off the engine. Before she could get out, the deputy hurried around to the driver's window and motioned for her to vacate the premises. She rolled down the window.

"Ma'm, you need to turn around. This is police business."

She flashed a card identifying herself as a reporter. "Why? I'm not obstructing anything."

"Please turn the car around."

"This is a public road."

"I don't care what it is or who you are, back up and leave."

That did it. Alexa had her notepad and cell phone in hand and whipped the door open. "Thanks for the warning." She marched past him with as much bravado as she could muster.

The patrolman was at a loss of what to do. "Hold on!" he cried. "Ma'm! Oh, ma'm!"

She paused as an ambulance drove up with flashers turning.

"I don't have a problem arresting you, lady. Get back in your car!"

Alexa wasn't budging. "Might as well throw the cuffs on, mister, 'cause I ain't goin' nowhere."

"It's okay, Larry, I'll vouch for her," hollered Tom Duckett. He closed the trunk to his patrol car and walked closer. "Sorry, Alex. Sheriff's orders. No one goes beyond the road without his permission."

A stretcher was removed from the ambulance and an emergency medical team rolled the stretcher part way, then, with the aid of Tom and another patrolman, carried it across a ditch toward the trees.

Alexa touched a number on her cell phone.

"News desk."

"Sam, I'm at the scene."

"Scene of what?"

"Not certain yet. Either a fatality or someone was hurt. Probably a fatality. An ambulance just arrived. I see four county patrol cars, the coroner's station wagon, one...no, make that two unmarked cars with state license plates, a truck from Mike's Tree Service, Sheriff

Pleamons' pickup, an unmarked van, probably carrying a forensic team, and four or five more vehicles."

"How in the world did you know where to go?"

"I followed a patrol car. What's interesting is the location. The missing person, didn't he work for Richard Macklin?"

"He did."

"What's his name?"

"Hang on." There was a rustling of a newspaper, a couple of groans, a turning of pages. "Ah…here it is. Wilfredo Pinoza."

"Gotta phone book handy? I'll see if there's an address on the mail box." She walked around to the front of the mobile home. "It's… 6766 Gills Pier Road."

Twenty seconds later, Sam said excitedly, "That's it! That's his address!"

"Why do you suppose they need a tree service?"

Sam made a humming sound—he didn't know.

"I'll call back when I have something," Alexa said. She closed the phone and turned her attention to the distant trees where another patrolman stood. She was tempted to greet the second patrolman as she did the first, but Larry, the cop, wouldn't have it.

"Don't even think about it," he cautioned.

Alexa occupied herself by taking notes. She made a few observations, then used her cell to take pictures of the unknown license plates, plus the telephone number to Mike's Tree Service written on the side of the truck. She paced back and forth as she compiled a list of que-tions when she noticed a car at the top of the hill. It was just sitting there, not moving. She asked the officer, Larry, if he had a pair of binoculars. He retrieved one and handed it to her. Cupping it, she focused on the driver whose face was obscured by shadow and sunglasses. Scanning down, she had less than two seconds to memorize the license plate before the white Mercedes backed up and drove away. Shaken, she handed the binoculars back to the patrolman.

"You all right, ma'm?"

"I'm fine. Thanks."

"That car, something about it bother you?"

"No, not really."

She wrote down a Pennsylvania license plate—91-A—on her notepad. By that time she saw four men struggling with the stretcher. Lying on it was a body covered with a sheet. Directly behind, a big man, familiar by his size and awkward gait, was Sheriff Aldrick Pleamons. Accompanying him were Tom Duckett, the coroner, four men wearing dark blue jackets with OBI written on the back, and two others wearing plaid shirts and blue jeans, carrying ropes and tree climbing gear.

At the first opportunity Alexa confronted the sheriff.

"Sheriff, could I have a minute?"

Shaking his head, Aldrick Pleamons stopped, consulted with another man, then grimaced as he made his way through the ditch. "Damn, lady, you do more popping up than anybody I've ever met. How'd you find out about this?"

"I followed a patrol car. What can you tell me about Wilfredo Pinoza? I assume that's his body."

Both men looked at one another. As the medical team carried the body to the ambulance, she could smell decayed flesh.

Alexa scribbled down more notes. The man standing beside the sheriff appeared to be listening to someone speaking into his earpiece. "How long has he been dead?" Alexa asked.

The two men conferred. The sheriff did a cursory introduction before the other man, Kenneth Frost, responded, "Miss Wilde, we're not prepared to make any statements just yet. I'm sorry."

"Why not? There must be something you can say. After all, he's been missing for a week. How did he die?"

The agent took two steps and halted. "What makes you think Wilfredo Pinoza is dead?"

She rolled her eyes. "Oh, come on! Why else would you cover the body?"

"Okay, let me rephrase it. Why do you think it's Pinoza's body?"

"Location. Circumstances. Everything fits."

"Will you at least allow us to notify his next of kin?"

"We're a weekly newspaper, Mr. Frost. I hardly think whatever you say will jeopardize the investigation. The letters on your jacket—OBI—what do they stand for?"

"Ohio Bureau of Investigation."

Sheriff Pleamons cleared his throat. "Miss, I think..."

"It's okay, Al," said Agent Frost. "She's right. I don't think a weekly publication will do any harm. Are you the young lady who's responsible for the stories in the newspaper?"

"A few."

"Why do you have to report his death?"

"Why do we report anything? Maybe people outside the family would like to know."

Agent Frost looked at the sheriff. "It's okay with me. How about you, Al? Should we give the lady a few minutes?"

The sheriff reluctantly gave his consent.

"Go ahead," said Ken.

Alexa held her pen, ready to write. "Do either of you know how he died?"

Ken looked at the Sheriff and shrugged. "Off the record?"

"I never put anything off the record," said Alexa, "unless it threatens an investigation."

"A tree," the agent confided.

"A tree? You mean, a tree fell? Crushed him?"

"No, a branch punctured his abdomen."

"Punctured?"

"A limb was sticking *through* it. Somehow his body was lifted into the air and thrown against a broken branch."

Her pen stopped. She looked up slowly. "You're kidding me, right?"

"I don't kid about things like that."

"I'm not sure I understand. Was the branch already broken, no longer part of the tree? Still attached? What?"

"I thought I made myself perfectly clear. A broken branch punctured his abdomen."

"Could you describe the condition of the body?"

"How gory do you want me to get?" said Sheriff Pleamons.

"Let's just say it wasn't pretty," added Agent Frost.

"Wasn't pretty *how*?"

Both men laughed, not that they thought it was funny.

Agent Frost resumed, "It's not exactly how you'd want to be remembered. Think of his friends and family, Miss Wilde. Think of a week-old cadaver, half a face missing, birds and animals chewing on rotting flesh. Not a pretty sight."

"Is that how long he's been dead—a week?"

Agent Frost deferred to the sheriff. "Six to seven days, the medical examiner estimates. He'll know more when he does the autopsy."

"So you needed a tree service to get the body down?"

"That's correct."

"Any idea how the body got up there?"

Agent Frost and Sheriff Pleamons traded stares.

"Soon as we know," said Ken, "we'll give you a call."

Both men started to leave.

She held up a hand. "Please. Just a couple of more questions. What exactly is the Ohio Bureau of Investigation? And what's its involvement in this case?"

"Just what you think it is," said Agent Frost, "the state equivalent to the FBI. And our involvement is to assist the sheriff any way we can."

"And how are they assisting you, Sheriff? In what capacity?"

"Manpower. Resources. You name it."

"Did you request their services? Or did you call the governor directly?"

"Sorry, we have other things to do," said the sheriff.

"Doesn't sound like an accidental death," said Alexa. "I assume, you've ruled that out?"

Neither man replied.

"Possibly a murder? Cult murder or something like that?"

Without excusing themselves, they walked to their respective cars.

"Is this case related to anything else, Mr. Frost? Sheriff? Wait, please!"

Too late.

Agent Frost had limited experience with reporters and the ones he had didn't turn out well. He felt the relationship between law enforcement and the fourth estate by its very nature was a clash of interests, one side fighting for transparency, the other guarded, hording information, mistrusting the accuracy and how events were portrayed. That's why when Agent Frost saw Alexa dialing her cell phone, he grew suspicious.

To the surveillance technician he said, "Did you hear the conversation we had with the reporter, Pete?"

"Yes, sir."

"Are you listening? Can you hear what she's saying?"

"Sure can."

"Who is she calling?"

"The newspaper. Hold on." After twenty seconds of silence, Pete said, "She talking to the editor. I'm recording it. I'll play it back when I'm finished."

Ken heard Alexa say she had an "exclusive," disclosing to quote the sheriff, "the *gory* details surrounding the mystery of Wilfredo Pinoza's death." After that, she relayed a message about a Pennsylvania license plate—91-A.

The agent slapped the hood of the car. "Damn it! I knew I shouldn't have trusted her! Pete, call the paper and tell the editor…" He hesitated, thinking.

"Tell him what?" said Pete.

"Never mind. It'll only make matters worse. Segedi, you listening?"

"Yes, I am."

"Call the Pennsylvania State Police and see if you can trace the registration to the license plate. Find out who 91-A is issued to. Pete, I want a fix on everyone involved. Richard Macklin, his son and daughter, and Walker. I want to know where they are and what they're doing."

The technician made no comment.

"You hear me, Pete?"

"Yes, I heard you. At the moment I can't locate any of them."

"Jesus H. Christ! Why the hell not?"

"The interference. We're not having visual problems as far as I can see. The cameras are working okay. It's the audio we're having problems with."

"And how do you explain that again?" asked Ken.

"I can't," said Pete.

Chapter 50

Agent Frost was getting impatient. A half a million dollars for a surveillance van—after two hours it still wasn't fully operational?

The frustration was very apparent when he said to the technician, "Check again, Pete. We put a tracer on both cars almost an hour ago."

"Nothing in the system, on the thermal or audio screens."

"That Black Hole thing again?"

"Could be."

"The locator on the daughter's Jeep—is it working?"

"Yep," said Pete. "Just sittin' in the driveway. Hang on. It appears we have a situation developing." When he spoke, he was excited. "Okay, here we go. I'm tracking a truck. Tracer One Vehicle is now on screen, traveling east on Route 2. Returning home."

"Anything to report?" Ken asked.

"Not yet. Oh, oh. We have another activity. Hmmm, that's interesting."

Agent Frost listened. The pauses were driving him crazy.

After a short delay, Pete said, "The computer thinks it heard a coyote."

"A coyote?"

"Maybe a wolf. I don't know. Ah, there it is again. Yep, it's a coyote all right. Listen! I'll play it back."

Through the earpiece there was a high-pitched howl, something between a bark and the cry of a wolf.

"Let's not get sidetracked," the agent remarked. "What's the location of Tracer One?"

"Pulling into the driveway as we speak. Hold on. They're talking." There were mumblings in the background between a man and woman. Pete did a quick interpretation. "The sister is going to the library to see a lady named Mae. Why, I don't know. That's pretty much it. Wait a second." There was ten seconds of dead air. "Something about a…huh? Let me run that back." After a short pause, Pete said, "Never heard a phrase like that."

"Like what?"

"Halting Place. The brother wants his sister to go to the library, to see if she can find any references to it. Evidently, he's staying home." There was ten seconds of silence. Pete was thinking. Or listening. "Oh, oh. The coyote. Just heard some dogs. They're barking. Same location. I think we've found our man."

"Walker?"

"No, Richard Macklin."

"Where?"

"Near a rock quarry, a quarter mile north of the farmhouse. By the way, the sister is leaving."

"Okay. Segedi, I want you to go to the library. Do some snooping around. Hurry, before it closes. Then meet with the Sheriff, see how he wants to handle this. G, call the deputies at the trailer and have them lock it down. And tell the coroner to call us as soon as possible. What's the status at the farmhouse, Pete?"

"Quiet. Just heard the dogs again. And whoever's with them. If it isn't Richard Macklin, I don't know who it is."

"Why didn't you mention this before?"

"I didn't think it was important."

"Why not?"

"I don't know. I thought someone was out hunting with his dogs."

"In late April? Come on! How long ago did you first hear them?"

"About twenty minutes ago. The computer didn't give it a high priority until now."

"Why do you think it's Richard Macklin?"

"Tone of voice. The way he talks to the dogs, whispers to them. If you ask me, it sounds like he's hunting the coyote."

Agent Frost put his clipboard aside. "Okay, everyone. Let's get moving. Got the coordinates, Pete?"

"Sure do."

"Segedi, report back as soon as you can. Fast and quiet we go, gentlemen."

Chapter 51

David tried to rationalize what he was about to do, but there was no justification other than being a case of curiosity. Plain and simple, it was an invasion of privacy. He walked into his father's bedroom, sat on the bed next to the nightstand, slid open a drawer, and pulled out a packet of letters written by his mother to Richard when he was Vietnam. That's when the guilt hit home.

Are you sure you want to do this? What if there are secrets you're not supposed to know? Intimacies young lovers share?

He untied a ribbon that bound the packet. Among the letters were newspaper articles, photographs, birthday cards. A pink rose, wrapped in cellophane, fell to the floor. He picked it up, unfolded a card, and recognized his mother's handwriting. "War will only make our embrace that much sweeter," she wrote. "Happy birthday, sweetheart."

Inside was a photograph of 'Dode' seated at a piano, elbows on the keys, hands under the chin, head turned, smiling, along with several more pictures of various poses. Seated in a swing. Sitting at an easel, paintbrush in hand, staring intently at the canvas. At a picnic, throwing a horseshoe with a note that said, "No ringers today. Wish you were here."

David discarded them and glanced at a newspaper clipping of an obituary stapled to a letter. In it, Dora had the unfortunate task of informing Richard his Aunt Blanche had died from lung cancer, having been a two pack a day smoker. At the bottom of the letter she wrote, "Funerals should be a celebration of life. We'll have a long and happy life together, Richard. When I die, don't put me in a pine box. I want to be cremated and celebrated, not mourned..."

David felt something stirring inside. He remembered the day his mother was put to rest, the long procession of mourners, the closed casket. He was a pallbearer. The casket didn't feel right. There had been a strange mood about the funeral, like she hadn't really died, and what was inside the casket wasn't really his mother. He couldn't quite put his finger on it.

No one took her death harder than David. She died his freshman year in college. His name was on the sports pages of the local paper every week, on the lips of everyone in Bertram County who had an interest in baseball. Baseball prodigy. Prolific in the field. Prodigious hitter. Parade high school All American. Wooed by scouts from every Major League team. The single most celebrated athlete in the tri-county area, ever. Perhaps in all of southern Ohio that year. Whenever his team played, it was an event. But no one knew the anguish he and his family were suffering at the time.

The Ohio Southern Tigers were undefeated, contending for the conference championship. An upcoming game against a rival college had the community buzzing and the Macklin household in an uproar. The doctor strongly advised against Dora's attendance. He said she was too weak, too frail, in no condition to travel anywhere. Having lost forty-five pounds in two months, she looked as if she'd aged a lifetime. The beauty may have faded on the outside, but not the inside.

He remembered the day she shuffled into the kitchen without a respirator or oxygen hose. Instead of a nightgown, she wore a loose-fitting sundress three sizes too big. David was eating lunch, or trying to.

He turned as soon as he heard footsteps. "Mom, what are you doing? You're supposed to be in bed."

She placed a finger over her lips. "Shoosh! Doing a few laps around the house. Don't want anyone to know." She reached into a kitchen drawer, pulled out a spoon, slid into a chair opposite him, and dipped the spoon into a bowl of tomato soup. "Mmmm, always tastes better when someone else cooks." She helped herself to another spoonful and slurped like a little kid.

"Yeah, right," said David. "All I did was add water."

She helped herself to a saltine cracker and munched. Two black cocker spaniel puppies pattered into the room, sat up, and watched them eat.

David noticed her hair was combed. A touch of lip gloss covered her lips. She never wore mascara, but her lashes appeared longer and darker. She looked healthier than she had in weeks and had done it on her own. The effort unfortunately left her exhausted. Wheezing, she fed a couple of crackers to Roscoe and Cinders, then slowly looked up. "Big day tomorrow."

She was referring, of course, to an upcoming game. David didn't have the heart to tell her he wasn't playing. The soup had lost its taste, so he pushed it aside.

Dora dipped a cracker into the bowl and chewed, then magically produced two decks of cards. "How about a little one-on-one?"

"Okay. What are we playing for?"

They always played for something. A trip to Hawaii. A privately chartered trip to the moon. A nickel's worth of gooseberry feathers. The loser never paid unless the bet was for something like who did the dishes or washed the windows. Mostly Double Sol was an excuse to get together, laugh, and have a good time.

Dora tossed a deck across the table, unboxed her deck, and started shuffling.

"How about a wish?" she proposed. "Winner chooses."

David grinned. "Okay, little lady."

The ground rules, having been established years ago, were simple. No cheating and no holding back. Slap the cards down as fast as you can. It was always a contest to see who could arrange the cards first. David smiled because he had two aces showing, a good hand. Dode frowned because her face-up cards were all black, spades and clubs.

On a count to three, the game commenced. As expected, David got the jump early. In keeping with tradition, whenever the pace quickened, he did a play-by-play—

"And *Little Momma's* on the outside, closing fast. Two lengths behind. The pace is torrid. She can't keep up. Oooo! Wicked move! Beat *Mister Davey* by doing the ol' slipperoo, folks. One length behind. Oh, oh! She's got the whip out. *Little Momma's* headin' for the turn. Givin' it all she's got. Ooooo! Double slipperoo! Got him again. They're neck and neck..."

Her nimble fingers did indeed gallop. Fluttered like a bunch of wild geese about to take flight. The table thumped as they threw their cards down. Giggles. Lots of giggles. He took one look at her and almost lost it. It was something he would remember for the rest of his life. Impish eyes darting from side to side. The tip of her tongue sticking out. The way she sat, grinning, lost in the heat of the moment. And loving it.

David was choking on emotion. It started somewhere in his belly, this great big floodtide of feelings. It rose uncontrollably into his neck, bubbling to the surface.

"Come on!" she cried. "Keep playing!"

It was hard. He couldn't get into it.

She was all over the place, two steps ahead. Hands flying. Bouncing up and down in her chair. Giggling.

"*Little Momma's* on a roll. *Mister Davey's* in trouble. Oh, oh. He doesn't know what to do. Oooo-weee! Look at *Little Momma* go! Girl's got giddy up! "

His emotion burst with a suddenness. Instead of crying, it was a peal of laughter. It shook his entire body.

His giddiness fed her giddiness and her giddiness fed his. She was hunched over, laughing. Once she took the advantage, she ran with it and never looked back. The game wasn't even close. She finished with a flurry and cried—

"I win!"

And then she coughed. She coughed until her face turned red. She held a fist to her mouth, gagging, fighting back the reflexes, unable to breath.

David ran to the sink and poured a glass of tap water. He practically forced it down her throat. Luckily, it did the trick. She was no longer hacking. Far from it. She was giggling again, humored perhaps by her frailty, but more so by the intensity and passion of the game.

He took a seat and waited until she recovered. "You all right?"

"Um-hmm." She nodded, then took another sip, gurgling like a little kid.

"Okay, so what's the wish?" David asked.

"No quitting."

"No quitting?"

"Neither of us can quit. However bad it gets, no quitting."

"That's not a wish."

"No, it's better. A promise."

David knew then what he had to do. A wish granted was a promise made. Tomorrow he'd be on a grassy field, hitting baseballs like…there was no tomorrow.

"And if you had won," she wondered, "what would you have wished?"

David thought for a second. "Haven't heard you play the piano in a while."

Without batting an eye, Dora got up from the kitchen table, shuffled down the hall into the front room, sat at the piano, and began to play. It was a melody—soft and sweet, her own composition. It was beautiful.

It was one of the greatest days of his life.

David fought back the tears.

Small dark shadows seemed to glide across the bedroom floor. A door squeaked in the kitchen. He could sense something, but didn't know what it was. Just then he thought he heard a chord from the piano, a note fading, the last bar of Gershwin's *Stairway to Paradise*. He could feel the hair on his arms stand up. The sound was interrupted by the front doorbell, which rang twice. He quickly stuffed the letters back in the envelopes, retied the ribbon, and put the bundle back in the night table. He rushed down the hall, paused to look at the empty piano stand, opened the front door, and with mixed feelings greeted Alexa.

"Hi. Come in." He knew right away something was wrong. "Want something to drink?"

"No thank you. Unfortunately, I have some bad news, David.

Wilfredo Pinoza is dead."

Chapter 52

Richard Macklin didn't consider himself a hunter. Occasionally, he shot quail or pheasant but never wild game, not unless he had to, and this was one of those occasions when he felt he had to. The coyotes were becoming a nuisance. The cattle had to be protected and without Tyson to do that the only way to protect them was to eliminate the source of the problem.

The past few days he was able to determine a pattern. The pack would wander in at night, looking for prey—rodents, rabbits, small deer—then return to their den in a wooded area north of the farmhouse. Thanks to the spaniels, finding the tracks was easy. It was keeping the dogs quiet that proved to be a bit of a task. At the slightest detection of an animal their ears would perk up, they'd growl, stand perfectly still, or, depending on the size and nature of the creature, become excited. It was a good thing Richard had them on leashes.

After entering the woods at the northern edge of the property, the search intensified. Roscoe and Cinders sniffed and growled, their eyes staring keenly at a distant point. When the dogs appeared to be in a constant state of agitation, he knew he was close. To his left, beside a brook, was a spot where a tree had fallen and seedlings withered under the forest canopy. There was no sunlight, only shade. It seemed as good a place as any to sit and wait. He tied Cinders and Roscoe to an oak, sat beside them, laid the shotgun across his lap, and reached into his back pocket.

It wasn't the taste of bourbon he liked. Just the effect. After two swigs, he turned the flask upside down and poured the remaining drops on the ground. In Vietnam he tried it all—marijuana, alcohol, a little opium. For a month after his wife died he drank heavily, then quit. But now…

He couldn't shake his addictions. He had to temper the loneliness somehow. That was his excuse anyway.

In disgust, he tossed the flask into the brush.

Something moved. A female coyote sprang from a growth of vegetation close to where the flask landed. She appeared uncertain as to what to do. The spaniels saw her, whined but didn't bark. Richard held out a hand to quiet them. Crouching on one knee, he raised the shotgun, but the coyote, sensing an intruder, trotted off, looking back once in a while to see if she was being followed, and disappeared into the woods.

It wasn't long before Richard heard a whimper much like the sound a puppy makes when it feels neglected. He barely heard it above the trickle of water running through the brook. Cinders heard it, too. Her ears curled as she listened. Roscoe stirred and did the same. Richard got to his feet, shouldered the shotgun, and looped his finger around the trigger. There it was again, except this time there were two whimpers. He thought they were coming from the other side of the brook. He stepped across the water—no more than three feet wide. Directly ahead, the trunk of a large oak was lying flat. He saw tracks, paw marks in the soil. Two more steps and he hesitated, listening. He could almost hear them breathing. He reached down and pushed aside a cluster of forest ferns And there they were. Baby coyotes. Two of them. Pups. Cowering timidly in a bed of hollowed out earth, beneath the tree trunk. They whimpered when their sleepy eyes saw him. They were so frightened they didn't think of running. Too young to know better, they just sat there, helpless, shaking.

Richard cleared the area of vegetation until the pups were no longer hidden. He raised the shotgun to his shoulder, squinting down the gun barrel. He stood there, thinking if he didn't do it now, he'd have to do it later. Might as well get it over with.

He looked at their eyes and saw the wildness, the innocence, and slowly put pressure on the trigger. He learned a long time ago killing should be swift. Anything else was cruel. Nature was cruel enough as it was. He found himself lowering the shotgun, then, reaffirming his resolve, held it tight against his shoulder, bracing for the kickback. A bead of sweat rolled into his eye.

Roscoe woofed.

A distant blare of a siren sounded—a quick burst, no more than two seconds.

His brow knitted in confusion.

A minute later the siren sounded again, a little longer, closer this time. Then it blared a third time, longer and closer still. He figured it had to be a signal. But why?

He lowered the shotgun and whispered to the pups, untied the spaniels, and led them to the edge of the woods where he peered through a break in the trees. He could see flashers spinning atop a car. A sedan was parked along a dirt road used for hauling crushed rock from a quarry. Standing outside the passenger door was the agent from the Ohio Bureau of Investigation. Agent Frost waved him closer.

"You looking for me?" Richard hollered. "How'd you know where I was?"

The agent ignored the question. "Wilfredo Pinoza, we found him. He's dead."

Richard showed no emotion. Only surprise. "Where?"

"All in good time, Mr. Macklin. We'd like to ask you a few questions first."

The dogs strained against the leashes. Richard gave them a hard tug as he approached the sedan. "How did he die?"

"He lost a lot of blood."

Richard was unable to hide his irritation. "Twelve years he worked for me. Twelve years. And that's all you can say?"

"It's a little more involved than you think, Mr. Macklin. It's only a guess, but the medical examiner thinks he died about a week ago. We found the body a few hundred yards from the trailer where he lived. I'll get into the details later. For now we'd like you to come with us."

"Why?"

"When someone's murdered, or should I say, if there's the suspicion of murder, that's what we do. We ask questions."

"Why me?"

"Mr. Macklin, please get in the car."

"Ask whatever you want. I'm right here."

"We want you to do a polygraph test. We don't have it with us. We'll have to go into town."

Richard looked at the dogs, then at the agent and gave up without a fight. "Suppose you'll be wanting this." He handed over the shotgun and unhooked the leashes as the spaniels stared up at him with sad, inquiring eyes.

"They can sit in the back with you," said Ken. "We'll take them home."

"No. They'll find their way. They're good dogs." Richard petted Cinders, then affectionately pushed her away. "Go home! You, too, Roscoe. Go on now."

The spaniels kept their eyes on Richard as he climbed into the backseat. Once the car was moving, they followed, cut away from the road, then trotted, confused, toward the farmhouse.

From the edge of the woods three coyotes watched with interest. They crept through the trees. Conditioned by years of stalking prey, their stealth and agility were amazing.

Chapter 53

Alexa stood in the hallway of the Macklin home, relating what she knew about Freddie Pinoza's death—who was at the scene, when the death occurred, where the body was found—while offering a few opinions of her own. She ruled out suicide and was pretty sure it wasn't an accident. How the body ended up in the tree, stuck to a limb, she had no idea.

"You think it was murder?" David asked.

"Had to be. I'll bet the sheriff thinks so too. Why else would the medical examiner be called to the scene?"

"Hard to say…"

The conversation came to an abrupt stop when they heard a loud cry.

David's body went rigid as he stared out the front window. He threw open the door and dashed down the front steps before Alexa knew what was happening. Across the street, in the field, there was another blood-curdling cry. The spaniels were running for their lives, pursued by a pack of coyotes. Although he was weaponless, David sprinted toward them, yelling and screaming as he crossed the road. The coyotes were gaining on the spaniels, in particular Roscoe. The lead coyote was snapping at his heels. Roscoe tried to dodge and swerve, but the coyote was too quick. It caught a leg. The spaniel tumbled and rolled, then got to his feet, and scrambled forward. The rest of the pack converged. Cinders sprinted ahead, out of danger—for the moment.

David felt his heart sink when the coyotes brought Roscoe down. They lunged at him, snapping their teeth while Roscoe howled, defenseless, twitching on his side, kicking at his attackers. Suddenly, Cinders did something completely out of character for a docile, domesticated animal. She turned and went into a rage, displaying a fierceness that was incredible. The coyotes appeared confused. Cinders stood facing the pack, barking and growling, threatening to lunge at the first coyote that dared to challenge her. David waved his arms and screamed…ran up, holding clods of dirt in his hands. The first clod he threw as a warning. Two coyotes backed away. A third bared its fangs. Another clod caught it flush on its side. The coyote yelped, stood its ground, and looked at David with a voracity that sent shivers up his spine. He walked closer, this time with a rock in his hand, cocked, ready to throw while Cinders kept barking. He saw Roscoe limping away...Alexa coming up behind him.

She picked up a handful of dirt, threw it, and yelled, "Git! Go away!"

The pack finally turned tail and ran.

When he knew it was safe, David called to Cinders, gathered her up in his arms, and looked around for Roscoe. Alexa was crouched over him. The black cocker was lying on its side, breathing heavily. She whispered softly, "It's okay. They're gone."

Roscoe was in bad shape. Blood was seeping from the wounds to his left leg and left side.

Alexa was about to touch him when David yelled, "Don't! He might bite. When dogs are in shock, they'll snap at anything that moves. Wait here. I'll get the truck."

"What if the coyotes come back?"

"They won't."

* * *

Pete recorded the sound portion of the attack, not the video.

His orders were explicit. If an incident occurred, he was told to alert the bureau, then the sheriff's office, in that order. Under no circumstance was he expected to deviate from the plan, which didn't take into account his love of dogs. Pete had a Jack Russell back home named Spud, a whirling dervish kind of dog, so lovable it made people coo and smile.

From a recorded conversation earlier, Pete knew Eileen Macklin was stopping at the library to see a lady named Mae. According to the tracking devise, her Jeep was parked along the street in front of the building. He Googled the phone number.

After four rings, a woman answered, "County Library. What department, please?"

"Actually, Operator, I'm looking for a librarian named Mae."

"Just a moment. I'll connect you."

A phone rang. "History. This is Mae. May I help you?"

"Yes," said Pete. "I'm trying to reach Eileen Macklin. Do you happen to know who she is...where I might find her?"

"Why, she's standing right here. Hold on."

A younger woman took the phone. "Hello."

Pete didn't know what to say. He stammered, "Uh...Eileen Macklin?"

"Speaking."

"You don't know me. I was driving by your family's farm. Sorry to break the news. I saw one of your dogs being attacked by a coyote. Your brother and a woman are taking the dog into town. To an animal clinic, I believe."

"You saw it?"

"Less than five minutes ago. If you hurry, you could be there about the same time."

"Same time where?"

Pete grimaced. He wasn't handling it well. He was talking too much, giving too much information. Information a stranger wouldn't know.

Elly repeated the question.

Pete didn't care. The health of the dog was more important. "I assume where you work. Linck's Veterinary Clinic."

There was a long pause.

"Who is this?" shey asked.

"Like I said, a passing motorist."

"How do you know where I work?"

"Doesn't matter. What I'm wondering is, does the clinic stay open after six?"

"No."

"Look," said Pete, "you're just going to have to trust me. There's an old truck heading your way. I assume there's an attendant on duty to take care of the animals."

"There is."

"Good. Then you better get moving."

"Wait! Is this some kind of joke?"

"No."

"How did you know I was here at the library? Are you following me? Who are you?"

"Your Guardian Angel. Hurry if you want to save the dog."

Chapter 54

Tom Duckett resented how the state had muscled in on the investigation. Granted, the Sheriff's Department needed help, but it didn't have to be delegated to a minor role.

In a back room of the Law Enforcement Center, in an adjoining office, Tom listened as OBI agents interrogated Richard Macklin. It was obvious Richard had been drinking. He was continually asked why he had been walking through a woods carrying a loaded shotgun. The agents seemed more concerned with that than the death of Wilfredo Pinoza—until they hooked up the electrodes and began the polygraph test. At that point Sheriff Aldrick Pleamons took a seat outside the interrogation room alongside Tom and watched the questioning through a one-way pane of glass.

Kenneth Frost, assuming the role of interrogator, stood glaring across the room. "Are you sure you don't want your attorney present?"

Richard shook his head.

"What, you're not sure," said Agent Brian Riddick, "or it's okay to proceed without him?"

Richard grinned. It was also obvious he didn't like Brian. "It's okay to proceed."

Agent Frost began the questioning. "Might as well get straight to it. Did you murder Wilfredo Pinoza?"

"No," Richard responded.

Ken glanced at the technician seated to his right. "Please answer, 'No, I did not,' if that's the case."

"No, I did not," said Richard.

The technician and Agent Frost exchanged glances.

Agent Frost continued, "Do you know who did?"

"No."

"One more time, Mr. Macklin. Answer, 'No, I do not,' if that's the case."

"No, I do not."

"When did you first know he was missing?"

"This past Monday when he didn't show up for work."

"Was he punctual, reliable?"

"Very. Never missed a day."

"What kind of relationship did you two have?"

"Excuse me?"

"Did you consider him a friend?"

Richard nodded. "I suppose you could say that."

"It's our understanding he borrowed quite a bit of money from you. Is that correct?"

"Borrowed? I gave him advances if he needed it."

"How much?"

"I didn't keep records."

"Did you have any disagreements over money?"

"Not really."

"Tom Duckett tells us you and Freddie fought in a bar. Could you tell us why?"

"He's dead. I don't see the point."

"The point is," said Brian, "we need to know."

Agent Frost circled the table, stood at the head of it, arms folded. "Did you have an argument about his late alimony payments?"

"I'd rather not discuss it."

"Not discuss it?" cried Brian. "You don't have a choice. Either you discuss it or we throw your ass in jail."

Agent Frost braced his arms against the table. "This is not a court of law, Mr. Macklin. Just an inquiry. You argued, didn't you? About money. The both of you got mad. It turned into a fight."

"He was late a couple of times. Once in a while he got a little belligerent."

"So you hit him."

"Slapped him. One time."

"That was it?"

"I gave him an advance the next day. We never talked about it since."

"I understand he had a drug problem—cocaine, marijuana—as well as alcohol."

"That has nothing to do with anything."

"Just answer the question," snapped Brian.

"He liked beer. So what? Occasionally, we had a drink together. He was always clean and sober when he worked."

"So you wouldn't know if he owed money to any drug dealers?"

"No, I wouldn't know that."

"A little while ago we described to you how we found his body, the location, the position of his arms, the broken branch sticking through his abdomen. I want you to picture it, remember it. Does it remind you of anything?"

Richard lowered his head without commenting.

Agent Frost repeated the question.

Richard rubbed his chin and replied, "No."

The technician flashed a negative look at Ken.

"Don't lie," warned Ken.

Richard shifted in his chair, ill at ease.

Ken moved closer, leaning over the table. "According to your war records, you fought in quite a few battles. Saw a lot of men die. I imagine it's not easy seeing someone dead. Arms twisted around his head. A tree limb sticking through his gut. Ever see anything like it?"

Silence.

Brian slapped the table. "Answer the damn question!"

Everyone flinched except Richard. He stared blankly at the floor.

"You saw a body like that before, didn't you?" said Ken.

The silence lasted for ten seconds.

Richard spread his calloused hands on the table. You could see the whiteness of his knuckles.

"Let me remind you," said Ken. "You're wired to a polygraph. I'll ask one more time and wait as long as it takes. Where did you see a body like that before?"

The word floated. A soft whisper—

"Vietnam."

"What? Speak up!"

"The war. Vietnam."

The mood in the room changed. The agents looked at one another as Agent Frost leaned closer. "Take me back. Tell me about it."

A nightmarish look passed across Richard's face, the look of demons resurfacing. He began a lengthy journey back to the jungles of Vietnam, a country ravaged by war almost forty years ago.

*   *   *

Roscoe was losing blood fast. Muzzled with a belt wrapped around his mouth, the spaniel was lying on a bath towel on the front seat, struggling to remain conscious, his body in shock. Alexa stroked the back of his neck as Cinders sat on the floor between her legs. Alexa and David had barely spoken.

"Did you bring your cell phone?" he asked.

The color drained from Alexa's face. She patted her pockets. "How could I be so dumb? Sorry. I left it in my car."

"It's okay."

She felt terrible, knowing a phone call could be the difference between life and death. "Where are we taking him?"

"The animal hospital where my sister works."

"Don't they close at six?"

"Somebody's always in the kennel. Least I'm hoping so."

As they approached the city of Mistwood, traffic picked up.

David eased up on the gas pedal, but not by much. "Once we get there, we'll make a few calls. It's almost six, so my sister might be in her apartment or on her way to the farm. She's the only one qualified to do surgery unless we call the vet at home."

Now and again David glanced at Roscoe to see how he was holding up. David was worried surgery might be too late. The bath towel was soaked in blood.

Once they entered the city, he kept the speedometer well over the speed limit. Linck's Veterinary Clinic was two blocks from the university in the south part of town. He couldn't believe his eyes when they pulled into the parking lot. Standing on the sidewalk, waiting at the rear entrance, was his sister.

Chapter 55

Six men crowded into Sheriff Pleamons' office. The last one in shut the door.

"Well, what do you think?" said Agent Frost.

The sheriff walked around his desk and sat down. "Interesting. Not sure what to make of it, but the polygraph doesn't lie."

"He's not delusional, that much we know," Tom Duckett remarked.

"Apparently not."

Someone knocked on the door.

"It's unlocked. Come in."

In walked Agent Roy Segedi, holding a file. He looked at Agent Frost. "I have the report on the Pennsylvania license plate."

Agent Frost explained what was going on, then said, "Go ahead, Roy."

"The plate is registered to a Hayden Crawford. Thirty-seven year-old white male. Jailed twice for illegal transportation of goods. One of three accomplices in a theft ring. All with records. They specialize in department store theft, stolen merchandise freighted across state lines. The guy's gone from bad to worse since being dishonorably discharged from the army. Two charges of rape. No convictions. Possession of narcotics, stolen weapons. Petty theft. Assault and battery. Also runs a private investigation service. Suspected of money laundering and trafficking. I could go on and on."

"Theft ring?" said Agent G. "The one in Pickett County?"

"Cops in Pickett County think so," replied Segedi. "They just don't have any proof. By the way, the accomplices are all related. Guess who Crawford's cousin is? Paul Heidtman. The guy who lives down the road from Richard Macklin."

Tom Duckett's interest suddenly grew. "Heidtman?"

The sheriff leaned up in his chair. "Tell them what you know about Heidtman, Tom."

"His family owned a saw mill. Mill burned down. Suspected arson. Not enough evidence to convict. Nice insurance settlement. Two months ago Heidtman worked for a collection agency. Got in a fight with a guy over money. Almost killed the guy. Lucky he didn't do time. Some hotshot lawyer got him out, clean. And, trust me, the legal fees didn't come cheap. Heidtman also faced a charge of suspected fraud, another of assault and battery. Both times the attorney convinced the court to rule in his favor. Everybody knows they're crooks. They're just good at covering things up. Oh, and the attorney I mentioned, he's from the same law firm that represents Mark Treshler."

There were a lot of perplexed looks around the room.

Duckett continued, "Treshler and Richard Macklin are in-laws. No love lost there. Treshler would do just about anything to get his hands on Macklin property, but Richard won't sell. He's been resisting a hostile takeover for months. When you peel back the layers, you begin to see a pattern."

"Maybe," said Agent Frost. "How does it tie in with what we just heard?"

"I'm getting to that. This past Tuesday I interviewed Heidtman. He's a tenant farmer. Raises pigs on the side. He said the night before the pigs got restless. He didn't get a minute of sleep. It's in the report."

Heads turned. More perplexed looks.

Duckett elaborated, "This morning we learned that Crawford was following the reporter you met earlier. She's been trying to dig up dirt in places she shouldn't. My guess is Treshler put a tail on her to shake her up, rattle her cage. Meanwhile, we suspect Heidtman is working some kind of scam on the inside while interests representing Mark Treshler are exerting pressure on the outside. That's where the leveraged buyout comes in. However you want to look at it, Richard Macklin is being squeezed."

"That's a bit of a stretch, isn't it?" said Agent Frost.

"Not really. I'd stake my reputation on it."

"I still don't see how these guys fit in with what's going on."

"Oh, they fit in all right," Duckett replied. "The puzzle is a bit cockeyed is all. The night I talked to Heidtman he said he had a dream about Desert Storm. One of the power units where he was stationed was sabotaged by Iranians."

"Are you saying there's some sort of connection?" said Agent Frost. "Huh-uh. No way."

"You asked the questions," Tom pointed out. "You heard the statements."

The floorboards creaked as Aldrick Pleamons drew back his chair. He stood up slowly. Made a big production of it. "You mean all these things are tied together through a series of dreams?"

No one said a word.

The sheriff's voice boomed, "Are we all frickin' nuts?" He sat back down and stuck his head in his hands, mumbling to himself.

Ken Frost glanced around the room, then directed his question at

Agent Segedi. "Did you get a chance to talk to anyone at the library?"

Segedi scratched the back of his neck and cringed. "Uh, 'fraid not. The lady I was supposed to see left early. By the time I got around to the rest of the staff, they were locking the doors."

Agent Frost hung his head in dejection. "Wonderful. Any suggestions? Questions? Anybody got anything?"

A lot of blank faces.

"Anything you want to add, Sheriff?"

Aldrick Pleamons cleared his throat. "Not right now."

"What about Richard Macklin?" Tom Duckett asked. "Can't keep him here all night."

"Let's see what the Medical Examiner has to say first," said Frost. "Then we'll release him."

The sheriff tugged at his belt and dismissed everyone. He and Agent Frost waited until everyone cleared the room.

When they were alone, Frost said, "Why do I get the feeling when we talk to the Medical Examiner, we won't know any more than we already do."

* * *

David was impressed. His sister had shown the poise and skill of a true professional. The care she administered to Roscoe was first rate. She had done everything she could, quickly and effectively—deadening the pain, sewing up the wounds, stopping the bleeding, and stabilizing the vital signs.

When Alexa excused herself to go the bathroom, David took the opportunity to ask his sister. "What did you find out at the library?"

Elly removed the surgical gloves, threw them in the wastebasket, and made an O with her thumb and middle finger, "Zero. Couldn't find a thing in the database or catalogues. Mae searched everywhere, asked everyone. No one heard of the term. But she agrees. *Halting Place* could be a burial ground."

"Well, that got us nowhere," said David. "Do me a favor. Would you and Alexa hang out here for a while? I've got an errand to run." He walked to the door.

"David?"

"Yeah?"

"What are you going to do?"

"Not sure yet." He left the room, satisfied Roscoe was in capable hands.

Once she freshened up, Alexa greeted him in the hallway. "I think your sister missed her calling. She should operate on people, not dogs."

"What can I say? She loves animals. Listen, Alexa. You mind staying here? I think Elly would appreciate the company."

"What about you?"

"There's something I've got to do. If you need a car, borrow my sister's."

"Okay, but…" She watched him turn to leave. "David."

"What?"

"Why did you call this morning?"

He shrugged, too embarrassed to answer. "Felt like it, I guess."

"Come on. You had a reason. What was it?" She saw a touch of shyness in his face. He was blushing.

David looked at her and could feel his pulse quicken. He had an irresistible urge to walk up and…

No, it would only complicate things.

"Tell me," she insisted.

He couldn't take his eyes off her. Emotions were running deep. Being alone in the hallway with Alexa only fueled those emotions all the more.

"Dinner," he said.

"Huh?"

"I wanted to know if you'd have dinner with me."

She stared at him, speechless, and laughed, "You mean, like a date?"

"What's wrong with that?"

"Nothing." Her mood suddenly changed. The hard veneer of a journalist was softening. "Are you thinking what I'm thinking?"

Now he was the one who was speechless.

She walked closer.

He wasn't blushing any more. Gushing was more like it.

"Do you need an answer right now?" she whispered.

She leaned closer. Their mouths were only inches apart. He could feel the heat of her, smell the sweetness of her skin, imagine the softness of her body pressed against his.

Her lips were drawing him closer.

Softer, quieter, she whispered, "Right this very second?"

Her lips were almost caressing his.

"Um-hmm," he murmured.

They kissed without touching anywhere else.

It was the softest, most pleasurable thing he had ever done. Innocent, but passionate. The perfect kiss. A promise of things to come.

Chapter 56

David couldn't get Alexa out of his mind during the ride home. He made two stops along the way, the first at Substation 12 where a utility worker informed him, "Power won't be back on until sometime tomorrow." The second stop was at Wilfredo Pinoza's trailer. A sheriff's patrol car straddled the road, blocking it. Yellow police tape tied between signposts designated the area as a crime scene. The realization of Freddie's death had a way of trivializing everything else, including Alexa. From that point on, David focused his attention on more urgent matters.

Five minutes later, when he pulled into the driveway, he saw a utility truck with a lift kit parked next to a telephone pole. The bucket was raised and a workman in hardhat was attaching a metal box to the top of the pole.

David thought nothing of it as he parked at the end of the driveway. After he opened the door to let Cinders out, he removed a piece of paper from a shirt pocket with a list of words and phrases he had written as reminders or subjects of interest. He glanced down the list until he came to an *abode of spirits*. Certainly a burial ground could be interpreted as an abode of spirits. Were they the same? If so, in what way? Which begged another question. What else could be considered an abode of spirits?

A cemetery?

An old barn?

If Old Serenity was haunted, he believed it was by mice and bats. Maybe a barn owl or two.

He leapt from the truck, leaving the engine running, the door open as Cinders trotted behind, wagging her tail. In the kitchen he picked up Elly's recharged cell phone and a flashlight, then grabbed a shovel from the lower barn, and hurried to the truck with Cinders following every step of the way.

Standing by the door, he looked at the two items in his hands.

Shovel? Flashlight?

Eeeny-meenie-miney-mo…

Cinders looked at him with happy, expectant eyes.

He glanced at his watch. 7:08 pm. His internal clock was ticking.

He laid the flashlight on the passenger seat, the shovel on the floor of the truck, then dialed his father's cell phone. It was temporarily out of service.

*   *   *

Tom Duckett felt he should be asking the questions, not Ken Frost. After all, he'd been on the case the longest and was the first one consulted whenever an opinion was needed.

He pleaded his case when the sheriff and Agent Frost returned from the Medical Examiner's office. They decided to give Tom a shot. Why not? What was there to lose?

The Medical Examiner listed the official cause of death as massive internal hemorrhaging, leading to heart failure. Death came instantly. Six days ago.

Tom walked into the interrogation room with two ice-cold cans of pop. He closed the door, offered a can of cola to Richard, and sat down.

"Tough week."

Richard pretended to laugh.

Tom noticed Richard's left shoulder was sagging. His eyes were languid, inert. He looked as if he was half asleep.

"How you feeling?"

"I want to go home," said Richard.

"What did you do to your shoulder?"

"I fell."

"Did you see a doctor?"

Richard nodded.

Tom got up. Started pacing slowly. "Are you taking any medication?"

A slight pause. "Yeah."

"What kind?"

"Painkillers."

Tom's expression didn't change. The topic did. "This morning... I'd like to go back over what happened one more time. When, or I should say, *what* woke you up?"

"I already told you."

"Tell me again."

"The cattle—I heard them stampeding."

"What else did you hear?"

"Nothing."

"You sure?"

"Yes, I'm sure."

"I understand you've been having dreams. Were you dreaming before you heard the cattle?"

"I don't remember."

The deputy sat down, propped his leg up on a chair, and put his hands together. "You understand why we keep asking you questions, don't you?"

"You must think I'm involved somehow."

"With...?"

"Whatever it is you're investigating."

"What's your theory?"

A shake of the head. A shrug. Richard didn't know.

"So what you're telling me is, you have no idea what's killing the livestock or what caused the bridge to collapse. They're all just one big mystery to you, is that it?"

"Sorry. What can I say?"

"That includes Freddie, of course."

"I told you what I know."

"Really? And the dreams...?"

"What about them?"

"I'm asking you."

"I don't know where they come from...why I have them."

"Think about it," said the deputy. "Vietnam. Didn't you tell Agent Frost you'd been dreaming about it for almost a week? And you can't say what caused it?"

A sag of the shoulders. Richard sat, brooding, searching for something to say. It started the night he found Caddo sitting beside a campfire by the old barn. The barn sitting atop the hill...

It was eight days ago, after sunset. Caddo had been acting peculiar, more peculiar than usual. He didn't eat much. For the past few months he hadn't slept in the basement. Two days a week he slept with Irene. Richard knew from the utility bills Caddo had moved into the old winemaker's shack, or 'cabin' as he now referred to it. As a gesture of good faith for being a good friend and diligent worker, Richard surprised Caddo by handing him a deed to ninety acres that included the cabin, winery, and surrounding area extending to the highway. Caddo had shown a great amount of interest in it, so Richard gave it to him as a gift. Caddo was so emotional he didn't know what to say. He became sole caretaker, an impassioned owner, presiding over the property with pride.

The day Richard made the offer Caddo took to the hills whenever he wasn't working. Richard would see small campfires burning at night and just assumed Caddo was doing what came natural to all Indians—communing with nature. He never questioned Caddo, never asked him what he was doing up there.

That's why last Thursday night, when there was a departure from the regular routine, Richard grew curious. After spotting the campfire on the hill, he took the spaniels for a walk. He and Caddo talked. There was an odor of something burning. Not wood or tobacco. Something sweet.

"Nice night," said Richard.

"Good night to be in the arms of a woman," whispered Caddo.

"Yeah, well, can't argue with that."

Caddo could sense a deep sadness in Richard, deeper than usual. "Irene has a friend. Nice lady. Just moved here from Tennessee. Maybe you two could get together."

"Maybe."

Caddo picked up a stick and stirred the ashes. The glow of the fire reflected on his face, giving it a mysterious quality. He seemed lost in thought.

It was easy to do on an evening like this. An infinite array of stars. The warmth of spring. Perfect conditions to let your mind wander, to dwell on life. Richard looked into his friend's eyes and what he saw—the deep concentration, the introspection—only made him more curious. The question even surprised himself—

"What are you doing up here?" Richard asked.

Roscoe stuck his head close to the campfire and sniffed. Buried among the embers was a carcass—a rabbit or some small animal. It wasn't being cooked. The fire was incinerating it to ashes in a type of ritualistic cremation. Caddo pulled Roscoe closer, petted his back, and said something in the language of the Pawnee.

"I'm afraid my Indian's a little rusty," Richard joked. "Could you say it in English?"

"I said the Evening Star is bright. Manitou is strong. Relaxing, that's what I'm doing."

Richard had the impression he was infringing on Caddo's privacy. He waved goodbye and was about to leave when Caddo said—

"Here, try this." He was holding a pipe.

"Haven't done that in a while," Richard replied. "When did you start smoking dope again?"

"This isn't dope."

"Smells like it. What is it?"

"Peyote."

"Peyote, dope. Same difference."

"Marijuana is a recreational drug. This is not."

Caddo handed over the pipe and a stick with a flame burning at the tip. Richard raised the pipe to his lips and hesitated.

"Make sure you inhale," said Caddo.

"I haven't gotten high in years. I'm not sure why I'm doing this."

"You're not doing it to get high. You're doing it to help yourself."

Richard held the flame to the pipe bowl and drew a deep breath.

The smoke choked his throat. He coughed. And coughed again. "Help myself do what?" he wheezed. He gagged and coughed again.

Caddo instructed him to take another hit. "This time, slowly. Not so much. Hold it in."

The tiny flame was sucked into the bowl. Richard held his breath, counting the seconds before he would explode. The smoke filled his lungs, bringing back memories of Vietnam when he and his platoon members sat around jungle trails and rice paddies, smoking Tai-sticks and Cambodian weed, some of the best marijuana in the world. One toke and you saw stars whether it was day or night. Music made you believe you could fly. You could consume food by the bucket loads. Eat pickles and ice cream at the same time and love it.

"Tastes so good...makes your tongue wanna slap your brains out," someone said.

Twenty guys, high on grass, burst out laughing.

Back then it was so surreal, almost like an out of body experience, as if you had entered a different world with altered sensibilities, clouded images that became crystallized within seconds. Creeping paranoia was mixed with a dose of adrenalin, clarity of thought with introspection and doubt. Imagination was let loose with aban-don and the whole fabric of your consciousness underwent a massive change. That's what drugs did to you in Vietnam.

Richard was experiencing it again—the high. The effect went straight to his brain. He exhaled and felt a touch of light-headedness. "What...what am I helping myself to do?"

"Understand," said Caddo. "Peyote is used by priests. They smoke it to see things differently. Among the sachem, it's considered strong medicine."

"It's also very illegal."

"Illegal in the white man's world. Not mine."

"Yeah?" said Richard. "How long have you been smoking this stuff?"

"Not long. Tonight is my...initiation you might say."

"Into what?"

"The culture of the Dream Maker. Vision Seeker. *Mana, manitou.*"

Richard took another hit, then another, holding the smoke in for as long as could.

He remained by the campfire a few minutes...an hour? He couldn't remember. Time was irrelevant. What he did remember was the quiet solitude of the night, the understanding that words need not be spoken. The peyote had affected him deeply, unlike any other drug he had ever experienced. Back then they called it a psychedelic experience, a hallucinogenic reaction. It was certainly moving and powerful whatever it was. Something had changed. Thoughts of Dora were more prominent than ever. To him she had become real again. But it wasn't just that. Something about the farm had changed. Not just the mood. The change wasn't physical. It was more... spiritual. Not only had he gained a new perspective of the land, he found a deeper meaning in it, in its history, a reverence shared by all Indians, and, of course, by Caddo. All because he had taken three or four hits of peyote?

As he was leaving, Richard looked at the sky and said, "Sure wish it would rain. Doesn't rain soon we can kiss this year's crops goodbye."

"I'll see what I can do," Caddo replied.

Later, while lying in bed, Richard could hear Caddo chanting, singing out back by the barn. The songs were lyrical, not sung with words, but a long succession of sounds, variances of voice, inflections, and tone. Richard had no idea what an Indian rain dance was, but to him that's what it sounded like—

An Indian rain dance.

"Mr. Macklin, did you hear me?"

Richard peered up at Tom Duckett who was standing beside him. "Sorry. What did you say?"

"This sudden occurrence of dreams, do you know what caused it?"

"No," Richard lied. "No, I don't."

Chapter 57

Once an Indian village. Home of the Dog People. Battleground of the War of Blood.

Henry Purdy's legacy, if true, had taken on a new meaning.

The family cemetery at Willow Creek had a wrought-iron fence around it nearly one hundred and fifty years old. The gravestones rose from patches of thistle and grass not far from the river. A rutted road led to it. Weeds grew from the cracks in clumps along the shoulders. The fact that the cemetery was generally neglected helped lead David to his assumption.

It had nothing to do with the location, more with what happened at Dora's funeral. Her parents wanted to place her in a cemetery of their choosing. Richard naturally wanted to bury her at Willow Creek, along with the rest of the Macklins. The two sides argued. Richard produced a letter signed by Dora allowing him to do as he saw fit. The signature was unquestionably hers. No one disputed that. How it was obtained was. Her father maintained it was done during the last days of her life when she was doped up on morphine, unaware of what she was signing or why. Richard denied it, of course.

The letter in the night table of his bedroom offered testimony expressing his wife's preference to being "cremated," not placed "in a pine box." It clearly stated she wanted her death to be "celebrated, not mourned."

Which led to David's assumption.

The dilemma was, what was he going to do about it?

Dora Ann Macklin's headstone stood at the far end of the cemetery. Carved in granite below her name was an intricate set of symbols, musical notes surrounding a single short-stemmed rose with the words, '*Artist & Musician*,' followed by, in bold letters, '*July 23rd, 1958 – Until…*' Below that: '*In our hearts Dode will never die.*'

David checked the pistol to make sure it was loaded. It was a long-nosed Smith and Wesson .38, fairly accurate at close range. He put the gun in the glove box, shut off the engine, opened the door, and said to Cinders, "Stay here. I don't want you wandering off." With shovel in hand, David walked down a stone pathway leading to the cemetery. Eighteen headstones were arranged in rows. Down a small embankment to his left was Little Bass River; to his right, a tributary known as Willow Creek.

David walked up to his mother's grave, knelt down, placed a hand on her tombstone, and told her how much he missed her. After paying his respects, he inserted the blade of the shovel into the ground and said, "Something I gotta do, Mom." Then quietly, under his breath he added, "God, I hope this is not a mistake."

* * *

The lack of food and lack of sleep along with several hits of peyote had placed Caddo in a state of consciousness seldom reached by anyone other than a sachem or priest, neither of which he was. He was on the verge of hallucinating. Colors sparkled. Everything had a clarity about it. He could see images in the context of everyday life and see them transformed into something extraordinary. Like a puff of smoke from the fire in front of him, he could see faces. Faces of the *Opirikut*. They rose from the shadows of the smoke, floating in constant motion, taking shape and form and quickly dissolving into nothing…just dark patches of air. And when he closed his eyes, he could feel the smoke as it drifted past his face. He could feel the cleansing quality it possessed. He was becoming purged of his inadequacies as a man.

He glanced down and saw the scratches on his chest and along his arms and felt no pain at all. Pain had no place in the spirit world, not where the *manitou*, *wakonda*, and forces of *wakan* existed, not where the Vision Seekers and men who hoped to become enlightened dared to go. He stood perfectly still and allowed his mind to wander. He relaxed and let his muscles go limp. Suddenly, he lost his balance and fell forward. He threw out his right foot and accidentally put his heel and arch on a hot rock, burning the skin like a slab of bacon. The pain was incredible. It felt like someone had struck him with a red-hot branding iron.

He leapt away from the fire, collapsing to his knees.

He closed his eyes.

In time the pain began to subside only because he was so tired. He knew the consequences if he slept, but he couldn't fight it any longer. A week with little or no sleep had left him exhausted, incapable of anything else but sleep.

Chapter 58

A light breeze swept across the hill, tossing a sea of grass about in waves.

David dug a little deeper and looked up. Ever since he entered the cemetery he had the impression he was being watched. He wiped the sweat from his brow and rubbed his hand. A blister had formed and he'd only been digging for a few minutes. With each shovel full, the guilt began to weigh more and more.

What am I doing?

Again and again he questioned his motive. Other than satisfying his curiosity and simply knowing, he asked himself—*What do I gain by finding out if she's buried here or not?*

Suddenly, he heard an unfamiliar series of ring chimes. He removed the cell phone from his pocket and looked at the caller I.D. No name was listed. Elly had the ring tone set up to sound like a normal phone, but this was no ordinary phone call.

Short bursts of music erupted. A guitar riff by the Moody Blues from a song titled *Your Wildest Dreams,* followed by a few chords of George Gershwin's *Stairway to Paradise*, then Procol Harem's *Whiter Shade of Pale*. Finally, nothing. Dead air. Each piece of music was significant. The Moody Blues, Gershwin, and Procol Harem were three of his mother's favorites artists and composers.

Before David could put the phone away, it rang again. This time it was a guitar solo from Eric Clapton's *Layla* by Derek and the Dominoes. Another of his mother's favorites.

David thought he was crazy for even thinking what he did.

Okay. Bad idea, Mom.

He couldn't bring himself to dig any more. He placed the phone on the headstone and, using the back of the shovel, scraped the dirt back into the hole. It took ten minutes to dig the hole, only two to refill it. After that, he did a little routine maintenance by pulling weeds and tidying up when Cinders started barking from the truck.

"Hush!"

Cinders had her front paws up on the dash, facing a field, snapping her jaws, barking non-stop. She paid no attention to David and kept barking.

"Quiet!"

She wouldn't let up. If anything, her barks were growing louder, more intense. He'd never seen her act like this and her behavior was only getting worse. She growled, barked some more, and leapt about excitedly, showing her teeth.

Then he knew why.

In the distance, beyond the trees, came a roar, a deep solitary cry so disturbing he froze. It sucked the wind from his lungs and his knees went weak.

A moment later, a blanket of fog began to roll down the hill. The condensation grew heavier, thicker, appearing like a morning mist over a swamp, only it was windblown, not calm. The air congested and churned as wave after wave kept roiling…foaming like breakers over a shore. Buried in the heart of it was a figure walking on all fours, a stout-legged animal, shaggy haired, bulging at the haunches with a mass of muscle, folds of fur rippling across its belly and flanks. Its movement was purposeful, not hurried, not slow. The sound it made, the loud grunt, was unmistakable. It was a bear, a brown bear, at least eight feet long and weighing eight hundred pounds. Lean yet hulking. Big boned. A carnivore with plantigrade paws and non-retractable claws used for digging, climbing, tearing, and catching prey. A creature capable of running twenty miles an hour or more. And it was lumbering flat-footed, head bent low, using its sense of smell to follow a scent.

The bear stopped and raised its head and roared again to serve as a warning: It was on the prowl and nothing in its way was safe.

David ducked behind a large headstone, six feet of sculpted granite, a monument to a great, great uncle. He reached behind at the small of his back for the .38 but realized he left it in the glove box. Glancing at the pickup, he wondered if he could make it in time, knowing full well he had probably waited too long.

Cinders kept barking and put her paws back up on the dash. The hair on the back of her neck stood up like a cat's. Sensing immediate danger, she jumped out the driver's window and crawled beneath the truck.

David could hear the plodding of feet, an occasional grunt, the hollowness of the its breaths. Crouching, he leaned to his right. The animal was sniffing and snorting, moving slowly to his left, using its senses to identify a scent. Deep grunts sounded a signal. The scent was growing stronger.

David didn't move. He wasn't sure he could. He was sweating, breathing hard, trying to catch his breath. His heart was almost in his throat. He had nine to ten seconds to weigh his options. Stay where he was and hope the bear would injure itself by climbing over the spikes of the fence. Run to the truck and risk everything. Stand his ground with a shovel against an eight hundred pound animal.

The possibilities were few and definitely not in his favor.

He knew bears were adept climbers, so climbing a tree was out of the question. Since they were also adept swimmers, escaping by way of water was chancy at best—a talent, however, he had perfected through the years.

Which left him only one option. The river.

He listened as feet rustled through the grass, no more than twenty feet away. From the sound of it—the heavy grunts, deep breathing, and snorting—he could tell the bear was highly excited. The grunts were getting louder and more frequent. The movement was slow and steady, coming closer. So close he could almost smell its breath. It snarled and growled in a threatening manner, the sound rising deep in its throat, like a motor idling, ready to launch into high gear.

He could hear it raise up...could hear the scrape of paws on the wrought-iron fence. It was climbing *over*.

David had four seconds at most.

His mind screamed, *Do something!*

He couldn't move. His feet felt like they were stuck in mud.

The river was sixty yards away, down an embankment. After seven weeks of drought, almost no spring rain and little winter snow, the water level had to have dropped. From eight feet to six, he guessed. The depth and sluggishness of the current made it even more risky.

No way would it deter a hungry predator.

The breaths and grunts were almost on top of him.

Now or never.

He decided to do the unthinkable. He popped straight up like a jack-in-the-box. The bear was standing on its hind legs, towering ten feet in the air. *Inside* the fence! It snarled and roared the moment it saw David. He cut left, dodged right like a tailback, racing past the headstones. Fueled by panic, he did a handspring over the fence, using his arms to catapult himself down the embankment, arms flailing, pin wheeling off balance.

He could hear the animal climbing the fence, hitting the ground with its massive weight, the plodding of feet as it ran through the grass, the exhalation of breaths coming in short, rapid spurts. The grunts were getting closer.

Don't look back! Just run!

Thirty yards.

Faster! It's right on your heels.

Twenty yards.

Head down! Okay now...get ready.

D-I-V-E!!!

He hit the water head first with a sidelong splash. He kicked.

Whipped his arms back and forth in desperation. It was only a matter of inches. He could hear the bear grunting and growling even though he was underwater. The water was dark and murky, muddier in the shallows. He swam along the bottom, kicking as hard as he could, reaching and pulling with his arms. He followed the current, hoping the murkiness would work to his advantage. He heard a muffled roar, a splash, a bellow of frustration. He could imagine the sharp eyes of the beast peering below the surface, the cat-quick claws poised to strike. If a bear could catch something as fast and slippery as a fish, the slow ponderous movement of a human was easy pickings.

His air was just about spent. David kicked once, twice, three times, holding his breath. He counted ten more seconds before his lungs were about to burst. Forced to the surface, he took a gulp of air and looked around.

The bear was gone.

He dove back under. Peered through the muddy depths, expecting to be attacked any second. Below the surface or above, he didn't see any movement, so he floated to the surface.

No bear was in sight. On land or in the water.

When he looked at the hill, the fog was receding, sucking back like waves into the ocean.

Chapter 59

Alexa was growing impatient. She didn't like waiting around an animal hospital listening to dogs barking all the time. According to the hall clock, it was 7:36. Less than an hour of daylight remained. She walked into the operating room and said to Eileen, "How's he doing?"

"Getting a bit fractious, I'm afraid."

"Fractious?"

"Unruly. Excited. When animals are traumatized, sometimes they'll bite." Elly pointed to a canister connected to a plastic tube and rubber mask sitting on a counter. "That's why I had to put him to sleep."

"Oh," said Alexa. She examined Roscoe. He was lying on a table covered in white linen paper. Gauze and bandages were wrapped around his back left leg and left side. Blotches of blood were smeared across the paper. A hypodermic needle, sewing needle and thread were lying inside a tray resting on a stool.

"Think he'll make it?" Alexa asked.

"Hope so. His vital signs are stable."

"So what do we do now?"

"Wait and cross our fingers." Elly turned to hide a tear. She washed her hands in a sink, picked up a paper towel to dry, and tried to keep her emotions in check.

Alexa didn't want to come across as being insensitive. Tactfully, she asked, "Anyone else around?"

"Brad's in the kennel. Why?"

"Just wondering how long we'd be here."

Elly reached into her pocket for a key. "Take my car if you need it."

"You sure?"

"Wouldn't offer if it wasn't okay."

"I'll only be gone an hour. I have a deadline to meet. How about if I bring us something back to eat? My treat."

"Sure."

Alexa walked to the door and paused. "Oh. I'm curious about one thing, Eileen. The guy who called...who told you to come here... how do you suppose he knew where you were?"

Elly removed her bloodstained smock and laid it on the table.

"Wish I knew."

"Do you think somebody's following you?"

"Now that you mention it, maybe."

Alexa opened the door and left without saying goodbye. At the end of the hallway, she stopped. She couldn't believe it. Sitting in the parking lot was a rusted, white Mercedes. She felt violated, angry, afraid. She ran to the reception desk, picked up the phone, and dialed a direct line to the newsroom. After four rings, a recorded voice asked the caller to leave a message.

She disconnected, then dialed Sam's cell phone. After two rings, he answered, "What's up, Alex?"

She was breathing hard, talking fast. "He's following me, Sam. The guy in the white Mercedes! I'm at an animal clinic. He's outside in the parking lot."

Sam was in his car, driving with the window rolled down. She could hear traffic, the wind whooshing past the window.

"I'm pissed off, Sam. The jerk's just sitting there!"

"Okay, stay calm."

"Calm? Why is he doing this? What do you think I should do?"

"Take a breath and listen. Our friend in the Sheriff's Department said they ran a trace on the license plate. The car's registered to a guy named Hayden Crawford. Big-time loser. He puts a new definition on the word, scumbag. Served in Desert Storm. Dishonorable discharge. Petty theft. D.U.I. Possession of narcotics. Stolen weapons. Accused of rape twice. Never convicted."

"Rape?"

"You name it, he's done it."

"So he's dangerous is what you're saying."

"Dangerous and stupid. A scary combination. And I haven't even gotten to the interesting part yet."

"What's that?"

"He's Paul Heidtman's cousin."

The name didn't seem to register.

"Richard Macklin's partner!" cried Sam. "The guy in the bar the other night, the one picking fights. Cops threw him in jail, remember?"

"Oh, that guy! They're cousins?"

"Um-hmm. Hangs out with a bad bunch, gutter rats who specialize in department store theft. They go from state to state, running scams, home improvement, that kind of thing. Charge outrageous sums to old ladies, take the money, and run."

"What're they doing here?"

"Who knows."

"You think Richard Macklin is behind this?"

"No. More likely his brother-in-law, Mark Treshler. Least that's what my source says."

"It doesn't make sense," said Alexa. "Why am I being followed?"

"You confronted Mark. He's trying to intimidate you."

The line went quiet. Alexa was thinking.

Sam knew her about as well as his own daughter. Both were headstrong. "Don't do anything crazy, Alex. This guy Crawford—he's no good. I'll call the Sheriff."

"Who's our mole, Sam?"

"Huh?"

"You heard me. Our mole—who is it?"

"You know I can't tell you that. Where are you? What hospital?"

"Tell me who the source is."

Sam laughed. "Ain't gonna happen. Seriously, where are you?

No answer.

Sam could feel the wheels turning in her head.

"Alex..."

She glanced at a broom closet. The door was ajar.

"Talk to me, Alex!" said Sam. "Don't do anything foolish. This guy—he's not somebody you wanna mess with."

She held the phone away from her ear, tapped her foot a few times while deciding what to do, and whispered into the phone. "Got to go, Sam. Talk to you later."

* * *

Slouched down in the front seat of the Mercedes, Hayden Crawford was smoking a joint. Having smoked one joint already, two cigarettes, and imbibed a thermos full of coffee, he was wired to the hilt with nicotine, caffeine, and THC. He took one more hit. Put the roach out in the ashtray. Removed his sunglasses. Looked in the mirror. Combed his red hair with his fingers, grinned, and sat back, thinking of lascivious things, lustful things he could do to Alexa. He thought of her breasts and rubbed his hand across his crotch. Suddenly, he heard a door to the clinic bang open. Out came Alexa, striding angrily, holding a broom handle. She was gritting her teeth, choking the handle, her face beet red with determination.

Out of nowhere a huge hairy face appeared at the front passenger window. The window was partially open. The huge hairy face barked and growled. Saliva dripped from the Doberman's mouth. Hayden jerked forward and yelled, almost hitting his head on the steering wheel. Another huge hairy face appeared, a German Shepherd, barking and growling and snapping its jaws. Both dogs were trying to get through the window. Behind them, a man held the leashes and screamed, "Sic him! Bite him! Rip his head off, Wiley!"

Hayden reached for the key in the ignition.

A second woman came striding behind Alexa. She was holding a hypodermic needle, wearing a surgical mask and smock with bloodstains on it. The dogs were barking. Saliva was dripping down the window. The guy holding the leashes was screaming, "Bite him! Sic him, Wiley!" And Alexa was now running, holding the broom handle like a baseball bat.

"Okay, buddy!" she hollered. "You asked for it."

Hayden turned the key. The engine sputtered, the cylinders making loud metallic pings. Alexa was only a few feet away. Hayden wasn't carrying a gun. A knife, yes. He felt defenseless. He closed the driver's window. Jerked the gearshift into drive. At the same time the broomstick came crashing down across the back window. The first time it struck metal, the second time glass. The rear window shattered as the tires burned rubber.

Alexa screamed as the Mercedes raced out the parking lot ramp, "Next time I'll be packing a gun, dickhead!"

The Doberman and German Shepherd stopped barking.

"Thanks, Brad," Alexa said to the guy holding the leashes.

"Anytime."

She looked at Eileen...saw the mask, the blood on the smock, the hypodermic needle, a twinkle in her eye...and lost it. Alexa burst out laughing while Elly did the same.

Chapter 60

Caddo had been awake for ten minutes. When he first woke up, he was groggy, out of sorts. He opened his eyes and groaned, aware of the scorching pain in his foot. He sat up and squinted at the fire, not knowing how long he'd slept. He wasn't sure if it was night or day. After a quick look outside, he estimated there was about half an hour of daylight left.

He hobbled back to the tepee, the Sweat Lodge, and threw a few pieces of wood on the fire and quickly got dressed. When he slipped on a pair of moccasins, there was no delicate way to do it. It felt like his skin was ripping apart. He limped to the rack where the dead raccoon was hung when he heard somebody whispering. Although the interior of the barn was dark, he saw a flicker of light. It passed by a stack of farm implements and disappeared. He wasn't afraid, but could feel a tingle in his arms, the hair standing up. Then he heard it again—the whispered cry, a shade louder than the wind.

He didn't move.

Didn't breathe.

The *wakan*. *Mana*. *Manitou*. He could feel it stirring…growing stronger.

He thought he heard footsteps, so he hurried into a horse stall and crouched behind a pile of junk to hide. A far door opened. He forgot to lock it. On the wall facing him to his right, there was a knothole in the wood about half the size of his fist. He peeked through it and saw someone walk in, carrying a flashlight. The beam danced around like a Jedi sword. In the pale reflection, he could make out the silhouette of a man. The glow from the fire lit up his face like a jack-o-lantern. David appeared like a specter, all cheekbones and hollow eyes.

David was swinging the beam side to side, not sure what he was looking for. He saw a painter's tarp shaped like a cone, a makeshift tepee. A tepee? A fire was crackling. He drew the flap aside and saw fresh logs burning. At the back of the barn, he heard something fall from the rafters. He pointed the beam of light at the roof and saw tiny eyes looking back at him. Bats. Lots of bats.

The entire barn creaked.

"Caddo, is that you?"

A mouse squealed and skittered across the floor, chased by a rat.

The barn creaked like an old wooden ship, the sea pressing against the hull. He felt like Jonah in the belly of the whale. A burst of light flashed near the base of a ladder to the hayloft. He thought it was a reflection of the flashlight coming off a piece of glass.

"Caddo, where are you? I know you're in here."

Then it happened again. A speck of light pulsed and faded.

The walls creaked—ocean currents knocking against the hull.

David turned the flashlight off. The light from the tepee bathed everything in shadow. He listened as he waited for his eyes to adjust. A glint of light blinked on and off like a firefly near a horse stall, followed by a whisper so quiet he could barely hear it. He walked toward the stables, shuffling past buggies and old wagons. A hint of illumination kept fading in one place, then reappearing in another, accompanied by a steady flow of whispers, a clipped series of soft S's that grated the nerves. The light drifted behind one of the wheels, then floated behind a wall that separated one stable from another.

The whispers died as he stared at an empty stall. All he could see was a board, dust, and hay piled in the corner. He turned the flashlight back on and tilted the board away from the wall and found nothing behind it. As he did, his eyes drifted across the floor. He almost knocked over an object as he stepped back. It was an old gray ceramic pot lying next to a wagon wheel. To his left, specks pulsed and faded every two or three seconds. He could hear someone breathing. His cell phone rang—four bars of *Stairway to Paradise*—which sent shivers down his back. A light reflected off the object at his feet as the music stopped. He felt his breath catch in his throat. He untwisted the lid to the ceramic pot and shined the light inside. It was empty, except for a few ashes at the bottom. And something else. He reached inside and pulled out a nugget. It was a charred bone fragment. And it wasn't a pot. It was an urn. A funeral urn, containing the last remains of someone's body.

David felt a sudden draft of cold air. The realization hit him as if he'd been sucker-punched. He staggered backward and tripped over a pitchfork and fell. He got up, heard a whisper…saw a halo of light flash behind a stall and got out of there as fast he could.

* * *

The driver's door to the surveillance van opened and closed. Liz said excitedly, "Our buddy, Homer…he's up to no good."

"Why do you say that?"

"He's drinking straight from the bottle. And I don't mean beer. We better keep an eye on him."

Pete twisted a knob on the computer console. A motor hummed

overhead. A camera mounted to the roof turned. He glanced at a monitor labeled #*Five*. A white farmhouse with junk piled on the porch rotated into view. Pete zoomed in closer. Scootch McPhee was wearing a dirty, sleeveless undershirt, overalls with suspenders, and drinking from a bottle filled with an amber-colored liquid. He looked to be in a bad mood and kept talking to himself, pointing a finger at the van, shaking it while sticking out his puny chest. He upended the bottle, took a healthy chug, staggered to the door, and disappeared.

Pete twisted another knob. Volume from a speaker crackled. He heard the drone of a generator rumbling from the basement...footsteps on a carpet, a man grumbling to himself, followed by a metallic thump, like a disc being slid into a machine. Pete put on a pair of headphones and killed the speakers. He heard a slurping sound, a woman moaning, not in pain, but in ecstasy. "Oh, yes. Yes! Yes!" Old Scootch, it appeared, was watching a porno flick. Pete shook his head and chuckled to himself.

"What's so funny?" Liz asked.

Pete removed his headphones. "What?"

"Why are you grinning?"

"No reason," he replied, clicking off the volume. "How was your walk?"

"Okay." Liz climbed into the back of the van and sat on a high-backed chair. Once she got settled, she glanced at the bank of monitors, then studied the screen labeled M.A.P.S. that listed various sounds and what they represented. Nothing appeared unusual. "So what's happening? Were you able to figure out why we can't penetrate the Black Hole?"

Penetrate the Black Hole?

Pete giggled, "No, not yet."

"What do you think it could be?"

He sat back, hands clasped behind his head. "That's the million dollar question, isn't it? It raises a very interesting point. What can distort, alter, or eliminate sound patterns? The problem appears to be electronic. As far as I can tell it's not the system. Everything's working fine."

"So it's a distortion, not a malfunction?"

"Yeah. Basically, sound waves occur by vibrating objects traveling through a medium like air or water. Nothing as we know it can make sound waves go away. But this, whatever it is, has the ability to mask them, hide 'em, make them seem like they aren't there, when realistically that's an impossibility."

"Is there something that could be the equivalent to a Black Hole as it relates to sound?"

"I'd say so." Pete nodded at the screen. "There's proof. At least in one respect."

"One respect?"

"Scientists contend a Black Hole is a highly condensed form of gravity. Nothing can escape it, including light. If that's true, then there wouldn't just be an absence of sound, but also of light, substance, trees, land, hills, everything. It would be a total void, an emptiness of space. What we're experiencing here is only one element of that void. Sound. What's creating the *sound vacuum* if you will, we don't know. Even a quantum physics theorist would have trouble explaining it."

Fingertips tapped a keyboard. Liz was seeking a clarification.

"What are you doing?" said Pete.

"Looking up Black Hole. Maybe the computer can tell us more."

"You're wasting your time. Metaphorically speaking, that's all I'm saying it is. A true Black Hole can only exist outside the galaxy. Not here. If here, we'd be a collection of vacuous fumes in a non-existent place."

Liz hit enter on the computer keyboard. Up popped a definition. She read a portion of it aloud, "'Black Hole…a region in space with concentrated mass so dense objects cannot escape its gravitational pull…origin and existence unknown.' So, no one knows how a Black Hole is created?"

"Hypothetically, they do. Or think they do. It's my understanding that, like most things in science, theories are based on two parts probability, one part educated guess, and one part fact. Some subscribe to the theory that Black Holes are formed by stars or a sun imploding, shrinking violently by degrees no one can truly fathom."

"Wow. One of the big mysteries of life."

"If we carry the logic further, I'd say our Black Hole, if we want to call it that, is a result of energy being discharged."

Liz gazed at the screen marked *M.A.P.S.* where sounds were categorized by color. In the center of the screen there was a blank circle stretching north and south from the interstate to the river, and east and west from the winery beyond the grain elevators, reaching almost to the farmhouse. Beside the larger circle she noticed a smaller one, also blank, encompassing the upper barn, the one that was old and decrepit, practically falling down. She pointed at the smaller circle. What do you suppose that is?"

Pete shrugged. "Don't know. More dead space? Another *systemic vacuum*?"

"Systemic vacuum?"

"Absence of sound. In an electronic sense."

Liz gave him one of those looks. "Huh?"

"Okay, Black Hole," he said. "We'll keep it simple."

She frowned and leaned closer to the screen, pointing at the smaller circle. "I wonder why it's so small."

"I'd say it's directly related to the source of power...how much power is being generated. The core of energy that exists."

Liz made a face. "Run that by me again."

"Whatever's disrupting the sound waves is generating power, exerting some kind of force. The sound waves aren't just vanishing on their own. In this case, one is weaker, the other stronger, strength being proportionate to the size."

"Of the circles, you mean."

"Yeah. The circles."

"Do you think they're related or independent of one another?"

"Independent. That would be my guess. Two separate entities. Two systemic vacuums."

Liz turned a dial labeled *Audio Input* and said, "Speaking of vacuums, let's see what our buddy, Homer, is doing."

"Ah, I wouldn't do that," said Pete.

Chapter 61

David stood on the driveway, bent over, hands on his knees, breathing hard.

What did I just see and hear? Am I losing my mind?

He didn't have time to think about it because the cell phone rang. He was hoping it was his father. The caller was listed as I. Vernath.

"Hello."

"Is this David?"

"It is. Hi, Irene." He could hear traffic. From the sound of it she must have been standing outside the café. David started pacing with the phone tucked to his ear.

"Would you mind if I came out there after work?" she asked. "I need to talk to you."

"About…?"

"This mornin', when I drove Caddo home, I saw somethin'. I can't discuss it right now. It's too complicated. Besides, somebody's watchin' me."

"Watching you?"

"A car's parked across the street. Has been for the last hour. And the two guys sittin' in it ain't bashful about it either."

"I hate to say it, Irene. They're not watching you. They're waiting for Caddo." She started babbling. He had to interrupt her twice to calm her down. "They're probably agents with the Ohio Bureau of Investigation," he explained. "It's okay. They can't hear us. What kind of car is it?"

"A gray sedan. Do me a favor. Find Caddo. I'm worried."

"Trust me. I will." David walked to the end of the driveway and looked at the telephone pole where a utility worker had attached a box to the top of the pole. The box swiveled…pivoted in his direction. He walked across the highway and said, "Say, listen, Irene. I'm glad you called. I need to ask you a few questions. I don't have much time." He looked at his watch.

"Short of time myself," said Irene. "Jake's havin' a fit. I'm takin' a break busiest hour of the day."

"This will only take a second. Have you ever heard Caddo refer to certain words, expressions that you would classify…as Indian?"

"I'm not sure what you mean."

"Words like *mana, wakan, manitou.*"

"Maybe. Why?"

"Has he ever mentioned the term, *Halting Place*?"

Reluctantly, she said, "Yes."

"How? In what context?"

Except for passing traffic, the line remained quiet.

"It's all right, Irene. Nobody's listening."

"I'm comin' out there," she replied.

"No. Don't do that. If you leave, they'll follow. Please, answer the question. It's important."

"It's a translation, from a poem he read. A book of poetry, written by Indians."

"Meaning...?" he asked. When she didn't reply, he answered his own question. "It means burial ground, doesn't it?"

Again, she said nothing.

"Did he give any indication as to *how* he found it?"

No answer.

"Whatever you say," he assured her, "I promise. It'll remain confidential." He stared up at the box attached to the pole. There were wires hanging from it, what appeared to be a styrofoam-padded microphone and a round flat lens. Then it dawned on him. It was a surveillance camera. But not a stationary one. It moved, swiveled on its axis, and followed his every step. A warning went off in his head.

"Don't say anything more, Irene. Go back to work."

"What?"

"Stay away from the farm."

"But...?"

"Promise me. Don't come near the farm tonight! Everything will be okay."

"Oh, oh. Here they come," she said, "the two men in the car."

David listened. He heard a man say, "Are you Irene Vernath?"

"Yes."

"I'm Agent Brian Riddick with the Ohio Bureau of Investigation. This is my partner..."

She disconnected.

David did the same.

He heard a vehicle approaching. Powered by a big loud V-8, it was a Dodge Ram extended-cab pickup, silver in color. The driver was Paul Heidtman. He had a passenger sitting beside him, a woman, a very attractive woman, young and dark-haired, with her arm around his shoulder. She was laughing. Paul slowed the truck down as it passed. It was crawling, moving less than ten miles an hour. He and the woman smiled. Her smile was innocent. His was not. Paul held his right hand up, thumb extended, pointing his forefinger like the barrel of a pistol at David. He pulled the trigger.

The Ram accelerated.
David heard them laughing as they drove off.

Chapter 62

The screen from the laptop cast a green, iridescent glow across his face. David had already changed into a fresh set of clothes—blue jeans, work shirt, and running shoes. He Googled security companies and surveillance systems, and eliminated those that didn't do both audio and visual surveillance, also companies outside the state. After cross-referencing, he came up with three possibilities and marked off two because the one he chose looked the most promising. According to its website, *Aerodyne Electronics* was a high tech company with a brief yet successful history with NASA, government agencies, and security organizations throughout the world. It touted itself as being "cutting edge."

Among the many capabilities it boasted were—

> *State of the art audio/visual equipment. We can see and hear what no one else can Our surveillance systems are foolproof, mistake-proof, so good Congress is considering outlawing them.*

David had to look no further.

If Aerodyne was monitoring a camera at the foot of the driveway, then it was probably listening, too. That would explain a number of things, including how a passing motorist notified Elly when the dogs were attacked by a pack of coyotes.

He glanced at his watch. 8:05 pm. Darkness was closing quickly. He poured a glass of milk, grabbed a handful of chocolate chip cookies, clicked on the speakerphone and said, "Dad, do you hear me? You there?" He listened. There was nothing but dead air. Discouraged, he dialed Linck's Veterinary Clinic.

Elly picked up after the fourth ring. "David?"

"Yeah. How's the patient?"

"So far, so good. He's resting right now. Brad's here, so I may take a break. There's nothing more I can do. Have you talked to dad?"

"Not yet. He's still out in a field somewhere."

"Can't imagine why he wouldn't call."

"He'll show up. What's Alexa doing?"

"She went to grab us something to eat." Elly explained the incident with Hayden Crawford, then said, "I doubt we'll see him for a while."

"Good. I'd advise you both to stay away from the farm."

"What about you?"

"Don't worry about me or dad. I'll find him." David figured the less she knew, the better. "I have to cut this short, El."

"David…"

"What?"

"Don't try to be a hero, okay?"

He disconnected, fed Cinders a chocolate chip cookie, drank the milk in one long gulp, walked over to the sink to rinse the glass, and noticed a note on the kitchen counter.

> *David,*
> *Call me. It's important.*
> *Coach K*

He grabbed a handful of cartridges from the hall closet, made sure the .38 was loaded, then exited the side screen door, accompanied, of course, by Cinders. Other than the backup generator, everything was quiet. The wind chimes on the porch hung still and cattle and chickens were resting comfortably in anticipation of darkness. Cinders peered up at him, begging for another cookie. "Nope, sorry." He showed her his empty hands, then walked across the driveway into the lower barn where he was about to do something rash, something risky, something that could easily backfire and get him killed, all because he wanted to see if there was any validity to a theory of his.

He sat down in a lounge chair by the doorway, propped his feet up like his father had done earlier in the day, and whispered to Cinders, "Wake me up if anything happens, okay?" He rested the .38 on his lap. Gripping the handle, he looped his finger around the trigger and closed his eyes.

The secret to sleep, he found, was learning how to breathe and relax while letting your mind go.

Cinders curled up on the floor beside him. She put her head on her paws and did the same.

Chapter 63

Alexa was sitting at her computer in the offices of the *Bertram County Sentinel*, putting the finishing touches on the story concerning Wilfredo Pinoza's death. When she was satisfied with the result, she printed a copy and placed it on her editor's desk for Sam to read, certain he would tone it down. By the clock on the wall she estimated she'd been gone for about forty-five minutes. In her haste to leave, she knocked her briefcase to the floor, spilling papers everywhere. "Oh, God!" Scrambling on her hands and knees, she started gathering the papers. Out of the corner of her eye she noticed through the front bay window a car driving slowly by, a car which happened to be an old, rusted, white Mercedes.

The offices were closed, the doors were locked, and she was alone. Only the computer screen and desk lamp were turned on. Still on her hands and knees, she reached for the phone and started to dial 911. But what would she tell the police? Hayden Crawford had just as much right to drive through town as anyone. He hadn't broken any laws. What could she do? She would sound foolish, like a hysterical woman, yet she believed Hayden had overstepped his bounds. He was stalking her. It was a blatant violation with intent to harm. You don't bust a window to a man's car, especially someone like Hayden Crawford and expect to get away with it. She was convinced he was dangerous.

Reaching up, she opened a drawer and felt around until she found a can of mace. After doing a four part series on rape, she felt it was necessary to have some kind of protection, especially in her line of work. Seated on the floor inside her cubicle, she dialed Sam Tully's home number, then his cell and left two messages, explaining the situation and where she was going.

At a side door facing an alley, she heard a loud rattle, like someone shaking the door, trying to get in.

Okay, if you want me to call the police, no problem.

But when she dialed, the line went dead, as did the computer screen and lamp. No doubt the lines had been cut. The offices turned black, except for the area in front by the windows that were exposed to the streetlights.

Don't panic, she told herself.

Slowly, she stood up, gripping the mace in her hand. She walked to a window facing the street, put her back against the wall, and waited. She could hear the rapid pounding of her heart. She was breathing so fast she was hyperventilating. Seconds passed with agonizing slowness. Her heart sped up even more when she saw a man's shadow fall across the floor. The shadow remained for about two seconds. She leaned to her left and glanced out the window and saw passing traffic and Eileen's yellow Jeep Wrangler parked along the curb. At least she didn't park in the alley or behind the building. She rushed back to her cubicle, grabbed the briefcase, and returned to the front door. Taking a deep breath, she opened it and closed it, made sure it was locked, and proceeded to the Jeep without incident.

Ten minutes later, after a brief stop at the Law Enforcement Center where she waited to see if she was being followed, she drove to a fast food carryout and ordered two fried chicken dinners to go.

* * *

Located halfway between the city of Mistwood and GlenRiver Valley on Route 2 was a bar called The Red Lion Pub. Students liked it because the beer was cheap. Locals liked it because it had good burgers and fries.

The most frequent customers lately were Paul Heidtman and his girlfriend, Gwen. A woman of subtlety and modesty she was not—a woman who wore skimpy, skin-tight shorts and low-plunging tank tops. Gwen was a flirt who flaunted her figure and teased men by a mere flash of her eyes. Since Paul was the jealous type, they made for a highly volatile couple. On this particular Friday night, the Red Lion wasn't as busy as usual. And the owner Cash McEwen didn't understand why.

"Farmer's Almanac," slurred a drunk named Cole Weaver. "Yes, sir. Predicted bad times this year. Seven-week drought. Grain elevators shut down. Bridge out. Livestock dead. Da'gum newspaper and sheriff ain't got a clue."

McEwen, who was tending bar, eyed Cole as Cole swayed on the barstool. Cole was so drunk when he went to light his cigarette the flame never touched the tip. Not a single puff of smoke entered his throat. He drew a deep breath anyway and coughed and hacked until his face turned red.

"That's it," said McEwen. "I'm cutting you off!"

Too late. Cole swayed on the barstool, leaned against Gwen, grinning, and wheezed, "How'd ya' do, miss?"

Disgusted, Gwen snapped, "Get off me, you creep!"

Before anyone knew it, Heidtman shoved Cole and Cole fell to the floor like a sack of bones. Sat there, woozy, grinning, burping.

McEwen and another bartender dragged Cole over to a corner. Set him in a chair. Sort of wedged him in it, hoping he wouldn't fall off. When McEwen returned to the bar, he said to Heidtman, "Poor slob. Don't know if he's afoot or horseback. Now why'd you go pushin' him like that? He wasn't hurtin' nobody. Any more rough stuff and you're outta here. Understand? Faster than you can count to two. You can count to two, can't you?"

Paul said nothing. Just grumbled, drank his beer, and looked around as if he were expecting someone. Sure enough, two minutes later a stranger walked in. Medium height, medium build. Slicked-backed hair. Gray slacks. White shirt open at the collar. He walked up to Paul, tapped him on the shoulder, and the two of them walked to the side of the bar to talk.

"Too much heat right now," said the stranger. "Hold tight until things settle down." He handed Paul an envelope. "Half now. Half later."

Paul slipped the envelope into his pocket. "They'll never catch me, you know. But I can wait. Old man's son will be gone soon. Old man can't work if his legs 're broken. I got a guy who'll cripple him for life."

"Shut up. Don't even whisper shit like that. You do it when we say so. We'll meet again in a few days."

"What am I supposed to do in the meantime?"

"Same thing you've been doing."

Paul grinned and glanced at Gwen who was enjoying the attention of several men. "Ain't been doing much…'cept her."

"Be careful," said the stranger. "Remember, if you get caught, you're on your own. We don't like mistakes."

"I don't make mistakes," said Paul.

* * *

Headlights appeared in the rearview mirror.

The speed with which they were gaining suggested two things to Alexa. Those were the headlights of an old, rusted Mercedes and she'd never make it to the clinic, not without being rammed from behind, or shot at, or whatever else Hayden Crawford had in mind. She had to think fast.

She considered her options. Stop and confront him face to face with a can of mace? *What if he has a gun?* Chances are, she couldn't outrun him. At least not on a paved road.

That's it! It's a Jeep. And what's a Jeep good for?

As soon as she spotted the open field, she hung a hard left. The Wrangler swerved across the highway, shot down an embankment, bouncing wildly as she pulled the shift lever into four-wheel drive. The embankment presented no problem whatsoever. She was up and over it in seconds. Behind her, she saw the headlights approaching.

Try following me now, sucker!

She drove across the field, never thinking of what the farmer might think. Never caring. When she thought she was far enough away, she stopped and watched the car pass. She killed the Wrangler's headlights, sat there with the engine running, and looked around.

Chapter 64

David was lost. Running for his life. Being chased—by what, he wasn't sure. From the sound of it, a creature plodding on all fours.

Beneath him, the trail was soggy and wet, the footing treacherous, covered in fog. It wasn't cold, just looked wintry, frost bitten, as if giant crystals had formed on the grass and trees. He had trouble keeping his balance. He kept running in place. Going nowhere.

All at once, hiding in the shadows, he saw a figure waiting beside a tree—a lady with a veil, wearing a silk windblown nightgown. She hovered, disembodied, motioning for him to follow, a wisp of air flowing from her mouth like a breath on a cold day.

He slipped, righted himself, and ran as fast as he could.

Suddenly, there were misty shrouds everywhere, trees blocking his every move. The deeper into the woods he went, the darker it became, and the more he began to panic. He couldn't keep pace. The woman kept drifting farther and farther away. Finally, he was alone, running aimlessly. The trail was impeded by branches and wild, gnarly bushes.

Stumbling, he broke into a clearing.

Somehow the Creature had passed him by. He could see it running toward two distant lights, the taillights of a car.

* * *

Darkness was closing fast.

Alexa was growing more nervous by the second.

Maybe it was the fog drifting past the window, being out in the middle of nowhere in a stranger's field, alone. She was worried Hayden Crawford might be hiding somewhere close by. There was also something else. A feeling that, perhaps, she wasn't alone after all.

She looked in the rearview mirror.

She thought she heard movement, footsteps, something plodding across the ground. The engine was idling. She slipped the gearshift into first and released the clutch. The Wrangler shot forward. After shifting into second, she turned on the radio, scanned the stations until she heard a symphony playing…what was it? Richard Strauss's *Also Sprach Zarathustra*. That was it. A rendition of *The Night Wan-*

derer's Song. At the same time she felt a rocking motion. The cabin of the Jeep was being tossed from side to side. The music was so loud she didn't hear a grating noise at the rear of the car—like sharp claws across a blackboard. She thought she hit a hole or mound of dirt because the suspension creaked. At the height of the musical score, there was a tremulous roar that appeared to come from the speakers. It didn't come from the speakers. Once she reached the highway, she felt safe and home free. Yet somehow the interior of the Jeep seemed strangely cooler than before, almost breezy.

* * *

The car was pulling away.

Aware of its pursuer, the Creature stopped, turned, and came lumbering towards him.

* * *

A hand nudged his shoulder. David's eyes fluttered open as he jerked forward and let out a muffled cry.

He heard a dog growling, chickens clucking, cows mooing.

Standing by the doorway, Caddo placed a finger over his lips and waved at him to keep quiet. Caddo was holding a bow with a quiver of arrows slung over his shoulder. He leaned outside, looked around the corner of the doorway, then in both directions, left and right.

David noticed it was dusk now. A light fog drifted across the driveway. It appeared to be thinning, withdrawing into the hills. In a few minutes it would be completely dark.

Caddo lowered the bow. "Your truck…I need the key."

Sensing something, Cinders barked and went racing from the barn. David whispered, "Come back! Cinders, come back!"

"It's okay," said Caddo. "It's gone…for the moment." He lifted a bloodied sack, hung it over his left shoulder, then walked to the truck while the cows stopped mooing and chickens quieted.

David leapt from the chair. "What's going on, Caddo?" He ran after him.

Caddo placed the sack, bow, and quiver of arrows in the truck bed and held out his hand. "The key. Hurry!"

"Not until you tell me what's going on."

"Then you drive."

Caddo walked quickly to a woodpile covered in a blue plastic tarp. He removed the tarp, placed the tarp in the truck bed, gathered an armful of firewood, and laid it carefully over the tarp, trying not to scratch the paint. David did the same. They each made two trips while Cinders came bounding playfully from the backyard, happy as can be. David ran to the driver's side, held the door open for Cinders to hop in, jumped in beside her and said to Caddo, "It comes during sleep when we dream, doesn't it?" He paused and added while Caddo took a seat, "I guess…in a dream, anything is possible."

"Drive," said Caddo. "We're wasting time."

*   *   *

Pete peered anxiously at the monitor. "Look! It's moving again!"

Liz adjusted her headphones, checked a computer readout, and glanced at the monitor. It showed a blank circle trailing away from the farmhouse. Just minutes ago, the circle identifying the Black Hole had changed position for the first time, straying off screen completely, only to reappear half a minute later. Now it was changing once more, moving back to where it originally started—high atop Birch Run.

"Any sound yet?" asked Pete.

"Not yet," said Liz.

"What the hell." Pete listened, leaning closer to the speaker. "Did you hear that?"

Liz shook her head, digitally enhancing the frequency. "I'm locking it in."

They waited until the Black Hole lifted clear of the farmhouse. Through a complex assortment of sounds, they finally heard an engine running, idling at the base of a driveway. Liz adjusted a knob, flipped another switch which read *Voice Activation*, and heard David say, "Okay, which way? Let me guess."

Appearing on screen inside the surveillance van, the truck identified as Tracer One turned west onto Route 2. Less than a mile later, it vanished into the outer cortex of the Black Hole.

"I think I saw two people in the truck," said Liz.

"You did," replied Pete.

Pete tapped the touch screen in front of him. "Let's see how good this system really is." He typed a message on the keyboard, asking the computer to amplify.

"What are you doing?" asked Liz.

"Fine tuning things, to see if we can hear the rest of the conversation."

"Is that possible?"

"We're about to find out."

Liz clicked a button on her battery belt. "Base, to all units. The Dead Zone…I mean, the Black Hole…it moved to coordinates off screen and just now reappeared. Unit One, do you copy?"

* * *

Alexa was surprised to see Elly smoking a cigarette.

After pulling up to the curb, Alexa cut the engine, opened the door, and reached across the seat for a drink tray and bag of carryout chicken.

"What took you so long?" Elly asked.

Alexa clutched the fast food in her arms and closed the door with her knee. "Long story. I didn't know you smoked."

"I don't."

"Here, take this." Alexa held out the bag, but Eileen just stood there, staring at the side of the Jeep.

"What's wrong?" asked Alexa. As she turned, she gasped.

Aside from a large smear of dirt, there were five long scratches in the paint, gouged into the metal above the wheel well, about two feet in length, an inch or two apart, like claws had raked down along the side of the Wrangler. When Alexa and Eileen walked to the rear of the Jeep, they saw more scratches, more claw marks on the back bumper, tailgate, a coating of mud on the rear tires, and, the most telling of all, a long gash in the rear plastic window.

Alexa dropped the drink tray and muttered, "I know Hayden Crawford didn't do that."

Chapter 65

David dialed a number, put the phone to his ear, and heard nothing but static. "Okay, we can talk now. How about if we start with this?" He removed a damp piece of paper from his shirt pocket. Turning on an overhead light, he handed the paper to Caddo. "Sorry. It got a little wet."

Caddo unfolded the paper and studied what was written under the glow of the dome light, not saying a word.

"Sooner or later you're going to have to talk to somebody," said David. "In case you didn't know, a mile back we passed a surveillance camera. All the traffic between here and the house is being monitored, day and night. Agents from the Ohio Bureau of Investigation are crawling all over the place. There isn't a law enforcement officer within a hundred miles of here that hasn't been put on alert. Trust me. Somebody will find you and when they do, they'll pick you apart piece by piece."

Caddo quietly stared at the damp piece of paper.

David was determined not to let his frustration show. "Why you've been avoiding me, I don't know. What I do know is this. A bridge is sitting at the bottom of a river and no one knows why. We've lost power twice. Livestock have come up missing. Or dead. I know what a Ghost Dance is, who the Dog People are. I know about Freddie, the War of Blood. Even learned a few words lately. *Yinglee, mana, wakan, manitou.* I know by *Halting Place* you mean burial ground. But what I don't know and what I'm having trouble with is you. Why do you sit there and keep your mouth shut when all I'm trying to do is help?"

"Enemy," whispered Caddo.

"What?"

Caddo referred to the piece of paper in his hand. "Charik waik-ta. It means '*the enemy is upon us.*' Charik means *enemy*. It's a war cry. Turn up ahead, to your left"

David almost missed it. They entered a fog bank, which seemed to be receding into the trees. He hit the brakes and made a left as the glare of the headlights shot across the unpaved road leading to the cabin.

Caddo leaned over the dashboard, watching, his eyes darting from side to side. "Stop for a second. Okay now…hit your brights."

Outside, the high beams intensified, reaching farther and wider, illuminating everything from the road to the trees beyond. As the truck idled, they stared ahead expectantly as the fog retreated from the road.

Ten seconds later, Caddo relaxed. "All right, what is it you wish to know?"

Dozens of questions flashed through David's head. "Everything."

"Very well," said Caddo, pointing. "A few answers lie inside there."

Caught in the glow of the headlights was an old building a city block long. Neglected for years, structurally it was still sound, constructed of white painted brick, covered by a gray slate roof. Two stories high, it belied the depths of it. The winery lay sprawled before them, abandoned, boards covering the windows.

* * *

They parked behind the building in case they were being followed.

As they approached the front door, David asked, "Don't we need a flashlight or something?"

Caddo pulled a key from his pocket, unlocked the door, and stepped inside. Cinders scampered forward, paws scraping the tile floor. A light appeared. Caddo was standing in the threshold, holding a kerosene lamp. He pulled the door open. It swung wide to an entranceway with a high arched ceiling. Surprisingly, everything inside had been cleaned and polished—from a glass display case filled with old wine bottles, to a crystal chandelier hanging from a gold metal chain.

David stared at Caddo, dumbstruck. He walked around the room, studying the display case, the bottles, and chandelier. The last time he remembered visiting the winery he was a boy. He didn't remember much, only that he was scared of the cold bleakness in the cellar below. From that day forward he vowed never to return. For almost two decades the place had been padlocked and chained. To his left was a winding staircase, covered by a threadbare carpet. The steps descended to a landing, then curved right, plunging into darkness.

Caddo led the way, holding the lamp. Cinders paused at the top step, refusing to budge while the two men walked down the stairway.

At the foot of the cellar, the lamp did little more than expose the dampness and shadowy impressions within.

The first thing that struck David was the aroma of tannic acid. There was a sugary sourness in the air, fumes of rich, full-bodied wine scented by fruits picked ages ago. It had an apple, buttery smell to it, suggestive of berries, a sweetness like vanilla.

As the light played upon the walls, David glanced around in wonder. "Bet I haven't set foot in this place in twenty years."

The sound of his voice echoed.

"Why is that?" asked Caddo.

"Just never had an interest, I guess."

The cellar extended beyond the shadows. Oak barrels rested on racks down five rows. A sixth row contained bottles, corked and sealed tight. The rafters were covered in dust and spider webs, the barrels and bottles as well. The closer to the racks, the mustier and richer the smell.

David explored every inch of it with his eyes. "Maybe it just depressed me. All the work my grandfather did. All the time spent. For what?"

Caddo walked to a door on their right. He opened it and gestured through the open doorway. "Inside is a book, a business journal written by your grandfather. If you want answers, take it home and read it." He placed the lamp on the floor and walked away.

"What happens if I read it here?" David yelled.

"I wouldn't suggest it. Not if you value your life."

Caddo was halfway up the stairs when David called to him, "This book of my grandfather's…is there any mention of a bear?"

Caddo froze. "What do you know of a bear?"

"Two hours ago, by the cemetery, I saw it. A big old brown bear. Eight foot tall. Looked like it had been in hibernation for years."

"Take the book home, Kiriki. It will tell you everything you need to know."

"Is there anything I can do to help?"

"No."

Chapter 66

He found it lying on the desk—bound in black leather, frayed at the edges, its corners worn thin. The first thing David noticed when he opened the book was the handwriting, how neat and precise it was. He could easily imagine his grandfather sitting in the chair, pipe in hand, composing the first entry—

14th of April, 1934 –
With an end to Prohibition, on this day forward, I begin a new venture. I owe three people a debt of gratitude. My father, Robert, and father-in-law George Bertram, for their financial support. And Girard Villion for teaching me the basic techniques of wine making. It is of great interest I embark upon this & so name our vineyard GlenRiver...

The next ten pages were devoted to the art of winemaking—from the selection of the grapes, the planting of the vines, cultivation, harvesting, pressing, fermentation, aging, bottling, and storing.
Wil also wrote about the lives and times of the Macklins, what was fast becoming more of a diary than a business journal—

27th of August, 1935 –
From seedlings to vines. Ultimately, to bearing fruit.
Our initial phase appears to be a success.
Congratulations to younger brother, John, for his engagement to Blanche Fischer. Houseguest, Henry Purdy, is back from Europe where he attended, of all things, a symposium on metaphysics. First spiritualism, now metaphysics.
What next, Henry?

29th of October, 1936 –
First Harvest is now history. Now I know how an expectant father must feel.

24th of May, 1938 –
What a sad, sad day. We found father lying on the front porch this morning, dead from a stroke. What a great, great man. What I have, I owe it all to him. Robert will be fondly remembered and sorely

missed. Need I say more?

7th of January, 1941 –
Brother John signed his enlistment papers today, a month after the bombing of Pearl Harbor. How disappointing for wife, Carolyn. Pregnancy tests continue to be negative.

From 1941 to 1944 Wil wrote very little. The early 1940's proved to be especially taxing with brother John serving overseas in defense of his country. Finding help was next to impossible. The winery basically was shut down and letters from John, who enlisted in the Marine's Fourth Regiment, stopped coming. Killed in action was what everyone feared the most.

Quoting from magazines and newsreels he had seen in movie theaters, Wil wrote—

3rd of August, 1944 –
News from the Philippines where the Fourth is serving is not good.
76,000 prisoners of war were taken captive by the Japanese & thrown into concentration camps. Mistreatment & conditions were worse than anyone could imagine. Beatings, dysentery, pestilence, torture, yellow fever, dehydration – each man endured one form of hardship or another.
Yesterday, Life Magazine did an expose on the Bataan Death March. '55 miles of Hell' was the headline. It described a five-day march by POWS in 1942 through the sweltering jungle heat of the Philippines without water and very little food. Along the way, American & Filipino soldiers were forced by sword-wielding guards to dig their own graves. The few times food was given, the prisoners were fed contaminated rice. Some were buried alive, beheaded for no reason at all, or bayoneted because they couldn't keep up or fell. Begging for mercy only received the sharp blade of a knife or bullet through the head. After reading it, I was so mad I was ready to reenlist.

9th of November, 1944 –
Great news! The military has informed us John is alive & is coming home!

23rd of December, 1944 –
A lovely snow has fallen.
In anticipation of our troops' triumphant return home, everyone gathered around the radio to listen to H. V. Kaltenborn who always begins a newscast by saying, 'Ah, there's good news tonight.'

Indeed, there was good news. And bad. The Third Reich is falling. Allied Forces discovered thousands of bodies at Auschwitz, Dachau & Buchenwald. Newspapers are calling them 'Death Camps.'

As we sat listening to the radio, who walks in? None other than old St. Nick, carrying a bagful of gifts. Behind that frizzy white beard & belly full of pillow, I could see old friend, Henry. Good times were had by everyone, especially Emily, our housekeeper. I dare say, I could see her face radiant with color when Santa, with champagne glass in hand, serenaded her. In French no less! Throughout the evening, Henry told stories of adventures through ancient Mayan tombs & crypts of the dead.

10th of March, 1945 –

With an end to the wars in Europe and the Pacific fast approaching, the economic climate here at home is definitely improving. Investment opportunities never come easy, but I believe it is time to become aggressive. Venture capital was denied by Farmers' First State Bank, thanks to old friend, Bill Treshler.

6th of April, 1945 –

Today we welcomed home brother John. His wife, Blanche, Carolyn, and I were waiting at the station when the train pulled in. When I first saw his shaved head & gaunt face, I cried. We all did. Whether from tears of joy or sadness, I do not know. Something inside John has changed as does with all men who witness the brutality of war. Something crawls into the soul and alters how you feel. One is never able to rid oneself of it. Every soldier who survived the Death March had it, including John. The look of a victim. All of us, to one degree or another, have it. The look in John's eyes is infinitely deeper, sadder, and more profound than ours.

David looked up sharply. He thought he heard something outside the room. He pulled the .38 from his pocket and waited. Beyond the open doorway he could see the outline of the wine racks and barrels, but that was about it.

The Journal once again drew his attention. The next entry was short and sweet—

11th of June, 1948 –

Carolyn is expecting a child—at age 44 no less. If I didn't believe in miracles before, I do now.

To celebrate, Wil sent a letter to Washington seeking federal assistance to build a complex of grain elevators. He also decided to invest more heavily in wine. He sought the services of an architect to expand production facilities and storage capacity and design a new facade for the winery, similar to a chateau found in Bordeaux.

February 27th, 1949 – Richard Allen Macklin was born, healthy and happy.

Six weeks later, Wil received approval for the Grain Elevator Project. Backed by father-in-law, George Bertram, construction was completed within ten months. A year after that, the Macklin brothers broke ground for their new production facilities. That's when their troubles began—

4th of April, 1950 –

Work crews arrived late this morning. As they began to dig the foundation for the new wing, an odd thing happened. A storm gathered, the likes of which I have never seen. A warm day turned suddenly cold. Work had to be suspended.

7th of April, 1950 –

Shortly after sunrise, I was called to the scene of the excavation. We discovered a section of earth removed & beneath it – bone fragments, arrowheads, & tools made from antler horns.

Henry believes it's an Indian burial ground. Normally I do not agree with Henry. Too often he is prone to exaggeration & a sense of the absurd. If not for his friendship, I would consider him derelict of his duty as a civilized man.

8th of April, 1950 –

I am beginning to see a change in the temperament of the workers. Drunkenness I can deal with. Inappropriate behavior I can excuse & hope to correct. But superstitions, however they manifest themselves, have no place here. Henry says we should choose an alternate site.

There it was again—that sound, just outside the doorway.

Clutching the .38, David eased from the chair.

What was that?

A scuffle? A foot scraping across the floor?

His heart was pounding. Somehow he found the courage to take a few steps.

A head appeared at the door.

"God almighty! You scared me half to death, girl!"

It was Cinders. She was shaking like a leaf.

Chapter 67

Tired, drowsy, and fed up with answering an endless number of questions, Richard Macklin sat in the patrol car, peering out the window at the darkness.

A hand nudged his shoulder.

"Hey!" said Tom Duckett who was sitting at the wheel. "Are you listening?"

"Sorry."

"You been saying that a lot lately, you know that?"

Richard almost said it again. The painkillers. That's what did it. Relaxed the muscles. Relaxed the mind. He could feel a slight buzz of medicinal serenity. It was wearing off.

"I said," Tom repeated, "you can always change your mind. I know half a dozen places where you could spend the night."

"No thanks. Don't think I could sleep anywhere else."

"Okay." The deputy suddenly sat up straight and squinted as if his eyes were deceiving him. "Well, take a look at that, will ya'."

Half a mile ahead, despite the power outage, a sign glowed in the darkness—Red Lion Pub—with an emblem of an old English Lion standing on its haunches, Derby hat tilted forward on its head, front paws raised like a boxer's.

Tom eased his foot off the accelerator. As they approached, he noticed a silver Dodge Ram pickup parked in front of the building. He pulled into the parking lot, leaving the motor running, and said, "Need some coffee. Be right back." After grabbing a thermos, he entered the pub and returned two minutes later with the thermos full of coffee.

"That old Irishman," said Tom, laughing, "he'd spend a fortune to make a buck. He bought a gas generator." He wedged the thermos between the door and seat and pulled out onto the highway.

"You didn't happen to talk to Paul Heidtman, did you?" Richard asked.

"No. Just got coffee."

"You didn't go in there for coffee."

Tom glanced at him and nodded. "You're right. I didn't go in there just for coffee." He drove for a while without speaking. "Tell me something. Has Heidtman ever given you trouble?"

"Not really," said Richard. "Why do you ask?"

"The department did a background check. He's been in and out of trouble since leaving the army. Dishonorable discharge. Assault and battery. Theft. Petty crimes. Did a little time. Got in a bar fight the other night. Did you know that?"

Richard shook his head.

"Cold-cocked a kid with a beer bottle. Hiedtman spent the night in jail. Nobody pressed charges. He's an animal. Sorry. No offence."

"None taken."

"I'm surprised they let him back in the bar," remarked Tom. "Heidtman threatened a bunch of people. Didn't like the way they were looking at his girlfriend. And believe me, she's a looker. Almost like those two go lookin' for trouble. She prances around, does the come-hither, and guys go crazy. Whenever Heidtman drinks, he gets violent. I told the owner to call me if anything happens. Mark my word. Trouble's brewin' in River City. Mind telling me how you got mixed up with a guy like that?"

Richard shrugged. "Mutual friend said he needed work. I needed money."

"Odd arrangement you two have."

"What do you mean?"

"You looked at his fields lately? Plough blade hasn't touched dirt all spring. How can you make money when you don't plant anything? What exactly do you think he's doing?"

"You tell me."

"Ain't good whatever it is. I'd watch my back if I were you."

"Thanks for the warning."

A female dispatcher called on the police radio, "Unit Four, this is Base. Do you copy?"

The deputy unclipped the microphone and pressed the transmitter. "Base, this is Unit Four. Go ahead."

"Sheriff wants a report every hour once you get settled, okay?"

"Ten-four."

"Sorry about your partner. He's sicker than a dog. Not too late to send somebody out."

"Not necessary, Base. I've been riding alone for years."

"Okay. Just be careful. Oh, in case you hear from Mr. Walker, let us know, all right?"

"Will do. Unit Four, over and out." After resetting the mike, Tom said, "Well, you heard the lady. You wouldn't happen to know where Caddo is, would you?"

"Not this moment," said Richard. "Why is it so important to talk to him?"

"Important to talk to everybody."

"You didn't talk to Heidtman."

"Not tonight. The other night I did."

"Did you give him a polygraph?"

"No."

"So it's all right to ignore a convicted felon, but not me."

"You agreed to it. You said it was okay."

"Yeah. I agreed to go to Vietnam, too, but that doesn't mean it was the smart thing to do."

"Look, law enforcement isn't about tact, Richard. Right now the only thing I'm concerned with is figuring out what the hell is going on."

The patrol car was approaching Substation 12 on the far left. Gas-operated lights made it look Christmassy. Opposite the compound, warning lights mounted on sawhorses blinked on and off while another patrol car was parked along the shoulders of the road.

Realizing there wasn't much time, Tom made one final plea. "So...anything you want to tell me, anything I should know?"

"No."

"You sure?"

A slow nod. Richard looked like he was getting sleepy.

"Have it your way then. Couple of things. We've got people—agents, deputies—stationed throughout the valley. In case anything happens, do you have a cell phone?"

Richard patted a side pocket.

Tom reached above the visor, pulled out a business card, and handed it to him. "Call if anything comes up. I'll be on duty all night. Don't forget your shotgun. It's in the back seat."

They traveled in silence the rest of the way. After arriving at the farmhouse, Tom offered a few words of advice, then drove away, flashers on, a quick whir of the siren, announcing his departure.

Once inside the house, the first thing Richard did was go to his medicine cabinet, open the bottle of pain killers, and pop three pills into his mouth.

The house felt like a morgue.

Where was everyone?

In the distance he heard the lonely baying of a coyote.

The shortage of fence wire compelled him to act. But first he needed refreshment. In the kitchen he picked up a pint of bourbon, a can of cola, glass of ice, flashlight, and stuffed them in the pockets of an army fatigue jacket. In a matter of minutes, he was lying on a chaise lounge chair inside the cattle yard with the shotgun leaning against the armrest. The buzz in his body became more pronounced. Pain was an abstraction now. It held no claim to the physical side of him.

Overhead, clouds floated past a full moon. He hugged the jacket around him, pulled up the collar, and sank deeper in the chair. At the far end of the yard, the cattle stood unmoving in the moonlight.

On a similar night eight years ago he might have enjoyed the peace and quiet of the moment. Not tonight. The last time he felt contentment was the day before the doctors told him his wife had cancer.

He poured a tall drink, bourbon mostly, and chugged it down. He closed his eyes and imagined Dora lying there, cozy and warm, snuggled close under the stars.

He closed his eyes. Five minutes later he fell asleep.

* * *

Parked beside the utility substation, less than a quarter mile away, Tom Duckett kept the engine running and heat on. He inserted his earpiece and said, "All set, Pete. Can you hear him?"

"Every breath he takes," replied Pete. "You let him go, huh. Think he's innocent?"

"Looks that way. No probable cause. No motive. No incriminating evidence. What about Walker? Heard from him yet?"

"Not a peep."

"Any idea where he might be?"

"Nope."

Tom stared at the valley. Nighttime had obliterated everything. The stars hung above in perfect symmetry.

At the opposite side of the intersection, a young deputy got out of his patrol car, lit a cigarette, and walked over. Tall and skinny, he had a bit of a swagger. "No use both of us being here. We're heading down to the river. Aren't you supposed to be riding with somebody?"

"Gus. He's sicker than a dog...home in bed. I'll be all right."

"Suit yourself." The young deputy took a drag from the cigarette and exhaled. "Wouldn't want to be alone on a night like this." There was something morbid in the way he said it. Like he enjoyed pointing out the obvious. After another puff, he swaggered back to the patrol car.

Tom watched him until he and his partner drove off. The only lights Tom could see came from a single farmhouse. Leaning forward, he cut the engine and turned off the headlights as the road ahead became swallowed by darkness.

"You there, Pete?" he asked while opening the thermos.

"I'm here." There was a slight reticence in Pete's voice. "Uh, Tom. Just so you know. The energy field..."

"Yeah?"

"It moved."

Tom almost spilled hot coffee on his lap. "Where?"

"Relax. That was a while ago. It's stationary now. You're nowhere near it. I'll alert you of any change."

"Good. Whatever you do, keep the channel open."

"Sound a little nervous. Everything okay?"

Tom poured a cup of coffee. His hand was shaking. "Wonderful. Couldn't be better."

Chapter 68

Cinders stood on her hind legs, pawing at David, wagging her tail. She whined as though she wanted a dog biscuit. Only it wasn't a dog biscuit she was whining for.

"What? What is it?" He put the lamp on the floor, petted her with one hand while holding the .38 in the other. "See this? Hollow points. Not to worry."

The spaniel stopped pawing, sat up expectantly, ears perked as if she heard something in the outer chamber.

David released the safety to the .38 and listened to the drip, drip of water from an old water pump. He was tempted to go exploring, but returned to the desk instead, took a seat, and pulled the lantern closer while Cinders curled up on the floor beside him.

According to the journal, the year was 1950. Wil Macklin was 53 years old, his wife Carolyn 45, and Richard a toddling one year old.

David glanced at an entry dated April 9th, then flipped to the next page—

10th of April, 1950 –
Work remains at a standstill while I decide what to do. Excavation of the new wing raises serious questions. Should we disturb what Henry says is an Indian burial mound? Leave it alone? Or consider another site?

Animal tracks were discovered late yesterday, possibly those of wolves or wild dogs. At several locations animals were found torn to pieces — muskrat, fox, deer — killed in a manner I have never seen before.

16th of April, 1950 –
A pack of wolves is running loose. A Rogue Pack. A professor at the university says there is no evidence to support the existence of rabies. "Judging from their behavior, however," he said, "they seem overly aggressive."

Meanwhile, armed guards have been hired to stand watch day & night until the project is completed. Weather is extreme, eerie at times, with fog so thick you can't see thirty feet in front of you.

29th of April, 1950 –

The animal attacks seem to be increasing. Henry thinks we should notify state conservation agents & invest in the services of a professional hunter.

In a related matter, there may be an even greater problem facing us. Last night, after another severe storm, a neighbor discovered the body of a cow, its chest split open, chunks of meat missing from its neck to hindquarter. Portions of the body, bone, & hide were scattered in a twenty-foot circle. Whatever attacked the cow gorged itself throughout the night. Based on the size & shape of the footprints, the predator appears to be a bear – a marauder. The only problem is, no bear has been seen in these parts in more than sixty years.

4th of May, 1950 –
Spring buds are beginning to show. Because of the amount of rain, the roots are rotting. Grapevines have been infested with aphids, tiny insects that feed on plant tissue & sap, causing uncharacteristic swelling, or 'galls,' in response to their feeding. What's so unusual about this is that insects of this type don't hatch until summer. Agriculturalists from the School of Agronomy hope to have a solution soon. Samples of the blight & insects have been taken to the university for analysis & testing.

6th of May, 1950 –
Agronomists from Ohio Southern called to say the aphid appears to be a new strain related to a green bug usually found in wheat or barley. This new aphid is highly resistant to pesticides. The damage in grape phylloxera is caused by root deterioration, an interruption in the vascular system, bacterial & fungal infection, & once devastated over two million acres of vineyards in France during the 1860's.
Where we go from here, I do not know.

7th of May, 1950 –
If I were to hand pick a professional, a hunter who looks the part, who has the scars to prove it — as evidenced by the many lions he stalked in Africa and grizzlies along the Alaskan Frontier, I would look no further than Blake Turner.

Unfortunately, Blake arrived one day too late. More deer were slaughtered during the night. State conservation agents are expected sometime soon. Livestock throughout the county are in jeopardy. We can hear wolves baying at night. During the day, workers feel unsafe.

Tomorrow we hope to put an end to this madness.

8th of May, 1950 –

Blake, Henry, John, & myself – along with several others -- have formed a plan to be executed at two locations: the first, here at the farm, to capture & kill the Rogue Pack; the second, in a secluded area half a mile from Route 2, to eliminate the bear. Blake suggested using a series of culvert traps, snares that are spring-loaded, constructed of cable, anchored to trees & then baiting them with fresh meat. "Once a bear has a taste for beef," said Blake, "he'll go to any length to taste it again."

9th of May, 1950 –

Two nights of little or no sleep. Twenty armed men stood waiting for hours, only to be fooled by the Marauder & Rogue Pack. More gore & more blood. They struck again, this time at opposite ends of the valley. Pigs, cows, as well as several horses, were mutilated.

Blake Turner has spent a lifetime hunting wild game. When we discovered the bodies, he said, "This wasn't done for food, but for the sake of killing."

David glanced at his watch and scanned the next few pages. The lamp was burning low. Cinders was asleep and the light in the room had a dark tinge to it—like smoke.

David was about to skip the remainder of the diary when he came upon this entry—

13th of May, 1950 –

We buried brother John yesterday.

Three nights ago, I had a nightmare, as did my wife. It was the first night she & I had slept together in weeks. I woke up, sweating and shaking. She was in tears. We both knew something terrible had happened.

"Go," was all she said. "I'll watch the baby."

I do not recall how I made it to my brother's house. When I arrived, it felt like I was returning to the scene of a crime. I walked to the back, knowing my worst fears would be realized. The back door had been shattered to pieces. I relived the moment, thinking I had stood in that very spot only hours ago. A trail of blood led from the kitchen through the hallway into the master bedroom. I followed it. There, at the door of the bedroom, I stopped. Morning, noon, and night, I can still see every detail – the breaking of the door, the chase through the house, what happened inside the bedroom. I cannot bring myself to describe it.

Brother John was buried in a closed casket, what was left of him.

Fortunately, the night before his wife, Blanche, left town to visit her sister in Napoleon. At the funeral she wore black.

Construction of the new production facilities is nearing completion.

Early this evening, Henry Purdy & Blake Turner came to see me in my study. We talked, but I do not remember what was said. After consoling Carolyn, off they went, carrying rifles.

It is a struggle just to make it through each day. Like Henry, I was never a religious man. I seldom read the Bible or went to church as often as I should, but now I pray to God for forgiveness so that I will make peace with myself, & more importantly, peace with my wife.

As David went to turn the page, he realized an entire section had been torn from the journal. Eight to ten pages were missing, the most crucial parts of his grandfather's story.

Chapter 69

David pounded his fist on the desk in frustration.

So many questions were left unanswered.

What happened to the Marauder? The Rogue Pack? Wil?

He'd heard certain things when he was little. Rumors about Wil's death persisted for years. Depending on the source, the stories varied, whether from family, the coroner, local newspaper, or neighbors. How Wil died was never the issue. Based on the evidence, everyone knew it was from a bullet to the head. Suicide or murder. That was the debate.

Desperate to find answers, David opened every desk drawer and went shuffling through papers, folders, and files, then froze when he heard a hiss and a squeal in the outer chamber. Cinders raised her head, staring beyond the open door, and gave a soft *woof*. David grabbed the .38. He couldn't see much. Most of the cellar was cast in shadow. Vaguely, he could sense something out there, hiding, a rat or a rodent. Or…

He cocked the trigger and waited. After a while he relaxed and sat back down and leafed through the book one last time. Pasted to the back cover were two envelopes. He opened the first and found a three-page letter discolored with age and several newspaper clippings. Carefully, he removed the clippings and glanced at each. The first contained a photograph of his grandfather. Beneath it was an obituary, listing his credentials: founder and former CEO of Farmers First State Bank; board member, National Bank and Trust Association; owner of Macklin Farms, GlenRiver Vineyards & Winery; former president of the Ohio Farmers Association; Trustee, Ohio Southern State College; contributor to the Ohio Conservancy."

A clipping in bold headlines reported—

> ***Local Businessman Dies of Gunshot Wound***
>
> *Wil Macklin, 53, was found dead Tuesday night from a bullet wound. Further details are not known at this time.*
>
> *Neither the coroner, Jerome Bishop, nor Sheriff Malcolm Whitney of Bertram County could be reached for comment.*

David read further, thinking newspapers didn't usually publish stories involving suicide, but Wil Macklin was highly regarded, often in the limelight. There was a great deal of interest in his death. Exercising confidentiality with respect to his family, the newspaper never mentioned "*foul play*," but did say the case was under investigation as the other clippings attested—

> *Investigation reaches dead end.*
> *Prosecution unlikely.*
> *No suspects found in shooting death.*

David put the clippings aside and unfolded the letter—

Dear Reader,
Please note the evidence surrounding Wil Macklin's death contains few facts and is rather contrite considering the nature of the subject matter. Since I know everyone involved in the case personally – from the newspaper editor, to the sheriff and medical examiner – I suspect theirs was a collaborative effort. To hide the truth, the intent.

Since you may be related to Wil or at least have some knowledge of him, having read the previous text, you may have been curious about the omissions at the end. It is only natural since I, too, have often wondered about the same. To some degree I will attempt to clarify those omissions and bridge the unfortunate events leading up to his death.

It came upon the heels of several tragedies, including the passing of his mother, Vera, who died of complications, some say a horrible nightmare while sitting alone in bed at night. On those few occasions when I had conversations with his wife, I learned that she, too, had nightmares, as did Wil, neither of whom showed a willingness to talk about them in any detail.

As noted in the previous journal a bear called the Marauder was prowling the countryside, despite the fact no bear had been in the area since the late 1800's. Time and again, cattle were slaughtered, their intestines slit open, their meat eaten with a voracity impossible to believe. The weather was always bad, always raining, or the wind was blowing, sometimes quite fiercely. One night, fully armed and more determined than ever, a professional hunter named Blake Turner and I positioned ourselves near the winery among a group of men hired as guards. The Pinkertons were as experienced as any men we could find – former policemen, soldiers, and such.

It was well past midnight when a shot rang out. We heard a scream, a growl, and then a roar. There was no mistaking it. It was the roar of a bear. Blake and I ran to a man lying on the ground, writhing in pain. His uniform was covered in blood. Part of his left side was missing, bitten off. He died in Blake's arms, choking, convulsing as much from agony as the loss of blood. Oh, what a horrible way to die!

In a woods behind us, we heard another roar – of triumph it seemed, in celebration of the kill. Moments later, opposite the trees, came yet another roar, followed by a scream and two quick shots. Blake raced ahead and found a Pinkerton lying on the ground, dead, slashes along his shoulders, chest, and back. While we stood there, a third guard panicked and ran away. We shouted at him to stop, but by now the storm was raging. The rain was so loud we could barely hear our own voices, let alone each other's. Above the patter we heard a third attack, more rifle fire, a scream, and a roar so chilling my heart practically stopped.

The next thing I knew Blake went running, screaming in frustration. He disappeared into the darkness while the storm raged on. An avid hunter like Blake, you would think he was smarter than to go dashing off like that. In the distance, I heard an explosion of a rifle, more screaming…snarling…growling.

Now I was alone, more frightened than ever. Blake was dead. I was sure of it, as were the others. The storm was intense, growing more violent by the second. A bolt of lightning struck, then a clap of thunder, and in the brief flash I saw the Creature standing at the base of a tree. When lightning struck again, It was on all fours, advancing towards me. By the third strike, It was gone. In Its place, I saw a shadow. Steadying my rifle as best I could, I almost pulled the trigger, but realized during another flash the shadow wasn't a bear, but a man.

Wil Macklin appeared before me soaking wet, holding a shotgun. Immediately, I could sense something about him that wasn't quite right. His manner was peculiar, far too calm than what the situation demanded. Unlike myself, he did not seem to be scared at all, even though at any moment either one of us could be attacked.

I remember him asking me if my rifle was my only weapon. It was not, I told him. I had a pistol in the side pocket of my overcoat. He told me to remove it. When I asked him why, Wil said something I will never forget. "I want you to kill me, using the pistol, not the rifle."

Of course, I was confused. Four men were dead and he was pleading with me to take his life? In my heart I knew I could not do it. Yet somewhere in the darkness I could sense a quiet plodding of feet.

"Do it now!" Wil shouted. It was like someone else was holding the pistol. "I can't!" I cried. To my left, I saw the Beast rise up. "I'm to blame for this, Henry," said Wil. "Hurry!" He pointed at the side of his head. "Shoot me! They'll think it was suicide!" As you can imagine, I was in shock. I had never killed anyone. A friend? Impossible!

The bear was now only thirty yards away, creeping towards us. "Kill me!" Wil shouted. "Once it only came to me in my dreams. Now it comes when I'm awake. It's in my mind, Henry! My mind! Kill me!"

My hand was trembling as I raised the pistol. I aimed but something was happening to me. I became hysterical, impassioned by the moment. When lightning struck, I saw an image flash before me, an image of a man hiding inside the skin of the Beast. An Indian. My old tormentor. The Mohawk chief, Standing Bear. We were face to face once again!

"Do it now!" Wil yelled. "Before it's too late!" Consumed with hatred, I couldn't help myself. Wil had his weapon aimed not at the Beast, but at me! I heard him shout, "There is only one thing you can do, Henry. Make your choice! Live or die!"

I saw something in the Creature's eyes that brought my hatred to the surface. I fired not at the Beast, but at my friend, and in the last second I saw a look fade from the Creature's eyes. I realized then I had denied the Beast the one thing It coveted the most—the kill.

Unfortunately, my aim was true. Wil was lying on the ground with a bullet through his head. By the time I looked at the Beast, It was gone. In Wil's hand I found a note, saying he had taken his life. The authorities could only come to one conclusion, that the blame fell solely on him.

So as to hide the truth and not implicate myself, I wiped my fingerprints from the pistol and placed it in Wil's hand.

It has been fifteen years since that night. I am an old man now, far too old for anyone to remember. Yesterday, posing as a passing stranger interested in architecture, I was granted entrance into this building by a young man I had known as a baby. Not knowing who I was, Richard Macklin allowed me, as it were, to return to the scene of the crime. Never having been accused of anything. Never convicted. Never arrested. Never suspected of the murder I had committed, my punishment being indescribable feelings of guilt, which, of course, is a terrible price to pay.

Only once was there any doubt about that night – or about me. Sheriff Malcolm Whitney, after seeing the note and questioning me the following day, kept shaking his head and looking at me suspiciously. Perhaps it was paranoia on my part. For whatever reason Wil's death was never discussed after that. Looking back, I realize there are inconsistencies...many things that do not make sense. Crimes of passion never do. How was I persuaded to do what I did? Was Wil insane? Was I? What made him do what he did? Most of all, what was the strange affliction that ailed him? To most of these questions I cannot give satisfactory answers. A few things I do know. Authorities did cover things up. The motive was simple – to hide the facts. Facts too impossible to be believed! People, of course, knew of a marauding bear. How It disappeared was a different matter. No one cared as long as the Beast no longer prowled the hills. As for the newspaper accounts, they were negligent by design. Journalism turned a blind eye, a deaf ear to it all for the sake of keeping peace in the community.

As for myself, portions of that night I remember quite well. Others, not so well. If there is a drug which allows for moments of lucidity during times of uncertainty, or a medication that masks bouts of depression, I have consumed it in quantity. Given the state of my mind at the time, it seemed the only plausible thing to do. I did it, willfully – with regret and guilt, of course. But none of that begins to explain the amount of pain that plagues me every day, every moment of my life, awake or asleep. All I can say is, the misdeed was done. Now I have to live with it.

There. Now I have set the record straight. It absolves nothing, but at least I will go to my grave knowing my confession was given freely.

Wil should never be blamed for any crime, any death, or any negative thing that happened during the last days of his life. In the end he sacrificed himself for the good of his family and community.

To Carolyn, his wife, who I understand is now living a sheltered life, I ask that you not judge me or hold me in contempt for what I have done. I did it for no other reason than to free Wil of himself and end his torture.

And to anyone who reads this, I give one final warning. These accursed hills are indeed haunted. Something lies beneath them, sleeping. Allow It to sleep. Let It rest unmolested and you shall live in peace. If not, Hell will surely find you.

As God is my witness,
Henry J. Purdy

David sat back, still not satisfied. Maybe Henry's letter answered a few questions, but it also raised many more.

As he unfolded the second letter, Cinders sat up, ears raised, eyes fixed on the open doorway.

Outside the room, in the chamber, there was a noise, what sounded like the shuffling of feet, the faint tinkling of bones so soft David almost ignored it. When he looked up, his heart practically jumped into his throat. He saw a barelegged man stooped over, dressed in bear skin and bear's head, wearing a breechcloth, standing in the doorway, staring at him with eyes that seemed to reach into the very heart and stop it from beating.

Chapter 70

The percussion of the .38 boomed, echoing throughout the room and outer chamber as David's hand vibrated from the aftershock.

Cinders jumped to her feet, barking wildly, the hair along her back standing on end. The figure darted to David's left, toward the stairway. The bullet was never meant to harm, only to scare. David reached down, felt the muscles tighten around Cinders' neck, and with a firm touch whispered, "Shhhh!" Instantly, she quieted, and then just as quickly she began to snarl and growl again. "Shhhh!" After a hard tug on her collar, she stood back, eyes locked on the open doorway, body rigid, legs prepared to spring.

David slid from the chair and weighed his options. The choices were few. Any mistake, any miscalculation could have deadly consequences. The apprehension was almost crippling, not knowing what was beyond the door. He turned his head to listen, expecting to hear the rattle of wolf teeth, the scrape of leather across the concrete floor, but there was a total absence of sound, except for the drip, drip of water from the old water pump.

From the brief glimpse of him, there was no doubt as to who or what it was. The intruder was an Indian. Stout-shouldered, thick-muscled, and surprisingly tall. He had slashes of paint on his face and squatted like an ape when he walked.

Where did he come from? What were his intensions?

Holding his breath, David waited with a finger curled around the trigger. He moved around the side of the desk and advanced slowly with Cinders a half step behind, growling weakly. It took ten, maybe twelve painstaking seconds to reach the door. David realized just then his shadow fell across the threshold. With the lamp at his back, he had exposed his position. It didn't seem to matter now. He'd made up his mind. Right or wrong, he lunged through the open doorway, did a rolling somersault, and came up crouching, legs spread, pistol clutched firmly in both hands, aimed at the stairway. He expected to come up shooting, but displayed remarkable discipline when no one was there.

Where did he go?

A quick look around confirmed his absence.

David never made rash decisions. Prompt ones, yes.

After retrieving the lamp, he walked cautiously up the stairs—

Cinders a step ahead, ready to bolt at any second. "Slow! Easy! Easy!" he whispered. She obeyed. Beyond the upper landing, the door was open. Outside, he was greeted by a blanket of fog, tinged with minute crystals that pulsed like a heartbeat, and the nauseous odor of sulfur and decayed flesh.

David noticed footprints leading to the trees bordering the highway. Holding the lantern high, he followed the tracks with Cinders at his side, head bent, doing what spaniels do best—

Following a scent.

Below the hill, in the direction of the river, he could see the glow of a campfire. The fire itself was hidden, obscured by fog.

As David walked through the field, a strange and slow-developing change occurred, which had to do with the size and shape of the footprints. At first the markings were clearly human. Before long the tracks went from a set of two to a set of four, the impressions becoming larger and thicker with claws that dug into the earth, the length of intervals between strides increasing, as if man or beast were running. Finally, there was a complete transformation. Instead of feet and toes, there was a large set of paws with five digits in front, claws extended and heel behind, the whole of it measuring fourteen inches.

The animal was enormous. Larger than a Kodiak or grizzly.

It was a startling realization.

David stopped and listened. The .38 at that moment no longer seemed adequate as a weapon. Cinders stood behind him, afraid to go another step. In the quiet chill of the night he noticed a slight change in the atmosphere. The fog was dissipating, thinning out. Yet he swore he could feel somebody watching. Then, in the blink of an eye, the tracks disappeared. Feet, paws, toes, claws—gone. Vanished right where he was standing.

Cinders circled, sniffing—confused.

The scent was gone.

* * *

"Uh-oh. We have movement."

Pete watched the monitor closely. It displayed a map of color-coded audio imprints identifying various types of sounds. It wasn't the color-coded imprints he had his eyes on, but an area just right of center, about a quarter mile in diameter which registered an absence of sound. It was totally blank, and this black mass he dubbed the *Black Hole*, or *Systemic Vacuum*, began to creep across the screen.

Pete noticed a large discrepancy in size and shape of the mass. When dormant, the Black Hole cast a much wider footprint, sometimes as much as a mile. When active or moving, the signal shrank to about a quarter of the size.

"Something's happening, guys," Pete announced. "Unit Two, what was it you heard?"

Static crackled through the headsets. Unit Two, Agent Roy Segedi and his partner, Dennis G, were parked along a gravel road between the river and grain elevators. Identifiable by his Bronx accent, Segedi responded, "A gunshot. West of us. Could barely hear it. Sounded like it was fired in an echo chamber."

Pete flipped a dial while watching the monitor. "Didn't register at this end. Keep me posted if you hear it again."

"Will do," said Segedi. He then addressed Agent Kenneth Frost who was teamed with Brian Riddick, their sedan parked along an unpaved road east of the rock quarry. "What do you want us to do, Unit One?"

Pete listened as Agent Frost answered, "Hang on for a second."

Pete's assistant, Liz, handed him a list of units with names written on a piece of paper. Each unit was strategically placed at various points throughout the valley, with two more units on call as backups if needed, parked outside the Watch Zone.

"Sure it was a gunshot, Unit Two?" Frost asked Segedi.

"Not a doubt in my mind."

"Okay. Stay alert, Unit Two. Pete, what type of movement is it?"

Pete rolled his eyes. "The Black Hole…"

"The energy field you were telling us about?" Agent Riddick said with skepticism.

"Correct," said Pete. He had briefed them earlier, but wasn't sure they believed him. Hell, it was hard to believe it himself. Why should he expect anyone to swallow such a far-fetched theory? A mass of energy that absorbed all sound electronically? Unfortunately, he had no other explanation.

Through the earpieces he could hear the agents grumbling.

Agent Frost told everyone to be quiet unless they had something constructive to say. He asked Pete, "This Black Hole, where is it?"

"Following Route 2, going east, half a mile from the farmhouse. It's not moving at the moment."

"What do you suggest we do?"

"Like you said, sit and wait."

"Maybe G and I should take a look," suggested Segedi. "See what's up."

"Not a good idea," cautioned Pete. "That's putting yourselves at risk. Right in the thick of things."

"Exactly the point," said Segedi.

There were a few seconds of silence before Agent Frost cut in.

"Okay, Pete. Since you're the closest thing we have to an expert, how dangerous do you think it might be…stationing them there?"

"Let's put it this way. Considering what little we know and the evidence we've seen so far, I'd say damn dangerous."

No one said a word.

Finally, Agent Frost broke in, "Still moving, Pete—the Black Hole?"

"No. Not this second. Staying put. But be advised. There's a good chance we may lose reception from Unit Two if they relocate."

"Hear that, Unit Two?" said Ken.

"Ten-four," said Segedi.

The lines remained quiet until Agent Frost said, "Okay, Unit Two. It's your call."

"Appreciate it," answered Segedi. "Unit Two is relocating."

"Proceed with caution," said agent Frost. "Use a flare gun if you need it. Any problems, send up a distress call."

"Will do. Unit Two proceeding with caution."

Pete shook his head, cupped his hand around the microphone, and said to Liz, "And fools rush in where angels fear to tread."

Chapter 71

He'd been trained against a silent and deadly enemy—in depths below the Bering Sea. In freezing water beneath thick layers of ice. In tae kwon do, karate, jujitsu. Against foes wielding knives, bayonets, and clubs. Against all types of surprises. But never one quite like this.

Not even a cocker spaniel bred for alertness and keen senses was aware of its approach. Shrouded by fog, the animal made its way stealthily, head slunk low, crouching, one silent step at a time.

There was a sound of something in flight.

A sudden yelp. A whimper.

David turned.

The coyote collapsed behind him, legs twitching, an arrow through its windpipe. It wasn't dead yet. Choking on its own blood, though. It would die soon. In a couple of agonizing seconds. Despite the fact it wanted to attack him, tear him to pieces, David felt sorry for the animal. He was about to shoot it with the .38, a mercy kill, when he saw it struggle for a moment, then pass away. Cinders stood over the body, assessing its condition as the legs contracted one last time before going limp.

David checked around to see if more coyotes were nearby. As far as he could tell, the area was deserted. For now he was safe.

Below the crest of a hill, silhouetted against the backdrop of a distant fire, he saw the shadow of a man, carrying a torch in one hand and bow in the other. Based on the limp, David knew it was Caddo. But not the Caddo of old. This was a man dressed in the traditional attire of his forefathers—moccasins, buckskin leggings, and leather shirt embroidered with porcupine quills. A beaded necklace hung from his neck—a necklace that rattled when he moved. All of it was accented by a band of feathers and a roach of some kind, dyed red, hanging from a shock of long, white hair. The most significant aspect about him, however, wasn't what he wore, but what was on his face. Two stripes of paint covered each cheek—red and black—about an inch long. What it symbolized, David could only guess. But there was no doubt in his mind it was…

War paint!

In keeping with his ancestors, Silent K had committed himself to an act of aggression. He had assumed the role of Warrior. Not the

Silent K of old, a survivor of a forgotten war, but a hunter, tracker, seeker of *mana*, the *wakan*.

Caddo walked closer, the torchlight flickering across his face. "Didn't they teach you in the Navy to watch your back?"

Wow, look at you!—David said to himself

He glanced at the bow and noticed it was more of a traditional design, not a high-tech metal monstrosity found in survivalist magazines. This was made of laminated wood with a pistol grip and a sight mounted to a shaft that curled at both ends, a serious, serious weapon—powerful enough, if shot at close range, the arrow would pass through a body. Using that as a gauge, in proportion to the depth of the wound, David estimated the range of the shot at eighty yards, which attested to the skill and virtuosity of the bowman.

David bent over to inspect the coyote. The skin around its mouth was drawn back, exposing teeth covered in saliva and blood, giving it the look of a crazed animal.

Using his bow, Caddo tilted the coyote's head to the side, facing him. "That's odd. Coyotes almost never attack humans. Looks like it hasn't eaten in days." He put his foot on the animal's neck, pulled with his right hand, and extracted a carbon-tipped aluminum arrow. He wiped the blood in the grass and put the arrow back in his quiver.

David's gaze shifted from the coyote to the Indian. "Rabies?"

"Rabies, no. Symptoms, yes. I'm sure if we did an autopsy, we'd find no disease."

"I don't understand. Symptoms but no disease? Why did it try to attack me then?"

Caddo peered at the trees along the highway. The fog was drifting away, unveiling a full moon. It was possessed. The rest of the pack is out there somewhere." He nodded at Cinders. "She's not safe here. *Poko*, go home!"

Poko? If David remembered correctly, that was an Indian word for dog.

Grabbing the dead coyote by the legs, Caddo dragged it a few steps and stopped. "Where's Roscoe?"

"At the clinic, having surgery. He was attacked..."—David paused for effect—"by a 'Rogue Pack.'" He was referring, of course, to his grandfather's journal. "Elly is sewing him up."

"How bad?"

David shook his head. "Bad enough to require stitches. He lost a lot of blood. She gives him a fifty/fifty chance." As he watched Caddo drag the coyote away, he said, "I saw him, you know. *It. Him.* Whatever *it* is."

The powerfully built Pawnee paused and mumbled something.

"Come look at these tracks." David motioned to an area behind him. "First they were human, then little by little they changed, mutated into claws, the paws of a bear. Then *poof*..." He snapped his fingers. "They vanished just like that!"

Caddo glanced at the full moon, then worriedly at David. "Do as I say, Kiriki. *Mana*—it's growing stronger. We have one hour. Two hours at most."

"To do what?"

Caddo dragged the coyote across the ground without replying.

"Don't you want to know what I saw?" said David.

"I know what you saw. Go home."

"Here...the house. What does it matter?"

Caddo whirled around. "You've interfered enough as it is. Go home!"

David stood up slowly, repressing his anger. Instead of venting it, he waved at Cinders and said, "Okay, Poko. Let's go."

* * *

Elly was pacing back and forth in the parking lot. She removed a cigarette from her shirt pocket and lit it.

"I thought you said you didn't smoke," said Alexa.

Elly took a puff, but didn't inhale. "Helps take the edge off."

"Bad day for all of us. Sorry I got you mixed up with that guy in the Mercedes."

"It's not your fault."

Alexa considered telling her about Hayden Crawford, how he tried to break into the offices of the newspaper, but a call to the Sheriff's office solved the problem. Alexa mentioned to a deputy on duty she suspected Crawford had been smoking marijuana in his car. Sure enough, when a patrolman pulled him over for driving over the speed limit, the deputy found a bag of weed hidden under a floor mat and two roaches in the ashtray.

Mr. Hayden Crawford was now spending the night in jail.

Therefore Alexa could now turn her thoughts to more pressing matters. She had been bothered all day by a number of questions, but the timing wasn't right or the situation didn't permit it. Now in full view of the Wrangler she had the perfect opportunity. "Sorry about your car. I wish I knew what scratched it."

Elly shrugged, pinched off the end of the cigarette, and let the matter drop.

"After last night, I don't know what to think," said Alexa. She paused a moment, wondering how to break the news. "Elly, I have something to tell you. They found Wilfredo Pinoza's body. I'm afraid he's dead."

Elly was too shocked to respond.

While Alexa offered her condolences, a door opened to the rear of the clinic. It was the night attendant, Brad. He didn't have to say anything. Eileen knew by the expression on his face—

Lovable little Roscoe was dead too.

"Go home," suggested Brad. "I'll take care of the body."

Elly was hurting too much to cry.

Chapter 72

David sat in his truck, arms hugging the steering wheel as he stared at the darkness. He turned on the overhead light, removed the damp piece of paper from his shirt pocket, and read a list of words he had underlined earlier.

Mana, manitou, wakan. All manifestations of the spirit world.

Near the bottom he wrote—*Okton*. Below that—*Oyaron*.

Scrawled in the margin was a name. *Aaron Caldwell*. And a phrase. *Greetings from the Land of the Silver Lakes.*

There was an obvious theme running through it all, which raised some interesting questions, most notably—what type of ritual was Caddo conducting?

David glanced at Cinders and said, "Well, what do you think? Should we go home or hang around here?"

Cinders barked once—right on cue.

"Couldn't agree more."

David reached for the door handle. A minute later he was standing face to face with Caddo who voiced his displeasure by snapping, "Go away!"

David took a piece of firewood, balanced it on end, and sat down. "Sorry. I'm not going anywhere until you and I talk."

Caddo stood with his hands on his hips, debating what to do. He bent down, removed a string of beads from a satchel, a pipe and a pouch, laid them aside, and did some busywork rearranging something in the satchel.

David studied him closely as well as the area around them. Lying beside the campfire was the dead coyote. A burlap sack soaked in blood rested between the fire and edge of a pit. Hanging from stakes outside the pit were four wooden masks. Their expressions were gruesome, having large, bulbous eyes protruding from furrowed brows, twisted mouths, and long, angular faces carved to effect horror. Their purpose, if David recalled, was mostly ceremonial, to cure sickness and ward off evil.

He pointed at one of the masks. "Why do they call it a False Face?"

Caddo ignored him and threw more wood on the fire.

"Least tell me this. Why is the house safer than it is here?"

Caddo dropped a string of beads into the fire and mumbled

something in Pawnee.

David was tempted to ask about the beads. Instead, he picked up a piece of gnarled wood lying on the ground and examined it. It looked like a walking stick or cane. It was old, made of mahogany or walnut, had markings carved on the sides, symbols and decorations that were undoubtedly Indian. It was about three and a half feet long and no thicker than the handle of a baseball bat.

"What's this?"

Caddo reached out. Snatched it from his hand. "Don't." And gently put it aside.

"A prayer stick, isn't it?" asked David.

No response.

David stood up, made a mental note of the items in and around the pit, and said, "Masks. Prayer stick. Fire. Dead animal. Cremation. What's it all mean, Caddo?"

David knew what it meant. They were objects chosen not at random, but very carefully, with one expressed purpose: to conduct a ritual.

But a ritual to do what?

As sincerely as he could, David said, "Tell me what to do. Just don't send me away."

Caddo turned and inclined his head as if he was listening.

"Why do you refuse to talk to me? Is it because I'm white and you're Indian?"

Caddo sighed. His shoulders sagged in resignation. "My silence isn't what you think it is."

"Oh?"

"I've taken a vow. Many vows actually. And I have broken almost every one. If I tell you what they are, I would be breaking another."

David stood next to the fire, close enough to feel the heat. "A vow of secrecy, you mean."

It was a rhetorical statement. Not a question.

Caddo said nothing.

If the implication wasn't clear before, it was now. David was meddling. But he refused to back off or give in. If anything, he was more determined than ever. As he considered what to do next, Caddo pulled a pinch of tobacco from the pouch, what appeared to be tobacco anyway, packed it into the pipe bowl, and said, "It has nothing to do with race or the color of your skin. It's here." He made a fist and tapped it against his chest.

David nodded. An idea was forming in his head. It came from Caddo's collection of books. In some respects, David realized, he was woefully ignorant of what was going on. On the other hand, he had gained some insight into the lives of Native Americans, their culture, the *sachem*, the Spirit World, and the things they worshiped.

In the end, however, it came down to three questions. Three simple, basic questions. One required tact. The others didn't.

Warming his hands by the fire, David said, "I read somewhere once 'there is no shame in not knowing, only in refusing to learn.'" He waited to see how Caddo would react. Except for his eyes, Caddo remained impassive. "I need to know...how this...*thing*, this Charik got here."

Caddo looked at the fire and stirred the embers with a stick. When it caught, he held the flame to the pipe bowl and inhaled. An odor of something sweet filled the air. After exhaling a long plume of smoke, he replied, "The farm needed rain, so I prayed for rain."

David was speechless. Caddo's casual way of expressing himself made everything seem trivial. *No big deal. I prayed. So what?* By seeking to help, he brought catastrophe. All because of a prayer?

It was absurd. Almost laughable. Only David wasn't laughing.

Then something strange happened. The timing was so peculiar, so uncanny, it had to be more than coincidence.

The fire popped and crackled, sending sparks and swirls of smoke into the air at the exact moment when David recalled a book title. It popped into his head, literally exploded into his consciousness as the fire erupted. His entire being felt a jolt of wonder, of realization!

Of course.

Rain dance!

Caddo had performed a rain dance!

It made sense now. It all fit together.

Only two questions remained.

David was almost shaking when he asked, "Why the Charik instead of rain?"

"I made a mistake," said Caddo. "Sometimes even a rain priest will say a wrong prayer or do the wrong thing. And I am not a rain priest."

Reeling from the impact, David began to pace back and forth. "But how? What can we do to make it go away?"

"I pray again, my friend. I pray again."

"But you might make another mistake."

"I might. Maybe you should pray that I don't."

So their hopes rested on a prayer?

David had a sinking feeling that prayer alone wasn't going to solve the predicament they were in. Before he could reply, Caddo cut him off by holding a finger to his lips. Without moving his head, Caddo rolled his eyes to the right, then to the left as he reached for a piece of firewood. At the same time Cinders started barking from the truck. David squinted beyond the light of the campfire, looking in all directions. He wasn't certain but he thought he saw a shadow moving among the trees. Then by degrees a figure emerged from the darkness, crouching. David reached for the Smith and Wesson tucked in the small of his back. As he did, Caddo took the piece of firewood and threw it. The coyote gave a brief yelp and retreated as two more coyotes crept closer. In an orchestrated move, Caddo picked up his bow and strung an arrow through it while David lifted his pistol and aimed.

"Not yet, Kiriki," cautioned Caddo. "Let them attack first, then shoot."

Chapter 73

"Attention, all Units! It's moving! Heading east on Route 2. No visual or audio. Fog's too thick. Do you copy?"

All Units responded in a positive way.

Unit One was doing a routine check when Unit Two, Segedi and Agent G, detected the acrid smell of sulfur.

"Unit Two," snapped Agent Frost, "what's the situation there?"

"Weird," Segedi answered as he drove. "Must be a gas leak somewhere. Smells like egg water."

Pete's voice rang through the earpieces, "Okay guys, it's slowing down. Crawling. Very little movement. Coming at you, Unit Four. Slow and steady. Unit Two, you're entering the Black Hole. Unit Four, do you copy? Do you hear me, Tom? It's coming your way!"

Agent G checked the shotgun to make sure it was loaded while Pete announced nervously, "Unit Two, you should loose reception any second now. I suggest aborting until we see what happens."

Somewhere up in the hills three shots were fired. *Pop, pop, pop!*

"What the hell was that?" hollered Segedi. "Hear that, Base? Three shots fired. Sounds like they came from the direction of the park."

Base didn't respond for a full five seconds. Finally, Pete came back on line, worried, a bit edgy. "What's that, Unit Two? You're fading in and out."

Unit Three, stationed at Fallen Oaks State Park, jumped in: "Confirm that. We heard shots. Awaiting orders, Unit One."

"Hold your positions," insisted Agent Frost. "Let's not go rushing into things. Unit Two, I agree with Base. Abort. Repeat. Abort. That's an order! Base, where is Unit Four? Tom, can you hear me?"

Three units and Base were suddenly speaking all at once. Confusion reigned through the headsets.

"Everyone, quiet!" cried agent Frost. "Tom, are you there? Do you read me? Copy? "

Agent G reached for a flare gun in the glove compartment as a gaseous cloud enveloped the windows. They had almost reached Route 2. There was a loud crackle in the earpieces, then static in and out.

Segedi yelled, grabbed his earpiece, and threw it.

Agent G was about to do the same when he heard a pop, almost like a firecracker, piercing his eardrum. He shrieked. It echoed with a loud, throbbing vibration that made him go deaf in his right ear. Snatching out his earpiece, he grabbed his ear and bent over in pain.

Unit Two was no longer in contact—with anyone. Segedi kept his foot on the gas pedal, but the engine stalled and the car came rolling to a stop, the headlights dimming until eventually they went out completely. Both Segedi and Agent G flung the doors open, coughing. Segedi raised the shotgun, pointing it in the direction of the highway. G cocked the flare gun and sent a rocketing glow of blue light spiraling toward the sky as another gunshot rang out from the hill.

* * *

Three miles away, Pete was screaming into the microphone, "How in the hell do I know? I told them not to go in there! I lost them! Contact with Units Two and Four have been cut off."

Agent Frost knew the situation called for action. "Unit Five, on standby. Can you hear me? Check out Unit Four."

"Will do. Unit Five responding."

Agent Frost: "Any suggestions, Pete?"

Pete lost it. He punched at the air and yelled, "Suggestions? Suggestions? I'm a technician for Christ sake! Not a cop!"

Then Frost lost it, too. "Stop yelling! Anything on visual?"

Pete looked at Cameras One and Two. No activity. Same with Camera Three, mounted to a telephone pole near the river. Camera Four, located near the Macklin residence, was completely covered in fog. Camera Five, mounted to the rooftop of the van, pointed at the old farmer's house. Appearing on screen through an infrared lens, Pete saw a door open. Out walked the old farmer, Norman "Scootch" McPhee, a.k.a. Homer, roaring drunk. Pete turned up the volume and heard a litany of cuss words, then noticed what Homer was holding. A shotgun.

"Holy crap!" Pete swore.

Liz jumped to her feet and yelled, "What's he doing?"

Staggering toward the van was what he was doing. His back was arched and sleeveless undershirt was torn and Homer was spitting out expletives like the raunchy old cuss that he was.

In the confusion, Agent Frost and his partner kept asking what was going on and both Pete and Liz kept blabbering, "What's he doing? What's he doing?" while ignoring their questions amid a profusion of shrieks and screams. It was pure bedlam, the closer Homer got to the van. At one point Liz couldn't take it anymore. She pushed the back door open, jumped, and ran like a scared rabbit. Left alone, Pete didn't know what to do. All he did was gawk in hushed amazement as Homer raised the shotgun.

"Oh, oh!" Pete hollered, hitting the floor. He sprawled, making himself go as flat as possible while in his headset he kept hearing the agents barking at him. Pete squinted one eye at Monitor Five and saw Homer swaying with the shotgun, pointing it somewhere in the vicinity of the satellite dish anchored to top of the van.

"Somebody, hurry!" Pete yelled. "The old farmer's drunk. He's got a shotgun. Somebody better get their ass up here. Get up here quick! Oh, my God!"

And all Pete could do was stare.

The shotgun exploded—*p-shoo-boom!*—pellets pinging, ripping holes through metal with a burst of hot lead. The screen to Camera Five went out like a light switch, its circuitry buzzing as it died.

Chapter 74

Like everyone else, Tom Duckett was at a loss of what to do. His electronic eyes and ears were gone, out of commission with the surveillance van. Twice he tried to hail Pete, each time with no response. Holding the police radio transmitter, he then hailed the Bertram County Sheriff's Department—

"Alert, Base One! This is Unit Four. Urgent! Are you there?"

A dispatcher named Lois, working the night shift, came on. This is Base. Go ahead, Unit Four."

Tom breathed a sigh of relief. "Unit Two may be in trouble, Lois. They went to investigate a possible Code Two. Heard anything?"

"No, not a thing. Not from Unit Two anyway."

"From anyone?"

"The surveillance van just sent out a distress call. Do you need assistance? Any Code Two sightings where you are?"

"Negative on both counts. All hell broke loose just a second ago. Don't know how you could have missed it."

"Sorry. We're keeping all channels open," said Lois. "The distress call involved some irate farmer. We're responding."

The deputy gave a brief description of what he heard from Unit Two before the system went down. Out of the corner of his eye, he saw headlights streaking through the darkness, coming his way. A patrol car driven by the young deputy hit the corner speeding, flashers on, tires screeching. He waved at Tom, yelled something out the window, and hailed all Units and both Bases, informing them he was answering the distress call. Tom, of course, didn't hear what he said. Seconds later, the taillights disappeared. Deputy Duckett was left alone. And he didn't like it, not one bit, and said so.

"Lois, on second thought, maybe you should send somebody out. Unit Five just drove outta here like a bat out of hell."

"Copy. You're breaking up, Tom. Unit Five is responding to the surveillance van. I'll see what I can do."

To relieve the tension, Tom joked, "Hell, yank old Gus out of bed if you have to. It's awful lonely out here. Make sure you keep this channel open."

"Roger, Unit Four. Don't worry. My orders are to monitor the situation."

"Remind the other guys I'm all alone, okay?"

"I understand. Call if you need help."

Tom put the transmitter down in favor of the coffee mug. He took a sip. Nothing like good Irish coffee to settle the nerves. He did a quick sweep with his eyes, making sure there were no surprises. And just to be sure, for the second or third time, he checked to see if the key was still in the ignition. Which it was. As he settled back, he checked the rearview mirror, then the side mirrors. It was almost unnoticeable at first. The air outside was still normal for this time of evening.

The red battery-operated warning lights at the intersection began to blink a bit faster. As he raised the coffee mug to his lips, the mug stopped an inch from his mouth and remained there. Half a second later, his eyes shot wide. The red lights began to pulsate in rhythm to his heart, faster and faster. His eyes twitched side to side as he lowered the mug. To his left, the gas-operated lights from Substation 12 began to dim and glow whereas before they just glowed. He didn't know whether to pick up the transmitter or grab the key. In his haste he tried to do both. The ignition turned, but that was it. The engine didn't start. All he heard was a metallic click. In desperation he pressed the transmitter. Whispering at first, he gradually raised his voice until he was hollering, "Unit Four to Base, do you read me? Lois, come in! You there? Something's happening! Calling all Units! Anybody listening? Hey, you guys, I'm all alone out here! Car won't start! Lights are going crazy...!"

The radio began to play music, short excerpts, from reggae to hip-hop to rock 'n roll. When he realized none of the other electrical parts of the car were working—starter, door locks, windows, interior lights. Then the interior lights started flashing, then the headlights, then everything began to flash all at once. Music surged in and out. Lights from the utility compound pulsed brighter and brighter. Tom sat with coffee mug in hand, shaking, wondering what in the hell was going on. He put the mug aside, grabbed the steering wheel, then the door handle. Each time he felt a jolt of electricity. He heard himself gasp and yell as his chest heaved in and out. At one point—he wasn't sure when—everything stopped, or went out, except the headlights. Utility lights, interior lights, red warning lights, radio—everything was cut off. The headlights blinked on and off, then slowed to a flicker until eventually they shut off as well. And just before they did, in a long protracted flash, he saw something down the road caught in the projection of the headlights that made his heart skip a beat. Big and burly, dark and lumbering, it was coming straight at him. In the next moment it was gone, only because the headlights had dimmed. Maybe not *gone*. He just couldn't see it. Outside, there was no light at all. The windows had clouded up—front, back, and sides—in a matter of seconds.

Then came the smell, that putrid stench of sulfur and rotting flesh.

Next, he heard a sizzle, tiny bits of hail pelting the roof and hood. Puffs of gently rolling haze drifted past the car. Specks of light shimmered here and there, floating in the breeze. A thick layer of fog gathered without his knowing it. As the flecks intensified, he began to feel a queasiness in the pit of his stomach. His eyes began to tear from irritation. He had trouble seeing.

Somewhere ahead, he heard a loud roar. A heavy weight fell on the hood of the car. The suspension gave, bobbing up and down. Then it happened again, once on the roof and once on the trunk, caving in the metal, as if something had leapt from the hood to the roof to the trunk, bending the roof so severely Tom bumped his head on the headliner. Whatever it was, as quickly as it came, it left. Tom sat there, expecting to be attacked any second. His entire body was shaking. Five seconds passed. Ten seconds. As much as he hated trying, he placed his hand on the door handle and pulled. No jolt of electricity this time. But the door wouldn't open. Panic set in.

Coughing and blotting his eyes with both hands, he started to feel a slight rocking sensation, thinking it was his body. It wasn't. It was the patrol car. The undercarriage trembled as though it were in a minor earthquake. The cabin was pitching. Car phone, radio, dashboard, seats shook as if the ground beneath were splitting open. A heavy camouflage of fog devoured the hood. The seat was bouncing, the car frame jostling back and forth, up and down. He screamed. The movement became more violent, flinging him from side to side, to the ceiling, to the seat, and back again to the ceiling. His head, shoulders, and back were being crunched between the roof and seats. He groped for the radio transmitter and somehow clutched it.

"Unit Four to Base! Unit Four to Base! Come in..."

He coughed. His head and shoulders were being battered. His body went careening around the front seat, harder, faster, his arms and legs flailing like a puppet's. Although he wasn't conscious of it, a force was pressing against the glass, squeezing inward, around the steel exterior. His skull struck the steering wheel. All the windows shattered, exploding inward with a sudden blast, spraying him with biting, glittery crystals. His hand dropped the transmitter as he fell across the seat. The steel frame started crumpling, chrome fenders buckling, chunks of metal whining as it was being reshaped.

Chapter 75

As a trained soldier, David had no problems killing another human being as long as that human being was the enemy and it was absolutely necessary. But an animal? That didn't sit well with him. He went deer hunting once. Shot a ten-point buck. When his sister heard about it, she railed into him something awful. Cured him of hunting of any kind. He never harmed another animal since. Until now.

After seeing the flare go up, he knew someone was in trouble and was about to go to the rescue when Caddo strongly advised against it. "No, Kiriki. It would be suicide. There's nothing you can do."

Even this couldn't dampen David's sense of urgency. As they dragged the dead coyotes near the campfire, he turned to Caddo and said, "And you? Exposed up here like this? In the military, we call it an 'untenable position.' Aren't you in danger?"

"I am, but that's a risk I'm willing to take."

"Then what do you suggest I do?"

Caddo went ruffling through his satchel as if he had no fear, no care, even though the situation appeared to call for immediate action. Almost with no compunction, he replied, "I suggest you drive as far away as you can, as fast as you can."

"But just a minute ago you told me to go home."

"I did. Not now. To do that..."—Caddo stood up and pointed east—"you'd have to pass through more untenable positions."

Hands jammed in his pockets, David paced back and forth. Having amassed information from his grandfather's journal, Henry Purdy's memoir, and passages from Caddo's books, he tried to make sense of it all. He stopped, turned, and asked Caddo, "Who is Aaron Caldwell?"

Caught off guard, the Indian blathered some unintelligible utterance.

"Aaron Caldwell...who is he?" David repeated.

"A writer. Teacher."

"Is that all?"

"No, a shaman. Tribal priest."

"Sachem?"

Caddo gave that knowing nod.

"Of what tribe?"

"Lakota."

"And as a tribal chief of the Lakotas, his beliefs are similar to yours?"

"The Lakota Sioux and Pawnee share certain beliefs, yes."

"And don't you both believe there's a...an *Okton*, I think you call it, a *malevolent presence*, and Guardian Spirit, a...a..."

"*Oyaron.*"

David repeated it phonetically, "*Oy-a-ron.*"

"Very good, Kiriki. You learned some new words today. As you believe in God and a demonic presence, in all societies there are opposites. Good and evil."

"Where do these 'opposites' live?"

Caddo gave him a blank look.

"An abode of spirits," said David urgently. "Isn't that where they...exist?"

Caddo nodded.

"And what happens when you destroy an abode of spirits?"

"The spirits leave."

"And once they leave, what happens?"

Again, Caddo gave him a puzzled look.

Too impatient to wait for an answer, David began to pace once more—hands thrust in his pockets, head bent in thought—and again just as he had done earlier, he stopped and stared at Caddo. "What I can't figure out is, how my father fits into all of this?"

Caddo was either playing dumb or he truly didn't know. He remained silent while David reworded the question—

"Indians have a word for someone who dreams. What is it?" Suddenly it came to him. "Conjurer?"

"No," said Caddo. The one who dreams is the *host*. Conjurer means magician. He is the one who creates the dream, shapes it as he desires."

"And conjurer in this case is the malevolent presence, spirit, or as you call the Charik, the enemy?"

Caddo nodded. He could see where this was leading. "Correct."

"Could his opposite, the Guardian Spirit, make him go away? In effect kill him?"

"If equal to the task. If he is powerful enough."

"Not he, Caddo. *She.*"

Chapter 76

The Friday night crowd at the Red Lion Pub was late in arriving. But arrive they did, in droves, like June bugs drawn to a light fixture on a hot summer's night. Having electricity helped as did the cheeseburgers and fries. The bar and grill were in full swing. The talk was loud, the music from the jukebox louder as ex-Beatle George Harrison sang '*My Guitar Gently Weeps.*'

Working on his sixth beer and fifth shot of tequila, Paul Heidtman was tired of listening to rock 'n roll oldies. He wanted country, something rip-roaring that got your feet stomping and, preferably, Gwen's luscious hips swaying.

Can't dance to George Harrison.

Paul staggered to the jukebox, slipped dollar bills into it like he was feeding a slot machine in Vegas. After pressing a series of buttons, Charlie Daniels belted out a song, his fiddle went to playin', and the whole place started rockln'.

"Hey, McEwen!" Paul yelled to the bar keep. "Crank up the volume!"

Everyone laughed.

Heidtman sidled up to the bar. Gwen was leaning with her back against it, elbows on the bar in a very seductive way, breasts peeking out of her tank top. She smiled and did the come-hither and Paul leaned against her, cupped a breast and they started going at it right there at the bar, mouth to mouth, tongue to tongue in front of ten guys who watched open-mouthed and wide-eyed.

The barkeep snapped, "Oh, no! Not in my bar! Go get a room!"

All the lights in the bar suddenly pulsed on and off. Bar lights, overhead lights, lights from the jukebox. Somebody it seemed was monkeying with the light switch. Music was disrupted like an old vinyl record skipping a beat or two, all of it occurring in the course of ten seconds before everything returned to normal.

The patrons groaned, then moaned in delight when they could hear old Charley playin' the fiddle and see their glasses of foamy beer.

Meanwhile, at the front door, at the opposite end of the bar, in walked a person of such shocking appearance, he nearly brought the house to a standstill. Slowly, one by one, everybody turned at the sound of tinkling bones. Conversations stopped. Fifty people shot a look of amazement at the stranger as he stood at the jukebox, staring at the twinkling lights, hands spread against the glass, head bent low. From head to foot, he was dressed like an Indian. Moccasins, leather breechcloth, bearskin vest, bear's head covering his head, and shrunken skulls hanging from a sash tied around his waist. He stood over the jukebox glaring at it, intrigued by the lights, feeling the strum of music coursing through his body when, all at once, every-one detected an odor of rancid fat.

One of the waitresses walked from the poolroom, holding a tray of empty beer bottles. As she passed the stranger, she froze. The tray tilted. One of the bottles fell. She almost caught it. It bounced against the foot of the Indian, rolled, and came to rest against his heel. The Indian didn't move. The waitress nervously reached down, picked up the bottle, and uttered a gasp. She looked at his face and trembled, almost too scared to move. The whole tray was shaking. She looked down and saw his dirty unkempt fingernails, his dirty skin, dirty clothes, a shock full of dirty, tangled, black hair hanging to his shoulders, but no distinct facial features. Only a suggestion of skin, nose, and mouth. He looked like a walking corpse.

Something in his eyes made her freeze and catch her breath.

The Indian turned his head slightly as Charley Daniels continued to play.

The waitress stammered, "Takes quarters. Or…or dollar bills. If you wanna play something."

He turned to the jukebox, tilting his head as he listened. The waitress backed away. Two steps later, she was practically running.

Standing at the far end of the bar, Paul Heidtman did a loud, "Ooo-wee! What do we have here?" Staggering toward the Indian, he slurred, "Trick or treat. Ain't it a little early for Halloween?" Paul looked him up and down, squinting, and said, "Is that a real bear's head you're wearin'? Hey, Sitting Bull. I'm talking to you. Is that a mini-skirt? Eh, girlie boy?" He laughed, then pretended to gag. "Man oh man, you could use a bath. What crawled outta your ass?"

Paul pinched his nose and stood there half grinning, half choking when the stranger turned, took one hand, pushed Paul to the floor, turned in the other direction, and exited the front door—skull bones rattling every step of the way—before anyone knew what happened.

From the jukebox, Tim McGraw started singing *'Live like you were dying.'*

Sprawled on the floor, Heidtman looked around and could see everyone staring at him, wondering what he was going to do. Be a bad ass, that's what he was going to do. No redneck Indian son-of-a-bitch was going to get the better of him. Paul went barreling out the door, yelling, "Hey, Indian! Sitting Bull! Hey, you!"

Gwen caught up with Paul and tugged at his shirt. "Paul, don't!

Let him go! Let him go, Paul! Please!"

Fog hung thick around the sign above as it pulsed red. The sign never pulsed. Until now.

Paul saw the Indian duck behind a truck and went staggering after him, yelling, "Hey! Hey, you! Geronimo!"

Gwen followed, pleading for him to stop, "Please, Paul! Come back! Don't! You might get hurt. Paul! Please!"

She saw her boyfriend slip behind the truck. She stopped short, hand clenched to her mouth, shaking.

There was a loud thrashing of bodies. A spurt of blood. Growls. Bones being crushed. A scream. A thud against pavement, then against a car door. The truck rocked back and forth. Another scream so frightening it stood the hair on end.

This time it was Gwen who screamed.

Chapter 77

David ignored Caddo's warning and drove home. He was basing everything on a hunch, a calculated guess. What it came down to really was hope, trust, and faith. Hope that he was right. Trust in his instincts. And faith in family.

If he was wrong, the consequences were deadly.

As luck would have it, it was a beautiful, warm spring night when he arrived at the farmhouse. With no time to spare, he would have one chance and one chance only, if his luck continued.

He led Cinders into the house and shut the door, ran into the barn, found two rakes and cut the wooden handles in half by using a hand saw. From a bin by the door, he grabbed a handful of rags and wrapped one layer around a rake handle, tied it in place with twine, and poured oil over the rags, careful not to soak the twine. He repeated the process three more times on each handle, then finished it off by pouring charcoal lighter fluid lightly over the outer layer of rags. Too much oil or lighter fluid and the flames would burn too quickly. One knot and the whole thing would fall apart in seconds.

A quick look outside to see if the air was still clear.

Good. All clear.

He listened, but all he could hear was the chug of the gas generator on the driveway and a slight pinging of wind chimes from the side kitchen porch.

He had time to do one more thing.

* * *

In spite of her brother's insistence and against her better judgment, Eileen jumped in her Jeep and drove back to the farm. Alexa refused to stay behind even though she was repeatedly warned she was risking her life, aside from being ridiculously foolhardy and stubborn. No haggling with Alexa.

As she put it, "Hey, if I'm being stupid, what about you?"

As they approached the Red Lion Pub, they noticed a sign blinking amid a shroud of fog. Surprised the bar had electricity, they slowed down, wondering if they should stop and turn around or continue on. They continued on, creeping along at ten miles an hour. Outside the bar, they saw people piling out the door. A crowd gathered around a truck. Elly heard screams. She rolled the window down and hit the brakes.

A man was holding a cell phone to his ear and yelling at a young woman standing next to him. "I'm trying! I'm trying, okay? The phone's not working."

Elly and Alexa glanced to the right of the front door where a dozen people were standing, staring in horror at something lying between the building and the road. Elly inched closer in her Jeep, then stopped. At the foot of the crowd was a body, slumped and unmoving, legs and arms twisted in awkward positions. Blood was splattered against the pavement, on the sides of the truck and the car next to it. Alexa and Elly suppressed a scream.

A person yelled, "Somebody call an ambulance!"

"The police!" shouted another.

Then everyone started pulling cell phones from their pockets and dialing 9-1-1. Panic spread when they realized they couldn't get a dial tone.

"There's no reception!"

"I can't get through!"

"Hey, lady! You in the car. Go get help! There's been a murder!"

Everybody was shouting and yelling at once.

Realizing they had no phones and how useless it would be if they did, Elly looked at Alexa, as if to say *'what should we do?'* Alexa yelled, "Go!" And off the Wrangler sped, pedal to the floor, peeling rubber.

The faster they went, the thicker the fog. A few miles later they saw a car parked beside the highway, sitting by an access road used by combines and tractors. It was a patrol car—a Bertram County Sheriff's patrol car—all buckled and bent and twisted as if the metal were made of putty.

Elly stopped and got out of the Jeep, as did Alexa. They ran to the patrol car. Through the broken windshield they saw a body slumped in the driver's seat. It was Tom Duckett. He appeared to be dead. A stream of blood trickled from his mouth and down his forehead. Elly tried the door, but it wouldn't open. She pulled again and again, her muscles straining. She pulled one more time, throwing all of her weight into it, and the door ripped open. Alexa caught the body as it flopped over.

Elly felt for a pulse.

A vein throbbed in Tom's neck.

He was alive.

Chapter 78

The herd was growing restless. Agitated.

When Richard Macklin opened his eyes, he was caught in the transition between nightmare and consciousness.

Fog choked the air as well as the stench of decayed flesh.

The cows went stampeding across the yard, mooing, shrieking. Richard leaned forward in the lounge chair and grabbed his shotgun. To his right, on his blind side, a figure came sprinting at him. All he saw was a glimpse of a body dressed as an Indian, with the head of a bear resting on his skull. Richard had no time to react. He was struck on the head with something hard. His knees buckled. And down he went, unconscious, his body limp. Not dead.

Richard was no good to him dead.

His attacker now had time to go on the assault. He chased after the herd. As he did, his body began to change. He heard a door slam in the distance, near the farmhouse. He could sense fear in the cows as well as a man. The Shape Changer thrived on fear. It was the sole purpose of his existence, to seek revenge and inflict pain on those who had once waged war against his race.

* * *

David ran awkwardly, holding the rake handles in one hand, a lamp in the other. A sack, containing a can of motor oil and a can of charcoal lighter fluid, was tied to a strap hanging from his shoulder. The sack kept banging against his side. When he heard the cows stampeding, he ran faster.

In a matter of seconds the night had turned ugly in every sense of the word. The moon had disappeared behind a rolling mass of fog. It was so dark he couldn't gauge where he was going. His depth perception was nonexistent. Even with the aid of the lamp, he could barely see in front of him. The lamp flame fluttered as he ran, casting a glow so weak he couldn't tell where his feet met the ground. It was like running in a cloud. His equilibrium was out of whack. The slightest change in elevation, a mound or depression, threw him off balance. He had to go by feel. Even then he wasn't certain of the direction. Toward the general vicinity of the river was all he could hope for now.

Judging from the movement and sound of the cows, the creature was close by. So far David couldn't hear any footsteps, but knew it was only a matter of time before one shape or another, man or animal, appeared. The Charik, he believed, could take the shape of a number of things, the most frightening being a creature consisting of nothing but air—brought to life by a dream. How do you kill something that doesn't exist in the sense of the real world? Or as David knew it? You can't. Yet, based upon what it had done in the past, the Charik could inflict pain, and, yes, could even kill. That was the most disturbing thing. It could kill and there seemed to be no defense against it.

Unless...

His only chance rested in the enemy taking the shape of a man or Beast. The only weapon at David's disposal was the .38. In a moment of panic, he stopped, placed the lantern on the ground, and reached behind at the small of his back where he had tucked the .38. Good. It was still there.

As he bent over to pick up the lamp, he heard a roar, a loud bellow of satisfaction. The cows were panicking, shrieking wildly, stampeding across the cattle yard.

He felt terror—unlike any he had ever felt before.

A voice in his head shouted, *Run!*

Head down, he sprinted.

His right leg was already cramping, the hamstring knotted, tightening with each stride. It was all he could do to maintain the pace.

He heard footsteps in the distance, the trample of plodding feet, those of the Beast.

The race was on.

Faster! Don't think of anything else. Just run!

David didn't see the rise in terrain. His feet got caught in the angle of ascent. He stumbled and plunged headfirst into the slope of the hill. The lamp slipped from his hand as he braced to absorb the impact. His shoulder took the brunt of the fall. He heard a breaking of glass. The glass globe shattered, spilling oil on the ground. The lamp flame trembled, shrinking, the light fading until there was nothing but darkness. He couldn't get his bearings. The feel of the slope provided the only direction.

Now came the hard part. Running uphill. He pinned the sack to his side with his elbow and started running.

He pumped his legs as fast as he could. It felt like one of his recurring nightmares where he ran in place but went nowhere. Every stride felt constricted. The slope now worked against him. It felt like he was moving in slow motion. Somehow he made it to the top of the hill. He staggered ahead, listening to the voice in his head—

Don't stop. Almost there. Oh, my God. My legs! I'll never make it. You won't make it if you don't try. What am I going to do when I get there? Who cares. The point is to get there.

There it is! The barn! Just a few more yards. Oh, no! It's right behind me. Don't look back! Okay now, grab the door.

A roar shook his concentration. He fumbled for the door handle. His hands were shaking.

His mind was screaming, *Open it! Hurry, David! Pull! That's it. Now close it! Latch it!*

Panting and gasping, he wedged the door jamb down inside the brackets.

A board two-inches thick stood between him and certain death, a board decades old, weathered by the elements, half rotted. He needed something stronger to reinforce the door jam. He looked around. It was pitch black inside…everywhere but one place. Through a small opening in the tepee he saw a reflection of hot embers from a fire, just an inch or two of light, a reddish glow shining through the gap.

David drew the flap aside. More light spilled from the fire, just enough to illuminate the shadows. He noticed a stack of rusted iron rods lying on the ground outside the tepee. As he went to grab them, something rammed against the door. The door gave, but didn't break. The entire barn shook…rocked on its foundation. Dust fell from the ceiling. A roar split the air, followed by an angry growl. Another crash shook the door. Wood splintered, then cracked, but the door jamb held. David shoved rod after rod down into the latch, realizing he was only delaying the inevitable. Four iron rods, half an inch thick, bolted the door, kept the intruder out—for the moment anyway. Now it was the hinges that worried him.

Again a wall shook from a body smashing into it, a massive body, not a lifeless form composed of air, but a Beast of incredible size and strength. No doubt It could break into the building at any time. But where?

Another roar rang out. The wall shuddered from a body crashing into it.

There was a flash of light at the far end of the stalls, a weeping sound so faint David could barely hear it.

He ducked inside the tepee and stuck the makeshift torches into the dying embers. They caught. The first thing he torched was the tepee. He doused the base with lighter fluid, held a torch against it, and watched the tarp flare up in a creeping wall of flame. To the carriages he went next, throwing handfuls of moldy hay onto the beds and sprayed the beds with motor oil. Flames whipped up with a loud *whoomph*. Alternating between the motor oil and lighter fluid, he ran here and there, igniting fires with one torch, then the other—in a corner where stacks of chopped wood lay, among the many scattered heaps of rubbish, to the horse stalls where mounds of hay were piled.

That's when the rats came out, dozens of them, running, squealing, trying to escape the heat of the spreading fires.

In the rafters above, bats were flying back and forth, screeching. Confused by the smoke, bodies could be heard striking a rafter, a wall, the roof.

The noises were constant now. There was a certain desperation in Its attempts to get inside. Walls, door, rafters, ceiling—everything shook from the repeated thumps and roars of the Beast.

Flames were enveloping the barn on all sides as David worked his way to the hayloft. Again, he heard the sound of someone weeping. A light, not of flame or glow from a fire, drifted from the hayloft to a stall below.

At the opposite end of the barn, the intensity of the Beast's desperation rose to another level. A body went banging against the door, once, twice, each time prying it farther from the hinges. The door finally split with a loud crack, the doorframe and door fell to the floor. David knew then the Beast had gained entry.

As he backed into a stall, he threw the torches aside. He reached for a pitchfork, held it under his left shoulder, reached behind for the .38, cocked the trigger, and waited.

Most of the walls and ceiling were engulfed in flames, burning with a brilliance so hot it was scalding from thirty feet away. Squealing mice and rats went skittering across the dirt floor.

He was sweating, shaking. He couldn't keep his hands still.

It was the waiting part that ate at him, the anticipation. The Beast was taking Its time, moving slowly through the fire-strewn building. On two feet or four, he didn't know. He had no idea which one It would be—man or Beast. Given a choice, he'd take his chances against a man any day.

The smoke was almost worse than the heat. Billows of smoke poured against the roof, choking the air. The torrid brilliance of the fires was running up the rafters, along the walls, spreading everywhere.

David estimated he had one minute before the heat and smoke got to him. He figured his only way out, if there was one, was literally through a wall. If he had to, he'd break through a burning wall like a linebacker and escape out the other side. At least that was the plan.

He could hear It breathing now. It was just outside the stall. Its shadow stretched across the threshold. David wasn't so much afraid as he was gripped by paralyzing anticipation. The degree of separation wasn't much. A matter of attitude. A coward versus a fool.

Feet shuffled...

And there It was—in full view. Not a bear. A man. Standing Bear by his Iroquois name, a Shape Changer, redeemer of the Indian race. He stood against everything the White Man had done to the Indian, all the bloodshed, the violence, the acts of brutality, the killing, the lands that were taken away. That's what this had come down to.

Standing Bear stared at David, watching his every move, breathing heavily.

David gripped the pitchfork and .38 and waited. There was less than half a minute before the barn would come tumbling down. They stood eye-to-eye, no more than twelve feet apart. David curled his finger around the trigger. The pistol was pointed at the Charik, at the abuser of Henry Purdy, murderer of John Macklin.

His body was covered in soot, as if he'd just crawled out of a hole, his hair stringy, disheveled, his face painted black from cheeks to chin. The only other part of him that was visible were his eyes. Eyes of the Devil Incarnate. Eyes that penetrated. Angry eyes—full of hate.

An odor smoldered of death. His feet were wrapped in the skin of a dead animal. His vest, taken from the hair and skin of a bear. His headdress was that of a grizzly. Ghastly, gory skulls hung from a sash around his waist.

"I understand why you're doing this, " said David. "I know."

As the man began to transform, to change into something inhuman, David pulled the trigger. The hammer clicked, but the .38 didn't fire. He pulled the trigger again. The pistol was useless. He threw it down. As it clattered against a board, the hammer triggered, sending a hollow point exploding against a wall.

There was a hint of a smile in Standing Bear's face. But those were not the teeth of a man any more, but the fangs of a bear. Everything was changing. Arms, legs, shoulders, face—widening, thickening. David could see the muscles expanding, the bones stretching as hair sprouted from Its skin.

All David had was a pitchfork. Somehow it seemed piddling as a weapon. But he had to try. At least die trying. Give it all he had.

He got his body behind it. Heaved it like a javelin. It flew through the air, prongs-first. Penetrated deep into the chest. There was a gurgling sound, of choking.

David saw pain.

The man reached up, pulled the pitchfork from his chest, and staggered backward when an arrow hit him square in the back between the shoulder blades. He growled and continued to change when a second arrow pierced his side. He faltered, turned, and looked over his shoulder when a third arrow struck his lower back. He wobbled and roared. Not a drop of blood poured from any of the wounds.

The Charik was almost a bear now, stretching to a height of seven feet to eight feet, all in less than ten seconds—from man to bear.

It had come down to this moment, the final sequence of dream-induced events, taken from the past. And it all depended on a feeling, a hunch. Nothing more. And that's where faith in family came in. If something as unreal as what David was witnessing now could exist, well…there was nothing to lose in hoping. If he was wrong, he was as good as dead.

"Mother!" he yelled. "Any time now, Mom. Any time!"

Rats and mice were shrieking from the heat of the fires. Amid all the confusion and noise a voice called weakly from the back of the barn.

The cell phone rang. He reached into his pocket, stared at the caller I.D.—'Caller Unknown'—and heard a chord from Gershwin's *Rhapsody in Blue*. The music was rapture to his ears. One long piano chord. The timing was perfect, eerie. He felt a rush. No, it was much more than that. It was *mana, wakan, manitou*. A rush of exhilaration! Unlike any feeling he ever had.

That's when he noticed a look in the bear's eyes, a look of fear, as It raised up. The Beast hesitated and within a split second there was a flash behind David, at the rear of the stall.

He felt dizzy, lightheaded. His eyes fluttered, then closed. And during that infinite pause between sleep and consciousness when the two become confused, that "dawning between wakefulness and sleep" as Henry Purdy once described it, David saw her. He saw his mother, Dora, as he once knew her, a beautiful young woman.

Her youthful appearance quickly dissolved into something much different, a disembodied spirit with hollow eyes, long-flowing scarf, locks of chestnut hair, and silky windblown nightgown. The woman who entered his dream the night of the accident had materialized out of the smoke and ruin of Old Serenity, no longer weeping, but laughing in the voice that seemed distant, far removed from this world.

A rafter against a far wall started sagging—on fire.

Soothing and quiet, a voice from the past whispered in David's ear, "It's all right."

A chill raced down his spine. *Am I dreaming?*

The bear was about to lunge. As It did, a hand pushed David aside.

A gust of wind came whipping through the barn. Fire and smoke were swept back. The light that flashed behind David now exploded.

Went surging forward, colliding with air, sending up a shower of sparks so blinding, he had to look away. There was a loud pop. Another explosion. Rafters were buckling. The entire building was in flames.

David felt a hand take his. He wasn't completely deaf or blind, but close to it. Sounds echoed from far away. He was disoriented. He didn't know if he was walking or floating. The hand guided. Led him through a corridor of wreckage, through heat, smoke and fire, up a ladder to the hayloft, across the floor, to the hayloft door.

The door opened, untouched.

There was a roar in the distance, a dying sound. It had a feebleness to it—sad and indefinable.

David didn't remember jumping.

He found himself kneeling on the ground outside, hunched over, coughing and hacking. A hand brushed his hair, a hand that had a familiar feel to it when he was kid. A loving touch. A gentle caress. As a mother would give a child.

"It's all right," she whispered so softly David thought he imagined it.

He turned. Blinked once, twice, a third time. The presence was gone.

He looked at the barn. All he saw was a massive sheet of whiteness, the outline of the building burning, flames licking up the sides. He could feel the heat. Parts of his shirt were singed, still smoking.

To his right, a figure came staggering through the thinning fog and mist, coughing, holding a bow. Caddo caught his breath and said, "Charik waik-ta no more!"

In the distance they could hear...what was it?

Sirens. They heard sirens.

Chapter 79

The questions kept coming and coming.

Agent Kenneth Frost proved to be as thorough as he was tenacious. He attempted to take apart every inconsistency, point by point. He probed, he picked, he prodded. But if you asked him, he came away from the experience more confused and more in doubt than he did going in.

David admitted to arson without malicious intent. He gave no reason other than to say he wanted to remove an eyesore. The charge of reckless "endangerment by use of unauthorized fire" brought a fine, the amount of which was to be determined by the Bertram County Sheriff's Department. Criminal charges were never filed because the fire was on Macklin property. No complaint had been issued and no crime committed other than a misdemeanor and no insurance claim was sought since the barn had no value, outside of sentimentality.

The general consensus was that the overall mood of the farm had changed. The proof lay in the monitors of the surveillance van. While one disc was damaged from a shotgun blast, the rest remained intact and the ability to collect data and monitor visual, thermal, as well as audio information was still working and the Black Hole was no longer visible on any of the screens.

Each of the Macklin family members, as well as both Caddo and Alexa, were questioned for two days during long, tedious sessions at the Law Enforcement Center.

Caddo received the most scrutiny. Wired to a polygraph, he was interrogated again and again about Wilfredo Pinoza's death.

"We know for a fact," said Agent Frost, "that you were in the vicinity where his body was found. We have you on tape. Why didn't you report it?"

Caddo narrowed his eyes. "On tape?"

"Yes, on tape," replied Agent Brian Riddick. "You said some cockamamie crap about, and I quote, "…May he rest while he sleeps in our hearts.' Now answer the goddamn question. Why didn't you call?"

Caddo remained calm and said, "I was going to report it once I removed the body from the tree."

Agents Frost and Riddick exchanged glances.

"And disturb a crime scene?" Frost said indignantly. "Cover up what you had done?"

"What did I do?"

"You committed murder!"

"Freddie was my friend. Why would I kill him?"

"You tell us." Once Agent Frost simmered down, he glanced at the man doing the lie detector test, then moved on, hoping to keep Caddo talking. "Okay, let's assume you didn't do it. Do you know *how* he was killed?"

"How he died maybe."

"Explain."

"It happened exactly the way it looked. Somehow he was lifted into the air and thrown against a broken branch."

"By whom? Or what?" asked Agent Frost.

"I don't know."

The agent put a foot on a chair, leaned closer, trying to intimidate and apply more pressure. "Were you a witness to any of this?"

"No."

"So an unknown person, or entity, picked him up…in your words 'lifted' him and threw him against a broken branch. Do you know how ridiculous that sounds?"

Caddo said nothing. He stared straight ahead, raising his eyes only when spoken to or asked a question.

The remainder of the session was just as unproductive. The polygraph proved his innocence. Caddo was challenged repeatedly but never broken.

The case involving Wilfredo Pinoza's death was never solved, even after weeks of processing scant evidence, following up leads, blood analysis, and detective work. Richard Macklin was the only one who offered a clue, having said earlier in a videotaped interview with electrodes strapped to his arms about an incident in Vietnam when a fellow soldier was seen hanging from a tree, impaled by a branch. The similarities, according to the Ohio Bureau of Investigation, were nothing more than coincidence.

As for David, one of his many concerns was his eyesight. He didn't know if he was going to regain it. Which he did. Alexa kissed him goodbye after posing a number of questions. He presented the facts and kept the details to a minimum. He explained that a bear—yes, a bear—followed him into the barn. Caddo shot it with a bow and arrow. End of story. The carcass was never found. David doubted Alexa would print anything because, in her words, the whole thing was "far too complicated and bizarre for public consumption."

Their date was set for Saturday night.

The next issue of the *Bertram County Sentinel* leaked a story concerning the bear's disappearance, how it was lured into the barn, then killed and destroyed by fire, leaving not a single trace of fiber or hair. The newspaper's intent was simply to put concerns to rest, but it only fired up more debate.

Pivotal to the investigation was Richard Macklin. He was found by agents lying unconscious beside a chaise lounge chair in the cattle yard. Two cows had been butchered, bone and tissue torn to shreds. The rest of the herd was as nervous and timid as mice, suffering from what Elly called "post traumatic syndrome." Other than a reference to a dream, Richard proved to be no help at all. He couldn't answer half of the questions, or explain how he got the bump on his head. When he saw the ruins of the old barn, he collapsed to his knees and sobbed uncontrollably. David tried to console him. In doing so he realized one of the horrible things that came out of it was the destruction of Old Serenity. Richard's tie to the past had now been severed permanently. David promised himself he'd do everything he could to help get his father back on his feet.

That night Richard wanted to be left alone to mourn his loss in private.

As for Caddo, Elly drove him to Irene's apartment in Mistwood in her yellow Jeep Wrangler. David sat in the back seat, Caddo the front. No one spoke. They rode in silence, respecting a vow of secrecy.

On the return ride home, Elly dropped a bombshell by announcing her engagement to a medical student who was doing an internship for Doctors Without Borders somewhere in Central America.

Eileen spent the night at the farm while their father drank himself to sleep. Drinking was another issue that had to be addressed. Richard wouldn't have made it through the night if it hadn't been for his children. He survived without incident through the darkest of hours of his existence, taking his first step on the road to recovery. The only time the war in Vietnam raised its ugly head was when he was awake, not asleep.

Ironically, Paul Heidtman's death and nine cases involving the slaughter of livestock received the most attention. The cases were attributed to bear attacks committed by a "Marauder" whose fangs were oversized, as were the Beast's voracity and fiendish intent to kill. Its den and hiding place were never found, its tracks never seen again. The cases were closed once every trace of the bear had disappeared.

Fueled by a morbid fascination, the day after the fire an endless parade of gawkers and curiosity seekers drove by, staring at the smoky ruins of the old barn. A firestorm of controversy spread through the community like a summer heat wave. What began as a simple fire grew into heroism of such magnitude, David's and Caddo's status in the community became legendary, so much so that *USA Today* did a three-paragraph article about the "killing of a bear" on the back page of the news section, compliments of Alexa Wilde.

Later Saturday afternoon, power was finally restored at Substation 12. A new chain link fence was erected, along with barbed wire and a surveillance camera. Signs cautioned violators of electrocution, plus a $2,500 fine for trespassing.

Soon after that Coach "Stumpy" Ed Kragan paid a visit in his high-top conversion van. "Boy, do I have good news for you. I left you a note. Why didn't you call?"

At the time David was feeding the chickens. "Been a little busy, Coach."

"Listen, kid. The scout with the Detroit team, Joe Reid—he's agreed to take a look at you. All you have to do is drive to Toledo next Tuesday and he'll put you through the paces. Got a farm team up there called the Mud Hens. Ain't the Tigers, but what the heck. Gotta start somewhere."

"Sorry, Coach. I can't."

The color drained from Stumpy's face. "Can't? Why not?"

"Prior commitments."

"It's the chance of a lifetime, kid. What happened to the dream?"

"It died."

"What do you mean 'died?' I have it all set up. It doesn't has to be Tuesday. I was just making that up. Monday, Wednesday, Friday. I could give a rat's ass. Hell, make it a month from now. Who cares."

"The dream's dead, Coach. One day you just have to wake up and trade one dream for another."

Stumpy whipped off his baseball hat, scratched his bald head, and looked dismayed. "Don't suppose you'd reconsider," he said as he slapped a cigar in his mouth. "Nah, I don't suppose you would. How long you stayin'?"

David shrugged. "Two weeks. A month. I haven't decided."

Coach Kragan chewed reflectively on his cigar. "Hope what they say isn't true. You're not tradin' a mitt for a golf glove, are ya'?"

"Not to worry, Coach."

Stumpy walked away, disappointed, muttering to himself.

That afternoon Jack Lorrigan and his partner, Matt, stopped by. Jack said he heard there was a good piece of property for sale.

"Where'd you hear that?" said David.

"Tom Duckett," replied Jack. "He said what worries we had, forget about them. They're gone."

"Is that what changed your mind?"

Jack hung an arm out the truck window. "Well, to be honest. The decision was pretty much made for us. Your uncle—he…a…took his proposal off the table. Not sure why."

As they were about to leave, Jack yelled, "Oh, yeah. One last thing. When working on a project, there is something I always do."

"What's that?" David asked.

"Give the golf course a name. In a book they call it a working title. If you think of one, let me know." Jack winked and drove away.

One more visitor stopped by late that afternoon. David saw a big black BMW with deep tinted windows pull up on the driveway while Richard was mowing the front lawn. Richard walked over to the car. Somebody rolled down a back window. The person in the back seat talked. Richard listened. Shook his head a few times. Came away smiling.

"Who was that?" David yelled once the BMW drove away.

"You're grandfather."

"What did he say?"

"He wants us to come to dinner Friday night. Said he has a surprise."

"What kind of surprise?"

"A *surprise* surprise, David. Hell, I don't know. He wouldn't tell me. Said it's worth a visit, though. Payment of an old debt." Richard laughed and shook his head. "After all these years…dinner at his place. Ha!"

He got back on the lawn mower and started whistling.

Epilogue

After the dust had settled and everyone went their separate ways, David took a long walk, a sentimental journey back in time to the winery. In the cellar of the processing plant where the wines were made, he found a hole in the wall where the bricks had tumbled to the floor. The hole was a foot below ground level, big enough for a man to crawl through.

David found an empty wine barrel, slid it to the wall, stood on top of the barrel, shined a flashlight through the hole, and saw mostly dirt, the remnants of a few bones, rocks, and tools chiseled from antler horns. On the floor among the rubble, he found an arrowhead. While inspecting it, he had the distinct impression of being watched. The impulse to run was overpowering.

Instead, he walked across the cellar to a room his grandfather once referred to as the "Asylum." David sat down and opened the journal to the back cover where two envelopes were pasted. The thicker of the two he already read. The other he slipped from the envelope and unfolded—

Dear Reader,
By now you should be familiar with the fact I have been influenced by events from a previous lifetime. Therefore I will proceed under the assumption you are reasonably acquainted with the subject matter.

Recently I decided to close a chapter of my life by addressing a subject that has haunted me for years. It began a few months ago when I had the pleasure of meeting a colleague of famed photographer Edward S. Curtis whose pictures and stories have captured the lives, hearts, and minds of many Native American Indians, particularly those of the Great Pacific Northwest. This historian of note, James Douglas, like Curtis, traveled the country interviewing Indians and becoming as he put it, "part of the fabric and essence of all things Indian." Through him I was able to discover a little known fact.

First I must lay some groundwork. I'm sure everyone has heard the phrase, "The only good Indian is a dead one." Not only is it inflame-

matory, but I find it exceedingly distasteful and insulting. History books too often portray the White Man as the good guy and the Indian as the bad. To contradict this, I offer two testimonials. The first concerns a famous Indian Chief —

"Judged by the primitive standards of the aboriginals, Pontiac was one of the greatest chiefs of which we have any record in our nation's history. His intellect was broad, powerful, and penetrating. In subtlety and craft, he had no superiors. In him were combined the qualities of an astute leader, a remarkable warrior, and a broad-minded statesman. His ambitions seemed to have no limit, such as was usually the case with an Indian chief. His understanding reached to higher generalizations and broader comprehensions than those of any other Indian mind. The first place that we hear of Pontiac is in an account of the expedition of Rogers' Rangers, in the fall of 1760. Rogers himself says, 'We met with a party of Ottawa Indians, at the mouth of the Chogaga (Cuyahoga) River, and they were under Ponteack (Pontiac)...their present King or Emperor. ***' He puts on an air of majesty and princely grandeur, and is greatly...revered by his subjects.' Pontiac forbade his proceeding for a day or two, but finally smoked the pipe of peace with Rogers, and allowed the expedition to proceed through his country to Detroit."

> Nevin O. Winter, 1917
> from the book – A History of Northwest Ohio

The second testimonial reads as follows—

"I do not recollect that I was ever insulted by an Indian, drunk or sober, during all the time I was with them, nor did any of them manifest any unkindness toward me...Indeed, I do not believe that there are a people on the earth, that are more capable of appreciating a friend, or a kind act done toward them or theirs, than Indians. Better neighbors, and a more honest people, I have never lived among. They are peculiarly so to the stranger or to the sick or distressed. They will divide the last mouthful, and give almost the last comfort they have, to relieve the suffering. This I have often witnessed."

> Rev. James B. Findley, 1821
> Missionary to the Wyandots
> from his private journal

For every negative story written about Indians, I could recite a hundred or more that spoke of their courage, their generosity, their kindness, and the decency shown to others not of their race. Regarding the negative perception of the Indian, ask yourself this. How would you like it if strangers invaded your village and for no reason at all told you to leave? And if you argued or protested in any way, no matter how innocent you were, they raped, pillaged, and killed. I doubt you would be pleased.

That's exactly what happened to several Indian tribes. I will explain...

After World War One, while living in New York City, I was able to borrow a mask from the Museum of Natural History to use at my discretion, a mask the Mohawk and Iroquois called a False Face. It had once belonged to a Mohawk tribe and was vital in summoning a 'person of interest.' At my request, we enlisted the services of several people, mainly the historian, James Douglas, and an individual of political prominence whose identity must remain anonymous. For purposes of simplicity I will call him the 'Hungarian'—a man who also happened to be a medium and possessed skills of a darker nature. These two men and I, along with several others, gathered in the basement of a house said to have a history of visitations. There, with Mr. Douglas acting as interpreter and the Hungarian as host and medium, we conducted the first of many séances.

They took place at night in an old New England country home facing the cold, harsh waters of the Atlantic. Our efforts were exhausting emotionally, each session lasting five or six hours. The first thing we had to do was to win our subject's confidence. After six days of persistence, leaving nothing to chance, we succeeded in securing a visit through our medium.

The Hungarian spoke a language understood only by Mr. Douglas. It was a strange affair, I must say. If I hadn't known the parties involved, my suspicions would have been aroused. As he played the part, the Hungarian was able to convey a great deal about our subject's personal life – where he lived, when, and the details regarding his family. He told us he was a priest, a mystic, a Shape Changer. We found him to be pleasant, a respectful and engaging fellow until he spoke of the tragedy that changed his life. He and several members of his tribe went hunting one day and returned home with enough deer to feed the entire village for weeks. They expected to be greeted with open arms and smiling faces, but as they approached the village it was strangely quiet. To their horror almost everyone had been killed – "...By white men dressed in buckskin," said a lone survivor. The massacre occurred because it was rumored the Mohawk were about to go on the warpath, when in fact they were about to smoke a pipe of peace. The leader of the hunting party found his wife, daughter, and two sons lying dead, their scalps taken as proof of a bounty. The taking of scalps, by the way, was mistakenly blamed on the Indian when in fact the evidence shows the opposite, that the White Man was responsible for the origin of this barbaric act—done out of greed for money.

Through our interpreter, our subject said what once began as a peaceful process, the engagement of whites and Indians, ended that day. Word soon spread throughout the Indian Lands that no White Man could be trusted. Hatred escalated into skirmishes, then all-out campaigns of war. Entire tribes were massacred, villages burned to the ground. Homeless and without a family, the Mohawk chief led his fellow survivors on a rampage, a campaign to organize all Indian Nations to take up arms against the 'yinlee' as he called them. This immediately got my attention.

I asked several questions of our interpreter while under the influence of the subject. One question in particular dealt with a former life when I was held captive by a tribe of little known Indians. I asked if he knew anything about a wagon train of settlers being attacked and two young white children, brother and sister, who had been captured, and an Indian named Jim. He admitted to knowing all three. I was stunned. As further proof of these statements, I asked the name of the tribe the Mohawks were visiting at the time. Our subject identified them as Mosopelea! Dog People!

I was in shock. No other conclusion could be reached. The person of interest was none other than my old nemesis, Standing Bear. Unfortunately that was the last we heard of him. He never spoke to us again. Both the Hungarian and Mr. Douglas said the pain they felt, the emotional pain that Standing Bear suffered, was devastating. It distorted all rational thought. One moment he was reasonable. The next, filled with so much hate he was driven to acts of violence! Of the power he possessed, they claimed it was "superhuman...a destructive force bent on retribution!" The loss of family sparked moments of insanity. He was a tormented soul who exercised those powers to exact revenge and do everything he could to punish the white race.

I understood then why he did what he did.

Long have I debated whether to put down these words in print. I have done so for two reasons. The first, to clear my conscience. The second, and more importantly, to paint a true picture of the individual who had a profound effect on me. Until now my brush has been anything but kind. I have called him many vile names. I have described him as a man of such evil that I know of no one in the annals of mankind I have hated more. Yet despite all my claims, I have done him a great disservice and an even greater injustice. I am as much to blame for these errors of judgment as I am for the shame I have brought upon myself.

Throughout my life I have considered myself a writer of sound judgment. My intentions always have been, and continue to be, honorable. When wrong, I am the first to admit it.

It turns out Standing Bear was not the monster I made him out to be. Nor should he be vilified for the things he has done to me. In his shoes, having experienced a loss of loved ones in the manner which he did, I certainly would have undergone changes of personality myself. His land was confiscated; his people violated, severely punished for offenses never committed, or if they had, they were only reacting to offenses committed against them. On moral grounds it can be debated – in theory anyway. In practice, who knows how anyone would react. An eye for an eye has always been a basic tenet. Ours is to forgive, is it not? If I can forgive him, perhaps he can forgive those who had nothing to do with the crimes against his people.

Now I have come to terms with our differences. I am at peace with myself, and at peace with my archenemy.

The question remains. Who were the victims and who were the villains in those early years before our country was founded? An innocent people who lived, for the most part, peacefully upon the land? Or the intrepid pioneers who blazed trails, albeit hell-bent, for the sake of discovery and colonization? I will let you be the judge.

I am an old man now, seventy-four years old. I am dying of cancer. Having lived many lives, I believe I have shared with you one of the more interesting of those lives. But do not grieve for me. I look forward to my next life, a life I hope that is not as exciting as the one I shared with the Indians.

> Sincerely,
> Henry J. Purdy
> As God is my witness

As David placed the letter back in the envelope, he noticed a slip of paper inside. He removed it and read a book review from the New York Post about a book of fictional short stories written by Henry J. Purdy, titled: *Mystiques of a Wandering Gypsy*.

The reviewer wrote, "...A dark literary voice. Mr. Purdy's imagination is as wild as the wind. What he lacks in narrative and characterization, he makes up in a deliciously skewed, robust view of horror that is mildly entertaining."

David thought to himself—*The Mystique*.

Not a bad name for a golf course.

* * *

Two nights later, David had another dream, remarkable in detail, cloaked in serenity and a peacefulness impossible to describe.

It was of a time and place unaffected by civilization. A forest swept across sun-washed hills not unlike those of southern Ohio. Only this land had a different feel to it, a gentler roll with mountains looming in the distance. There was a swift-moving river passing through a valley. A village rested on a far bank. Lodges and campfires dotted the clearing along the shore of a sandy basin where children waded naked in pools of warm water.

Most of the activity centered around a dance ground where Indians of all ages sang and danced in costumes made of buckskin, accented by colorful ribbons, sashes, and feathered bonnets. Drums pounded a steady rhythm to keep the dancing vibrant, the singing joyful.

It was impossible to say what was more impressive—the sights or sounds. Song inspired dance and dance inspired song.

High above a bluff, a tall broad-shouldered young man stood looking down at the village. He was dressed in full regalia—buckskin leggings, porcupine quills hanging across a leather vest, and wolf-teeth necklace. His hair was cut in a scalp lock, topped by a band of black and white feathers. A war club was tucked in his waistband. A painted leather sash hung to his knees and he was holding a ribbon of feathers of black and white.

He looked magnificent and proud, his pride coming from the roots of the trees, the river, the sky, the sun above—the world of the *mana, wakan,* and *manitou.* The celebration below made him happy. It filled his heart with joy.

He turned and gestured with an open hand.

A woman stepped into view. She was wearing a bright yellow sundress. A matching sunbonnet flapped in a slight breeze. Both the bonnet and dress seemed out of place, more in character with a different time, a different setting. Yet somehow from the look of her and the way she carried herself, you knew she was beautiful, a contemporary woman thrown into the wilds of a virgin land long ago.

The two stood side by side, not holding hands, but it appeared they were comfortable in each other's presence as they watched and listened to the singing and dancing in the village.

The man held out the ribbon of feathers. The woman took it as an offering of peace. She held the ribbon in one hand and removed the sunbonnet with the other, letting strands of her light chestnut hair blow in the breeze.

The music was infectious. The drums beat like thunder and voices sang to the beat of the drums.

The man gestured with an upraised hand.

He said two words in the tongue of the Mohawk. "My people."

He smiled.

And Dora Macklin smiled back at him.

In a dream
anything is possible

— The End —

About the author—

Robert C. Wahl is a former television news reporter in Augusta, Georgia where he also worked for a few short years at the Augusta National Golf Club. He currently lives in his hometown of Toledo, Ohio.

He has published two children's books and another novel titled *Ride the Giant Wolf* by BearManor fiction.

Sources and Acknowledgments

I wish to thank the following for their contributions—

Jan Wahl. Brother. Fellow author (of children's books). It is brother Jan, a collector of films from silents to talkies, who showed movies in our basement on his 16-mm projector often late at night, which helped shape my interest in film. At age five I had a deliciously wild and harrowing experience watching Henry Hull, disguised as a half-man, half-wolf, creeping up a wall to the balcony of his aunt's flat (to do what, I wasn't sure, but it was spooky) in the classic film *The Werewolf of London* (1935).

Two other movies influenced this novel—

Northwest Passage (1940) with Spencer Tracy cast as Major Richard Rogers. It was Rogers who led a rag-tag militia called Roger's Rangers through a wilderness occupied by Indians in search of a passage linking the Atlantic to the Pacific.

Forbidden Planet (1956) with Walter Pidgeon, Leslie Nielsen, and Anne Francis. This horror classic has all the ingredients a good film must have in order to achieve popularity. The very core of my novel, the influence of dreams, was borrowed from this movie.

Jerry Tasker and his wife, Carolyn. It is their generosity that enabled me to revive a stagnant writing career.

Michael Wahl. Brother. It is Michael and his wife, Beth, who sent me books and information on subjects pertinent to the subjects I was writing.

Douglas Wahl. Brother. The first to read my manuscript. Also its first critic.

Peter Wahl. Nephew. Who helped put the whole thing together, acting as book consultant and computer guru. He and wife, Parul, continue to be supportive.

Michael Richardson. Who helped navigate my way through the Internet and Microsoft Word.

Don Cellini, Janice Dempster, David and Kerry McMurray who proof read the manuscript.

Brittney Conklin, artist, designer of the book cover.

Back cover photograph by Penny Gentieu.

Many books added to the richness of my life and served as references and inspiration—

Black Elk Speaks by John G. Neilhardt
Pawnee, Blackfoot, and Cheyenne by George Bird Grinnell
Indian Days of long Ago by Edward S. Curtis
In the Land of the Head-Hunters also by Curtis
Sacred Legacy and the North American Indian also by Curtis
To Build a Fire and Other Stories by Jack London
The Call of the Wild also by London
Northwest Passage by Kenneth Roberts
One Flew over the Cuckoo's Nest by Ken Kesey
H.P. Lovecraft's *Book of the Supernatural*
The Religions of the American Indian by Ake Hulkrantz
The Myths of the North American Indians by Lewis Spence
American Indian Myths and Legends edited by Richard Erdoes
  and Alfonso Ortiz
The Hobbit and *Lord of the Rings* by J.R.R Tolkien
A Pictorial History of the American Indian by Oliver La Farge
The Native Americans, the Indigenous People of North America
  written and edited by contributing members of the Smithsonian
  Institution
Man's Rise to Civilization as Shown by the Indians of North America
  by Peter Farb
The Encyclopedia of Ghosts and Spirits by Rosemary Ellen Guilley

Made in the USA
Middletown, DE
30 November 2015